"Blume succeeds in capturing the condition of an entire community. . . . No one captures coming-of-age milestones and stomach butterflies like Blume, and those scenes are worth waiting for." —*The Boston Globe*

"Judy Blume's writing is simply a delight. . . . Blume is a master at presenting the complexities of life. This novel is entertaining, heartbreaking, and redeeming."
—*The Missourian*

"Heartwarming." —*New York Daily News*

"Satisfying, heartfelt. . . . Delivers on the warm nostalgia that we remember from Blume's earlier books and will appeal to her admirers—of which I am absolutely one— who regard any new book by this trailblazing literary and cultural icon as a celebratory event."
—Melissa M. Firman, *Pittsburgh Post-Gazette*

"A powerful journey through the grieving process. . . . Riveting, heartfelt." —*Toronto Star*

"Blume creates characters who are real and sympathetic."
—*St. Louis Post-Dispatch*

"Excellent and satisfying. . . . Has all the elements of Blume's best books: the complex relationships between friends and family members, the straight talk and lack of shame about sex, and, most of all, the compassionate insight into the pleasures and pains of growing up."
—*Chicago Reader*

"Has [Blume's] signature warm, personal touch."
—Vogue.com

"Vividly rendered. . . . Blume deftly demonstrates just how different the personal fallout from tragedy can turn out to be. . . . As Blume proves over and over again not just in *In the Unlikely Event* but in all of her fiction, life *does* go on in spite of hardship. We love. We lose. We fail. We may fall. But the lucky ones, we try our best to endure."
—*The Oregonian*

"Soars. . . . It's Judy Blume and, therefore, it's gold."
—*The Star-Ledger* (Newark)

"Judy Blume is revered. She is claimed, and cherished, and clutched close to the hearts of American adolescents and former adolescents, everywhere that books are read. . . . Blume's great gift is [her] personal touch; her unflinching but reassuring voice—that of a no-nonsense big sister who gives it to you straight, then gives you a hug."
—*The Buffalo News*

"Characteristically accessible, frequently charming, and always deeply human."
—*Publishers Weekly*

"Compelling. . . . Smoothly written. . . . A new Blume novel will always be big news."
—*Booklist* (starred review)

JUDY BLUME

In the Unlikely Event

Judy Blume is one of America's most beloved authors. She grew up in Elizabeth, New Jersey, and was a teenager in 1952 when the real events in this book took place. She has written books for all ages. Her twenty-eight previous titles include *Are You There God? It's Me, Margaret*; *Forever*; and *Summer Sisters*. Her books have sold more than eighty-five million copies in thirty-two languages. She is a champion of intellectual freedom, working with the National Coalition Against Censorship in support of writers, teachers, librarians, and students. In 2004, Blume was awarded the National Book Foundation's Medal for Distinguished Contribution to American Letters. She lives in Key West and New York City.

www.judyblume.com

In the
Unlikely Event

In the
Unlikely Event

A Novel

JUDY BLUME

SEAL BOOKS

Seal Books and colophon are registered trademarks of
Penguin Random House Canada.

IN THE UNLIKELY EVENT
Seal Books/published by arrangement with Doubleday Canada
Doubleday Canada edition published 2015

Grateful acknowledgment is made to Alfred Music for permission to reprint
an excerpt from "How High the Moon," lyrics by Nancy Hamilton and music
by Morgan Lewis, copyright © 1940, copyright renewed, by Chappell & Co.,
Inc. All rights reserved. Reprinted by permission of Alfred Music.

Library and Archives Canada Cataloguing in Publication Data is
available upon request.

ISBN 978-1-4000-2684-5
eBook ISBN 978-0-385-68508-5

Text design by Cassandra J. Pappas
Cover design by Carson Dyle
Cover photograph © Aflo Co., Ltd./Alamy
Printed and bound in the United States of America

Seal Books are published by Penguin Random House Canada.
"Seal Books" and the portrayal of a seal are the property of
Penguin Random House Canada.

www.penguinrandomhouse.ca

10 9 8 7 6 5 4 3 2 1

Penguin
Random
House

To George,
My Henry Ammerman

Principal Characters

THE DEMETRIOUS FAMILY

Christina Demetrious, *high school senior, with an after-school job at Dr. Osner's office*

Nia Demetrious (Mama), *Christina's mother, owner of Nia's Lingerie*

Nico Demetrious (Baba), *Christina's father, owner of Three Brothers Luncheonette*

Yaya and Papou, *Christina's grandmother and grandfather*

Athena, *Christina's older sister*

Jack McKittrick, *Christina's boyfriend, brother of Mason McKittrick*

THE STEIN FAMILY

Phil Stein, *Steve Osner's best friend*

Kathy Stein, *Steve's girlfriend, cousin of Phil Stein*

Mrs. Stein, *Phil's mother, Kathy's aunt*

THE BARNES FAMILY

Mrs. Barnes, *Fern Osner's babysitter, mother of Tim Barnes, a pilot*

Laura Barnes, *Tim's wife*

Thirty-five Years Later

———————————————

February 10, 1987

Even now she can't decide. She thinks about flipping a coin. *Heads* she goes, *tails* she stays. But isn't indecisiveness an early sign of mental illness? Didn't she cover a story about that a few years ago? Or is it that she's conflicted? Conflicted is better than indecisive. Why is she thinking this way? A voice inside her head says, *You know damn well why.*

She steps up to the bank of phones inside the departure lounge and dials her fifteen-year-old daughter, Eliza, at school, but gets her machine. She supposes it's good news that Eliza has gone to her early morning class. She'll try her again later when she gets there, if she goes. Otherwise she'll call from home.

She's still weighing the pros and cons an hour later when the flight to Newark is announced and the first-class passengers are invited to board. She feels the panic rising—the dry mouth, the pounding heart, the urge to run. The moment of truth. Once she gets on the plane there will be no turning back. A hot flash washes over her body. *For god's sake, not now,* she tells herself, wriggling out of her coat, as sweat pools between her breasts. She takes a deep breath, grabs her carry-on bag and heads for the gate. She's going to do this. She's not backing down.

Once she's seated with her seat belt fastened, she thinks about taking a Valium to help her sleep on the long flight. But when has she ever slept on a plane? The guy next to her, in the window seat, is already loosening his tie, slipping a sleep mask over his eyes. No chitchat for him, which is fine with her. She's about to pull out the book she's reading, *The Prince of Tides*, but instead grabs the classy leather-covered journal her friend Christina gave her for her birthday. Each of them has been asked to share something tomorrow, a few personal words, a poem, a memory. This is her only entry.

After enough time it fades and you're grateful.

Not that it's ever completely gone.

It's still there, buried deep, a part of you.

The stench is gone from your nostrils now

Unless someone leaves the kettle on to boil and forgets about it.

The nightmares have tapered out.

There are more pressing things to dream about, to worry over, to keep you awake at night.

Aging parents, adolescent children, work, money, the state of the world.

Life goes on, as our parents promised that winter.

Life goes on if you're one of the lucky ones.

But we're still part of a secret club,

One we'd never willingly join,

With members who have nothing in common except a time and a place.

We'll always be connected by that winter.

Anyone who tells you different is lying.

Part One

December 1951

Elizabeth Daily Post

CHRISTMAS TREE DAZZLES

DEC. 11 (UPI)—The 82-foot Christmas tree at Rockefeller Center dazzled last evening as its 7,500 red, white and green lights were flipped on in the traditional ceremony to inaugurate the season. An onlooking crowd of 2,000 holiday shoppers and homeward-bound office workers wrapped in winter coats for the chilly weather "oohed" and "aahed" as the lights blazed on. The voices of the Rockefeller Center Choristers filled the air with Christmas carols, and skaters twirled on the ice below.

A nationwide audience shared the ceremony, which was televised for the first time on NBC's Kate Smith show. Miss Smith highlighted the event with a rendition of Irving Berlin's "White Christmas." The tree will be lighted every day from twilight to midnight until Jan. 2.

1

Miri

Miri Ammerman and her best friend, Natalie Osner, were sprawled on their bellies on the thick, tweedy wall-to-wall carpet of Natalie's den, waiting for the first-ever televised lighting of the famous Christmas tree. The den was Miri's favorite room in Natalie's house, not least because of the seventeen-inch Zenith, inside a pale wood cabinet, the biggest television Miri had ever seen. Her grandmother had a set but it was small with rabbit ears and sometimes the picture was snowy. The furniture in the Osners' den all matched, the beige sofas and club chairs arranged around a Danish modern coffee table, with its neat stacks of magazines—*Life, Look, Scientific American, National Geographic.* A cloth bag with a wood handle, holding Mrs. Osner's latest needlepoint project, sat on one of the chairs. A complete set of the Encyclopaedia Britannica took up three shelves of the bookcase, along with family photos, including one of Natalie at summer camp, in jodhpurs, atop a sleek black horse, holding her ribbons, and another of her little sister, Fern, perched on a pony. In one corner of the room was a game table with a chess set standing ready, not that she and Natalie knew how to play, but Natalie's older brother, Steve, did and sometimes he and Dr. Osner would play for hours.

She and Natalie sang "White Christmas" along with Kate Smith, then oohed and aahed with the crowd, with the whole country, when the tree was lit, signaling the start of the holiday season.

Later, Miri found out her mother had been there to see it live, one of the two thousand spectators. Rusty told Miri she'd been pushed and shoved as the crowd pressed forward until she'd decided it wasn't worth the effort and left to catch her train to Elizabeth. She could see the tree any old day on her way home from work.

FOR MIRI the real start of the holiday season was her mother's birthday. Miri was sure Rusty had felt robbed as a kid, having a birthday so close to Hanukkah, but Rusty assured her that no, she'd never minded having a holiday birthday. It made it more special.

This year Hanukkah fell at the same time as Christmas, something Miri thought should be the rule, not the exception. She vowed she wouldn't wait until the last minute to do her shopping, but here she was on Saturday, the day before her mother's birthday, on a mission that took her downtown to Nia's Lingerie, a shop on Broad Street. Neither she nor her second best friend, Suzanne Dietz, who smelled of Noxzema year-round and had the best skin of any girl in their crowd, had ever set foot in Nia's. Just the word *lingerie* was enough to send them into fits of laughter. It sounded like something Mrs. Osner would say in her southern drawl instead of *underwear*. Underwear was what Miri and Suzanne bought at Levy Brothers, one of two department stores on Broad Street. Underwear was white cotton. But *lingerie—lingerie* was something else. Not that there was anything suggestive in Nia's windows. Not a bra or girdle in sight. And nothing black. Navy blue was as close as it got. Still, who knew what they'd find inside? Miri had clipped an ad from the *Daily Post*: THIS SEASON GIVE HER NYLON TRICOT BY VANITY FAIR. She wasn't sure about nylon tricot but the ad from Nia's showed a half-slip for $3.99, something her mother might appreciate since she'd been complaining about the worn-out elastic waistbands of hers.

A single chime announced the opening of the door as Miri and Suzanne entered the shop. Inside, it was busy with holiday shoppers but not overwhelming the way it would be at Levy's or Goerke's, the other downtown department store.

The shoppers, all women, talked in hushed voices. A small white Christmas tree with silver ribbons threaded through its branches, topped by a silver angel, sat on the display table. Satin bedroom slippers and delicate bed jackets in pale colors were arranged around the tree. Who wore bed jackets? Rusty had a woolly robe and two flannel nightgowns for winter, and a seersucker robe and a few cotton nightgowns for summer. Maybe movie stars who were served breakfast in bed wore bed jackets. But there were no movie stars in Elizabeth, New Jersey. None that Miri knew of, anyway. Even Mrs. Osner didn't have a bed jacket. If she did it wasn't hanging in her closet, because Miri had been through that closet a hundred times, ever since she and Natalie had become best friends two years ago. Miri and Suzanne were still babysitting partners and ate lunch at the same cafeteria table every day—they just weren't *bests*.

"Can I help you?" a pretty young woman asked Miri.

"Are you Nia?" Miri hadn't planned to say that. It just slipped out.

"I'm Athena, her daughter. What can I show you today?"

Athena—Miri didn't know anyone named Athena. Such an exotic name. Wasn't Athena the Greek goddess of wisdom, arts and something else, maybe war? She'd loved her book of Greek mythology in fifth grade. Uncle Henry had given it to her. Every night they'd taken turns reading myths to each other.

"Are you looking for something special?" Athena asked.

When Miri didn't answer, Suzanne nudged her.

"It's my mother's birthday," Miri said, coming back to

the moment, "and I was thinking of a half-slip, maybe a nylon tricot half-slip."

Before Miri had the chance to dig the ad from her purse, Athena said, "I have just what you're looking for. What size does your mother wear?"

"She's either a small or a medium, depending."

"Really, a small?" Athena said, as if a mother couldn't possibly be a small.

"She's five-five, a hundred and fifteen pounds." Miri knew everything about her mother, every detail of her life, except for one, and she wasn't going to waste her time thinking of that today.

Athena brought out a few half-slips. "Double slits," she said, holding up one. By Vanity Fair, $3.99. "This is the nylon tricot. Feel how soft it is. It won't cause static." She laid a size small on top of the medium to show Miri the difference.

"My mother wears a medium," Suzanne said quietly, as if she were giving away top-secret information. "And she's bigger than your mom."

"Go with the small, then," Athena advised Miri. "She can exchange it if it's the wrong size. What color? We have it in white, pink and navy."

"She goes to business in New York," Miri said. "She wears dark colors, especially in winter. So I think navy."

"An excellent choice," Athena said. "Can I show you anything else?"

"I need to get her something for Hanukkah, but—"

"Hanukkah is like Christmas," Suzanne told Athena.

"Yes, of course," Athena said.

Miri gave Suzanne a look. Why would she bother to explain? Not that Suzanne didn't pride herself on knowing all about the Jewish holidays, not that she didn't love throwing around the Yiddish expressions she'd picked up from Miri's grandmother. Suzanne knew way more about the story of Hanukkah than Miri knew about Jesus.

"I can't spend as much this time," Miri told Athena. Both she and Suzanne had saved their babysitting money for holiday shopping. They'd already chipped in to buy the little sisters they babysat a box of five finger puppets for $1.50. The girls were going to love them. But at this rate Miri wasn't going to make it through her list.

"How about stockings?" Athena said. "You can never have too many, especially when you go to business."

"But stockings are so boring." Miri turned to Suzanne. "Don't you think stockings are boring?"

"I don't know," Suzanne said. "I was thinking of getting my mother stockings for Christmas."

Miri backtracked. "I didn't mean they're not a good idea." Suzanne's mother was a nurse. She wore white stockings with her uniform. But Suzanne chose the new seamless stockings by Lilly Daché, three pair in "Dubonnet Blonde," nicely packaged and tied with a red ribbon.

Miri was thinking of a less practical gift, something that would make her mother laugh. Something Rusty could show her friends at work, saying, *My daughter gave me this for Hanukkah. My daughter is such a card!* When she was little she'd always made something at school, a painted clay ashtray, a decorated coaster, a pin made of buttons. Rusty had saved every one of her handmade gifts. But now that she was a month from her fifteenth birthday, painted clay ashtrays were a thing of the past.

Suzanne checked her mother's name off her neat, alphabetized list. Miri's list was in her head and was neither neat nor alphabetized. But at least she had a good birthday present for Rusty. At least she had that.

"I hope you'll shop with us again," Athena said.

"We will," Miri told her.

Then she whispered to Suzanne, "The next time we need to buy *lingerie*," making Suzanne laugh as they opened the door and stepped out into the icy wind and blowing snow from yesterday's storm.

Rusty

On Sayre Street, a brisk fifteen-minute walk from downtown in decent weather, a ten-minute bus ride on a day like today, Rusty Ammerman had already finished the laundry and vacuuming. The two-family house on a street of other two-family houses, each with a small, neat front yard, was divided into an upstairs apartment, where she lived with Miri, and a downstairs one, where her mother, Irene, lived with Rusty's brother, Henry. But the doors between the two floors were never locked and Miri spent as much time at Irene's as she did upstairs.

Rusty was putting the finishing touches on the Hanukkah gifts she was wrapping for Miri. The Lanz nightgown was at the top of Miri's wish list, not that Miri had told her in so many words, but Rusty knew. All the girls had Lanz nightgowns. She'd seen that in the photo from Natalie's slumber party, with four of them in Lanz and Miri in ordinary pajamas.

She hadn't planned on the white angora mittens with leather palms, but she couldn't resist when she saw them in the window of Goerke's last week on her way home from the train station. They certainly weren't practical, but Miri loved angora. The next best thing to having a pet, Miri said, since the dog or cat she wanted was out of the question. The house was too small, no one was home all day, and pets were a responsibility, not to mention an expense. Besides, Irene wouldn't hear of it. Rusty should know. She'd lobbied for a dog when she was a girl, when they'd lived on Westfield Avenue in a single-family house with a backyard, close to her father's shop, Ammerman's Fine Food Emporium. She'd recruited Henry to beg with her.

"We already have a cat at the store," her mother had said. "You can play with Schmaltzie anytime you want to."

What kind of name was Schmaltzie for a cat? Rusty's father had named him. "Because he's fat," he'd explained. "Because he looks like he eats too much schmaltz." Her mother used chicken fat—*schmaltz*—in the chopped liver she made every Friday.

"Schmaltzie catches mice," Rusty had said. "That's why he's fat."

"That's his job," her father told her. "But he still likes to play."

"I want a different kind of cat," Rusty told him. "One who lives at home, or else a dog. A dog would be even better."

But then the market crashed, and in the Depression that followed a pet was the least of their concerns.

Rusty hid the wrapped presents in the corner of her closet, on the highest shelf, not that Miri would snoop around the way she had when she was little, but still, there was something satisfying about hiding them.

Now that she'd finished her housework for the week, a

little luxury was in order, starting with a long, hot bath. As the water ran in the claw-foot tub, Rusty chose her bath salts carefully, sniffing each one. Was she in a lavender mood, vanilla, musk? Yes, musk. Something to remind her she was just turning thirty-three. She was still young. It wasn't too late. She stepped into the steamy bath, then lowered herself, sinking lower and lower until only her face was above water.

Irene

Downstairs, in her first-floor apartment, Rusty's mother, Irene Ammerman, poured a bottle of Harveys Bristol Cream into a crystal decanter, to welcome the holiday shoppers she hoped would flock to her house from four to eight p.m., despite the falling temperatures. She'd sent out penny postcards, inviting all her regular customers, encouraging them to bring friends.

This morning, before he left for work at the newspaper, Henry had opened her dining room table to its full length, big enough to seat twelve. She'd created a tabletop display with fluffy cotton, white as fresh snow, arranged the Volupté compacts just so, then scattered sparkly snowflakes around. The snowflakes would make a mess, she knew, and she'd be Hoovering tomorrow morning, but they were worth it. This year's line featured a style to appeal to every taste. If you wanted gemstones, there were gemstones. If you preferred gold accents on silver, fine. And if you wanted simple but elegant, there were plenty to choose from. She set the Ronson lighters, the other line she carried, in small groups, ranging from large silver tabletop models to small, pocket-size squares.

There was still time to have the Ronsons engraved, but not much.

She had to be careful what else she put on the table. Last year she'd used her leaded crystal candlesticks to add height to her display, along with a few colorful antique bowls. A mistake, since customers assumed they were also for sale. So she sold a few bowls, making up prices on the spot. But the candlesticks—no. She didn't have much left from the old days, when they were flush from the store, and these she was keeping for Rusty, or Miri, or even Henry's wife, if he married, which she hoped he would.

Yesterday, she'd splurged on a wash, set and manicure at Connie's Beauty Salon. She needed to look as stylish as the gifts she was hoping to sell. Presentation was presentation, and that included her. She moved the family photos, usually lined up on the sideboard, to the top of the spinet to make room for her famous coffee cakes. Her customers would expect a nosh. She touched her lips to Miri's photo and stood it next to one of Max, her husband, who'd died two weeks before Miri was born. *Boom boom boom*—just like that—Rusty turned eighteen, Max died, Miri was born. She was forty-one at the time and in one month she'd become both a widow and a grandmother.

Bad things happen in threes, her cousin Belle reminded her, but Irene couldn't say that Rusty having a baby at eighteen was a bad thing, or maybe it was, given the circumstances, but the baby herself was not. The baby, Miri, was a precious gift, with her grandfather's high cheekbones and dimpled cheek. Not a beauty like Rusty, not yet, but growing into her looks. The eyes, she knew where they came from, but she kept that to herself. She hoped to god she would never again come face-to-face with the person responsible for those eyes. If she did she didn't know what she might do. He'd better hope she wouldn't have a carving knife in her hand. If she kept thinking of him she might need a nitro under her tongue. She brushed off her hands as if brushing away bad thoughts and poured herself a small glass of sherry.

RUSTY CAME DOWNSTAIRS to help at the open house. Irene looked smart in a simple gray wool dress with a white collar. She was at her most charming, chatting with her customers, offering a glass of sherry to the few husbands who'd accompanied their wives, and to the women, too. "It will warm you up," she told them. Was anyone better at this than her mother? Rusty didn't think so. Irene had once confided to Rusty she'd had the opportunity, when she was young, to marry into the family who'd started Volupté. But her parents thought Max Ammerman was a better catch. He was fifteen years older and already established in business. If she'd married the Volupté boy she'd be powdering her nose in the best clubs and restaurants, instead of selling compacts wholesale from home.

It was still early but already it looked like Irene would get a good turnout. Rusty replenished the stock from Irene's closet, handled the cash and the occasional check, and was available for gift-wrapping. When the phone rang Rusty excused herself and picked it up.

"Irene?"

"No, this is her daughter, Rusty."

"Oh, Rusty, dear, I haven't seen you in ages. This is Estelle Sapphire from Bayonne. I can't get to Elizabeth tonight. I'm busy packing, leaving for Florida in the morning, but I was hoping Irene could put away six compacts for me. My husband will pick them up tomorrow on his way back from the airport. He's driving to Miami but I'm flying."

Lucky Mrs. Sapphire, Rusty thought, to be escaping this weather. She wouldn't mind a trip to Florida, but she took her two weeks of vacation in the summer so she and Miri could spend time together down the shore.

"Any special design?" Rusty asked.

"No, dear. Whatever Irene thinks."

"Price range?"

"Mid. Really, I'm just taking them in case I meet someone, a good hairdresser, a pleasant maid. You know. As a way to say thank you. So much nicer than giving money."

"Of course," Rusty said. "I'll get them ready for you right now."

"Thank you, Rusty. Please tell Irene I said hello."

"I will." Rusty was willing to bet the *pleasant* maid or the *good* hairdresser would prefer cash, but a gift was better than nothing.

"Rusty, darling," Irene said, handing her four compacts and two Ronsons. "Could you gift-wrap these for Mrs. Delaney? Red ribbon."

Red ribbon was a code for Christmas, not Hanukkah, which would be blue ribbon.

Rusty knew Mrs. Delaney's son, a good-looking guy who worked at the branch bank on Elmora Avenue. He always flirted with her. Sometimes she flirted back, just to keep up her skills, though she knew he was married with four children. Not to mention Catholic.

Steve

A few blocks down East Jersey Street from the Martin Building, where Steve Osner's father had his dental office and you could get a great-tasting burger at Three Brothers Luncheonette, Steve was shooting baskets at the YMHA with his best buddy, Phil Stein, both of them seniors at Thomas Jefferson High. They'd been born two weeks apart at Elizabeth General Hospital and bar mitzvahed a week apart at Temple B'nai Israel, across the street from the Y. A couple of regulars were playing with them in a pickup game, and one of them must have brought Mason McKittrick. He seemed like a nice enough kid, not that Steve knew him well, since he was just a junior, but he had good moves and a great hook. "You should go out for the team next year," Steve told him. "Bet you could make varsity."

"I work after school," Mason said, "at Edison Lanes—not much time for practice."

"You set up pins?"

"Yeah, that and other stuff when it gets busy."

"I'll look for you next time we go bowling."

"You in a league?"

"No, just bowl for fun."

Mason nodded.

In the locker room, Steve asked Phil, "You want to grab a burger at Three Brothers? I'm starving."

"Nah. My mother's probably got dinner in the oven."

"Okay, but come over later."

"You have a plan?"

"Don't tell me you forgot already?"

"Remind me."

"My sister's party."

"We're going to your sister's party?"

Steve swatted him with his damp towel. "I have to chaperone. My mother thinks if I'm around there won't be any trouble. What a joke! Remember ninth grade? That's the first time I copped a feel."

"You were always ahead of the rest of us," Phil said.

If only that were still true, Steve thought. A lot of the guys talked about how much they were getting. Their girlfriends let them touch *and* look. Steve had touched but no one had ever let him look. He didn't have a regular girlfriend. He liked playing the field. Maybe he just hadn't met the right girl yet. He knew girls who'd invite you into their houses to neck on the sofa in the living room, but it never went any further than that. Maybe he was doing something wrong. It might be different if they went to a coed high school. Theirs was the only city in New Jersey with sex-segregated public high schools, Jefferson for boys, Battin for girls. Even St. Mary's was coed and those kids were Catholic.

"I'll set up a card table in the laundry room," he told Phil. "We'll play a little acey-deucey. You in?"

"Why not?" Phil said.

Mason didn't say anything.

"You know what they do at their parties?" Steve said.

"Who?" Phil asked.

"Jeez, Phil, my sister and her friends! Who do you think?"

"No idea."

"They play Rotation," Steve said. "The musical chairs of making out. That's a prelude to sex if ever there was one." It was one thing to make a joke of it with Phil, but if he ever found some guy messing around with his sister, he'd tear him to shreds. Not just Natalie, but Fern. The men of the family had to be vigilant. It was their job to protect the women. That's the way it was, whether the women liked it or not. The family's honor was at stake. No one told him this in so many words, but he understood what his mother expected of him. To be an honorable man. He was his mother's favorite and he knew it. Natalie and Fern were more daddy's girls. He had ten years before he had to worry about Fern. She was just in kindergarten. By then he'd be, what—twenty-seven, almost twenty-eight? He'd probably be married, maybe with his own kids. Jeez, that was a scary thought.

"So what time tonight?" Phil asked Steve.

"Around eight."

"I'll be there." Phil turned to Mason. "You want a ride home? I got the car outside."

"Yeah, sure," Mason said. "I just have to pick up my dog. The janitor's watching him in the basement."

Steve had a car outside, too. But they were going in different directions.

Mason

Phil took Mason home for supper, introduced him and his dog, Fred, to Phil's parents. Phil swore it would be okay, said his mother liked dogs, and it was true—she took to Fred right away, scratching him behind the ears like she knew what she was doing. "Look at this little fellow. What a darling boy you are," she said to the dog, who cocked his head at her. "I miss my dog Goldie very much," she told Mason.

At the dinner table, Fred sat at Mrs. Stein's feet, looking up at her, hoping for scraps. There was no more talk of Goldie and Mason didn't ask any questions.

Phil's father was some big-deal executive. He and Phil talked about football over the roast beef. They were New York Giants fans and had tickets for tomorrow's game, the last of the season, against the New York Yanks.

"Are you a fan, son?" Phil's father asked Mason.

"Yes, sir," Mason answered.

"What team?" Phil's father asked.

"Yours, sir, the New York Giants."

"Attaboy!" Phil's father said, clinking his fork against his glass.

Mason preferred baseball to football but he kept that to himself. He still couldn't believe Joe DiMaggio was retiring.

After dinner Phil asked Mason if he wanted to go to Steve's. When Mason hesitated, Mrs. Stein picked up Fred. "It's too cold for such a sweet little fellow to be outside. He can spend the night here and you can get him tomorrow." Fred didn't complain, didn't even run to the door when Mason left with Phil.

Natalie

The Osners' house was down Shelley Avenue on the left, across the street from School #21, where Natalie had gone to elementary school.

"I don't see why Steve needs to be a chaperone tonight." She was arguing with her mother in the upstairs hallway. "I mean, really, what do you think is going to happen? You know all these kids. I've been going to school with them since seventh grade. They've been here a million times."

"Boys can get rambunctious, especially this time of year," her mother said, her southern drawl more pronounced during an argument. "The holiday season makes them crazy. I don't want any trouble. We have a responsibility to the other parents."

"But it's not like you won't be home. You'll be in the den."

"Steve will be unobtrusive."

"I hope you know you're ruining my get-together. I hope you know that."

"You won't even know he's there. He'll be in the laundry room."

"The laundry room?" This almost made Natalie laugh. The laundry room was next to the finished basement and almost as big.

"With some of his friends."

"His friends? I don't want his friends anywhere near my get-together."

"I just told you—you won't even know they're there."

"I'll know. I just hope *my* friends don't find out. If Daddy were here he'd understand."

"I'm sure your father would agree with me."

"I doubt it. And keep Fern upstairs. Please! All I need is Fern walking around with her cowboy bunny. It's hard enough to be fifteen without your family making it worse."

"You're not fifteen yet, Natalie Grace Osner."

"But I will be soon, unless I die of humiliation first."

Just before the party began Natalie confronted Steve in the laundry room, where he was setting up a card table.

"Just stay out of our way. Don't ruin my get-together with your wisecracks."

"I'll bet your girlfriends wouldn't mind. They like my wisecracks."

"Stay away from my girlfriends!"

Steve laughed. "As if I'm interested."

"You're just three years older than me, big shot. Remember that. Your wife will probably be younger than I am. The girl you're going to marry is probably Fern's age now."

"Gee, I wonder if she has a toy rabbit."

If Natalie had had a bottle of soda in her hand she'd have shaken it and squirted it in Steve's face. But she didn't, so she couldn't.

Ruby

In Sunnyside, Queens, Ruby Granik was giving herself a facial, massaging gray clay into her delicate skin. Her hair was wrapped in a towel. She was careful not to let the clay drop onto her chenille robe, as warm and comfy as a childhood blanky. Her suitcase sat open on her bed, a pale-pink cardigan sweater with pearl buttons thrown on top.

Her family was going to celebrate Christmas tonight, ten days early, because she was leaving tomorrow morning, on her way to Miami to dance at the Vagabond Club on Biscayne Boulevard. She'd just appeared at Café Society in New York, though she was still waiting for her check on that one. All in all, not bad for a local girl.

Her gifts for her mother and father were wrapped. She just needed to tie them with ribbon. For her mother, the same pink cardigan with pearl buttons as the one in her suitcase but in a larger size. Her mother loved wearing the same things as Ruby, something about being a twin, Ruby thought. When she was little her mother made them mother-daughter dresses. But the day she'd turned ten Ruby had balked. "I'm not your twin!"

"I know that, Ruby. You're my daughter."

"I don't want to wear the same clothes as you."

"Well, if that's the way you feel, you don't have to."

"You and Aunt Emmy can wear the same clothes. You're twins."

"Yes, we are. But we're grown-up twins now and we only wear the same clothes if we're going to a family party."

Even that struck Ruby as strange, but as long as she didn't have to wear matching dresses anymore, she was satisfied. Funny, because now that she'd grown up herself, she didn't mind, from time to time, buying two of something, since her mother's life was difficult and it gave her so much pleasure. For her father, she'd found a large magnifying glass in a leather case. Her father was confined to a wheelchair since his foot was amputated in August, a complication of diabetes. Now, with his failing eyesight, another complication, her mother had had to quit her job to stay at home and take care of him. These days Ruby was their sole support. Not that she brought in much, even when she had a steady job, but she was sure that was about to change.

She felt a twinge of guilt for leaving her parents over the holidays but she had a career to think about. Her aunt was coming from New Jersey, from Elizabeth, where she and her mother had grown up singing in the church choir.

The singing Konecki twins. Emmy and Wendy. At least she wouldn't be leaving her parents completely alone. Her mother and father could argue about anything and everything and having Aunt Emmy in the house would help. Her father liked Emmy. He called her the reasonable twin, which sometimes infuriated her mother and other times made her laugh.

From downstairs she heard her mother call, "Ruby . . . do you need me to iron your white blouse?"

"Thanks, Mom, but I'll do it later. I have a few other things to press."

"I don't mind. Bring them down."

Ruby gathered a pair of shorts, two skirts, and an off-the-shoulder blouse. She ran down the stairs with them just as the doorbell rang. She pulled the door open, expecting to see Aunt Emmy. Instead it was Dana, Ruby's best friend, another long-legged dancer.

Dana burst out laughing. "You look cute," she said, reminding Ruby her face was still covered in gray clay.

"Dana, you're frozen," Ruby's mother said, greeting her daughter's friend. "A cup of coffee or tea?"

"Thanks," Dana said, "but I'm okay."

Dana followed Ruby up the stairs. They'd met and roomed together on the national tour of *Kiss Me, Kate*. Ruby wasn't sure she'd ever have that much fun again.

"Looks like you're all packed," Dana said.

"Almost. I was just finishing wrapping presents for my mom and dad."

"Give me the ribbon. I'll do it. You get that goo off your face. I can't take you out for a holiday drink like that."

"We're going out for drinks?"

"We are."

Ruby passed the red and green ribbon to Dana. "Give me ten minutes. So long as I'm back for supper with the family. You should stay. My mother's making pierogi."

"I love your mother's pierogi."

"She'll be happy to have another guest. Aunt Emmy's driving in from Elizabeth."

"With handsome Uncle Victor?"

"Afraid the handsome fireman has to stay at home. He's on duty. Anyway, he's old enough to be your father."

"I like older men."

"My uncle is off-limits."

"As if I don't know."

They laughed as they walked arm in arm to Billy's, the tavern on the corner, where they sat in a booth. Ruby's skin was glowing from the facial. Without makeup she could pass for a high school student.

"What can I bring you lovely ladies?" Billy asked. Billy was bald, short and round, but he moved fast.

"Two hot toddies," Dana said.

"With pleasure, though neither one of you beauties looks old enough to be legal." He knew they were. Billy had known Ruby's family since before she was born. Knew she'd turned twenty-two over the summer, just before her father's surgery. Billy knew almost everything about her family, and he kept it to himself.

When they were served, Dana held up her glass. "Cheers. Here's to a great year for both of us!"

Ruby clinked glasses with her. "I'll second that."

They talked for forty-five minutes over a second hot toddy, taking turns feeding nickels into the jukebox. When they tired of holiday songs they started on Broadway musicals, singing along with "Why Can't You Behave?," reminding them of their good times on the road and entertaining the few customers who were seated at the bar.

When it was time to leave, Billy called, "Have a good trip, Ruby."

"Thanks, Billy. And don't let my father have more than one, if anyone brings him in."

"Don't worry, sweetheart. And a Merry Christmas to you."

"You, too, Billy."

Miri

That night, Suzanne's father dropped Miri and Suzanne at Natalie's house. Mrs. Osner answered the door. Small and pretty, she wore a single strand of pearls whether she was in a skirt and sweater, like tonight, or a cocktail dress on her way to the country club. Miri liked to think of her as Corinne. She liked thinking of all the adults in her life by their first names. It made them seem more interesting, less like parents and more like regular people with stories of their own. Steve and Fern were dark-haired like Dr. Osner, but Natalie was blond, with short, soft curls like her mother, and the same gray-blue eyes.

Even though Natalie's family was Jewish and attended Temple B'nai Israel on the High Holidays, same as Miri's family, they had a big, beautiful tree in their living room, which they called a Hanukkah bush. It was decorated with handmade wooden animal ornaments. On Christmas Eve Natalie and Fern would hang up stockings by the fireplace and Fern would leave out milk and cookies for the Jewish Santa, who flew through the sky wearing a blue suit with silver Jewish stars. Instead of reindeer his cart was pulled by camels because he came from Israel, not the North Pole.

Dr. Osner didn't approve of celebrating this way, but Mrs. Osner, who came from Birmingham, Alabama, had grown up with the custom and refused to give it up. Miri wished her family celebrated the Jewish Santa, too. She would have enjoyed decorating a tree and leaving milk and cookies for him even though she was way too old to believe.

"The young people are downstairs," Corinne told Miri and Suzanne, as if they didn't know.

Natalie wasn't the only one in their crowd to have a finished basement, but if they put it to a vote Natalie's would win by a mile. It wasn't just the red leather banquettes, the knotty-pine walls, the red and black floor tiles, or even the oval bar with its flip-top counter and glasses in every size imaginable lined up neatly on mirrored shelves. Forget all that. What made Natalie's basement take the prize was the jukebox.

"It's not new," Natalie always said, as if it would be a crime to have your own *new* jukebox, the kind with swirling colors and flashing lights. Natalie still got to change the records herself and nobody had to put in a coin to start it up. You just had to push the button. Dr. Osner brought home the jukebox with all the latest hits thanks to one of his patients who was in the music business. *Some gangster*, Natalie once confided to Miri.

When Natalie pushed the button and the jukebox came to life, the dancing began with something swingy, something they could Lindy to—*Hey good lookin', whatcha got cookin'?* It left them laughing, breathing hard, ready for more.

But when Nat King Cole came on singing "Nature Boy" the mood shifted. Miri was wondering who she'd dance the first slow dance with, when out of nowhere a dark-haired boy, someone Miri had never seen before, came up to her, wrapped his arms around her and held her close, as if they'd been dancing together forever. Well, swaying was more like it, but even so . . . *There was a boy, a very strange enchanted boy* . . . She could feel the pack of Luckies in his shirt pocket. She didn't *know* they were Luckies but she imagined they were. She wondered what he felt holding her that way and hoped it wasn't her Hidden Treasure bra. *Give a girl a Peter Pan and she will grow, grow, grow* . . . Not likely Nat King Cole would record that one.

She had to stop herself from talking, from asking questions the way she did when she was nervous, because she sensed this boy didn't want to talk. She prayed the palms of her hands wouldn't sweat, that her deodorant was working, that the faint scent of her mother's Arpège would reach his nostrils. His breath was near her ear, making her tingle. Then the song ended and he was gone, like Cinderella racing from the ball, but without a shoe, glass or otherwise, left behind to help her find him. She didn't even know his name. She doubted he knew hers, either. She hoped her blue angora sweater—the one she kept in a garment bag on the top shelf of the fridge—had shed just enough onto his flannel shirt to remind him of her.

When someone turned out the lights Miri snuck away and headed upstairs to Natalie's bedroom. She wasn't in the mood for playing Rotation after dancing with the sexy stranger.

Upstairs, she lay on one of Natalie's twin beds, the bed

she slept in almost every Saturday night, but not tonight, because tomorrow was her mother's birthday and she needed to be home to bring her breakfast in bed, a tradition started three years ago, when permission to use the stove was finally granted. Miri liked to pretend this was *her* room. The starched organdy skirt on the dressing table was as pretty as any summer dress. Attach a couple of straps and she could wear it to the ninth-grade prom in June. She knew that inside the dresser lay piles of cashmere sweaters. Miri had once counted them. Fourteen. Natalie was embarrassed. "We get them at a discount. From the cashmere sweater lady. You should come over next time she's here." As if Miri could afford to buy cashmere sweaters, even at a discount.

More than once Miri had allowed herself to fantasize being a part of Natalie's perfect family. If Natalie's mother died—not a gruesome, slow death, but something fast and dramatic, say a car crash—Natalie's father could marry Miri's mother, who was young and beautiful and single. Then Miri and her mother and grandmother could move into Natalie's big red-brick house and Miri and Natalie would be sisters and Miri could start collecting cashmere sweaters like Natalie. Not that Miri didn't like Natalie's mother. Mrs. Osner, Corinne, had always been very nice to her. She treated Miri almost like another daughter, which was just one reason this fantasy left Miri feeling ashamed and sick to her stomach. She didn't want to be a disgusting and immoral person.

Fern suddenly appeared in the doorway to Natalie's room, clutching a toy rabbit dressed in cowboy gear. Fern called him Roy, for Roy Rogers, the singing movie cowboy. Fern was obsessed with Roy Rogers. "*Oh, give me land, lots of land under starry skies above . . . don't fence me in . . ."* she sang.

Fern was wearing flowered flannel pajamas with feet. "Is the party over yet?" she asked.

"No," Miri said. "Does Mrs. Barnes know you're running around?" Mrs. Barnes took care of Fern and cooked dinner for the family four nights a week. She made dishes Miri had never heard of, dishes with foreign names like boeuf bourguignon and veal marsala. They tasted better than they sounded.

"She's not here tonight," Fern said. "Mommy and Daddy are here. They're in the den."

"Oh."

"Roy Rogers has a penis," Fern said, waggling Roy Rabbit in Miri's face. "Did you know that?"

"Yes," Miri said. She'd heard it often enough, every time she was at Natalie's house, but she still wasn't sure how she was supposed to respond. Fern was just in kindergarten.

"I've seen two penises," Fern said. "Daddy's and Steve's."

Miri hadn't seen any penises and she wasn't in a hurry to, either. "How about I tuck you into bed?" she said to Fern.

"Okay."

Miri followed Fern down the hallway to her room, the beige carpet plush under their feet. Fern climbed into bed and Miri pulled the blankets up to her chin. "Roy Rabbit doesn't have a penis, even though he's a boy bunny."

Miri wanted to get out of there. She'd had enough penis talk.

"Don't forget to kiss me," Fern said.

Miri dropped a kiss on Fern's forehead. Her skin was cool and smelled sweet.

She returned to the party just as it was breaking up.

"Where were you?" Natalie asked.

"Upstairs. I had a headache. I guess I fell asleep."

"Are you better now?"

Miri nodded. "Who was that boy I was dancing with?"

"What boy?"

"That boy with the dark hair."

"I didn't notice. Maybe one of Steve's friends. He had a card game going in the laundry room and he was supposed to keep his friends away from my party."

Mason

Steve was pissed about him dancing with that girl. "She's my sister's best friend, asshole, so stay away from her. I didn't even invite you here."

"Hey," Phil said to Steve. "Take it easy. I invited him."

"I didn't know we weren't supposed to dance," Mason said. "Nobody told me."

"We're chaperones," Steve told him. "You know what that means? Or don't they teach you that in junior year?"

"Okay, Steve," Phil said, standing between him and Mason. "We get it. Off-limits. It's your house. You get to set the rules."

Too late, Mason realized it had been a mistake to come to Steve's house so he hightailed it up the stairs. In the kitchen Dr. Osner was scooping Breyers ice cream into two bowls. "Everything all right?" Dr. Osner asked.

"Yes, sir," Mason answered. "Everything is fine." He hoped Dr. Osner wouldn't recognize him from that day his brother had dragged him to his office, his face swollen with a toothache. His brother's girlfriend worked for Dr. Osner, but no one was supposed to know they were going together. Something about Christina's family being Greek and Jack's being Irish. Their secret was safe with him. He had plenty of secrets, and he kept them all to himself.

He grabbed his jacket and was out of there, glad his dog was spending the night at Phil's house. What really bothered him was that he didn't know he was doing anything wrong when he'd danced with that girl. He'd caught a glimpse of her doing the Lindy with some boy who barely came up to her chin and he'd liked the way she looked, liked the dimple in her cheek when she smiled, the long hair flying. He just got a feeling that it would be nice to hold her. When he did, she didn't talk, didn't say a word. And neither did he. Just the music and the feel of her in his arms. Yeah. That was all. She didn't flirt, didn't play games, just moved with him. Just that.

Miri

Suzanne was spending the night at Robo's house on Byron Avenue. So Natalie's father drove Miri home. Miri was sure when Mr. and Mrs. Boros named their daughter "Roberta" they never expected her to be called Robo.

She enjoyed having Dr. O to herself. "What's new and

exciting, Miss Mirabelle?" He had a special name for her, but when it came to new and exciting she couldn't tell him about the mystery boy, so she didn't say anything.

"Still working on the school paper?" Dr. O asked, and he seemed really interested.

"Yes, but we never get to cover any exciting stories. Just the same old Christmas pageant and the annual food drive."

"Say you were interviewing me," he said. "What would you ask?"

"I'd ask what made you become a dentist."

He laughed. "Really, you're interested in teeth?"

"I'm interested in people."

"That's what I like about being a dentist," he said. "My patients."

Miri was his patient. So was the rest of her family. "Were you always checking your friends' teeth when you were young, saying, 'Open wide'?"

He laughed again. "I was more interested in music. But my brothers were dentists. They encouraged me to go to dental school. We practiced together for a while."

"Where are they now?"

He hesitated. "They moved away."

"Do you miss them?"

"Yes, I do."

They pulled up to Miri's house. "Thanks for the ride," she called, getting out of the car.

"My pleasure, Miss Mirabelle."

Dr. O was everyone's favorite, which is why Miri couldn't help wishing she had a father just like him. Somewhere Miri had a father but she didn't know where.

What kind of guy leaves his seventeen-year-old pregnant girlfriend and never even sees his baby?

She'd asked Rusty more than once when she was little, "Where is my daddy? Who is my daddy?"

She could tell, even then, Rusty wasn't going to answer that question.

JOY TO THE WORLD

DEC. 15—The blanket of snow dumped on Elizabeth over the past two days seems not to have deterred bundle-laden shoppers. With Christmas lights strung across streets, stores gaily decorated for the season, and the ever-present sound of carols, shoppers seemed bent on proving they could have a good time no matter what the weather.

Leaving their cars behind because of dangerous driving conditions, they waited last night for buses downtown on Broad Street, contributing to the heavy burden already placed on public transportation during and after Friday's snowstorm.

"It's Christmas," said Myrtle Carter, trying to balance her packages while keeping track of two young children. "Joy to the world, and all that."

2

Miri

Sunday was frigid, gray and windy. At Newark Airport a new low of six degrees was recorded at 7 a.m. But Miri, asleep in her bed under a puffy quilt, didn't give two figs about the weather. She was dreaming of the mystery boy she'd danced with last night. She was good at that, at deciding what she'd dream about, then doing it.

When her alarm went off at 8 a.m. she reached out and turned it off. She threw on her robe and hustled to the kitchen where she prepared two eggs boiled exactly three minutes, dark rye toast slathered with butter, fresh-squeezed orange juice and coffee with real cream and two sugars. She decorated the tray with a paper doily and a flower plucked from the arrangement on the hall table, a gift from Rusty's boss and his wife. Her mother's real name was Naomi, but because of her auburn hair, which was long and thick, everyone called her Rusty. People turned to stare when she walked by, as if maybe she was a movie star. Too bad Miri didn't get her mother's hair or her green eyes. Nobody stared when she walked by.

When she presented the breakfast tray, Rusty acted all surprised, like she'd forgotten it was her birthday. Miri thought about the bed jackets displayed at Nia's. If she had had the money she'd have bought one so Rusty could have breakfast in bed in style on her birthday.

"That was delicious," Rusty said when she'd finished her breakfast.

Miri held out the gift from Nia's Lingerie.

"Breakfast in bed *and* a present?" Rusty said. "Should I open it?"

Miri nodded. What else would you do with a present?

Rusty untied the ribbon and rolled it up, then carefully removed the wrapping paper, so it could be reused. Finally she opened the box and pulled out the half-slip. "This is exactly what I wanted!"

She sounded as if she meant it. Miri was pleased.

"And in navy," Rusty said. "It's perfect."

"It's nylon tricot," Miri told her. "And if it's the wrong size you can exchange it."

"Thank you, sweetie," Rusty said, reaching for Miri. She hugged her and gave her a forehead kiss.

"You're welcome, Mom."

After Miri cleaned up the kitchen, she decided she'd finish her homework so she wouldn't have to do it later, but she couldn't keep her eyes open, so she climbed back into bed and snuggled under the covers.

Ruby

Ruby sat on the stool at the counter at Hanson's Drug Store on Fifty-first Street and Seventh Avenue in New York City, savoring a scrumptious strawberry ice cream soda topped with whipped cream, chopped nuts and a Maraschino cherry. She saved the cherry for last. When she bit into it, Jimmy, the soda jerk, said, "You're not supposed to eat those things."

"Why not?"

"They're for decoration. Too many of them will kill you."

"But just one will make you happy, right?"

"If you say so."

Hanson's was a celebrity hangout where Ruby was sometimes recognized—not that she minded—and where she often chatted with other entertainers, many of them famous, way more famous than her. But on this Sunday morning it was quiet, probably because of the miserable weather. She'd been a morning guest on WJZ, broadcast from Howie's Restaurant on Sixth Avenue between Fifty-second and Fifty-third, and from there she'd walked over to Hanson's. So what if she ordered an ice cream soda before lunch? Who was going to tell her she couldn't have exactly what she wanted? Being the only customer gave her the chance to flirt with Jimmy, a Broadway gypsy who worked behind the soda fountain between shows. Jeez, he was so cute. Once upon a time Ruby and Jimmy had shared a backstage kiss. But it never went any further. Ruby knew better than to fall for a dancer. Besides, she'd heard he liked boys as much as girls.

Anyway, she was romantically involved with Danny Thomas's brother Paul now. She didn't know yet if it was going to turn into something more serious or not. Her mother was always nagging, "Get married while you still have your looks, Ruby. And for god's sake, marry up. Having money beats the dickens out of being poor."

As if Ruby didn't know. Sorry, Mom, but she was nowhere near ready for marriage. She had a career to think about. And she expected to have her looks for a long time. Her agent was trying to get her on *Ed Sullivan*. He thought she had a good shot. A movie musical wouldn't hurt, either. Maybe Danny Thomas would put her in his next picture. Nothing wrong with pulling a few strings while she was dating his brother.

"What time's your plane, babe?" Jimmy asked.

"Last time I checked it was two hours late." She looked down at the watch Paul had given her for her birthday, a pink-gold Bulova. The tiny hands told her it was almost ten-thirty. "Oops, I'm supposed to be at the airport before noon," she said, collecting her things and paying for the ice cream soda.

Jimmy leaned in to give her a goodbye kiss on her cheek. At the last second she turned her face so his kiss landed on her lips, surprising him.

"Mmm . . . strawberry . . ." Jimmy said, licking his lips,

making Ruby laugh. "Have a good trip, babe, and come back soon."

"You know I will." Ruby blew him a flirty kiss.

Ruby loved to travel. Give her an airline ticket and she'd be on the next plane. She liked staying at hotels, where someone made the bed for her every day and brought her clean towels. Even when the hotels were less than classy, even when they were on the sleazy side, which was often, she still liked being on the road.

Miri

Just before noon Rusty found Miri still asleep in her bed. She shook her gently. "Come on, honey . . . get up! Let's go to an early show at the Elmora."

Miri rolled over but didn't open her eyes.

"Hurry or we're going to miss it."

Being the only child meant Miri was often her mother's companion. And if Rusty wanted to go to the movies today, she'd go with her. After all, it was her birthday. Miri threw on dungarees, a turtleneck, a heavy sweater over that and thick white socks. She tied her saddle shoes, ran the toothbrush over her teeth, not bothering to brush up and down the way Dr. Osner had taught her, pulled her hair back sloppily and got into her winter jacket, mittens, red and black striped Rutgers scarf and fuzzy earmuffs.

Miri and Rusty walked the mile up to the Elmora Theater. No bright winter sun today. Just gray sky and freezing cold. Until this year Miri could still get into the movies for a quarter, but not anymore. This was both good and bad. Good because she looked older, bad because she had to pay full price for a ticket. She'd be the first of her friends to turn fifteen, the age at which she was sure life would fall into place and at least some of her dreams would come true, starting with the *strange enchanted boy* from last night's party.

At the concession stand Rusty bought a Milky Way for Miri, not bothering to ask if Miri had had a proper breakfast, which she hadn't, and a box of Goobers for herself. "What the heck," Rusty said to Little Mary, who worked behind the counter, "it's my birthday."

"Happy birthday, hon," Little Mary said. "I'd give you a soda on the house but then I'd be fired."

The 12:30 show was a double feature. First, *You Never Can Tell*, with Dick Powell and Peggy Dow. A dog dies and is reincarnated into a private eye. Rusty loved screwball comedies. Miri preferred her movies torrid and dark. The feature attraction was *Across the Wide Missouri*, with Clark Gable. Halfway through Rusty leaned over and said, "Time to go. We have to change for dinner." Now Miri would never find out what happened to Clark Gable or his Indian wife.

Ruby

At Newark Airport the Miami Airlines plane was delayed again with no explanation. No wonder Dana had tried to dissuade her from taking the non-scheduled flight to Tampa, then Miami. "Non-skeds are unreliable," Dana said.

Ruby argued how much cheaper this flight was than the others. Really, what was the difference? An airplane is an airplane. It gets you where you want to go. So non-skeds don't have a regular schedule like a train or a bus.

Who cares? Besides, she was impatient. The sooner she got to Florida, the better. She'd been dreaming of balmy beaches and soft moonlit nights. She couldn't wait to get away from this awful weather. So what if she had to wait another hour or two?

She took a seat in the departure lounge, adjusted her skirt and pulled the book she was reading from her over-size purse, glad she had a gripping mystery to distract her. She was aware of the glances coming her way, at the sight of a pretty girl reading *I, the Jury*, by Mickey Spillane, known for his racy language, but Ruby didn't give a hoot. Let them look. Let them stare. It was nothing to her.

Across from her an older couple were talking in voices loud enough for her to hear. The wife said, "You have a long drive. You should get going, and don't forget to pick up my Voluptés from Irene Ammerman. You remember where she lives?"

He said, "I'm not leaving until I see you on the plane."

"That's sweet, Ben, but it doesn't make sense."

"It makes sense to me."

She laughed. "You're such a romantic."

"Me, you're calling me a romantic?"

"Maybe not every day but when it counts."

He laughed and kissed her.

She said, "Ben, people can see . . ."

"So? I'm not allowed to kiss my wife in public after thirty-five years?"

Ruby smiled to herself. She couldn't remember a time when her parents kidded around that way.

"Excuse me," a young man said, "but is anyone sitting here?"

Ruby sighed and moved her bag, meant to discourage

other passengers from sitting next to her. He sat down, hoping to start up a conversation, she could tell.

"My mother thinks I'm driving to Florida," he said, "either that or taking the train. I have six brothers. Every one of us served overseas. I'm the youngest."

"I thought there was a rule about not allowing all the sons in a family to serve."

"Well, they took us. We wanted to serve. And we all came back." He smiled at her. "What about you?"

She didn't feel like telling him she was a dancer. So she said, "My fiancé is in Miami. He was in the war, too. I'm going down for the holidays to stay with him and his family." The look on his face said it all. Surprise and disappointment. After all, she wasn't wearing a ring. She felt bad. He seemed like a nice boy but there was no point. "I'll bet you'll have a great time in Miami," she said.

"Do you have any single friends there?" he asked. "Maybe your fiancé has a sister?"

"No, sorry. But I'm sure you won't have any trouble meeting girls. You're a very nice-looking young man."

"Not so young. I'll be twenty-five on my next birthday."

"I never would have guessed."

"How about you?"

"Twenty-two."

"Could have fooled me."

"Younger or older?"

"Younger, of course."

She laughed. "Of course."

"I'm Paul Stefanelli, by the way," he said, holding out his hand.

"Ruby Granik," she told him, letting him shake hers.

"How's the book, Ruby?" He nodded at the book on her lap.

"Can't put it down," she said. "So if you'll excuse me . . ."

"Sure. I get it." He got up and wandered away.

Leah

Leah Cohen was hoping Henry Ammerman would pop the question soon, maybe over the holidays. She was going to his house later today to celebrate his sister Rusty's birthday. Henry's mother sold Volupté compacts wholesale. A girl could never have too many Voluptés. She'd probably get a few from the mothers of the children in her second-grade class. Last year she did. They sure beat fruitcakes, which she gave away, or bad perfume, which she poured down the toilet.

She knew in order to win Henry she'd have to win the rest of his family, and she felt she was doing a pretty good job of it, mainly by keeping her mouth shut. They thought she was shy, quiet, a nice girl from a nice Cleveland family. A teacher. And she was all that, wasn't she?

She'd been seeing Henry for almost eighteen months. She'd met him at a party given by one of the other teachers at her school after she'd moved to New Jersey to live with her aunt Alma. Her mother swore the only way she'd let Leah leave Cleveland was if she lived with family. Alma, her mother's sister, liked the idea of Leah sharing her house and helping with the expenses. As far as Leah was concerned, anything was better than staying in Cleveland and living with her parents. Aunt Alma was a retired school secretary who'd never married. A maiden aunt, Leah's mother called her, but one who played canasta with her friends three afternoons a week, and volunteered at the hospital every Friday morning.

Alma approved of Henry and had told Leah's mother so. Well, who in her right mind wouldn't approve of Henry, a reporter for the *Elizabeth Daily Post*? Henry was smart, kind, funny and very attractive. When he'd first enlisted, right out of high school, he hoped to serve as a reporter for *Stars and Stripes*, since he'd been editor in chief of the *Monticello Times*, the school newspaper at Jefferson High. But after just three months of training he'd been sent into battle. He said he was lucky to get out alive. Most of his company didn't. He was in the hospital for two months with a shot-up leg. After that he got his wish, a desk job with *Stars and Stripes* in London, until six months after the war ended. He said he learned more from those journalists than he ever did at college.

As much as Aunt Alma said she liked Henry, lately she'd been warning Leah about men in general, and Henry, in particular. *Why should he buy the cow if he can get the milk for free?* Aunt Alma's advice, when it came to romance, was so old-world. Besides, Henry never pushed her to go too far. She might not have minded a little push. It wasn't like they were teenagers, after all. Henry had turned twenty-eight over the summer and she would be twenty-four on her next birthday. And guess what, Aunt Alma? He wasn't getting much at all, never mind for free. Though, honestly, if she turned twenty-five and she still wasn't engaged, she saw no point in saving it. She might as well enjoy it while she still could. She was pretty sure Aunt Alma had never enjoyed hers.

When the notice had come around at school asking for volunteers, especially teachers who had experience with young children, to chaperone a holiday party at the Elks Club in Elizabeth, Leah thought her principal might be impressed to see what a community-minded young woman she was, willing to give her time on a Sunday afternoon the week before Christmas.

Another teacher at her school, Harriet Makenna, also volunteered and, better yet, offered to drive Leah, saving her from waiting for the bus from Cranford to Elizabeth in this weather. When she told Henry, he said he'd be covering the event for the *Daily Post* and he'd have a photographer with him. So Leah chose a pretty dress in a deep winter blue, even though she knew the picture in the paper wouldn't be in color. At the last minute she tied on an apron. You never knew when some child was going to be sick or fling something that would land on you.

More than a hundred kids came to the holiday party. There were plenty of volunteers, many of them parents, and they divided the children into groups by age. She and Harriet and two of the mothers took the four- to seven-year-olds and handed out Dixie Cups to get things going. Right away a little girl shouted, "I got Lassie!" She licked the cover of her Dixie Cup clean to show Leah.

Another began to cry. "I want Lassie, too."

"Let's see who you have," Leah said, wiping the child's tears. "Go ahead and lick it clean so we can see." She did and held it up to Leah.

"Ooh, you have Natalie Wood!" Leah told her. "You're lucky because Natalie Wood is a very famous movie star, and look how pretty she is. And you know what? She was a movie star when she was your age."

"I'm six."

"Well, that's swell. Six is a good age to be."

When Henry arrived with the photographer, who didn't look old enough to drive, Leah took off her apron, smoothed out her blue dress and reapplied her lipstick. Harriet, who knew Leah and Henry were seeing each other, whispered, "You look good enough to be the photo on a Dixie Cup."

"As good as Lassie?" Leah whispered.

"Nobody can compete with Lassie."

Leah laughed, then clapped her hands to get the children's attention. "Boys and girls," Leah said. "This is Mr. Henry Ammerman. He's a reporter for the *Elizabeth Daily Post* and he's going to write a story about us." She liked saying his name out loud. *Henry Ammerman.* When she did, Henry waved at the children.

"And this is Todd Dirkson," Henry said of the boy photographer. "He's going to take a picture. Maybe you'll see it in tomorrow's paper." Todd held up his Speed Graphic, so the children could see his camera.

Henry and Todd conferred, then suggested they gather around the piano.

Leah sat down and began to play the introduction to "Rudolph, the Red-Nosed Reindeer." She motioned for the children to sit on the floor around her. Some were still eating their Dixie Cups with the little wooden spoons, some faces were already smeared with chocolate frosting from the cupcakes. Harriet ran around with a damp cloth trying to wipe their faces clean, knowing the parents would want their children to look their Sunday best in the paper.

"All eyes here, please," Leah said, as she continued to play and sing. *"Then one foggy Christmas eve, Santa came to say . . ."* Half of the children sang along with Leah, the other half were more interested in the camera or looking out the windows. Todd clicked while Leah was at her most animated. Henry waited until she'd finished the song, then called, "Thanks, everyone. Thanks, Miss Cohen!"

"You're very welcome, Mr. Ammerman!"

"Happy holidays, Miss Cohen!"

"Same to you, Mr. Ammerman."

Oh, she really, *really* liked Henry Ammerman! She might say *loved* but she was superstitious about using that word too soon.

Ruby

In the departure lounge at Newark Airport Ruby was nodding off. She'd been up since 5 a.m., finishing her last-minute packing before rushing into Manhattan for the radio show. The ice cream soda at Hanson's felt like eons ago. She pulled out the sandwich bag her mother had packed for her and lifted out a cream cheese and pimento sandwich on white bread, crusts cut off as if she were still a little girl going off to school. She was so hungry she wolfed down that sandwich plus another, turkey and Swiss. And then an oatmeal-raisin cookie. All of that made her thirsty, but her mother had filled a thermos with chamomile tea. Her mother was a big believer in the powers of herbal teas.

When they finally boarded, close to 3 p.m., Ruby was seated on the right side of the cabin, next to a girl about her age traveling with a baby. The girl's mother was seated across the aisle, holding a toddler on her lap. Ruby offered to change seats so she and her daughter could be together. "Thank you, dear," the mother said, "but we both want to be on the aisle."

Ruby was fine with that. She liked the window seat.

She saw the lady whose husband was driving to Miami board, and right behind her, the young man with six brothers. He waved and gave her a big smile. While her seatmate burped the baby, Ruby opened her book and picked up reading where she'd left off.

"He's seven months, almost eight," her seatmate said, though Ruby hadn't asked. "The older boy is two. My husband's coming down in a few days. It's the first time we've been apart. We're going to visit family for the holidays." She glanced over and eyed the book Ruby was holding. "Oh, Mickey Spillane! He grew up in Elizabeth. My uncle taught him at the high school. Not that I've read it. My husband says it might be too much for me." Ruby could swear her seatmate blushed. "This is my first flight," she confided. "What about you?"

"I've flown a lot." Ruby shuddered at the thought that this girl's life could be hers, except for her talent and determination.

The stewardess, blond and pretty, with a lisp—*Fathen your theat belths*—sashayed up and down the aisles, checking on them. When they finally began to roll, the young mother's face went white. "I'm a little bit nervous," she whispered to Ruby.

"Take deep breaths," Ruby told her.

But as soon as they took off, Ruby knew something was wrong.

"Does it always feel like this?" her seatmate asked.

Ruby didn't tell her that, no, it didn't feel like this. They were too low. They should be climbing. Why weren't they climbing?

"Can you hold the baby for a minute?" and she shoved the baby at Ruby. "I think I'm going to be sick."

Ruby took the baby. He clutched her necklace, a golden strawberry on a thin chain, while his mother retched. The chain broke. So what?

For seven horrible minutes, seven minutes that felt like hours, years, a whole lifetime, everything seemed to be in slow motion. Ruby heard only the thump of her own heart, not the screaming, not the wailing, not the two-hundred-pound wrestler seated behind her reciting the Lord's Prayer.

This is it? This is how it's going to end? No, it has to be a mistake. Please, God, make it be a mistake. She held the baby close, feeling the warmth of his little body, kissing his soft cheek. He looked right into her eyes.

Outside the window the wing broke away from the plane.

Then they were falling . . . falling diagonally out of the sky.

Henry

As Henry and Todd came out of the Elks Club and started down the long flight of stairs to the street, they heard a roaring sound. "Jesus, is that what I think it is?" Todd asked, looking skyward. He opened his camera, framed the image, then clicked. Henry hoped he'd captured the plane trailing smoke, flames billowing back nearly to the tail, maybe one hundred feet above them and banking steeply to the left.

"Your car or mine?" Todd shouted.

"Mine. Let's go!"

Henry already knew this would be his first front-page story. He drove with his hand on the horn, following the path of the plane. "Get everything you can," he told Todd, who had no experience but was the nephew of the managing editor. "Every detail. Don't stop to think—just do it or you'll miss your chance." He was talking as much to himself as to Todd.

Miri

Outside the theater, the weather had grown even worse. Miri and Rusty locked arms and walked quickly with their heads down. Miri had never felt so cold, so weak from hunger. The candy bar at the movies was the only thing she'd had to eat today. A few more blocks and they'd be home. She could almost smell the leg of lamb rubbed with garlic and rosemary that would be waiting, with pan-roasted potatoes, mint jelly, and green beans, plus a wedge of iceberg lettuce with Russian dressing. Irene would have already frosted the birthday cake she'd baked for Rusty. Miri's mouth was watering just thinking about it.

At the corner of Westfield Avenue and Lowden Street a small child, one of the Bell kids, probably, was sledding in front of her house. There was a Bell in every grade. Miri knew at least four of them. Suddenly the child screamed and pointed to the sky. Miri and Rusty looked up to see a ball of fire rushing toward them.

Miri could feel the heat from above as Rusty grabbed her, pulling her across the street. They ran as fast as they could but the fireball kept coming. They heard a deafening roar. Then a splintering crash, followed by two explosions only a second apart. They were knocked down by the force, Rusty covering Miri's body with her own, trying to protect her.

When Miri opened her eyes she saw feet, dozens of feet, and at first she was so disoriented she didn't know where she was. She couldn't hear anything. There was a ringing in her ears. From every direction people were running toward the flames that were shooting up, toward the thing that had crashed and was burning in the frozen bed of the Elizabeth River.

Rusty helped Miri to her feet. "Go home and tell Nana we're okay," she shouted. "Hurry!" Rusty gave her a gentle shove. "Go, Miri!"

She ran for home. Her feet were numb in her saddle shoes. Snot ran down her face and froze on her upper lip, on her chin, as she rounded the corner of Sayre Street and raced up the front steps. "Nana," she called, bursting into the house. "Nana, where are you? Nana!" she shouted. "Nana!"

She found her under the dining room table. "A bomb?" Irene asked.

"No," Miri told her. "Something crashed in the river. They say it's a plane."

Irene clutched her chest. Miri grabbed her pills from the kitchen counter. Irene put one under her tongue. "Rusty?" she asked.

"She's okay."

"Thank god."

"I have to go back," Miri said.

"Over my dead body!" Irene told her.

"Nana, please . . . I have to help!"

Irene came out from under the table. "Not without me." She pulled galoshes over her shoes. Miri helped her into her coat, all the time arguing, "It's too cold for you, Nana." Cold wasn't good for Irene's angina. But Irene wouldn't listen. She wrapped a wool scarf over her mouth and nose so the wind wouldn't take her breath away.

Outside, Miri held her arm, afraid Irene would slip and fall on the snow that had turned to ice from Friday's snowstorm. When they got to the crash site, Irene looked around and gave one cry. Her hand went to her heart. Miri shouldn't have let her come. She was afraid to let go of Irene's arm, afraid someone would knock her over. She didn't see Rusty anywhere. But she recognized Rabbi Halberstadter standing with a couple of priests, all of them stomping their feet in the cold.

And then Uncle Henry saw them and ordered Miri to take Irene home. "Now!" he barked, and Miri wasn't about to argue with him.

Henry

He'd had to elbow his way through the crowd to where the plane lay on its back in the Elizabeth River, belly ripped open, rubble spilling into the frozen stream and onto the banks. The river was a mass of roaring flames shooting a hundred feet into the air and surrounding the mangled wreckage, one wing pointing straight up.

Firemen, policemen and other rescue workers swarmed to the scene, armed with cutting torches, grappling hooks, blankets, stretchers and bags. A white-clad intern, stethoscope around his neck, went with them, but he didn't stay long—just long enough to know he wasn't needed.

When they started separating the debris, a few bodies, or parts of them, became distinguishable. The bodies were brought out in bags and folded blankets. Workers formed a chain to hand up the remains.

A woman who had somehow evaded police lines and tumbled through the snow too close to the carnage was sick and had to be helped away.

As darkness gathered, floodlights were set up on either bank of the river. The cutting torches went deeper into the tail. More bodies were brought out.

The plane just missed taking down the water company offices, where fifty employees worked during the week. Hamilton Junior High was only a block away. These details would make it into his story.

Miri

None of them was hungry that night but Irene insisted they eat something. She whipped up scrambled eggs and toast while Henry's girlfriend, Leah, told them how close the plane had come to the Elks Club.

"Henry had just left when we saw it. I ran out after him but he was already gone. So I went back inside and started playing the piano really loud. I played a march and told the children to pretend they were elephants. One of the volunteers pulled the velvet drapes closed so the children couldn't see anything. We didn't want to frighten them, so we just kept singing and playing games until their parents came to take them home. We heard the explosions but we pretended to be lions in the jungle, roaring. No one told the children to use their indoor voices. No one told them to settle down. For once they did whatever they wanted, making as much noise as they wanted. And all of them in their party clothes. All those patent-leather Mary Janes. Really, I didn't know what I was doing. My friend, she went crazy. She saw it out the window and just slumped to the floor. One of the mothers had to take her to the ladies' lounge to lie down. What could I do? I was responsible for all those children. One hundred children. It could have crashed into—"

Rusty covered Leah's hand with her own, like a big sister. "But it didn't and the children are fine, thanks to you and your quick thinking."

Until then Miri hadn't thought about how close the plane had come to her school. Suppose it had been a weekday instead of a Sunday? Suppose the plane hadn't made it to the frozen riverbed?

Henry came home just long enough to drop a kiss on Leah's cheek, scarf down some food and change into dry clothes. He must have gotten wet at the crash site. Miri could tell by the way he was walking that his leg hurt. He had a cane but Miri had never seen him use it. "I have to get back," Henry said. "It's the second worst air disaster in this country, the worst disaster since . . ." He looked around the table, shook his head and left.

The worst disaster since what? Miri wondered.

The doorbell rang as Miri was clearing the supper dishes. "I'll get it," she called, running to the front door. It was Natalie, with her mother and little sister. They stepped into the foyer. Natalie hugged her and gushed tears. "I was . . . we were . . . so worried. I couldn't get through on the phone and I thought . . . I thought . . . you know . . . because you live so close . . ." She took in a big breath. "We were at The Tavern when we heard but we didn't stay to finish. They wrapped our food and we took it with us because Daddy had to . . . had to . . ."

Corinne finished for her. "Dr. Osner was called in to help identify the bodies."

Miri stiffened.

Fern said, "Babies died."

"They say you could hear them crying," Natalie added.

"No," Miri said. "I was there and you couldn't hear anything."

"Oh, my gosh!" Natalie cried. "You were there?"

"I was coming home from the movies with my mother. We saw it."

Corinne hugged Miri. "Oh, honey . . ." she said in her southern drawl. Miri teared up, wishing she could apologize for her fantasy. She'd feel guilty forever for wishing something bad would happen to Corinne, who was kind and good and smelled expensive.

"Miri, who is it?" Rusty called.

"Come in," Miri told Corinne.

"Oh, no, we don't want to intrude," Corinne said. "We just wanted to make sure you were all right."

Suddenly, it seemed important for Natalie and her family to stay, to help celebrate Rusty's birthday. "It's Rusty's birthday and we're going to have cake."

"I love birthday cake," Fern said.

"Well . . . just for a minute," Corinne told Miri, following her into Irene's dining room. Leah jumped up and brought extra chairs to the table.

"Please . . . sit . . ." Irene told them. "Let's be happy we're all together."

"Except for Henry," Leah said.

"But thank god Henry is safe," Irene reminded her. Irene could always find something good to say about a situation. And for the moment Miri was grateful for both her mother and her grandmother.

When Irene lit the candles on the cake and set it down in front of Rusty, Miri began to sing, *"Happy birthday . . ."* The others joined in. Rusty blew out the candles on her cake, thirty-three of them, plus one for good measure, with tears streaming down her face.

"You're not that old, are you?" Fern asked.

Rusty laughed. "No, I'm not *that* old."

Then they all laughed, as if it were a real party, as if nothing bad had happened or would ever happen. Miri forgot to ask what became of the leg of lamb.

Rusty

Rain, shine or disaster, Rusty was on the 7:32 train to New York. The day after the crash was no exception. She hadn't missed a day of work in fourteen years and she wasn't about to start now, just because a plane crashed into the Elizabeth River. Never mind that she'd hardly slept, that Miri had spent most of the night in her bed, both of them tossing and turning, dozing off, then waking with a start. When Miri asked if she believed in God, what was she supposed to say? "Of course I believe in God," she'd told her.

"But how could God let such a terrible thing happen?"

"It's not God's job to decide what happens," she'd said. "It's his job to help you get through it." If only she really believed that.

On the train her hands shook and her teeth chattered. The man seated next to her assumed she was cold and offered his coat. "Maybe you're coming down with something."

"No, it's not that . . ." She thanked him but refused his coat. Maybe she should have stayed home, but then Miri would have wanted to stay home, too, and it was important for her to set an example, to show Miri that no matter what, you take your responsibilities seriously.

She'd landed the Employee of the Year award more than once, and not just because of her exemplary attendance record. If Irene hadn't stepped up to the plate when Miri was born, Rusty wouldn't be executive secretary to Charles Whitten, senior partner at Whitten, Granger and White, one of the most respected law firms in the city. Rusty was lucky to have such a good job, such an important job, given that she'd never gone to college. She'd planned to go, had been accepted to Douglass, the women's school of Rutgers University, but things happen, things that can change your life overnight. Not that she was going to dwell on that. She'd learned a long time ago to look ahead, not back. What's done is done. Make the best of it and move on. And she had, hadn't she?

None of the girls at the office asked her about the crash. They knew she commuted from New Jersey, but they were chatting about their weekends—about how their boyfriends couldn't believe Joe DiMaggio had announced his retirement. Only Mrs. Yates, head of the secretarial pool, said, "You live in Elizabeth, don't you, Rusty?"

"I do."

"I heard about the crash. Tragic."

"Yes, it was."

"Glad you were able to make it to work today."

"Me, too."

And that was it except for her friend Naomi. Rusty's family called her the "Other Naomi." They met for grilled cheese sandwiches at the coffee shop around the corner from their offices. Naomi wanted to talk about the crash but Rusty kept changing the subject. Turned out she didn't want to talk about it, after all, or even think about it. Instead, she bummed a Chesterfield off Naomi and asked for a refill on her coffee.

Miri

Miri expected school to be canceled on Monday morning but there was no announcement on the local radio station. She wished she could stay in bed under the covers with the quilt pulled over her head. She'd slept fitfully last night, waking every hour, finally winding up in Rusty's bed, the two of them watching over each other. She'd never get rid of the stench in her nostrils, no matter how she washed them, sticking the soapy washcloth up as far as it would go, making her sneeze twenty times in a row. She'd tried telling herself it hadn't happened. If she went to the river today there would be no sign of a plane. It had all been a bad dream.

Even before she got downstairs the aroma of freshly baked coffee cake wafted up from Irene's kitchen. And if it hadn't happened, why would Irene be up and baking this early?

"For the Red Cross, darling," Irene told her, while Blanche Kessler, home-service chairman for the Elizabethtown chapter, packed the cakes into boxes.

"To serve at the hospitality table," Blanche Kessler said, "outside the makeshift morgue behind Haines Funeral Home."

If she still had any doubts, they vanished when she got to school. They were all buzzing about it in the hall outside their homerooms. *Where were you when you heard the news? What were you doing?*

SUZANNE: My mother and I had just sat down to Sunday dinner when we heard the roar, then the explosions. We put our faces into our dinner plates—pork chops, mashed potatoes and beets. You should have seen us when it was over. Beets stain everything. I swear, I thought it was a comet. It sounded like a comet.

ANGELO VENETTI: That was no comet—that was a bomb inside the plane.

PETE WOLF: That was no bomb. It was something from outer space, some alien thing, maybe Martians.

DONNY KELLEN: It's a Commie plot!

ELEANOR (*baiting Donny*): You sure Senator Joe McCarthy didn't take the plane down?

DONNY KELLEN: McCarthy's the one person trying to save us from the Commies.

ELEANOR: McCarthy is an evil man. A bully.

DONNY KELLEN (*shouting*): I can't help it if you're too thick to see the truth, bitch.

ELEANOR: Idiot!

Eleanor Gordon was the most sophisticated in their crowd. She read *The New Yorker*. When it came to McCarthy, Miri's family agreed with Eleanor.

Donny Kellen was always ranting about the Commies and how they were trying to take over the world. When the Dianetics were kicked out of town for starting a medical school without permission, he'd ranted about that, too, but Miri didn't think the Dianetics had anything to do with the Commies, though she couldn't be sure. Uncle Henry had covered the story for the *Daily Post*. That's how Miri found out Donny's aunt had left town with them, to follow some guy named L. Ron Hubbard to Kansas.

WHEN THE BELL RANG they headed for their homerooms, Suzanne, Miri and Eleanor to 9-201, Natalie and Robo to 9-202, but that didn't stop them from jabbering.

"Settle down, boys and girls," Mrs. Wallace, their homeroom teacher, said. Mrs. Wallace was so small, not even five feet, they called her "Tiny" behind her back, not Theresa, her real first name. Rumor had it she weighed under ninety pounds. Yet she was married and had two children, both of them in elementary school. In addition to teaching English, Tiny was the adviser to the school paper, *Hamilton Headlines*. Eleanor was editor in chief. The paper came out just three times during the school year and the stories covered only school-related activities. Nothing about the rest of the world, or even the rest of the city. Miri had very little interest in the stories she was assigned to write, but she did her best, getting in the *who, what, where, when* and *why*.

On the day the paper came out most of the kids just glanced at it, then tossed it into the wastebasket. Some didn't even bother to look before throwing it away. It galled Miri to see that, because even if it wasn't exciting to read, it was still a lot of work.

Tiny said, "I can see you're upset about yesterday's situation, but now it's time to get back to normal."

Situation? Miri thought. *Normal?*

"Mrs. Wallace," Suzanne called, waving her hand in the air.

"What is it, Suzanne?" Tiny asked.

"Miri was there. She saw it happen."

Why did Suzanne think she had to tell the whole world she was there? Natalie had let the girls know last night. Not that it was a secret, not that she didn't want her friends to know, but having Suzanne announce it in homeroom felt wrong, it felt like a betrayal, as if your friend blurted out one of your deepest secrets, something you never wanted anyone else to know.

Everyone turned to look at Miri, including Tiny. "Then it's only right that Miri should get to choose today's psalm," Tiny said.

Every day since they'd started junior high, the morning routine in homeroom was the same—Pledge of Allegiance, followed by the singing of "My Country, 'Tis of Thee," the reading of a psalm, then reciting the Lord's Prayer together.

Tiny walked to Miri's desk and laid the Bible on it.

"Psalm one hundred," Miri said, without opening the book. It was the only psalm she knew by heart, the one she chose whenever it was her turn to read from the Bible.

"Would you read that for us, Miri?" Tiny said.

Miri thumbed through the Bible until she came to it. She cleared her throat and began very quietly. "'Make a joyful noise unto the Lord, all ye lands . . .'" Usually the words meant nothing to her but today every word left her picturing the crash, hearing the explosions. The ringing in her ears returned. She couldn't finish. She felt like she might cry or scream or both. Suzanne took the Bible from her and finished reading the psalm.

"I'm sorry," Suzanne said when the bell rang and they left for their first-period classes. "I didn't know she'd make you read the morning psalm."

"It's okay," Miri told her. "Just, please, don't tell anyone else."

"I won't."

No other teacher mentioned the crash.

Right after fifth-period algebra, Natalie took Miri aside in the girls' room and said, "I have this buzzing inside my head."

"You want to go to the nurse?"

"No, it's not like that."

"Maybe it's your period," Miri said.

"This is different," Natalie told her. "And when the buzzing stops, Ruby starts talking to me."

"Ruby?"

"The dancer who was on that plane. Didn't you listen to Walter Winchell last night? He spent half his show talking about her." As soon as she admitted Ruby was talking to her, before Miri even had the chance to take it in, Natalie grabbed her shoulders. "Swear you won't tell anyone what I just said."

What could Miri do? Natalie was her best friend. She had no choice but to swear she would never tell. For the rest of the day, whenever the other kids were buzzing about the crash, Miri was thinking about the buzzing in Natalie's head.

OBITUARIES—Mrs. Estelle Sapphire of Bayonne was among the first identified at the makeshift morgue set up in the two garages behind Haines Funeral Home. She was identified by her wedding ring. Her husband, Benjamin Sapphire, collapsed at the scene and was taken by police car to the home of a friend.

THE CHRISTMAS PAGEANT WAS just days away, and Miri had choir rehearsal after school. When she got home she found a strange man in Irene's living room, sitting in the wing chair, wrapped in one of Irene's crocheted afghans, his feet soaking in a pan of warm water, his trouser legs rolled up to reveal the hairiest legs Miri had ever seen. Even his toes were covered with dark hair. If she didn't know better she'd have sworn they were animal legs.

"Miri, darling, this is Ben Sapphire," Irene said, handing him a steaming cup of tea, or maybe it was soup. "He was freezing cold," Irene told her. "His hands and feet were blue. I thought for sure they'd have to take him to the hospital."

He was still shivering but he managed to say, "Irene was serving home-baked coffee cake."

"Which one?" Miri asked. "Sour cream with cinnamon and walnuts, or streusel?"

He looked to Irene for an answer. "Sour cream," she said, leading Miri into the kitchen where she whispered, "We knew each other in the old days, in Bayonne. He lost his wife in the crash."

Miri didn't want to think about the crash. "I'll be upstairs," she told Irene. "Call me when it's time to set the table for supper."

She and Rusty and Uncle Henry ate at Irene's every night. Irene was a great cook, which was Rusty's excuse for never having learned. Instead of encouraging her, Rusty said Irene shooed her out of the kitchen. Rusty was always harping that Miri should learn to cook, that Irene would have more patience with Miri than she'd had with her. Learning to cook from Irene would be a lot better than making lumpy and disgusting white sauce in the required cooking class at Hamilton Junior High.

THE LEG OF LAMB materialized as lamb stew that night. Tasty, with little potatoes, green beans, carrots and celery, seasoned with rosemary. Ben Sapphire joined Miri and Rusty at Irene's table. He broke down several times, covering his eyes with his hand, blowing his nose with a handkerchief. "I can't think of her inside that plane . . . my darling wife, my Estelle . . ." Irene patted his hand.

"We took a place in Miami Beach for the season," he told Rusty. "She was flying down early to get it ready. I was going to drive down with the luggage. She gets carsick—got carsick—never liked long drives." He broke down again.

"I'm so sorry," Rusty said. "I spoke with her on the phone on Saturday. She ordered six Volupté compacts to take to Florida."

"The compacts," he said, hitting his forehead with his hand. "I forgot about the compacts."

Again, Irene patted his hand. "Never mind about that."

"No, I want to pay."

"Please, Ben . . ." Irene shook her head.

Miri stole a look at Rusty, who took *her* hand under the table and gave it a gentle squeeze. Rusty's fingers were warm.

Henry came home as they were finishing what was left of Rusty's birthday cake. He was flushed with excitement, dropping a stack of papers on one end of the table, then handing each of them a copy of the *Daily Post*, with his story and byline on the front page.

He had no idea who Ben Sapphire was but he passed a copy of the paper to him, too. Ben Sapphire took one look and turned gray. He excused himself from the table and Irene helped him to the bathroom.

When she came back without Ben, she told Henry, "His wife, Estelle, was on that plane."

"How was I supposed to know?" Henry asked.

"Sometimes you have to assume," Irene said. Then she turned to Miri. "Darling, give me that paper."

But Miri held on to it.

"She's been through enough," Irene said to Henry. "She doesn't need the gruesome details."

"She was there, Mama," Henry said. "She saw it happen."

"And that's bad enough."

"You don't think she's going to read the paper tonight?" Henry said. "You don't think she'll want to read my story?"

Miri wasn't sure she wanted to read Henry's story but she didn't say so. She didn't say anything. On the one hand, she wanted to forget it ever happened. On the other, she wanted to know who else was on the plane besides the dancer and Ben Sapphire's wife, Estelle. She wanted to know why it crashed.

"Tomorrow there'll be a story about Paul Stefanelli, the youngest of seven brothers," Henry said. "Came through the war without a scratch and died on that plane. He worked at Ronson's. And later this week I'm interviewing Ruby Granik's family. I'm talking to anyone who has a story to tell, and so far, that's pretty much everyone."

Miri wished she could tell him about Natalie. She was betting Natalie was the only one who heard Ruby's voice. "What about us?" Miri asked. "Are you interviewing Mom and me?"

"Would you like me to?" Henry asked.

"No," Rusty said. "Enough is enough. She's too young to understand. None of *us* can make sense of it—how can you expect a young girl to?"

"Not by sweeping it under the rug and pretending it didn't happen," Henry said.

"Since when are you the expert?" Rusty asked. "When you have a young, impressionable daughter we'll discuss it."

Until then, Miri had never heard an angry word between Rusty and Henry. She couldn't believe they were talking this way in front of her, as if she weren't sitting right there. This was a first after a lifetime of silences, of secrets, of pretending everything was fine.

Irene pushed her chair back from the table, signaling the end of this argument. "I'm going to check on Ben."

"Miri, don't you have homework?" Rusty said.

Oh, sure. Homework. The answer for everything.

Elizabeth Daily Post

56 KILLED AS FLAMING PLANE CRUMPLES, FALLS INTO FROZEN RIVER

By Henry Ammerman

DEC. 17—Elizabeth, long fearful because of its proximity to Newark Airport, gained a permanent listing in the annals of aviation tragedy at 3:09 o'clock yesterday afternoon when a two-engined non-scheduled airliner plummeted in flames into the east bank of the Elizabeth River, only seven minutes after its takeoff. All 52 passengers and the four crew died, the most tragic civil catastrophe in Elizabeth's three centuries of existence.

Thousands in streets already flooded with holiday shoppers turned their eyes skyward to the thunderous roar of a low-flying plane in trouble. They gaped in horror as a thin streak of smoke turned to flame, and the plane struggled to return to the airport, before its right wing collapsed.

The plane hurtled earthward into the heart of the city like an angry, wounded bird. It sheared off part of an unoccupied house at 70 Westfield Ave., crashed into a brick warehouse of the Elizabethtown Water Company, and landed on its back in the frozen riverbed, a mass of twisted fiery wreckage.

It was one of the only open areas in a mile-square radius, perhaps a silent tribute to the deceased pilot's skill.

3

Miri

Miri sat on her bed reading the beginning of Henry's front-page story, then had to lower her head to the floor. She couldn't breathe, couldn't remember how to take a breath. When she felt the blood rush back to her face she sat up and took a sip of water. Then she lay back against her pillows and thumbed through the paper until she came to her favorite section.

> Debutante Judith Merck, daughter of Mr. and Mrs. George Merck of West Orange, a student at Sarah Lawrence College, will be presented tomorrow night at the Grosvenor Ball. After, Miss Merck will be heading anywhere there's snow for some holiday skiing.

She closed her eyes, picturing Miss Judith Merck in her white ball gown at the Grosvenor Ball, dancing the first dance with her father. She tried to imagine herself wearing a beautiful long white dress, dancing with *her* father, though she'd never seen a photo of him.

She was glad she didn't have her father's last name. *Monsky*—ugh! No one ever said his name. She still wouldn't know it if Henry hadn't taken her to Spirito's for a pizza last April, on the day President Truman had relieved General MacArthur of his command. The whole school had been called to the auditorium to listen to MacArthur's speech. *Old soldiers never die—they just fade away.* Eleanor was allowed to cover the story in the school paper, because of the special assembly.

She explained why President Truman had fired General MacArthur, had kicked him out of the military for insubordination after MacArthur voiced disagreement with his policies.

Most kids dumped the paper in the trash, as usual. But Miri had read every word. She'd asked Uncle Henry about it. He'd been surprised but pleased by her interest. Between bites of pepperoni, he'd explained. "I want you to know the truth, Miri. Always."

So she'd gathered all her courage and asked him about her father, just *la-di-dah*, as if they were still talking about the president and the general. She prayed Henry couldn't tell how fast her heart was beating. He swallowed the food in his mouth, swigged some Pabst Blue Ribbon, wiped his mouth with a napkin, and told her. Not everything. She knew he was holding back, but for now, she was satisfied just to know her father's name, Mike Monsky, that he and Rusty had gone out for a few months and—*Bingo!*—she was pregnant. She didn't say what she was thinking—*You can't get pregnant from playing Bingo*.

Once, when Miri was in sixth grade, she'd tried asking Rusty. "So this father of mine . . . is he alive or dead?"

The color had drained out of Rusty's face. "I don't know."

"Come on, Mom . . ."

"Honestly, Miri, I don't know."

"Were you married to him?"

"That's a hard question to answer."

"Either you were or you weren't."

"I *said* that's a hard question to answer, Miri."

"I just want to know if I'm a bastard or not."

Rusty exploded. "Don't ever let me hear you using that

word! That word has nothing to do with you." Then she choked up. "You were loved from the moment you were born." That was the last time Miri asked her mother about her father. Because what was the point? At least no one said he was *a no-good son of a bitch*, the way she'd heard Cousin Belle describe her daughter's husband. They didn't say anything, which in a way was worse.

"This talk has to be a secret between us," Henry had said that night last April as they'd walked to his car, each of them with an ice cream cone. "Okay?"

She didn't tell him how much she hated secrets. Hated them with a passion. Were adults ever honest with kids? Aside from Henry, none had been honest with her—not Rusty, not Irene. They lived in a world where children, even teenagers, were protected from the truth for their own good. That's how they got out of saying anything. Ever since she could remember, the adults would stop talking when she walked into the room. They'd smile at her, then change the subject.

Now here was Henry telling her *she* had to keep this a secret from Rusty and Irene. *With pleasure, Uncle Henry.*

"I'd be in big trouble for breaking their rules. Who am I to say you have the right to know about your father? I don't have kids. I don't know how I'd feel if I did."

"Thank you, Uncle Henry." She didn't ask any of the hundreds of questions already forming inside her head. She'd save them for another time.

She wondered where Mike Monsky was now. Maybe he'd been a passenger on the plane to Miami yesterday. Maybe Dr. Osner would have to identify him by his teeth and dental X-rays. Rabbi Halberstadter would pray over him, even though there would be no next of kin for the rabbi to comfort. Who's to say Mike Monsky hadn't bought a huge insurance policy on his life before he'd boarded the doomed flight and once they discovered *she* was next of kin, she would get the money? Would she take it? She didn't have to think twice. Yes, she'd take it! For Rusty and Irene and Henry, who had raised her without a dime from him. Just don't expect her to visit his grave, Rabbi. She'd give him the same thing he'd given her. Not a second thought. Even if he'd bought that policy she knew it was just because he'd felt guilty for all the years he'd neglected his daughter. If he even knew he had a daughter.

Henry

Hadn't Rusty told her anything? She had a right to know. It was *her* life, her history. He may have been young then, but he remembered how Irene had argued with Rusty over calling Mike's family. Rusty wouldn't hear of it. "He's gone, Mama. He's probably on a ship in the Pacific by now. Anyway, I don't want to marry him."

"You should have thought of that sooner," Irene told Rusty, one of the only unkind remarks he'd ever heard from his mother.

Irene shipped Rusty off to Aunt Ida's in Santa Monica, California, where Rusty supposedly met and married a boy who was going overseas. When Max had the second stroke Rusty took the next train back and Irene didn't try to stop her. She needed all the help she could get.

He remembered the murky stories Irene concocted to

explain to anyone who had the guts to ask how Rusty happened to be pregnant, or later, how Rusty happened to have a baby, or even what happened to the boy. When Rusty balked, Irene told her, *Too bad*.

He loved his sister, he admired her, he took her side, but he didn't think this was fair to Miri.

Elizabeth Daily Post

CONTROLLERS SAW SMOKE FROM ILL-FATED PLANE

By Henry Ammerman

DEC. 18—The Miami Airlines C-46 that crashed here on Sunday was a doomed flight. It had been turned over to maintenance personnel just one hour before its scheduled departure that morning. They worked furiously behind the scenes as passengers fretted in the departure lounge. The flight was delayed five hours.

It was not long enough. As the aircraft climbed, air controllers saw smoke trailing from the right engine. They called the pilot and authorized him to return on any runway. He never answered that call, but witnesses saw the landing gear lowered. The pilot struggled to turn in the fatal moments before the flames and a collapsed wing deprived him of control.

Parts of the plane rained down on residential neighborhoods. Home owners on Verona Avenue, a mile from the crash, found pieces of aluminum and belting material in their yards. Joseph O. Fluet has been placed in charge of investigating the disaster for the Civil Aeronautics Board. He has put out a call for any found parts to be turned in to the police.

4

Miri

Some parents suggested it might be seen as inappropriate to hold a Christmas pageant this year. Others asked what could be more appropriate than celebrating the birth of Jesus and the spirit of the holiday season.

The principal decided the show must go on. It would be performed twice—once in the afternoon for the kids at school and the parents who didn't work, and again that night, for working parents and friends. That's when Rusty would come.

Miri marched in the choir. She loved the green choir robe with the white collar, and carrying the slim pencil flashlight that looked like a candle. The sound of their voices singing together gave her goose bumps it was so beautiful. She felt the same when she listened to the choir at Temple B'nai Israel but that was just on the High Holidays, the only time her family attended services, except for seventh grade, when the boys in her class had been bar mitzvahed and every week there was another celebration. Then she'd had to go with her friends to Friday night and Saturday morning services. The parties were lavish affairs at catering halls or places like Chi-Am Chateau.

But no matter how thrilling it was to Miri, she couldn't convince Irene to come to the pageant. Irene said it hurt to hear Miri singing songs about Jesus. Miri explained over and over that the songs didn't mean anything to her. They were just songs. So what if they were about Jesus? He was a Jew, wasn't he? They'd had this discussion every year since Miri joined the choir at Hamilton. Every year Irene told her it was against her principles. Why didn't they celebrate the story of Hanukkah and sing Hanukkah songs, too? Deep inside, Miri knew Irene was right. It was unfair to celebrate only one religion. Still, she continued to march down the aisle singing "Adeste Fideles" in Latin.

Natalie's mother didn't mind that Natalie was portraying Mary, mother of Jesus, in the Christmas pageant. *It's about acting*, Corinne said. *Not about believing.* If only Miri could convince Irene of that.

On the day of the afternoon performance of the pageant, halfway through, something happened onstage, something Miri couldn't see because the choir was seated in front of the stage, facing the audience, and the pageant was unfolding behind them. A murmur went through the audience, and when Miri turned to see what was going on, Natalie was sobbing. This was not part of the pageant, although the audience didn't know it yet. Natalie wasn't supposed to talk or cry or do anything but look holy while cradling the baby Jesus, who was played by a doll swaddled in a blanket.

"I hear the babies crying," Natalie said once, clearly, before she ran offstage. The audience still didn't get it. They were probably thinking this was some new, hastily added tribute to those who had lost their lives in the crash—until the other Mary, the nighttime Mary, Lois Morano, took Natalie's place onstage. When Lois picked up the baby Jesus the pageant continued.

Miri was both surprised and not surprised. Since the crash Natalie had been acting weird—that business about the buzzing in her head and Ruby talking to her. Natalie could be overly dramatic but she would never give up the chance to be onstage. Miri caught sight of Corinne, rushing out of the auditorium as the choir sang "O Little Town of Bethlehem." She wondered if she should leave, too, because, after all, she was Natalie's best friend. But that would be awkward since she was seated smack in the middle of the middle row of the choir.

After the recessional, when the choir marched out singing "Joy to the World," Miri tried to find someone who could tell her what happened to Natalie. Mrs. Domanski, the choir director, explained that Natalie had suffered stomach pains, probably brought on by stage fright, and had gone home with her mother. Miri knew that Natalie never suffered stage fright, though she often had stomach pains.

She hadn't expected to see Henry. "Thank you for coming," she said, hugging him. She knew how busy he was.

"I was in the last row. Missed the processional, but caught the change of Marys onstage. What was that about?"

Miri shrugged. "I don't know."

Henry was the only one in their family to own a car—a '38 green Chevy coupe with a rumble seat. But today was no day to sit in a rumble seat, unless you wanted to wind up frozen to death, so Miri sat up front with Henry and asked him to drop her at Natalie's house. He glanced over at her but didn't ask any questions.

MRS. BARNES WAS TALL, with excellent posture, and wore her silvery hair pulled back in a bun. "Natalie is upstairs, resting," Mrs. Barnes told Miri, when Miri rang the bell.

Miri didn't ask for permission to go up. She took the

wide stairs two at a time, but before she reached the landing, Mrs. Barnes called, "Miri!"

Miri stopped.

"I hear you were there when the plane crashed."

She nodded.

Mrs. Barnes said, "My son Tim is a pilot."

She nodded again. Mrs. Barnes was always talking about her son, the pilot.

"He says the pilot of that plane tried to avoid the residential area. That's why he brought it down in the riverbed. He saved a lot of lives."

"I know. My uncle wrote about it in the *Daily Post*."

"I forgot your uncle is a reporter. He should talk to Tim. He says it was maintenance. That's the problem with those non-scheduled airlines—you don't know who's doing the maintenance. They don't have the same standards as the majors. It's a risk to fly them. Tim flies with American. Top-notch. You can trust them."

"I've never flown," Miri said.

"When you do."

"I doubt I will."

"Of course you will."

Miri shook her head. When she learned the fiery thing that fell from the sky was a plane, she vowed she would never set foot on one.

Natalie was lying on her bed, her pale curls fanned out on the pillow. She looked like an angel, her cheeks still rosy from stage makeup, the Pixie Pink lipstick not yet worn off. Miri sat on the edge of the bed and reached for Natalie's hand.

"I made a complete fool of myself," Natalie said. "I'll never be able to go back to school."

"Everyone will understand."

"Understand what?"

"You know."

Natalie looked at Miri, waiting for her to spell it out.

"Understand that you're . . ." Miri began.

"What?"

"Understand that you're sensitive." Miri was proud for coming up with such a good word.

"Is that like saying I'm dramatic, or crazy?"

Miri was careful now. "*Sensitive* is better than *dramatic*, and it's definitely not as bad as *crazy*."

"*You* saw the crash but *you* didn't cry in the middle of the Christmas pageant."

"Everyone is different." Miri didn't add, *You don't know what's inside of me. You don't know about the smell in my nostrils, you don't know how I have to sleep in bed with my mother half the night, or that the only thing she'll say about it is,* It's over and it's never going to happen again.

Natalie held on to Miri's hand, and looked around as if there might be someone else in her room. Then she lowered her voice to almost a whisper. "You know that dancer, Ruby Granik?"

"My uncle is interviewing her family," Miri said.

Natalie let go of Miri's hand and sat up, intrigued by this information. "Do you think he'd interview me?"

"He's only talking to people who knew her. Family. Friends. People who worked with her."

Natalie's voice went very low. "What I could tell him is just as important, maybe more important. Not that I'd want him to use my name."

"Like what?"

"Swear you'll never tell?"

"I already swore I wouldn't, remember?"

"She's the one who cried in the middle of the Christmas pageant today because she'll never have another Christmas. She's the one who keeps telling me about the babies inside the plane." Natalie jumped off her bed. "I have to get ready for dance class. Come with me."

"Wait, I thought . . ."

But Natalie grabbed her hatbox-shaped dance bag and ran down the stairs, with Miri trailing behind her. Natalie was full of surprises today, Miri thought. One minute, falling apart onstage, the next, with enough energy to light up the whole house.

"Tell Mom I've gone to dance class," Natalie called to Mrs. Barnes.

Mrs. Barnes met her at the kitchen door. "I thought you weren't feeling well."

"I'm better now," Natalie said. "And Miri's coming with me. We'll take the bus. Mom can pick me up at the usual time."

At tap class Natalie was the best. Her feet led the way and the rest of her body followed. Double pullbacks, traveling time steps, wings—she could do it all. No one in her class could begin to keep up with her.

After class, Natalie gave her teacher, Erma Rankin, her Christmas gift, which Miri guessed from the size and shape of the box was a Volupté compact, tied with the same holiday paper and red ribbon her grandmother used.

Miss Rankin said, "Thank you, Natalie. I'm going to miss you. I hope you'll still come to visit from time to time."

"What do you mean?" Natalie asked.

"I've taught you all I can. As I told your mother a few weeks ago, you're ready to study with the masters. I'm going to suggest a few teachers in New York."

"You told my mother?"

"Yes, just after Thanksgiving." Erma Rankin read the look on Natalie's face. "Oops! I'll bet she was saving that as a holiday surprise."

"Did you hear that?" Natalie asked Miri in the changing room. "Did you hear what she said?"

Miri nodded. "Yes."

"Do you know what this means?" Natalie asked.

"It means you have talent."

"Yes," Natalie said. "But it's Ruby's talent. Don't you see? She's dancing through me now. She's living inside me."

"But Miss Rankin said she told your mother at Thanksgiving."

"But she didn't tell *me* until today. Because today I was so much better than I was at Thanksgiving."

Even though she swore she wouldn't, Miri wondered again if she should tell someone about Natalie. But who would she tell and what would she say? She was still thinking about it at the pageant that night, and after, when Rusty took her to Schutt's, the ice cream parlor on Morris Avenue, for a hot fudge sundae.

Elizabeth Daily Post

THAT GIRL

By Henry Ammerman

DEC. 19—She was 22, with the longest legs he'd ever seen. "She could dance," Jimmy Bower said. "She could really dance! That girl was going places."

That girl was Ruby Granik, on her way to dance at the Vagabond Club in Miami when she boarded the ill-fated Miami Airlines C-46 on a bitterly cold Sunday afternoon. The flight had already been delayed two hours and Ruby and the other passengers waited another three before they boarded.

"I begged her to wait," her best friend, Dana Lynley, said, "but she insisted on taking the non-sked. It was less money and money was tight. She hadn't been paid yet for her last job and she needed to get to Miami. You didn't win an argument with Ruby. Once she made up her mind there was no going back. That's how she lived her life."

"I knew her since she was born," Billy Morrison, owner of Billy's Tavern and family friend, said. "I served her her first legal drink, a pink lady. I made it weak but it still made her tipsy. Her father was my best friend. There are no words," he said, visibly shaken. "None."

Her uncle, Fire Captain Victor Szabo, of Elizabeth Engine Company #3, said, "I knew Ruby was on that plane. I knew it and yet when the call came in and my unit sped to the scene of the crash, I had to force myself not to think of her inside that broken pile in the Elizabeth River. I had to do my job. It was the hardest thing I've ever had to do. My wife and Ruby's mother are sisters. My wife had gone out to Queens to keep

Ruby's parents company for a few days. We have no children so we thought of Ruby as our daughter, too. We couldn't have been more proud. It's a devastating loss." He paused and turned away, using a handkerchief to dab at his eyes. When he regained his composure he said, voice breaking, "There was nothing left of Ruby but that Bulova watch and the infant in her arms."

The infant belonged to Ruby's seatmate. At 7 months, he was the youngest member of a family—his mother, his grandmother and his 2-year-old brother—all of whom died when the C-46 crashed and exploded.

Ruby's last stop before leaving New York for the airport was Hanson's Drug Store. Jimmy Bower, who worked behind the counter and had once danced with Ruby in a show, was distraught. "She loved all things strawberry," he said. "I made her a strawberry ice cream soda. I kidded her about eating the Maraschino cherry on top. She enjoyed it down to the last lick. Sunday was the saddest day of my life. A lot of the dancers who hang out here feel the same way. Ruby lit up the room, always ready to enjoy a joke, always with that dynamite smile."

The owner of the Vagabond in Miami, where Ruby was heading, said there was no replacing Ruby. "Oh, sure, there are plenty of dancers out there, but Ruby had that certain something. That je ne sais quoi, if you'll pardon my French," Frank Viti said. "She made the audience feel special, as if every dance move was just for them. Not that many dancers connect on a personal level, but Ruby Granik gave it her all."

Her mother said she was an ambitious girl. "Since she was a child she knew what she wanted and she figured out how to get it. She didn't depend on anyone to hand it to her. Not Ruby. We named her for Ruby Keeler, my favorite movie star. Who knew our Ruby would also be a dancer, a star? When our family hit rough times and I had to give up my job to care for my husband, Ruby became our sole support. But our girl never complained. She was a gem, just like her name."

Her boyfriend, brother of actor and entertainer Danny

Thomas, declined this reporter's request for an interview. He was in seclusion, according to family members, mourning the loss of a wonderful girl.

5

Christina

Christina Demetrious was done in by that news story. *Ruby was an ambitious girl . . . she knew what she wanted*, Ruby's mother said. She couldn't get that line out of her head. If *she* died suddenly, would her mother say that about her? She didn't think so. Her mother didn't know who she was or what she wanted. And that thought made her cry as much as the story in the paper.

Christina and her family had been at an anniversary party for her aunt and uncle in Metuchen on the day the plane crashed. The next morning, when Papou, her grandfather, had taken out the trash, he'd found pieces of the plane in their yard. Her father dropped them off at the police station on his way to work at his restaurant, Three Brothers Luncheonette. Baba was disappointed she wasn't coming to work with him at the restaurant after graduation. She might have if there weren't already four male cousins waiting to take over when Baba and her uncles retired. None of them believed a girl had any place working in a restaurant except as a waitress, a cashier or maybe a bookkeeper. Athena was smart to go into business with Mama, where she had a real future.

Christina was sure Dr. O would cancel the annual holiday outing to New York. She could see the toll the crash had taken, the way Dr. O worked all day, then rushed to the makeshift morgue to help identify bodies by their dental records. That would take the steam out of anyone. Sure, Dr. O still told jokes in the office—the one about the guy with the carrot in his ear was his latest—and he still whistled his patients' favorite tunes while he worked on their teeth, but she could see it in his eyes, a sadness that was never there before.

This was the third year Christina had worked for Dr. O after school. He'd asked her to work for him full-time starting in June, when she graduated from Battin High School, and she was going to take him up on his offer.

If her mother knew who sometimes came to Dr. O's office she would faint. Faint and then forbid her ever to return. Or maybe the other way around. Forbid, then faint. Her mother lived to see her girls safely married to Greek husbands, as if then nothing bad could happen to them. She already had her eye on someone for Christina, Zak Galanos. He was a senior at Newark State, majoring in education. Next year he'd be teaching. His father worked at Singer's and was known around town as the Sewing Machine Man because he could repair or recondition any Singer. Christina's father thought she could do better. A businessman, maybe, or a lawyer.

If her father knew she'd met Longy Zwillman, New Jersey's most notorious gangster, at Dr. O's office, let alone held a dental mirror in his mouth, she didn't know what he'd do. But it wouldn't be good. Now that Longy had a fancy society wife, two children, and lived in an ivy-covered mansion in West Orange, he was considered a wealthy businessman, not a gangster. He was active in the community, philanthropic, giving money to synagogues and other Jewish charities. No more talk of murder or other crimes. Still, everyone in her parents' generation knew about him.

We don't discuss what happens in the office, Daisy always reminded her. Daisy Dupree had worked as Dr. O's secretary forever, since he set up his dental practice nearly twenty years ago. She was considered family by the Osners. Christina was learning from Daisy how to be discreet. *Discretion.* A word most of her classmates had never heard, and certainly never practiced.

Yesterday, Daisy had taken her aside to explain the rules for this year's holiday outing. "Mrs. Osner has imposed a moratorium on crash talk," Daisy said. "And, Christina . . . why don't you wear the sweater set Mrs. Osner gave you for your birthday? I know she'd like to see it on you."

She'd be happy to wear the sweater set. It was beautiful. Mrs. Osner's gifts always were. As for happy talk, she could do that. Who wanted to talk about the crash, anyway? Who wanted to think that only eight people could be identified by their faces? *Only eight.* They all needed a break, didn't they?

THE TRIP FROM ELIZABETH to New York on the train took twenty-three minutes, with one stop in Newark. Christina brought along her knitting. She was making argyle socks for Jack for Christmas. The contrasting colors hung on dangling bobbins, not easy to keep straight on a herky-jerky train. She couldn't work on them at home, except alone in her bedroom, because everyone knew you knitted argyle socks only for a boyfriend. When she was with the family she worked on the scarf she was knitting for Jack's younger brother, Mason, or the matching coat for Mason's dog, Fred. If Mama asked, *Who is that for, Christina?* she could say it was for Mr. Durkee, her favorite teacher, and Mama would approve.

Daisy, who was sitting next to her on the train, leaned over and said, "I love those socks!"

"They're for Jack." Daisy knew Christina had a boyfriend. She'd met him once, when he'd brought his brother to the office. Christina was proud of Jack. He knew how to shake hands and look a person right in the eye. Plus, he had a great smile without ever having had orthodontia. She couldn't tell Mama or Baba about Jack because he wasn't Greek, which was too bad, because she was sure they'd like him.

"Lucky Jack!" Daisy said. Then she went back to the book she was reading. Christina couldn't see the title because Daisy covered her books in oilcloth to keep them clean, the same pattern as the covering on the kitchen table at Christina's house.

This year Natalie brought her friend Miri on the holiday outing, and the two girls sat together in their matching camel-hair coats, yakking away. They seemed so young to Christina, even though she knew they'd be in tenth grade at Battin next year. Had she been that young three years ago? She didn't think so.

Steve was reading that new book *The Catcher in the Rye.* Christina had no idea what the title meant. Some of the girls at school went on dates to Staten Island, where you could be legally served at eighteen. Some of them had fake IDs. They drank rye-and-ginger ales. Maybe that's what the title meant. *The Catcher in the Rye and Ginger Ale.* The idea made her laugh. If she wanted to know more she'd have to go to the public library and reserve a copy of the book. Maybe she would.

The train swerved, causing Christina to drop a stitch. She rested her knitting on her lap and looked over at Mrs. Osner, who sat with Fern. She didn't get why they let Fern drag that cowboy bunny everywhere, and even worse, let her tell people he had no penis. In Christina's family Fern would get her mouth washed out with soap just for saying that word out loud.

Mrs. Osner was wearing her mink coat and alligator pumps. She carried a matching alligator pocketbook. A small mink hat was perched on top of her short blond hair. Her nails were perfectly manicured. She used just a touch of makeup to accent her eyes and a bit of rouge to give her a healthy glow. Christina couldn't help imagining Mrs. Osner's underwear. She'd grown up playing on the floor of her mother's shop, Nia's Lingerie, with the packing boxes from the girdles and brassieres as her toys. She'd watched as her mother had gently guided excess flesh into boned and padded girdles, lifted sagging breasts into brassiere cups, telling each customer to take a big breath and hold it as she hooked the bottoms of the brassieres into the tops of the girdles. But Mrs. Osner was trim and probably wore just a panty girdle, bra and slip. No bones or hooks for her.

She shifted in her seat and picked up her knitting. She felt bloated. She'd doubled her pads, sprinkled them with baby powder, and neatly pinned them to her sanitary belt. Her mother had forbidden her to use Tampax until after she was safely married. "It could spoil you," Mama said. Christina got the message. It's good her mother didn't know how far she'd already gone with Jack.

EVERY YEAR their first stop in the city was lining up to see the Christmas windows at Lord & Taylor, followed by the viewing of the huge, beautiful tree at Rockefeller Center and the skaters in the rink below. Christina sometimes skated on the frozen pond in Warinanco Park, but she had never worn a velvet skating skirt or learned to twirl with her head tilted back.

Then it was time for lunch at Lindy's. Christina had learned to order a hot turkey platter, something she could eat with a knife and fork, instead of one of their signature sandwiches piled high with corned beef and pastrami.

She was glad she'd taken Daisy's advice and worn the sweater set Mrs. Osner had given her on her last birthday. Mrs. Osner was pleased to see it. "That style suits you, Christina. And I like the collar."

"My grandmother embroidered it for me." All the girls at school were envious of Christina's collar collection. Yaya embroidered them with tiny flowers to match her sweaters.

"An elegant touch," Mrs. Osner said.

She wasn't sure Mrs. Osner meant it but Daisy had taught her you never second-guess a compliment. She was lucky to have a grown-up friend like Daisy to help her navigate the world that was waiting on the other side of high school. When she looked over at Daisy, Daisy smiled at her.

. . .

CHRISTINA RELAXED for the first time that day when, finally, it was time for the Christmas show at Radio City Music Hall. She sank back into the plush red seat and let her eyes close for a minute. The movie was *I'll See You in My Dreams* with Doris Day and Danny Thomas. She loved Doris Day. If Christina could be anyone, she might be Doris Day. Doris was so perky and had such a good voice. Christina sang in the shower, pretending to be Doris, belting out one song after the other. But she knew she didn't sound anything like her, no matter how hard she tried.

After the show they made a stop at Hanson's, the drugstore where Ruby Granik hung out before she got on the plane. Even though they weren't supposed to talk about the crash today, a visit to Hanson's was the one thing Natalie wanted for Hanukkah—that and dance classes in New York.

Christina needed another Midol. She needed to get to the ladies' room to change her pads.

Daisy

Daisy had three thoughts on the train coming back from New York.

One: She could see plain as day that to Christina, the holiday outing was a chore, something to get through without appearing to be suffering. She understood her discomfort around the Osner family. What did Christina have in common with any of them? She and Steve might be the same age, but they'd never gone to school together and didn't share the same friends. And to Christina, Natalie was a child. She didn't seem smitten by little Fern, either, though personally, Daisy found Fern irresistible.

But she appreciated the effort Christina was making, going overboard in telling Corinne and Dr. O how much she'd enjoyed the movie, how Doris Day was her all-time favorite movie star, how the songs in the movie were so beautiful she'd be humming them in the shower for years to come. When she compared the ice cream at Hanson's to the homemade ice cream at Schutt's in Elizabeth, Daisy put an arm around her shoulder to gently shut her up.

In all her years with Dr. O, Daisy had never allowed herself to grow emotionally attached to the young assistants who came and went, working a few years before marrying, having babies, then sending pictures of their growing families every Christmas. But she had to admit, she felt maternal toward Christina. She could not imagine having a better daughter. Kind, loyal, bright, hardworking. She had to hand it to her parents for raising such a fine young lady. She knew Christina's father from his restaurant. Most days she'd go down to Three Brothers to get Dr. O a sandwich and coffee for lunch. He'd eat in his tiny lab, sitting on a high stool, thumbing through the lastest issue of *Esquire* or one of the other magazines he subscribed to. She brought her lunch from home and ate at her desk, between patients.

Recently, Dr. O had asked her about Christina's boyfriend. She told him Jack McKittrick struck her as a fine young man, an electrician with a good future. He was responsible and mature for his years.

"But they're so young," Dr. O had said.

That was certainly true. Christina just turning eighteen, Jack, what, maybe twenty-one? Daisy liked Jack. She sensed something different about him. And she liked the way he'd treated Christina the few times she'd seen them together.

Daisy so wanted the younger generation to enjoy themselves today, for Dr. O's sake. The annual holiday outing was his idea, and because it was important to him, Daisy did her best to organize the events and tickets. Dr. O needed a good day right now, a day to celebrate life and family and friends, a day without death. *So follow Christina's example, kids, and show some enthusiasm!*

Two: She should be pleased Steve was reading *The Catcher in the Rye*, and she would be if she hadn't selected the same title for his Hanukkah gift, wrapped and waiting in her car. She'd planned to hand the bag with their holiday books to Corinne when they said goodbye at the train station in Elizabeth, so Corinne could put them under the Hanukkah bush. Steve could take it back to the bookshop and exchange it for another book, not that there was another as perfect for him as *Catcher*. She wondered who had given it to him, or had he taken it out of the library? If so, she should be doubly pleased. But she wasn't.

Three: She needed a stiff drink, the sooner, the better.

Christina

When they got back to Elizabeth, Daisy offered Christina a ride home from the train station. It was already dark and Christina was grateful she wouldn't have to take the bus. When Daisy dropped Christina off at her house, she handed her a wrapped gift. "You might not want to put this one under the tree. It could be too personal."

Christina thanked Daisy and tucked it under her coat.

As soon as she was safely in her room, with her back to the door, she ripped the paper off Daisy's gift. No surprise that it was a book. Daisy bought all her gifts at the Ritz Book Shop, just up the street from the office. Christina didn't know anyone who bought books the way Daisy did. Once, Christina had asked Daisy why she didn't use the public library. Daisy said, "Oh, but I do. The bookshop is for books I just have to own." Daisy didn't buy just any book. She gave a lot of thought to each of them. Christina had never heard of this one, *Love Without Fear*. Daisy's note said,

> Dearest Christina,
>   I wish someone had given me this book when I was your age. I had so many questions but I was too afraid to ask them. Merry Christmas to a special young woman. It's a pleasure to work with you.
>
> > Daisy

There was also a small separate package with a key to the office in a purple leather key holder. Her own key to the office. That meant they trusted her. It meant they thought she was mature enough to handle emergencies and to lock up after hours if she was last to leave. The key meant more than the book. Until she looked at the book. The book shocked her. And it made her wet down there. She'd have to keep it hidden under her mattress and read it only at night before she went to sleep.

She would write a friendly thank-you note to Daisy, making a big deal out of the key and a smaller deal out of the book.

Elizabeth Daily Post

LITTLE THINGS SAY A LOT

By Henry Ammerman

DEC. 21—When Elizabeth firemen hacked their way through the underbelly of the wrecked C-46, they piled the shoes, gloves, eyeglasses and other salvage into boxes that were carried into the Elizabethtown Water Company's garage.

The items revealed stories that for a moment made the victims seem alive. A set of medical records told of a soldier who had survived the Korean battlefield, only to perish here. A pile of press clippings and photographs of a man described as a "212-pound Brooklyn wrestler" reminded us that the strong fall with the weak.

Other pieces of salvage, though anonymous, told their own stories. A pair of high-powered binoculars, the carrying case burned off, would never be used at a Florida race-track. A child's twisted bicycle would never be ridden in the warm afternoons. An anticipated Merry Christmas was evidenced by the gay holiday wrapping on a set of men's pajamas.

"Handle with care" was the admonition scrawled on the remains of a photo album.

If only it could have been.

6

Miri

Was it wrong to go to a holiday dance just a week after something horrible had happened in their town? None of her friends thought so. They hardly talked about the crash anymore. They wanted to dress up and dance and have a good time. There might be boys from the Weequahic section of Newark at the Y, older boys who wouldn't necessarily know they were just ninth graders.

Miri wore her favorite dress, red wool with a full skirt and metallic buttons down the front that either were or weren't made of old coins. Rusty thought they were. Her boss's wife saved their daughter's best things for Miri. Miri used to think Rusty bought them at a snazzy shop, Bonwit Teller, because that's what the labels inside said. But last year Miri met Mrs. Whitten, the boss's wife, at an office party, and when Mrs. Whitten admired Miri's dress, Miri jumped at the chance to say it came from Bonwit Teller. Mrs. Whitten said, "Yes, dear, I know. We get almost all of Charlotte's good clothes at Bonwit's."

How embarrassing that until then she'd had no idea Rusty was bringing her hand-me-downs from Charlotte Whitten. What must Mrs. Whitten have thought? But when she'd confronted Rusty about Charlotte's dresses, expecting, she wasn't sure what, Rusty said, cheerfully, "I never said I *bought* them, honey."

"You never said you didn't."

"They're beautiful dresses. What's the difference if Charlotte wore them half a dozen times?"

So Miri learned to adjust, to be grateful to Charlotte Whitten for being her size, for having good taste, for taking care of her clothes. But she didn't tell her friends. She wasn't sure she ever would.

Some of the girls wore Cuban heels to the dance and others wore saddle shoes or ballet flats, but Miri carried Rusty's black pumps with heels and changed into them in the coatroom at the Y.

"Just don't get them wet," Rusty had said, before Miri left the house.

"Don't worry. I'm not walking outside."

"Even from the car to the Y, wear your flats."

"Okay."

They weren't Rusty's best shoes. These were leather and scuffed around the heel, though Rusty kept them polished. Miri was hoping to attract the attention of the older boys with her heels, and she did, for a minute—until they realized she was just in ninth grade and was friends with Steve Osner's younger sister.

At first the boys stood around surveying the room. The girls stood around talking to one another and pretending not to notice the boys. Then someone put on the first slow dance of the night—Nat King Cole singing "Unforgettable." That was the moment Miri would always remember, the moment she thought of as changing her life, because *he* was there, the mystery boy from Natalie's party, and he was heading her way. When he put his arms around her to dance, she melted into him, praying the song would never end.

> *Unforgettable, that's what you are*
> *Unforgettable, though near or far . . .*

But like all songs, it did end, and when it did, he took a step away from her and looked deep into her eyes. His were blue. Miri held her breath. "You're taller than I remembered," he said.

"It's the shoes."

"Oh, the shoes." He smiled at her, a smile so disarming she melted on the spot.

She smiled back. "I'm Miri."

"I know."

He knew?

"I'm Mason." His voice was gravelly, as if maybe he had a sore throat.

"Mason." She tried it out. She'd never known anyone named Mason.

"Mason McKittrick."

McKittrick. Miri tried to hide her disappointment. He wasn't Jewish. Irene wouldn't approve. Okay, she wouldn't tell her. She wouldn't tell anyone. He would be another of her secrets. She was beginning to enjoy having secrets from her family.

While Natalie danced to every song with Winky Herkovitz, the best dancer in ninth grade, who dipped her, flipped her from knee to knee and twirled her, while Suzanne, the shiksa the Jewish boys loved, danced to every song with a different partner, while Eleanor, who still had braces on her teeth and refused to smile for photos, had a deep conversation with a chaperone, a teacher Uncle Henry's age and Robo, well developed and athletic, made out in the cloakroom with Pete Wolf, who believed in Martians, Miri danced only with Mason.

After a while he led her outside so he could have

a smoke. She'd been right. He did smoke, and his brand was Luckies. *Lucky Strike Means Fine Tobacco*. He offered one to her. She shook her head. She'd tried it once and had almost choked to death. Almost vomited in front of everyone. But she liked the way he held the cigarette between his teeth. When he'd had enough he tossed it to the ground and stepped on it, crushing it like a bug.

He kissed her then, outside the Y in the freezing-cold December night air, with neither of them wearing a coat. Her teeth were chattering but she wasn't going to suggest they go back inside, not as long as he was holding her that way, not as long as he was kissing her that way and she was kissing him back. They kissed a second time and her legs turned to jelly. She'd heard that expression a million times, but until now she hadn't understood it. She'd never been kissed by a boy like Mason. No sloppy tongue shoved halfway down her throat, no washing out her ear. Just perfect kisses. Two, three, four—she lost count. If she died then she was sure she'd die happy.

They went back inside for the last dance. The lights had been dimmed and she and Mason danced cheek to cheek, thanks to her mother's heels, their arms wrapped around one another. *In the meadow we can build a snowman* . . . She was glad it wasn't "Goodnight, Irene," often the last song at a dance. She loved her grandmother but she didn't want to think about her tonight.

"Can I walk you home?" Mason asked while they, and everyone else, scrambled for their coats.

Miri nodded. "I just have to tell my friends."

Outside, Robo's father was waiting for them. The girls

had already piled into the car. "I'm walking home with Mason," she told them.

"Who's Mason?" Natalie asked.

"The boy I've been dancing with, the one from your party . . . remember?"

"Yeah, but *who* is he?" Natalie said while the other girls hung on every word.

"Mason McKittrick. He goes to Jefferson," Miri said. "He knows Steve."

All this time Mason was standing next to her, listening. "Hey . . ." he said, giving a small wave to her friends.

"Where does he live?" Natalie asked, ignoring Mason.

Miri didn't know where he lived or why it mattered.

"I live on Salem," Mason said. Then he whispered to Miri, but loud enough for the others to hear, "They don't trust me."

"They don't *know* you," Miri told him.

Robo said, "As soon as we get home I'll have my father call your mother so she doesn't worry."

"No, don't do that," Miri said. "I'll call her myself."

She borrowed a nickel from Mason and used the pay phone inside the Y.

Rusty answered on the second ring. "I'm walking home from the Y, okay?"

"I thought Robo's father was picking you up."

"He is, but I'd rather walk home." She knew Rusty was waiting for more. "With a very nice boy," she added. "You don't have to worry."

"Okay," Rusty said, just like that, surprising Miri. "But don't dawdle. If you're not home in half an hour I'm calling the police."

"Mom . . . it's a long walk."

"I know exactly how long it is."

"Okay."

"And not in my shoes."

"I've already changed out of them."

"Okay then."

Miri was grateful for Rusty's good mood.

She took off one of her mittens and stuffed it in her pocket so she could hold Mason's bare hand as they walked home. His skin was rough, probably chapped from not wearing gloves in this weather. He had a strong grip. Some guys held your hand like it was a fish they wished they could throw back.

Mason spoke first. "That was Dr. Osner's daughter, right?"

"Yes, Natalie."

"My brother's girlfriend works for Dr. Osner."

"You know Christina?"

"She got me an emergency appointment one day when I had a toothache."

"He's my dentist, too," Miri said, then wondered why they were talking about teeth when the moon was shining and the sky was full of stars. Maybe he was wondering the same thing because after that they stopped to kiss at every tree, her back pressed up against it, Mason leaning into her. When they came to the site of the crash, they stood silently, his arm hugging her shoulder.

"Where were you when . . ." he said.

"I saw it happen," she told him. "I was coming home from the movies with my mother."

"Jeez . . ."

"What about you?"

"I was at work . . . at the bowling alley on East Grand.

We didn't hear anything but we felt it. I thought it was an earthquake."

"We don't have earthquakes in New Jersey, do we?" Right away she regretted asking such a stupid question.

He shrugged. "There's a first for everything."

There's a first for everything, she repeated silently, and he was a first for her.

When they got to her house he asked if her number was listed.

"Yes. N. Ammerman. That's my mother. Or I can give it to you now."

"I don't have a pen."

"I do." She dug a leaky pen out of her bag and handed it to him. He stuck the top in his mouth, holding it between his teeth, the way he had with the cigarette. As she recited her number he wrote it down on his arm, just above his wrist. Miri had never seen anyone do that, would never have thought of doing it herself.

He kissed her goodnight, touching her face. "Miri Ammerman," he whispered.

For the first time her name sounded musical. It sounded like a love song. What did it mean that he said her name that way? What did it mean that he touched her face? Did it mean he was in love with her the way she was with him?

Mason

Phil was the one who told him if he wanted to see her again to go to the dance at the Jewish Y, that she'd probably be there. It didn't cost anything to get in, he said. And you didn't have to be Jewish. Nobody asked. Nobody cared. He said he and Steve wouldn't be there. They'd been invited to a party given by Phil's cousin Kathy Stein, in Perth Amboy. Kathy was a freshman at Syracuse, and aside from the two of them, everyone at the party would be older, would already be at college. It wasn't necessary for Phil to make excuses about why Mason wasn't invited. But Phil was a decent guy.

There was a holiday dance at the YMCA that night, too, and Mason planned on going until Phil told him about the girl from the Osners' party. Miri. That was her name. And as long as Steve wouldn't be there to get all hot under the collar about him dancing with his sister's friend, why not go?

At the YMCA he'd have known all the girls, most of them, anyway. And they'd know him, dance with him, laugh with him, but none of them would feel the way Miri had in his arms. He couldn't explain it. He half hoped she wouldn't be there tonight. Because he sensed he was just looking for trouble. She was young. He had to be careful. Above the neck only. And only if she wanted him to kiss her. Only then.

And there she was, in that red dress, and her mother's shoes making her three inches taller, and when it came to kissing, it turned out she was more than willing.

Miri

Mason wasn't a secret love for long. During the ten days of vacation, she saw him whenever he wasn't working. She was allowed to stay out until 10 p.m. as long as Rusty knew exactly where she was—a get-together at Robo's house or Eleanor's, or at the movies with Suzanne and Natalie and the other kids. Miri had to introduce him to Rusty—that was the deal—then to Uncle Henry and finally, to Irene, who'd had a conniption fit when she first heard his name, but not, thank goodness, in front of him.

"For god's sake," Rusty said to Irene later. "She's not getting married. She's in ninth grade."

"Be careful," Irene warned Miri. "All boys want the same thing."

So do girls, Miri thought. But she was never going to make the mistake her mother did. She wouldn't go all the way until she was twenty-three or married, whichever came first. And they'd use protection. A funny little rubber circle called a diaphragm that you somehow had to shove up there, like Corinne used—Natalie had shown it to her in its circular container. "I'm not sure how well it works," Natalie said, "because I think Fern was a mistake. Or maybe my mother got it after Fern was born."

Last year Robo had snitched one of her father's rubbers from under his shirts in his dresser drawer. They'd stretched it over a cucumber. "Do they get *that* big?" Suzanne asked. "Because if they do, I'm never doing it."

"Maybe we should have used a carrot," Robo said, and they all laughed.

Now Irene told her, "Be a good girl. Promise me you'll be a good girl."

"I am a good girl," Miri said. "So stop worrying."

Rusty didn't say anything.

Mason

If he wanted to see her he had to meet her mother. And not just her mother but her uncle, maybe to prove there was a man around the house, and her grandmother, who looked like she'd swallowed a lemon when Miri introduced him and she'd heard his name. "McKittrick?" she'd said, like she'd never heard it before.

He knew to shake hands with them. He knew to call the uncle *sir*. Jack had taught him all that. He had no idea who'd taught Jack. He knew to tell them exactly what their plans were and that he'd have her home by ten o'clock or else she'd call to explain.

The mother didn't ask the questions he was expecting, starting with, *What do your parents do?* She didn't say, *Maybe I know them*, like some of the girls' parents from the YMCA so he didn't have to give his standard answer, *I don't think so. No, you wouldn't know my parents. No, we're not new in town. I was born here at St. Elizabeth's.* He might not have told the truth if she'd asked those questions, so he was glad she hadn't.

Miri

In the middle of vacation Miri had an appointment at Dr. O's office for a checkup and to have her teeth cleaned. As Christina attached the bib around her neck, Miri said, "You know Mason McKittrick, right?"

Christina was surprised. "He's my boyfriend's brother. Why?"

Miri wasn't sure how to answer. "No reason."

"Are you going with him?"

Was she going with him? Did being in love for a week count?

Christina didn't wait for her to answer. "He's a nice

boy," she said. "A hard worker. He wants to get out of Janet Memorial and as soon as Jack can move into a better place . . ."

But Miri didn't hear the rest of what Christina was saying. She was stuck at *Janet Memorial*.

"It's temporary," Christina continued. "Like I was saying, as soon as Jack moves into a better place he'll be able to take Mason to live with him. In the meantime, you want to do something nice for Mason—take his dog, Fred."

She had no idea he lived at Janet Memorial, the orphanage on Salem Avenue. He hadn't told her anything about his life and she hadn't asked him any questions. But so what? She knew how she felt when they were together. Wasn't that enough?

Fred was a different story. Mason took Fred everywhere, except to work and to school. One day over vacation he asked if she could keep him for the afternoon, while he was at work. She'd told him sure, without thinking about what she'd do with him. She couldn't risk bringing him home. If Irene caught her with a dog in the house she'd be in big trouble.

So she'd gone to Suzanne's, whose parents were both at work. She'd had to hold Fred in her arms to keep him from setting foot on the floor or, worse, jumping onto the furniture. In Suzanne's room they'd made a little bed for him out of a box and some rags. Barking was off-limits. Suzanne lived in an apartment house on Chilton where dogs weren't allowed.

After her visit to Dr. O's office she told Mason she'd had her teeth cleaned and that Dr. O had found a small cavity. "I have to go back to get it filled. He said I won't need Novocain."

Mason wasn't impressed. "I've had teeth pulled without Novocain and it hurt like hell."

"Dr. O would never hurt you."

"That's where I'm going from now on."

They were walking home from the movies. "So I was wondering," she said, not able to stop herself, "where does Fred live?"

A shadow fell over his face. Why was she doing this?

"He lives around," Mason said. "He stays with one of my friends. But I pay for his food and I walk him every day. I can't have a dog at Janet, if that's what you're getting at."

She hated herself for putting him in this position. "I'm sorry."

"For what?"

"That you're an orphan."

He forced a laugh and grabbed her hand, pulling her behind him as he ran.

Elizabeth Daily Post

C-46 HAS A CHECKERED HISTORY

GIs Nicknamed the Transport "The Flying Coffin"

By Henry Ammerman

DEC. 26—The C-46, the aircraft that crashed into the Elizabeth River on Dec. 16, began life with a bad name. It was rushed into military service in 1943 to fly supplies over the Himalaya "hump" from India to Burma. Allied pilots called her the "flying coffin," with at least 31 known instances of fires or explosions in flight between May 1943 and March 1945. Many others went missing and were never found. Disabled C-46s were stranded at bases from Kansas to Karachi. It was standard procedure to save two of every five that reached the theater just for parts.

The plane was gradually modified and improved, and in 1948 the Air Force made surplus C-46s available to airlines for rental at the very attractive rate of $300 a month. Here was a transport that could be modified to carry 52 passengers, enabling non-scheduled airlines to offer cut-rate service across the country, and between this area and Florida in the winter.

Despite the improvements, a summary of aircraft accidents shows 45 involving the C-46 between January 1947 and October 1951, 11 of them fatal, taking 137 lives. The need for careful maintenance is obvious, yet like any plane, it makes money only when flying.

Miami Airlines, the non-scheduled operator of the ill-fated Dec. 16 flight, is already in litigation with the Civil Aeronautics Board for flying an excessive number of flights between Newark and Florida. But because the crash is still under investigation it is too soon to say whether pressure to keep the plane in the air contributed to the disaster.

7

Miri

The fathers took turns driving their daughters to and from events, a get-together in someone's finished basement, a dance at the Y, a Saturday night movie. Miri was the only one without a father. Not that any of her friends asked about him. They figured either he was dead or her parents were divorced. Either way, they understood she didn't see him, didn't talk about him, and that was enough. Once, when they didn't know she was in the girls' room at school, she'd heard them speculate that maybe he'd died in the war. She sometimes hoped he *had* died in the war. That would simplify everything.

Mothers might drive them somewhere during the day, but at night it was strictly fathers. Anyway, Rusty didn't drive. She'd never had a car. She and Miri walked or took the bus around town. Sometimes Henry would give them a lift, but only in decent weather, because one of them, almost always Miri, would have to sit in the rumble seat.

Ben Sapphire, on the other hand, drove a big black Packard. The car was new. It was the car he'd planned on driving to Miami Beach. Miri had seen photos of his wife standing next to it. Not that she wanted to see his family photos, but he'd brought an album to Irene's one day and she knew Irene expected her to be polite. She couldn't tell him that when she pictured his beloved Estelle, it was inside the ball of fire that had fallen out of the sky. No, she could never tell anyone that. Well, maybe Natalie, since she claimed to have a special connection with Ruby Granik, but if Ruby knew anything about Estelle Sapphire, Natalie hadn't shared it with Miri.

They'd held the funeral for Estelle three days after the crash. Irene had baked for the shiva at the Sapphires' house in Bayonne, and now Ben Sapphire's sons were headed back to Chicago and Los Angeles with their wives and children. Once they'd left, Ben offered to drive Miri and her friends to the Y, or wherever they wanted to go, in his fancy new car, but Miri wasn't about to let him drive her anywhere. He was too old, too hairy and sometimes—you never knew when—he'd break down and cry. It was dangerous to drive that way, wasn't it? She understood he was sad. She understood why. But she wasn't ready to accept a ride from him. "Thank you," she said to his offer, "but my friend's father is driving us tonight."

He nodded. "Maybe another time."

"Yes, another time."

Ben Sapphire

He'd open the door to the house in Bayonne, the house where he and Estelle had raised their family, calling out, *Stellie, honey, I'm home*—but no one ran into his arms, no one slept curled around him, telling him every night before they went to sleep how much she loved him. Estelle was gone, gone forever. He wanted to believe he'd catch up with her on the other side but he didn't believe in the afterlife. It was all shit. Dead is dead. Dead and buried.

All he had left was his memories and their children and grandchildren. He and Estelle had vowed long ago they would never become a burden to their children. The children had their own lives. And he wanted it that way.

He didn't know what his future held. Only that he had to get out of that house. He'd already made the decision to put it on the market. His daughters-in-law had disposed of Estelle's things. They'd taken the good jewelry and furs for themselves, with his blessing. The new leather gloves, gloves Estelle hadn't yet worn, they gave to Irene for the compassion she'd shown Ben since the crash. He could see Irene didn't want the gloves. But what could she do? She was a mensch. She thanked them for thinking of her. Now Ben would move to the Elizabeth Carteret hotel until he found an apartment that suited him. In the meantime, there was always Irene's couch.

After the funeral, he wanted to talk to the rabbi about something so personal, so shameful, it was eating away at him. But he couldn't admit it to this rabbi, who had bar mitzvahed his sons, who had married one of them, this rabbi who thought of Ben Sapphire as a loving husband and father, a pillar of the community. Instead, he went to a Catholic church in Elizabeth, where no one would know him, and sat for a long time before he told the priest he had something to confess.

He had not been faithful to Estelle. *Men are different*, he'd explained early on, *men have needs*. And she'd understood. Not that she hadn't cried the first time, until he'd taken her in his arms and reassured her. *I will never leave you. You understand? I will always be here for you and the boys.* The others, he didn't love them, they weren't worth the hem of her dress. He just couldn't help himself. Couldn't ask her to do the things he could pay for, things that made him feel dirty. She was his wife. Now he was done with all that. He'd been done with it for years. Couldn't remember the last time. But there it was, gnawing at him, giving him sharp pains in his left side, as if he'd eaten popcorn and set off his diverticulitis.

The priest listened as Ben explained he was a Jew but too ashamed to talk about this with his rabbi. The priest was kind and forgiving. He asked Ben to think of others before thinking of himself, to help others before helping himself. To do good with the time he had left. Ben promised. He made a generous donation to the church and another to his synagogue.

He visited the cemetery every day to talk to Estelle, to apologize for the things he'd done, to tell her she'd been his one and only love. *If I could do it over . . .* he'd cry. *Please, Stellie, give me another chance to prove how much I love you.* But Estelle never responded. He stood alone as the winter wind whipped his hat off his head, hoping for a sign—a falling leaf, a dove flying by. He'd have settled for a pigeon. But there was nothing. This was why he cried.

𝕰𝖑𝖎𝖟𝖆𝖇𝖊𝖙𝖍 𝕯𝖆𝖎𝖑𝖞 𝕻𝖔𝖘𝖙

Editorial

NEW YEAR, BUT OLD BUSINESS

DEC. 31—We watched while giant machines of the air skimmed our rooftops in ever-increasing numbers. We warned against that inevitable day when disaster would follow in their wake.

They said it couldn't happen. They said we were attempting to block progress.

We watched as the last twisted wing of the plane that had claimed 56 lives was dragged from the banks of the Elizabeth River. We waited in vain for a solution that would make recurrence impossible.

We are still watching and waiting.

When will a concern for the safety of our citizens take precedence over a concern for the business of the Port Authority's Newark Airport?

8

Miri

Every year Corinne let it be known that Miri was welcome to bring her mother to the Osners' New Year's Eve party. Every year Miri explained to Corinne that Rusty never went out on New Year's Eve because New Year's Eve was when Rusty's father had died.

"I'm sorry," Corinne would say. "But maybe this year . . ."

"I doubt it," Miri would tell her. Not that she ever extended Corinne's invitation to Rusty. Why would she? It wasn't like the Osners and Rusty socialized, it wasn't like they were Rusty's friends, or Rusty's second family, the way they were hers.

Henry dropped Miri at Natalie's house on his way to pick up Leah. They were going to the Riviera nightclub in Fort Lee, the place where Frank Sinatra sometimes sang, where Martin and Lewis did their comedy act and Pupi Campo and his band played Latin music. Henry looked dashing in his rented tux. Miri wished she could see Leah. Would she be wearing velvet, taffeta? Would she look like Doris Day in *I'll See You in My Dreams*? Sometimes Leah had that Doris Day look, other times she was more Debbie Reynolds, peeking out from under her bangs.

When he pulled up in front of the Osners' house, Henry turned to Miri and said, "Tonight's the night," which embarrassed her at first, until he dug a small black velvet box out of his pocket. "I'm proposing to Leah at midnight." He opened the box to show Miri the ring.

Miri felt herself choke up. She knew the ring. How many times had she gone with Irene to the vault when she was younger to watch as Irene checked the contents of her safe deposit box, making sure the ring was still there, along with her diamond pin and her important papers? The ring and the pin were the only pieces of good jewelry Irene had left from before 1929, before the stock market crash, a different kind of crash from the one in the Elizabeth River two weeks ago—back when Irene and Max

Ammerman still had money, before Max lost his fancy food emporium, before Irene sold the rest of her jewelry to pay the bills, before Max had the first stroke, and then the second, the stroke that killed him on New Year's Eve, 1937, just weeks before Miri was born. Rusty named her for him. They always lit a *yahrzeit* candle for Max on New Year's Eve and another when the notice came from the synagogue listing the date of his death on the Hebrew calendar.

"It's beautiful," she told Henry. And it was. A lacy design of small twinkly diamonds. Irene had always let her try it on. And even though Irene had said, *Someday, when Uncle Henry finds the right girl, he'll give her this ring,* she remembered exactly how disappointed she was at age nine to learn it would not be hers.

"You're the first to know," Henry said.

"Nana doesn't know?"

"Maybe tomorrow, if Leah says yes."

"Of course she'll say yes," Miri told him. "If she doesn't she's crazy and you wouldn't want to marry a crazy person, would you?" She hugged him.

"Happy New Year, Miri. I hope someday I have a daughter exactly like you." He ruffled her hair.

I am your daughter, Miri told him inside her head.

"I know," Henry whispered, as if he'd actually heard what she hadn't said. Then he hugged her again.

MIRI WAS NOT HAPPY when Rusty showed up at the Osners' party. And even less happy to see she was wearing her good black dress, her dress shoes and stockings with seams. Then there was the hair. Rita Hayworth hair. To her shoulders. Heads turned when Rusty came into the living room. She waved at Miri but Miri turned away. "What is my mother doing here?" she asked Natalie.

"My mother wants to introduce her to Cousin Tewky from Birmingham."

"Tewky? What kind of a name is *Tewky*?"

"Some family nickname. He's my mother's first cousin, from the banking side of the family. You know, Purvis Brothers Bank."

Miri didn't know.

"My mother's from the department store side."

Miri didn't know that, either. "You should have warned me," she told Natalie.

"How was I supposed to know your mother didn't tell you she was coming?"

Corinne greeted Rusty and led her straight to a man, a man who must have been Tewky Purvis, balding, not especially handsome, but not ugly, either, with a mustache. Well, half the men in the room had mustaches, including Dr. O. She couldn't hold that against him. They were talking now, her mother and Tewky Purvis, and laughing, maybe even flirting. Miri didn't like it. She didn't know how grown-ups judged each other, especially how women judged men. It never made sense to her. *It's about character*, Rusty once told her. *Strength, goodness. A sense of humor doesn't hurt, either.*

She didn't ask how men judged women because she already knew. It was obvious, and Rusty looked glamorous tonight. "That's not all of it," Rusty had once argued. "But you're right—looks are certainly a starting point. Chemistry, too." Miri understood chemistry now. Chemistry turned your legs to jelly and made your insides roll over.

If Mason hadn't had to work tonight Miri might not be at the Osners' party. She hoped she'd never have to choose between her best friend and the boy she loved. Since seventh grade, New Year's Eve had been for just the two of them, Natalie and Miri. She didn't think Natalie would have invited Mason. Maybe someday when Natalie was also in love, they'd invite dates to the Osners' party, but not now. Rusty must have thought that Miri would be out with Mason when she accepted Corinne's invitation. Now she'd have to deal with her daughter keeping an eye on her.

Rusty

She decided to go to the party at the last minute when Irene urged her to get out and enjoy herself. Seeing the worry on Miri's face now, she began to regret her decision. Maybe it had been a mistake to keep the men in her life a secret. Not that there had been many. But she'd never brought a date home. Not one man in fifteen years. She hadn't done a thing to get Miri used to the idea, to the possibility. In all these years, there had been just two serious boyfriends. One of them had been married. She certainly wasn't going to introduce him to her family. She knew from the start he would never leave his wife and children. She knew she wasn't his first affair. Yet she kept seeing him. For five years she saw him every week. If you asked her about him today she wouldn't be able to explain it. Just that she'd been young and she'd enjoyed the attention, the thrill, the sex.

The second man was decent and available. He'd proposed after a few months, with a diamond as big as her thumbnail. For a minute she thought she could learn to love him, could be happy with his promise of a big house in the suburbs, a maid to clean and cook, summer camp for Miri. But when it came time to introduce him to the family she couldn't do it. They would see right through her. They would see the truth—she didn't love him, wasn't the least attracted to him and didn't want to marry him, not even for an easier life.

Sometimes she wondered about her first love, but not often. A girl gets in trouble, she marries the boy. They wind up hating each other, resenting each other and finally they get a divorce. By then it's taken its toll on both of them and their children. No, she never wanted that, which is why she'd refused to allow her mother to call the Monskys and force Mike to marry her. Maybe she would fall in love again. If and when that happened she would introduce him to Miri. But until then, what was the point?

Miri

The Osners' living room glowed. The Hanukkah bush was gone, replaced by a fire in the fireplace, and, at the baby grand from Altenburgs on East Jersey Street, Dr. O sat on the upholstered bench, covered by a needlepoint canvas hand-stitched by Corinne. His fingers danced over the keys, never hesitating, the same fingers that worked magic in his patients' mouths. The guests were singing around the piano, glasses of Scotch and rye and bourbon resting on coasters to avoid getting water marks on the polished ebony. If anyone was careless, Mrs. Barnes was there in a flash, slipping a coaster under a glass here, scooping a crumpled cocktail napkin into her pocket to be deposited in the trash in the kitchen, where Mrs. Jones and her daughters, Rhonda and Jamison, were stacking up Sloppy Joe sandwiches on silver platters.

Mrs. Jones was also the Osners' laundress, spending every Thursday at their house, washing and ironing the Osners' clothes, their bed linens. At the end of the day Natalie's blouses, every one perfect, would be lined up on hangers in her closet. Never any last-minute ironing with the ironing board set up in the Osners' kitchen, the way it was at Miri's, so that when you put on your blouse it was still warm. Mrs. Jones ironed their pillowcases, the tops of their sheets and Suzanne once told Miri that Mrs. Jones ironed their towels, but Miri hadn't believed her. "Why would anyone iron towels?"

"I don't know, but she irons Natalie's dungarees, too. You can see the creases. And Corinne's underwear. I've seen her ironing Corinne's slips and nightgowns."

Sometimes, when Miri was ironing one of her Ship 'n Shore blouses she pretended she was a laundress, like Mrs. Jones. But the one time she'd tried to iron a bra it had melted into nothing. *Poof*, and her pretty blue nylon bra was gone forever.

Miri and Natalie joined the singers around the piano. When someone called out the name of a song, Dr. O didn't hesitate. He moved right into it. For the first time every song spoke directly to Miri. *He dances overhead, on the ceiling near my bed*. Yes, she thought. One day you're a regular girl, two weeks later, you're someone in love— and wasn't that also the title of a song?

When Rusty and Tewky came to the piano, Miri stopped singing. Rusty knew every word of every song and sang them too loud, smiling at Tewky, enjoying herself. Not that Rusty didn't sing in her room, or when she was in the bathtub, but out in public? This was something new to Miri, and she found it embarrassing.

By then the dining room table was laden with platters. Not just the Sloppy Joe sandwiches, but a chafing dish of spicy meatballs in sauce, brisket sliced as thin as paper with white horseradish, cucumber salad, potato salad and pickles. There were trays of cookies and tarts. And rugeleh from the Jewish bakery.

Fern ran around the table in circles, like a small, badly behaved dog, and if not exactly barking and snapping at people's ankles, then close to it. Mrs. Barnes tried to catch her but Fern was too fast.

After the buffet supper the guests headed downstairs to the finished basement, where she and Mason had first danced together. She wished he could see it tonight, with gold and silver half-moons and stars hanging from the ceiling. At the bar, bottles of Champagne sat on ice waiting for midnight toasts. And the music—instead of Nat King Cole singing "Nature Boy," the jukebox was filled with dance music for Corinne and Dr. O's crowd—the samba, the rhumba and the newest craze, the mambo.

"You'd think Pupi were here himself," Miri heard one of the guests say, reminding her that Uncle Henry was dancing with Leah to the real, live Pupi at the Riviera.

Miri had to admit Tewky Purvis was a good dancer, the way he twirled Rusty but never lost control, the way Rusty was able to follow his every move. As far as Miri knew, the only place Rusty danced was in her bedroom, though sometimes she'd turn on the record player in the living room and try to get Miri to be her partner. As a little girl, Miri had loved to jitterbug with her mother, but not anymore.

Miri preferred to watch Steve Osner dancing with Phil Stein's cousin Kathy, who wore a dark-green strapless velvet dress. She laughed a lot, and when she did, her dark eyes sparkled and crinkled up. You could tell Steve was gaga over her. Maybe she was gaga over Steve, too, even though she was a year ahead of him, already a college girl. Miri could recognize love now, or maybe it was attraction she recognized—either way, she knew it when she saw it. She could feel it when it was in the air and it was in the air around Steve Osner and Kathy Stein.

Natalie gave her a nudge. They were sitting on the steps leading up to the kitchen. "See those earrings my mother's wearing?" Corinne was dancing with Dr. O. "Daddy gave them to her for Hanukkah. She let me try them on. She said someday I'll find a husband who'll give me diamond earrings. Then she reminded me for the millionth time, it's just as easy to fall in love with a rich boy as a poor boy, which is interesting, considering Daddy was a poor boy who had to work his way all through school. She said even though some people say diamonds aren't important, they are. I didn't tell her I'm never getting married."

"Since when?" Miri asked, surprised.

"Since I promised Ruby my career as a dancer would always come first."

"Do you think you should be making promises to someone who's . . ." She stopped herself just in time.

"I told you," Natalie said, annoyed. "She's not *dead*. She's living inside me."

"But what does that mean?"

Natalie shook her head. "You're not even trying to understand."

Miri wanted to understand what Natalie was trying to tell her. For all she knew it was possible. Just because she'd never heard of having a dead person living inside you, didn't mean it couldn't happen. She'd read about spirits, about ghosts. Not that she believed they were real. No, she argued with herself, this thing with Natalie was crazy. It was impossible. Natalie was going nuts. Maybe she should tell someone. But Natalie trusted her with her secret. If she told, she'd be betraying her best friend, wouldn't she? Or would she be helping her? Miri wasn't sure. This was a secret she wished she'd never heard.

The conga line zigzagged around the room, everyone laughing as they one, two, three, kicked! Dr. O led the way. Rusty was sandwiched between him and Tewky Purvis. Kathy Stein held on to Tewky's waist, and Steve held hers, followed by Corinne, then Dr. Reiss.

"Come on," Natalie said, dragging Miri out to join the fun. They broke in between Dr. O and Rusty so that Miri held Natalie's waist and Rusty held hers. Not the way she would have planned it.

Dr. O turned off the jukebox and switched on the radio for the countdown to midnight. Corinne handed out party hats and noisemakers, and as the clock struck midnight corks popped, the guests cheered and everyone started kissing.

Miri watched Steve Osner kissing Kathy Stein, his hands on her naked back. When she and Mason kissed they were almost always wearing winter coats. She tried to imagine how it would feel to have his hands on her naked back. Just that thought was enough to make her legs so weak she had to sit down.

She was grateful her mother wasn't kissing Cousin Tewky or anyone else.

"You don't have to worry," Natalie said.

"Who's worrying?"

"It's written all over your face."

"What is?"

"He's not interested in getting married."

"Suppose he falls for Rusty?"

"I'm telling you, that's not going to happen. So you can relax and wish me a Happy New Year."

"Happy New Year, Nat."

"Happy New Year, Mir."

They hugged.

While the Champagne flowed, welcoming in 1952, the guests told one another it was going to be a great year. Miri hoped they were right.

Part Two

January 1952

Elizabeth Daily Post

INVESTIGATION

Stewardess Who Perished in Crash Warned Sister

By Henry Ammerman

JAN. 8—A highlight at the CAB hearing yesterday was a report that the stewardess on the C-46 that crashed on Dec. 16 had telephoned her sister just five minutes before the plane took off, telling her that the plane was "unfit to fly." She said that passengers on the aircraft's trip in from the West Coast suffered because cabin heaters had been inoperative.

Joseph O. Fluet, heading the investigation for the CAB, dismissed this as conjecture. He focused attention on a graphic presentation showing the course and probable altitudes flown by the plane. This had been carefully compiled from eyewitness reports and the locations of parts from the plane that fell to the ground. Experts on the C-46 have been brought in to examine the wreckage, with particular attention to the right engine, which had been streaming smoke.

9

Kathy

At Syracuse, Kathy Stein told her roommate, Jane Krasner, that she'd met someone over the holidays. "And I think . . . well, I really liked him."

They were on their beds with the pink and red plaid spreads they'd bought during orientation week on sale at Dey Brothers. They'd become friends right away, decorating their tiny dorm room, figuring out how to share the only closet and the personal items they'd brought from home—Kathy's clock radio, Jane's foldable clothes dryer. Every night Jane diligently hand-washed her heavy wool socks in Woolite along with her bra and underpants and hung them on her wooden clothes dryer. Kathy collected her laundry for a week before using the washing machine in the basement of their dorm. Now, with finals coming up, they were studying, Kathy wrapped in the hand-knitted afghan her mother had made for her, Jane in her flannel robe.

"That was fast," Jane said. "Where does he go to school?"

"Okay, promise not to laugh?"

"Promise."

"He's a senior in high school but he's coming to Syracuse next year, assuming he gets in."

Jane just looked at her.

"He's mature for his age. Actually, we're just a few months apart because he has a winter birthday and mine is November. So I want to get home for break after finals to see him again."

"You better make your reservations now."

"Come with me. I'll introduce you to my cousin Phil. He's Steve's best friend. We'll have fun."

"Where am I supposed to get the money to fly?"

"I'll bet my dad would spring for your ticket," Kathy said. Her father was an orthopedic surgeon.

"Don't do that. Don't ask your dad to pay for me. I can take the bus."

"But that would take all day, and another day getting back."

"That's why I might not come."

"That'd be a disappointment."

"You're going to see a boy. You don't need me around."

"But it's more fun when you're around."

"Thanks."

"Wish me luck," Kathy said. "I'm going to call home now."

"Good luck."

Kathy went out to the pay phone in the hall to dial her parents.

PELHAM GIRL HAS BEST POSTURE

Cites Muscular Control

JAN. 10—The annual Posture Queen award at Barnard College was given yesterday to Miss Marjory Schulhoff of Pelham, N.Y. Freshmen were judged on the basis of carriage, poise and ease of movement, both walking and sitting. Miss Schulhoff, a prospective art major, was also queen of the Columbia College rush last fall.

She attributed her success to sleep, good food and muscular control. "Exercise alone won't do it," she said. "I know plenty of football players who walk like apes."

"You know," the newly crowned Posture Queen added, "I'd feel better if it was an academic award."

10

Miri

Usually, January was the longest month, dragging on and on, the weather cold and dreary, school routine and boring, everybody's noses runny, their throats sore. But this January everything was different. Mason called Miri every night, sometime between nine and ten o'clock, whenever he got a break at the bowling alley. If she'd finished her homework she might be watching TV at Irene's with Rusty and Ben Sapphire, who sometimes slept over on Irene's couch. Miri would leave the door between her house and Irene's open so she could hear the phone. When it rang she'd run up the stairs, pick up the phone and drag it by its long knotted cord under the bathroom door, locking it behind her. Then she'd sit on the edge of the tub in the dark, smelling Rusty's bath salts—lavender, citrus, musk— listening to Mason's breaths and her own, until she could feel him breathing into her ear right through the phone.

After they'd said goodnight, she'd turn on the bathroom light and look at herself in the mirror on the medicine chest. Her face was always pink and warm. She'd splash it with water to take away the blush. Then she'd flush the toilet for no reason except to announce she'd finished in case anyone was interested, return the phone to the hall table and run down the stairs to catch the rest of whatever TV show they'd been watching. Irene wouldn't say anything. Neither would Rusty. But Miri was sure they'd had plenty to say while she was gone, unless it was Wednesday and they'd been watching Kraft Television Theatre. Then they wouldn't have talked at all except during commercials.

EVERY OTHER SUNDAY NIGHT Miri and Suzanne babysat for the Fosters, seven-year-old Penny and four-year-old Betsy. Mr. Foster managed an appliance shop on Route 22 and Saturdays left him too tired to go out. It was okay with Rusty and Suzanne's mother as long as they had their homework finished and were home by ten-thirty. The girls liked it because it left them free on Saturday nights.

Mrs. Foster had an impressive collection of hand-knit cardigan sweaters to wear over crisp white shirts, and this night her cardigan was in a cobalt blue and had brass buttons. She wore the same shoes every time they babysat, black pumps with medium heels. She was usually easygoing but tonight she went over everything with Miri and Suzanne two or three times before leaving, while Mr. Foster, annoyed, checked his watch. She handed them lists with numbers of who to call in an emergency, including the Branford Theatre in Newark, where *Bright Victory* was playing, and the Weequahic Diner, where they always stopped for supper after the movie. Mrs. Foster felt more secure knowing Suzanne's mother was a nurse. And she liked having two of them babysit, not just because she got two for the price of one. She said it was a comfort to her.

"Let's go, Jo!" Mr. Foster called.

Penny and Betsy loved that. "Let's go, Jo!" they squealed.

Mrs. Foster didn't find that funny. "I'll be right there, Monty."

"I'll be right there, Monty," the little girls sang, mimicking their mother.

"Stop that right now," Mrs. Foster told them. And this time they did.

"Suzanne and Miri have heard the spiel before," Mr. Foster called, tapping his watch.

"All right, Monty!" Mrs. Foster said. Then, quietly, to Suzanne and Miri, "Betsy has sniffles. It could be the beginning of something, or nothing. But check on her every half hour after she goes to sleep, okay?"

"Okay, sure," Miri said and Suzanne nodded.

Mrs. Foster kissed Penny and Betsy. "You girls be good."

"Joanne!" Mr. Foster called, and this time Mrs. Foster hurried to the door.

Once they heard the door close behind them Suzanne let out a sigh.

As soon as their mother was out of sight, the girls started racing through the house. Miri chased them, a game they loved. "Eeny, meeny, miney, moe, catch a tiger by the toe. Which little tiger will I catch first?" The girls shrieked until Miri caught one, then the other, carrying them back to the living room. When they calmed down Suzanne painted their toenails and Miri brought them milk and gingersnaps from the kitchen. Later, when they were in their twin beds, tucked in just so, Miri and Suzanne took turns reading to them from a stack of library books. Mrs. Foster had been a first-grade teacher before the girls were born and stressed the importance of reading aloud to children.

After that, Suzanne turned on the radio, both girls took out the homework their mothers thought they'd finished earlier and settled down on the living room floor.

Mr. and Mrs. Foster returned happy, holding hands. It must have been a good movie. Usually Mrs. Foster asked for details of how the evening had gone. But not tonight. Mr. Foster drove them home, each with $1.50 in her pocket, a bonanza! Now that the holidays were over, Miri was saving her babysitting money for her ninth-grade prom dress. She figured $15 would do it, including shoes. When Mr. Foster started humming a tune, Suzanne leaned close to Miri and whispered, "I'll bet they went to a motel instead of a movie."

This thought had never occurred to Miri. Why would a married couple go to a motel when they said they'd be at the movies? No, Miri didn't believe it. She was sure Rusty would never do such a thing. Not that she was married. She didn't even have a boyfriend. And Miri liked it that way.

Capricorn

Born on January 15, you are a natural leader and problem solver. You have the intelligence to understand any situation and the discipline to follow through in pursuing a solution. Coupled with the trait of great loyalty, it makes you respected by all who know you. There is no better friend to have than a Capricorn.

BY THE MIDDLE of the month Fred knew Miri so well he'd jump up and down, barking, the minute he saw her. She'd scoop him up, letting him lick her face. Unless she had an after-school activity, she'd meet Mason at Jefferson High and walk him down to Edison Lanes. Then she'd deliver Fred to Phil Stein's house, either walking all the way to Westminster or taking the bus if the weather was bad, hiding Fred inside her winter jacket, the way Mason had taught her. She loved having his little body next to hers.

Phil's mother enjoyed Fred, so even if Phil wasn't home it wasn't a problem. Mrs. Stein was glad to see Miri, and always invited her in, offering a Tastykake, or a piece of fruit, or even a sandwich. If Miri accepted, Mrs. Stein would have something to eat, too, just to keep her company, laughing about whatever new diet she was going to start the following Monday. She liked flipping through her family photo albums, pointing out pictures of her dog, Goldie, who had died over the summer. "This is Goldie as a puppy. And here she is as a sweet old girl. A whole lifetime in twelve years."

In one photo Miri thought she recognized the girl in the green velvet dress from the Osners' New Year's Eve party. "That's my niece Kathy," Mrs. Stein said. "A wonderful girl. She's a freshman at Syracuse." So it *was* Kathy Stein from New Year's Eve.

Mrs. Stein seemed lonely to Miri, especially when she talked about her children. "I miss my daughter. She's away at college. University of Michigan. And next year, when Phil leaves, I don't know what I'll do."

"Maybe you should get another dog," Miri suggested.

"I've thought about that," Mrs. Stein said, "but what would we do when we travel? My husband is hoping to spend more time traveling once both children are at college."

"Where does he want to go?" Miri asked.

"Oh, he has some *meshuggeneh* idea about adventure, about exotic lands," Mrs. Stein said, helping herself to a second Tastykake. "Maybe India. Maybe Israel. Frankly, I'd rather see California. I'm not sure my stomach could handle India. I have a sensitive gut. You know what that's like."

As far as guts were concerned, Miri knew only that certain foods, like raw tomatoes, triggered Irene's heartburn, and when they did, she'd drink a glass of Alka-Seltzer.

"Anyway, my husband doesn't want another dog. He's afraid I won't want to leave a puppy at the kennel when we travel. It's true I never liked leaving Goldie, even when she was grown." She sighed and looked out the window. "It feels like snow, doesn't it?"

"I hope it does. I'd like to have fresh snow for my birthday."

"Your birthday?"

"Yes, tomorrow. I'll be fifteen on the fifteenth."

Mrs. Stein brightened. "Fifteen on the fifteenth! That's sure to be a lucky sign. You have to take every bit of luck that comes your way and turn it into something bigger, something lasting."

Miri was mulling that over when Mrs. Stein touched her arm. "Come with me. I have something for you."

"Oh, no, really . . ." Miri said.

"Oh, yes . . . really." Miri had never seen Mrs. Stein so animated. Fred trotted up the stairs behind them to Mrs. Stein's bedroom. Until then, Miri hadn't seen much of the Steins' house, which was on the fanciest street in town, where all the houses were big and old and set back from the street, surrounded by stately trees. She was familiar only with the back porch and the kitchen. But this—Mrs. Stein's bedroom—was bigger than Miri's living room and bedroom combined, with a chaise longue and two chairs grouped around a coffee table stacked with books and magazines spilling onto the floor, waiting to be read. At the other end of the room were two beds pushed together, attached to a single carved wooden headboard. Mrs. Stein disappeared into a walk-in closet behind the bed and came out with a small white box tied with a slender pink satin ribbon. She handed it to Miri. "Happy birthday."

Miri was embarrassed.

"Open it," Mrs. Stein sang. Miri half expected her to clap her hands and jump up and down, she seemed so pleased.

Miri opened the box. Inside was a bracelet. Gold with—were they garnets, her birthstone? "But you can't give this to me. You should save it for your daughter."

"Her birthstone is opal," Mrs. Stein said. "Mine is garnet, like yours. And I've got more garnet bracelets than I can count. I want you to have this one. It's delicate, like you."

Miri had never thought of herself as delicate and wasn't sure she wanted anyone else to, either. She supposed that next to Mrs. Stein, with her ample bosom, wide hips and plump arms, she could seem delicate, but she wasn't.

"Thank you," Miri said. "It's beautiful."

"So are you," Mrs. Stein said.

No one outside the family had ever told her that.

"Have a wonderful birthday." Mrs. Stein leaned in and kissed her cheek.

Fred barked until Mrs. Stein turned her attention to him.

MIRI WAS ALMOST SURE Rusty wouldn't approve of Mrs. Stein giving her a gold bracelet with garnets, so at first she didn't show it to her. But what was the point of having it if she could never wear it? That night she waited until after Rusty's bath, when Rusty seemed relaxed and happy, humming to herself. "Mrs. Stein gave me a bracelet for my birthday. She said it doesn't fit her anymore and she has more birthstone bracelets than she can possibly use."

"Let me see that." Miri passed her the bracelet. Rusty turned it over in her hand, studying it the way an appraiser might. "Which Mrs. Stein?"

"Phil's mother. They live on Westminster."

"Who is Phil?"

"Phil Stein. He's Steve Osner's best friend. He was at the New Year's Eve party."

"And what's the connection between you and Mrs. Stein?"

"I drop Fred off at the Steins' house a couple of days a week."

"Fred?"

"Fred. Mason's dog."

Rusty breathed deeply through her nose. "So this is about the dog?"

"Yes. Mrs. Stein likes having Fred around. They had a dog, Goldie, but she died."

"Does that make Mrs. Stein a better mother than me?"

"What? No." This wasn't going well.

"Mrs. Stein probably doesn't go to business," Rusty said.

"She doesn't."

"You see?"

Sometimes no matter what Miri said or didn't say, Rusty acted as if it reflected on her as a mother. She should have told Rusty that Mrs. Stein would like to work. That she'd like to be a librarian or a clerk at a book-store. Instead she wound up saying what she thought Rusty wanted to hear. "You're the best mother."

"You're just saying that so you can keep an expensive bracelet she had no right to give you."

"I don't care about the bracelet."

"Good. Then give it back. It's inappropriate for a stranger to give you such an extravagant gift."

"She's not exactly a stranger," Miri muttered under her breath as Rusty walked away with the bracelet. Miri chased her down the hall. "Mom . . ."

"What?"

"You took the bracelet."

Rusty handed it to Miri.

The next day after school she returned the bracelet. She didn't want to offend Mrs. Stein. But as soon as she began, "My mother doesn't think . . ." Mrs. Stein gave her a kind smile, a knowing smile, and took the box.

"Maybe I will give it to my daughter, after all."

"I'm sure she'd like it."

"She's hard to please."

"Even so."

"Thank you, Miri."

There. She'd done what she had to do. She would tell Rusty she'd returned the bracelet and she hoped that would satisfy her. Rusty could be moody but her bad moods rarely lasted.

BEFORE THE FAMILY sat down to Miri's birthday dinner, Rusty gave her a small box wrapped in blue paper and tied with a white ribbon. "Happy birthday, honey."

Inside was a gold and garnet bracelet, not exactly the same as Mrs. Stein's, but close enough. "It's beautiful," Miri said, slipping it onto her wrist.

"Now you see why . . ." Rusty began.

Miri hugged her mother. "I'm sorry."

"There's no need to be sorry," Rusty told her, smoothing her hair. "I love you."

"I love you, too."

Miri would never know if Rusty had already bought her the bracelet when she showed her the one from Mrs. Stein, or if she went out and bought it that day. "It looks really pretty, doesn't it?" She held up her arm for Rusty to admire.

Rusty smiled at her. "It does. It's delicate enough to go with anything."

Miri resisted the urge to laugh. At least Rusty hadn't called *her* delicate.

LATER THAT NIGHT, Mason stopped by with a birthday present for Miri. After Rusty greeted him, she went into her room, closing the door behind her, so the two of them could have the living room to themselves. "Fifteen minutes," Rusty called. "Four feet on the floor at all times." They couldn't help laughing over that rule, and when they did, Rusty laughed, too.

The present was wrapped in layers of tissue paper and tied with red and white bakery string. Miri opened it carefully, stealing looks at Mason. But he was looking down at the floor. At first she wasn't sure what it was except it was made of wood. Beautiful polished wood. A spyglass? She held it to her eye. No, it was a kaleidoscope with exquisite pale stones, regrouping into intricate designs as she turned it. This was nothing like the toy kaleidoscopes she'd had as a child. She'd never seen anything like it. She couldn't put it down. Finally, he took it out of her hands. "It was my mother's."

His mother's. "It's beautiful. Thank you." She wanted him to tell her more but she sensed he wasn't going to.

When Rusty knocked from inside her bedroom door, signaling their fifteen minutes were up, Miri walked Mason downstairs to the front door. "This is the best present anyone has ever given me," she told him.

"It's the only thing my mother had to leave me."

"I'll keep it safe for you," she said. "If you ever want it back—"

"Don't say that." He kissed her goodnight. Then he whispered, "Don't ever say that."

Rusty

Fifteen minutes, Rusty thought. They couldn't get into trouble in fifteen minutes, not with her just a room away. Besides, she could hear them talking softly the whole time. They'd known each other what—a month?—but she knew it felt like much longer to them. Everything was heightened when you were young and in love. And she could see they were in love. And so sweet together. It was that sweetness that got to her. She wasn't going to warn Miri that it couldn't last. She wasn't going to warn her they were too young, like the song. Why spoil it? There would be heartache when it ended but Rusty would help her through it. Maybe it was better for Miri to experience first love now than in a few years, when *she* wouldn't have as much control over them. Fifteen minutes. Plenty could happen in fifteen minutes when no one was watching and you were in a Nash with a seat that folded back to make a bed.

She picked up the copy of *From Here to Eternity* she'd

checked out of the penny library at the confectionery on Morris Avenue. It was a thick book. She'd better get in more reading time. At the rate she was going, she might as well have bought it.

Miri

It snowed again overnight on Friday, so Miri awoke to more fresh snow on the day of her slumber party, a birthday celebration planned with her girlfriends before she'd met Mason. That afternoon she went sledding on Wyoming Avenue with Suzanne, Robo and Eleanor, while Natalie was in New York at dance class. Donny Kellen and his brothers were their usual obnoxious selves, steering their sleds into the girls, trying to knock them to the ground, where they would wash their faces with snow if they got the chance. Miri hated the Kellen boys. She hated them even more since she'd read *Ethan Frome* in English class. Suppose they forced her to crash her sled into a tree and she wound up like Mattie Silver in the book? What would Rusty do then? Quit her job and spend the rest of her life taking care of Miri, or would Irene have to "step up to the plate" again? Both scenarios filled her with dread.

But Miri and her friends survived and arrived cold, wet and happy at Miri's house, where Natalie joined them. They changed into their nightgowns, leaving on their underwear since they weren't going to sleep for hours, and enjoyed pizza from Spirito's, thanks to Uncle Henry, who brought three large pies home for them. Only Natalie resisted. She'd given up sweets and bread for dancing. "Something every dancer has to do," she told them. "And

I don't mind. I've never had a sweet tooth and bread just leaves me feeling bloated."

Robo told them her mother goes to a diet doctor every week, Dr. Kalb, who gives her pills. "It's like a candy shop at his office. Except instead of candy the bins are filled with different-colored pills. He scoops them into a brown paper bag and tells my mother how many she should take a day, and what colors. Some of them give her diarrhea."

"Ew . . ." Suzanne said. "Not while we're eating."

"I don't need pills," Natalie said. "I have willpower."

"Too bad you can't bottle that," Eleanor said. "You could make a fortune."

"Mmm . . ." Natalie said, concentrating on her salad of iceberg lettuce and green grapes. Miri prayed Natalie wouldn't act weird tonight, and she didn't, except for not even tasting Irene's delicious birthday cake, Miri's favorite, dark chocolate with mocha frosting. Miri wrapped a piece for Mason. She would bring it to him Monday after school.

Later, they went down to Irene's to watch *Your Hit Parade*. Eddy Howard sang the number three song, "It's No Sin."

"Now, that's a beautiful song," Natalie said. "If we're lucky we won't have to hear 'Slow Poke' or 'Shrimp Boats' again."

Miri agreed. She imagined dancing with Mason to "It's No Sin." The thought was enough to give her shivers.

Back upstairs in Miri's room, the girls gave her their present. Her first cashmere sweater from the cashmere sweater lady, in a beautiful shade of aqua.

"It's from my mom, too," Natalie said.

Miri understood. Corinne had shelled out whatever

extra the sweater cost after the girls had pooled their money.

"Try it on," Robo told her.

"Now?" Miri asked.

"Yes, now!" the other girls sang.

She stepped behind her closet door, let her nightgown drop from her shoulders, pulled the sweater on, then gathered the nightgown around her waist so she could model the sweater for them. They whooped and cheered. Robo and Suzanne whistled. She couldn't wait to wear it for Mason.

"Wait until Mason *feels* how soft it is!" Robo said, as if she knew what Miri was thinking. It used to be Natalie who knew what Miri was thinking, but not anymore. Natalie was distant now, living in her own world. The other girls laughed until Robo switched gears. "I have something to tell you."

They could see from the look on her face it was serious. Miri pulled off the sweater, rebuttoned her nightgown, and sat on the floor with her friends, waiting for Robo's news. She hoped it wasn't serious, as in someone was going to die. She didn't want to hear anything bad on her birthday.

"We're moving," Robo said. "To Millburn."

They gasped.

"But why?" Suzanne asked. "You already live in a beautiful house."

"My parents say it's because of my father's job. He's building one of those new shopping centers nearby . . . but I think it's because of . . ." She trailed off.

"Let me guess," Eleanor said. "The crash."

"Well, yes, even though they won't admit it. Instead

they say things like the schools in Millburn are really good." Then, embarrassed, she added, "Not that there's anything wrong with the schools here."

"But the crash is over," Suzanne argued.

"I know, but what can I do?" Robo wouldn't look at them. Her friends. They'd been together for almost three years. At Battin they'd have three more.

"I thought you have to be really rich to live there," Suzanne said.

"Only on some streets," Robo said, growing defensive. "You'll come visit. It's not that far away. Just twenty minutes or so by car."

"Only another planet," Eleanor said.

"There's a Lord & Taylor," Robo said, trying to find something positive to say. "We can go shopping."

"You can go shopping." Eleanor didn't add that Natalie was the only one of their crowd who could afford to shop at Lord & Taylor. Until now. Who knew Robo's parents—Milton and Pamela Boros—were rich enough to move to Millburn?

"You sound angry," Robo said to Eleanor. "Are you angry?"

"No. Yes." Eleanor shook her head and shrugged. "Maybe."

"Because it's not my fault."

"I know it's not your fault," Eleanor said. "I'm just . . . I don't know . . . disappointed because I always thought the five of us would be together all through high school."

Miri never would have guessed Eleanor cared so much. She had her whole life planned out, including winning the Nobel Prize in math or science.

"I can't control my parents," Robo said. "If you want

the truth, they didn't even ask me. They took me and my sister for a ride last week and pointed to a house. 'This is our new house,' my father said. We're moving before Lincoln's birthday."

"Now?" Suzanne said. "You're moving in the middle of the school year?"

Robo flushed. "I have no choice."

Natalie said only, "We'll miss you." Just that. Just the perfect thing to say.

"Thank you, Nat."

They set their hair in pin curls, or socks, depending on the length, spread out their sleeping bags on the floor of Miri's room and turned out the lights. Then, on cue, her four friends serenaded her in the dark.

> *They try to tell us we're too young.*
> *Too young to really be in love . . .*

Something about that song, something about the tender way they sang it to her, made Miri tear up. She loved her friends. She loved her family. She loved Mason. She couldn't bear the idea of losing any of them. Ever.

Elizabeth Daily Post

TRUCE TEAMS STILL WRANGLE OVER KOREA
TAX INCREASES LOOM

MUSAN, KOREA, JAN. 16—Truce negotiators kept tempers in check today as they wrangled fruitlessly over terms of a Korean armistice. The only outburst came from a Chinese delegate who referred scornfully to America's allies as "running dogs." U.S. casualties to date total 104,084, with 15,950 killed, 75,374 wounded and 12,760 missing or held as prisoners.

On the home front, facing a budget deficit because of the Korean War, President Truman has again proposed increasing taxes, the fourth time since the hostilities began. "We have to be fiscally responsible," a presidential spokesman explained. But Congress seems more intent on finding ways to cut spending, especially in an election year.

11

Steve

On Thursday, January 17, Steve Osner and his father flew to Boston for college interviews at Brandeis and Tufts. Steve had been to Syracuse with Phil Stein and *his* father, a Syracuse alum, a fraternity man, who was treated like the BMOC he must have been. Steve already knew Syracuse was his first choice but his father insisted he look at other schools, too. "Keep your options open, son."

He'd applied to the two Boston-area schools and he liked what he saw, but not enough to change his mind. His father took him to lunch between interviews at a Harvard Square restaurant. It was good to be alone with his father when he wasn't *on*, singing to his patients or telling jokes. Even at home his father was always performing for Fern and Natalie, making them laugh at the dinner table. His mother was more proper, more concerned with doing things the right way, which was *her* way. Deep down he knew he was more like his mother, even though there were times when he wished he could be more like his father.

"Nice-looking coeds," his father said of the college girls at the restaurant.

Steve agreed. Nice-looking coeds. But none so nice as Kathy Stein.

He knew it had been very different for his father, who had grown up poor but strong-willed, working his way through college, then dental school. He knew he was supposed to feel grateful that life was easier for him, though sometimes he wasn't so sure it was. Sometimes he felt he was carrying a heavy load, that he'd never be able to be a good enough person. His parents' expectations for him were too great.

Is that why he'd shouted at Mason McKittrick the night of his sister's party? Phil wanted to know what had gotten into him. He remembered only that he'd been filled with rage when he saw Mason dancing with Miri. He would have killed Mason if he could have, but he didn't know why. What made him feel that way?

By midafternoon it was snowing pretty hard. At the airport they learned their plane back to Newark had been canceled due to the weather. "This isn't good," his father said. "I have to get back. I have a full day tomorrow."

"And I have a test in chemistry," Steve told him.

"Let me see what I can do," his father said. "Wait here and watch our stuff."

What stuff? Steve wondered. They had no bags, except for one with college scarves for Natalie, who collected them, and another with a little wool hat in Tufts colors, blue and brown, for Fern.

His father was gone for half an hour and came back looking pleased, waving around two boarding passes. "Snagged two tickets," he said. "We board in fifteen minutes."

It wasn't until they'd taken off and reached their cruising altitude that his father leaned close and said, "You can never tell your mother we flew on a non-sked."

Steve looked at him. Was he kidding?

"She'd never forgive me," his father said.

"We're on a non-sked?" Steve asked.

"You didn't know?" his father said.

Steve shook his head.

"It's not a C-46," his father said. "I'd never fly with you on a C-46."

Was that supposed to be reassuring?

"Even so, you know how your mother is, so this has to be our secret."

When Steve didn't say anything, his father gave him a playful punch in the arm. "Man to man. Agreed?"

"Sure," Steve said. "Agreed." But he couldn't believe his father had risked *his* life, the life of his only son, because he had to get back to the office, back to his precious patients. You'd think, after spending night after night trying to identify burned and dismembered corpses, his father would never fly again, let alone take a non-sked.

INSIDE HOLLYWOOD

By Virginia McPherson

JAN. 20—Hollywood is still digging itself out of the muck and mud from the latest West Coast storm disaster—and some marooned movie stars haven't scooped out yet.

Humphrey Bogart waded hip-deep into muddy water on Sunset Boulevard to direct traffic. Hasn't had so much fun in years. "Couldn't get home for three days," he grinned. "Just holed up in the Beverly Hills Hotel bar and stayed spiffed for 72 hours."

Until his spouse Lauren Bacall phoned irately, "You get home tonight, with milk and orange juice for your son . . . or else!"

Bogie got.

12

Miri

Miri was on her bed, reading her favorite columns in the Sunday paper, when the doorbell rang. She ran down the stairs to answer it. She was in a sour mood because Rusty wouldn't let her invite Mason to dinner at The Tavern, where they were going to celebrate Henry's engagement to Leah.

"It's not appropriate," Rusty told her. "This is just for the immediate family."

"Nana is bringing Ben Sapphire," Miri reminded her.

"Yes, but she's hosting this party, so if she wants to bring Mr. Sapphire, she can."

"He's not immediate family."

"He's picking up the bill."

"So you're saying I should ask Mr. Sapphire about inviting Mason?"

"Damn it, Miri! Don't push me. And don't you dare ask Nana or anyone else about inviting Mason."

So when the doorbell rang, Miri was more than glad to get away from Rusty. She wasn't sure who she expected to find on the other side of the front door, but certainly not this woman in slacks and a matching wool coat with a big fox collar. A yellow Cadillac was parked in front of the house. Miri had never seen a yellow Cadillac on her street. The only yellow Cadillac she knew of belonged to one of the Levy brothers, who owned the department store on Broad Street.

"Are you Miriam?" the woman asked. Her voice was smoky, her lipstick red, not a strand of her dark hair moved in the wind.

"Do I know you?" Miri asked. No one called her *Miriam*.

"I'm Frekki Strasser but my maiden name was Monsky. I believe I'm your aunt."

Miri grabbed hold of the door to steady herself.

Rusty called from the upstairs window, "Who is it, Miri?" Jazzy music floated down from Rusty's radio.

When Miri didn't answer, the woman called, "A voice from your past."

Miri didn't turn, didn't take her eyes off the woman, but she could hear her mother's footsteps on the stairs. Rusty had been vacuuming. Her hair was carelessly tied back. She was in an old shirt with the flaps hanging out, worn slacks and beat-up moccasins.

The woman held out her gloved hand. "Hello, Rusty. It's Frekki Monsky Strasser."

"Frekki?" Rusty went pale. She made no move to shake Frekki's hand, which floated in midair, until Frekki shoved it into her coat pocket.

Rusty stood in front of Miri as if to protect her from this stranger. "What are you doing here?"

"Unexpected events . . ." Now she used the same gloved hand to gesture toward the sky, and Miri knew it wasn't God she was talking about. "Well, it made me stop and think, I have a niece, I should know her."

Rusty turned to Miri. "Go upstairs."

"But I—"

"Right now."

Miri moved toward the vestibule as Rusty said, "How did you know I have a daughter?"

"It's not a secret, is it?"

"Fifteen years later you decide you want to know my daughter?"

"Better late than never," Frekki said.

"I'm not sure that's always the case." Rusty turned back to Miri. "I *said* go upstairs. Now."

Irene appeared at the door wrapped in a shawl. "What's all this?"

"Hello, Mrs. Ammerman." The woman held out her hand again. "Frekki Monsky."

Irene's hand went to her chest. "You have the nerve to show up here, at my house?"

"Now, Mrs. Ammerman—"

"Don't you *now*, *Mrs. Ammerman* me!"

Miri had never heard such anger in her grandmother's voice.

This time Rusty shouted, "Go upstairs, Miri!"

"I'm going to get Nana a pill."

"I don't need a pill," Irene said.

"Yes, you do," Miri told her. "I can tell."

"Why don't you invite me in?" Frekki said. "I mean no harm and it's freezing out here."

"That looks like a warm coat to me," Rusty said, hugging herself.

Miri came back with Irene's pill, but Irene waved her away.

"All right," Frekki said. "If that's how it's going to be . . ." She pulled a creamy envelope out of her purse. "This is for Miriam. An invitation to lunch and a show at the Paper Mill Playhouse. I hope you'll be reasonable about this, Rusty. I live in South Orange now. I'm married to a doctor. I'm in a position to be a positive influence in Miriam's life."

Miri felt sick to her stomach. But at the same time, excited.

Frekki

Frekki's husband, J.J., had a cousin in Elizabeth who owned Strasser Sports. How many times had she brought the boys to their store for their team uniforms, for the expert in athletic shoes, said to be the best in the state, to fit them properly? More than ten years of shopping trips for summer camp, and to make sure they had the best equipment for baseball, basketball, football, never mind the hockey skates, the cleats. They'd built a special closet in the finished basement just for the boys' athletic equipment.

In September, during the annual trek to Elizabeth, Sherry Strasser, the cousin's wife, invited Frekki to lunch. "Leave the boys at the store and come out with me."

The *boys*, who were now seventeen and nineteen, were capable of looking after themselves, so she'd accepted Sherry's invitation to lunch at Dorothy Dennis, a ladies' tearoom. "We don't get to see you often enough," Sherry said.

"I know. J.J. and I were just saying the same thing."

After their sandwich plates had been cleared and the tea served, Sherry said, "The store is so busy this time of year I help out as much as I can, and last week I saw a young girl, maybe fifteen, with eyes exactly like your brother's."

Frekki wasn't sure how to respond.

"She's friends with the Osner girl. You know the Osners, don't you? He's a dentist."

"Yes, I've met them at the Club."

"So while the Osner girl and her friend were trying on sneakers I told them they looked so cute together I just had to snap their picture with my new Polaroid camera." She fished a photo out of her pocketbook and passed it to Frekki.

Frekki was surprised, but tried not to show it.

"What do you think?" Sherry asked.

"Makes me wish I had a daughter," Frekki told her. "About the resemblance, I mean."

"I don't see any resemblance."

"Really? I've always thought your brother had the most unusual eyes, almond-shaped and hazel. And so does she. Of course I haven't seen Mike in ages, not since he left town in a hurry."

"He didn't leave in a hurry. He enlisted."

"Either way. We went to all the same parties that spring. He and Rusty Ammerman were crazy for each other. She was in my class at Battin."

"I don't remember that name." The redhead. She hoped her face wasn't giving anything away. Mike had brought her to the house in Weequahic a couple of times. And Frekki had been to the Ammermans' house, too. Had enjoyed Mrs. Ammerman's delicious chocolate cake.

"She's still around," Sherry said. "And this is her daughter, Miri."

"What are you getting at?"

"Do I have to spell it out?"

"What you're suggesting isn't possible."

"Are you sure? There was a story going around back then that Rusty had run off and married a boy that summer, a boy who was going overseas."

"She didn't marry my brother."

"Well, she's never married anyone else that I know of."

"I think you should forget about this, Sherry. There's no truth to it and all you can do is make trouble for both families." Frekki glanced at the photo again. "She looks like a nice girl."

"She is. The Osners love her like a daughter."

Frekki dabbed at her mouth with the napkin, applied

fresh lipstick and pushed back her chair. "I have to get back to the boys. Thanks for the lunch. Next time it's on me." Before she put on her jacket she said, "Oh, do you mind if I keep the picture?"

"Of course," Sherry said. Was that a smirk on her face?

Frekki called her brother that night, made sure he could talk privately, then told him the story. "I just want to know one thing. Is it possible, yes or no?"

"No," her brother said, convincingly.

She probably would have let it go if it hadn't been for the plane crash. She didn't need any more *tsoris* in her life. But by then she knew where Rusty lived, and how close the plane had come to her house and that beautiful young girl with Mike's eyes, that girl who very likely was her niece. She couldn't sleep that night thinking about it, or the night after that. Which is how she came to ring Rusty's doorbell on Sunday morning.

Miri

Rusty and Irene were masters of cleaning up, putting everything away, keeping things in order—things they didn't want to think about, as if they had a box in the closet and they could open it, shove in Frekki and her yellow Cadillac, close the lid, lock the box, put it back on the top shelf and be done with it. Sometimes Miri tried to imagine she, too, had a secret box on the top shelf of her closet, covered in burgundy velvet, a place to hide every hurt, every bad thought, every worry that she couldn't do anything about—but it didn't work as well for her as it did for Rusty and Irene. Still, she was good at pretending, good at putting on a happy face. She'd learned that much from her mother and grandmother. So she dressed in her best skirt and the sweater her friends had given her for her birthday, and went off to The Tavern restaurant in Ben Sapphire's black Packard with Irene seated up front and she and Rusty sharing the back.

A few hours after Frekki Strasser came to their door, you would never have guessed anything unusual had happened that day. Neither Rusty nor Irene said a word to her about the unexpected visit. And Miri knew better than to ask them any questions today, a day they were celebrating the engagement of Henry and Leah.

Elizabeth Daily Post

POLIO CHAIRMAN NAMED

JAN. 20—Mr. Ronald T. Stein was today named chairman of the Union County division of the Annual March of Dimes Polio Drive. Mr. Stein is Chief Executive of Steinmack Trucking, a company he founded in 1938. With headquarters in Elizabeth, the firm has branches throughout the state. He resides in the Westminster section of Elizabeth with his wife, Sarah, and two children, a son, Philip, a senior at Thomas Jefferson High School, and a daughter, Deborah, a sophomore at the University of Michigan.

Long committed to community service, Mr. Stein is a Member of the Board of the Watchung Hills Children's Home, which specializes in the care of polio patients. He is also on the Board of the Janet Memorial Home.

"Though polio cases have surged in recent years, we now see hope for a vaccine to prevent this dread disease," Mr. Stein said. "We must redouble our efforts to raise funds to provide care for the afflicted and finance the research to end it."

13

Miri

Everyone Miri knew considered The Tavern, in the Weequahic section of Newark, the best restaurant in New Jersey. Some families, like the Osners, treated The

Tavern like a club. They were Sunday regulars. Other families, like Miri's, celebrated only the most special events there.

Miri wasn't surprised to see the Osners lining up just as she and her family arrived. The Tavern didn't accept reservations. Miri had had Sunday dinners at The Tavern with Natalie and her family more times than she could count. She knew what they would order before they even sat down. Corinne, Natalie and Fern would start with consommé and they'd slice dill pickles into it. Slicing dill pickles into chicken soup struck Miri as disgusting but Natalie swore it was delicious. Every time Natalie said, *Have a taste*, Miri would say, *No thanks*. Miri supposed dill pickles in chicken soup was another tradition Corinne had brought with her from Birmingham, Alabama, like the Jewish Santa. Probably Tewky Purvis sliced dill pickles into his consommé, too.

When Irene had asked Rusty about the New Year's Eve party, Rusty told her Tewky was the best dancer she'd ever danced with. "A lovely man."

Irene brightened. "And . . . you're going to see him again?"

"He lives in Birmingham, Alabama. His family owns a bank there."

"A bank!" Irene sang. "So what's a few miles between friends?"

"Unfortunately, he's a confirmed bachelor."

Irene paused. "He told you so?"

"He did."

"Did you ever hear that meeting the right girl can change all that?"

"I've heard it but I don't believe it."

A confirmed bachelor? So Natalie was right. He was never getting married. Well, that was a relief.

At 4 p.m. the line to get a table at The Tavern was already long, extending down Elizabeth Avenue all the way past the Krich-Radisco building, where Fern would tilt her head back to see her reflection in the mirrored overhead. Families laughed and talked while waiting as if the wait were part of the whole experience, even in winter. Rumor had it the only person who never had to wait was Longy Zwillman. No one complained about that, either, at least not to the owner, Sam Teiger. They all wanted to stay on Sam Teiger's good side. Not that Miri had ever laid eyes on Longy, but she listened when his name came up.

Miri introduced Leah to the Osners. "We're celebrating our engagement today," Leah said, holding up her hand as if she couldn't believe it was *her* hand, with polished fingernails, a white orchid wrist corsage and, to top it all off, the ring. Corinne called the ring a *truly elegant heirloom piece*. Leah looked pleased. "Yes," she said. "It is, isn't it? Thank you so much."

"It was my grandmother's," Miri told Natalie.

Natalie said, "My mother wears my grandmother's ring, too. But she had the diamond reset to look more modern."

Miri would never change Irene's ring. She hoped Leah wouldn't, either.

After forty-five minutes of waiting outside in the cold, they made it to the heated vestibule of the restaurant, where they shed their winter coats. Ben Sapphire helped Irene out of her Persian lamb, worn only on special occasions. Miri had always liked the way it smelled from the cold. When she was little she once napped on it at a family party. Lately she'd been thinking about how before it was a coat it was a real lamb, a little black lamb, maybe more than one little black lamb, and that thought haunted her now whenever Irene wore the coat, which was older than Miri. Every few years the furrier on Bergen Street in Newark would update it, making any necessary repairs. Last year he'd relined it with black-on-black patterned silk, embroidering IRENE AMMERMAN in shocking pink just inside the waist, like a fancy name tape, in case someone went home with the wrong coat.

Both Irene and Leah's aunt Alma had purple orchid corsages pinned to their suit jackets. Alma had never been to The Tavern but, like everyone else, she'd heard of it.

Sam Teiger greeted everyone. "Doc," he said to Dr. O, "have a little something," as a waiter passed around a tray of hors d'oeuvres in case a person got hungry while waiting for a table.

Alma helped herself, daintily wiping her mouth with a cocktail napkin. "Delicious," she said.

Dr. O introduced Henry to Sam Teiger. "Henry is the star reporter who's been writing about the crash of the plane in Elizabeth. If you haven't read his stories, you should. I hear he's considered so good the paper is doubling his salary and giving him his own byline. Is that right, Henry?"

"Byline, yes," Henry said. "Doubled salary?" He laughed. "Haven't heard that one."

"He's being too modest," Dr. O said. "And this is Henry's fiancée, the lovely . . ."

"Leah Cohen," Henry told Sam Teiger. "We're celebrating our engagement today."

Leah held up her left hand so Sam Teiger could admire her ring, which he did. "Heirloom," Leah told him.

"Lovely," Sam Teiger said. "And so are you."

"Why, thank you, Mr. Teiger," Leah said, looking up from behind her bangs, with her most Debbie Reynolds look. Miri half expected her to burst into song. Then they'd all dance as if they were in a movie musical.

"This calls for Champagne!" Sam Teiger snapped his fingers and a captain appeared, like a genie out of a bottle. Sam asked, quietly, "How many in your party, Henry?"

"Seven," Henry answered. "But we can squeeze around a table for six."

"And we're five," Dr. O said, though no one had asked. "But we could squeeze around a table for four. Back-to-back tables would be good."

"Let me see what I can do," Sam Teiger said, nodding to the captain.

Two minutes later both families were being shown to their tables, one a table for six with an extra chair added, the other a table for six with one chair removed. The big room was attractive, but simple, noisy, but not too noisy. At their table Miri sat between Rusty and Aunt Alma, who was skinny, and, Miri thought, nervous, her hands trembling slightly.

Across the dining room Miri caught a glimpse of Mrs. Stein with her husband, who wanted to travel to exotic lands, and their son, Phil. She hoped Mrs. Stein wouldn't come over to their table. She didn't want to have to introduce her to Rusty. She didn't want to risk how Rusty might react—all that insecurity about not being a good enough mother. She didn't have to worry. Mrs. Stein acknowledged her with a small smile and a slight gesture of recognition that could have been missed by anyone but Miri. She was grateful to Mrs. Stein for that.

Sam Teiger sent over Champagne, as promised. "A magnum!" Ben Sapphire was impressed. "Sam Teiger is a real sport."

The waiter popped the cork and poured it, filling Miri's glass halfway before he realized she was underage. But no one took it away from her.

Irene made the first toast. "Thank you, Henry, for choosing Leah. I can't imagine anyone I'd rather have for a daughter-in-law." They all clinked glasses.

"Thank you, Mother Irene," Leah said. Miri had never heard Leah refer to Irene as *Mother Irene*, as if she were a nun. Or would that be *Sister Irene*? She'd have to ask Suzanne, even though Suzanne was Protestant, not Catholic.

"Please, call me Irene."

"Or Mama," Henry said. "Because she's a wonderful mama." He leaned over and kissed Irene's cheek. "There's never been a better mama."

"Such a son!" She hugged Henry.

Alma said, "My sister, Leah's mother, is also a wonderful mother. It's a shame she can't be here today. But it's such a long trip from Cleveland and with Sy's arthritis . . ."

"But they'll come for the wedding," Leah said.

Leah

She was embarrassed her parents weren't here, leaving Aunt Alma to cover for them. She knew darn well it had nothing to do with her father's arthritis, which was mild, and everything to do with his pocketbook. He was such a cheapskate when it came to his wife and daughters. And not just with money, but with time, with affection. Now that he was retired it was all about playing the ponies at Thistledown, kibitzing at poker with his buddies or hanging out in the bookie's room behind the paint store. His daughters never stood a chance with him. *Girls, what good are girls?* he'd supposedly said when she, and then her sister, were born. Her mother had no guts, never stood up to her father, kept her mouth shut to keep the peace. She'd had to scrimp and save out of her weekly allowance, serving hamburger instead of steak to buy her girls a pair of shoes. She felt sorry for her mother but she'd learned from her, too, learned to speak her mind, to make sure she would have a life apart from her husband's. Sometimes she hoped her parents wouldn't come to the wedding. Her father would only make trouble. She'd already told him they didn't expect him to contribute to the cost, and he hadn't argued. She and Henry were going to foot the bill and Irene was taking care of the liquor and the cake.

Henry's family was so close. It worried her sometimes that she was fourth in line after Irene, Rusty and Miri. Not that they hadn't welcomed her into the family. But he was so attached to them. She'd learned quickly never to say a critical word about any of them. As far as Henry was concerned, they were perfect. A hard act to follow.

Miri

Rusty gave a little cough to get the attention back to the toasts. She held up her glass. "Here's to the best brother a girl could ever have. And you know I mean that, Henry.

May you and Leah enjoy health and happiness always."
Then she choked up.

"Here, here . . ." Ben Sapphire said. Miri was surprised when he held up his glass because it wasn't like
he was one of the family. Still, no one stopped him from
speaking. "Leah," Ben Sapphire said, "you are joining a
kind, generous, loving family. They rescued me when I
thought my life was over and helped me find a reason to
keep going."

Now Miri was really surprised. She'd never heard Ben
Sapphire say much of anything, let alone something so
deep. At least it sounded deep to her. She was trying to
think of what she could possibly say after that when Alma
clutched her arm. Miri could tell she was growing more
and more anxious. Now her hands shook as she passed
Miri a note card. "I can't make speeches," she whispered.
"Will you do it for me?"

So Miri held up her glass the way the others had, and
read, "Aunt Alma is so happy that Henry and Leah are
marrying." Miri glanced over at Aunt Alma, who gave her
a nod and a small, grateful smile. "And she looks forward
to the day you bring your children to her house to play
in her yard."

"Please," Irene said. "Don't rush them. They're not
even married yet." Then everyone laughed, except Alma,
who was embarrassed by what she had asked Miri to say
for her.

Miri didn't say any of the things she might have said to
Henry alone. He was just thirteen years old when she was
born. All of her childhood memories involved him. He
was gentle with her and always kind. He never lied, never
shied away from taking her questions seriously. When he

went away to war she couldn't stop crying. Every morning and every night she prayed for him. She prayed to a god she didn't know, not the god from the High Holidays, but some other god, who wouldn't be too busy to listen. Every night when she sat down to supper with Rusty and Irene, they joined hands, bowing their heads and closing their eyes. That meant they were thinking of Uncle Henry, who was *over there*.

Irene pasted a blue star in her window, signaling she had a son in the military. When they had air raid practice at night, when the sirens went off and they lowered their blackout curtains, Rusty would lie next to her in bed and tell her stories about Uncle Henry when he was a little boy. She'd always end by promising Miri the war could never come to Elizabeth and no enemy could harm them or any of America. Miri believed her until recently. The day Henry came back from the war was the happiest day of Miri's life.

WHEN HENRY ORDERED broiled lobster, Alma surprised everyone by saying she'd have one, too. "My friend has a cottage in Maine and when I visited we bought lobsters right off the dock."

"I've never been to Maine," Rusty said.

"I highly recommend it," Alma told her.

Miri watched, fascinated, at the way Alma dissected her lobster, meticulously removing every bit of meat before eating a bite, dipping each piece into butter, uttering small sounds of satisfaction as she did. She was the last to finish her meal.

As the waiter was clearing their plates, Miri saw a tall man come up to Dr. O. Dr. O jumped up from the table. The men shook hands warmly, the taller one squeezing Dr. O's shoulder. Then Dr. O guided the tall man over to their table. "I'd like to introduce you to Henry Ammerman," he said. "He's been covering the crash for the *Daily Post.* He's about to become famous."

"You should write for the *Newark News,*" the tall man said. "You want an interview, I can set one up." Then he put out his hand and introduced himself. "Abner Zwillman. Abe, to friends. Very pleased to meet you." His suit and tie and polished shoes looked expensive. His dark hair was threaded with silver and slicked back. In his hand he held an unlit cigar. He looked around the table. "And who is this ravishing young lady?"

Miri thought he was talking about her because of the *young lady* business—but then she realized he was focused on Rusty.

"Rusty Ammerman," Dr. O said, making introductions. "Henry's lovely sister."

Abner/Abe took Rusty's hand and kissed it. "*Enchanté,*" he said, making Rusty blush.

"You know who that was?" Henry said to Rusty, when Abner/Abe was gone. "That was Longy Zwillman."

"Oh, my gosh," Rusty said, blushing an even deeper shade of pink. "That was Longy? Longy kissed my hand?"

"Yeah," Henry said, "but that wasn't all he was thinking of kissing."

"Henry, stop!" Rusty pretended to swat him with her pocketbook.

Aunt Alma looked shocked. But not so shocked that

she wouldn't have liked a handsome man to be *enchanté* over her, too.

Then the waiter arrived with a dessert tray. "Banana cream pie, coconut cream pie and The Tavern's signature cheesecake, to die for." They all protested. They were too full. But not for just a taste.

Ben Sapphire poured the last bit of Champagne into his glass, stood up and made one last toast. "To Leah and Henry. Terrible things can happen in this life but being in love changes everything. It gives you something to hold on to. From now on only good times, good health, good news!" Then he leaned over and kissed Irene on the cheek.

Yes, Miri thought, being in love changes everything.

Elizabeth Daily Post

WINTER BREAK PRESIDENT TRUMAN VISITS LITTLE WHITE HOUSE

JAN. 21 (UPI)—The President flew to Key West, Florida, yesterday for a lengthy visit to his "Little White House" retreat on the Navy base at the southernmost point of the United States. His arrival was greeted with full presidential courtesies—simultaneous 21-gun salutes from USS Gilmore and USS Yosemite in the harbor, and the playing of ruffles and flourishes followed by the national anthem by the Marine drum and bugle corps.

The President is able to continue working at this remote location thanks to thrice-weekly mail courier service from Washington. The USS Williamsburg, equipped with duplex radio teletype equipment, was dispatched ahead of the President's visit and moored at the Navy base. It will provide a classified circuit to the Navy Department and the White House.

This morning President Truman enjoyed his daily walk to the beach one mile away, where he swam in the Atlantic Ocean and watched his staff engage in a vigorous volleyball match. The movie "The Model and the Marriage Broker" will be shown in the living room this evening.

Mrs. Truman remained in Washington at the bedside of her mother, who is ill, and was unable to join her husband. They spoke on the telephone last night, which they will do every evening. He also spoke on the phone with his daughter, Margaret, who is performing in Birmingham.

14

Kathy

On Tuesday afternoon, January 22, Kathy Stein sat at her desk finishing her final exam in English lit, stealing glances at her watch, praying she'd finish in time to make her plane from Syracuse to Newark. She had a taxi lined up to deliver her to the airfield, and the second she turned in her blue book she raced out of Slocum Hall, taking the steps two at a time, never mind the ice, and was relieved to see the cab waiting. She tossed her bag into the backseat and told the driver to step on it. He handed her a line about the weather. "You want to get there in one piece, or not?" Well, yes, she wanted to get there in one piece, but she *wanted* to get there. The driver had the heat turned up to what felt like 100 degrees but there was nothing to do about that but roll down her window. "It's not enough I have a sore throat?" The driver coughed to make his point. "You want me to get pneumonia?"

She paid him, leapt out before he'd come to a full stop and ran for the field. When she saw that her plane would be half an hour late, she relaxed. She was one of four students from Syracuse waiting to board American Airlines Flight 6780 heading to Newark Airport. Like her, they'd finished their exams and were going home for a break before second semester began. Kathy was the only girl among them, making her wish her roommate, Jane, had been able to come. She kidded around with the boys while they waited, bought a pack of Juicy Fruit and a copy of *Silver Screen* to distract her during the flight.

The weather was nasty, but who cared? Her cousin Phil would be meeting her at Newark, and he'd promised to bring his friend Steve Osner. Not that she and Steve had talked about officially dating or anything, but he liked her—she could tell. There was definitely an attraction between them. Not to mention that sweet Happy New Year kiss. She wasn't going to worry about the difference in their ages. Everyone knew that wives outlived their husbands.

The plane had already picked up passengers in Buffalo and Rochester when it finally landed in Syracuse. Kathy boarded and was seated next to an older man, who introduced himself as Robert Patterson. When he asked what she was studying she hid her movie magazine, not wanting him to think she was some dumb girl. He was very friendly. Told her he had a son and three daughters. Told her he was the former Secretary of War under President Truman. Gads, Kathy thought, he was someone important, someone famous.

He wanted to know her plans for the future. Said it was never too early to have goals. She was embarrassed. She'd never really thought beyond graduating from the college of home economics, marrying someone with possibilities and having a couple of kids. "I'm going to work for a food magazine," she said, trying to impress him. Working for a magazine sounded glamorous to her. She'd have to live in New York. She was pretty sure that's where the magazines had their offices. Or she could commute.

By the time they began their descent into Newark, she had it all worked out in her head. She'd marry Steve Osner, work for a magazine in New York until they had children and live in Elizabeth, in the same pretty neighborhood as Steve's parents, where the streets were named after poets—Kipling, Browning, Byron, Shelley. When she'd mentioned to Steve that she loved the names of the streets around his house Steve had seemed surprised. "Really?" he'd asked. "English poets?" Oh, well, the required freshman English lit course would fix that.

It had been a bumpy trip, and she was starting to feel queasy. "I don't like it when I can't see the ground," she told Secretary Patterson.

He told her to focus on something straight ahead. Don't look out the window. She figured he knew, being a former Secretary of War and all. So she focused on the fasten-seat-belt sign, willing herself not to give in to the waves of nausea rolling over her. *Focus . . . focus . . . think about Steve, who'd be there when she landed. Should she give him a hug? Would that be too forward?* "I actually hate it when I can't see the ground," she said.

Secretary Patterson took her hand. He smiled at her. "It will be okay," he said in a very reassuring voice. She nodded. It would be okay.

Steve

Steve and Phil cut American history, their last class of the day, to meet Kathy at the airport. After umpteen years of American history they still hadn't made it to World War II, never mind Korea. Phil borrowed his mother's car that morning, a blue Ford convertible, but given today's foggy, rainy weather, they couldn't put the top down the way they'd planned. Who in their right minds would put the top down in the middle of January, anyway? Assuming Steve and Phil were in their right minds, and some people might dispute that, starting with their American history teacher.

He and Phil couldn't wait until graduation. They already had summer jobs lined up at Shackamaxon Country Club as parking attendants. Both the Osners and the Steins were members. Maybe Phil's cute cousin would spend time around the pool. Yeah, that'd be good. He wouldn't mind getting a long look at Kathy in a bathing suit. Ever since they'd kissed on New Year's Eve he'd been thinking about her. He and Phil were already trying to decide which fraternity to pledge when they got to Syracuse next fall. Kathy had given them the lowdown on each. Not that they'd know if they were accepted at the college until April, but with their grades, SAT scores and sports, they weren't worried.

Newark Airport was just three miles from Jefferson High School. They hit some traffic on Route 1 because of the rain but they still made it in plenty of time. They parked in the airport lot, then ran from the car to the terminal. No umbrellas for them. Only pansies carried umbrellas, they told themselves, shaking the water off their heads. They planned to meet Kathy at the gate. Instead they met her mother, Phil's aunt, who decided to pick up Kathy after all. "In this weather I didn't want you boys to have to drive all the way to Perth Amboy, then back to Elizabeth."

Steve tried to hide his disappointment. He'd had a different idea about how the afternoon would go, and it didn't include Kathy's mother.

Laura

Laura Barnes didn't like this weather. She looked out the window of her first-floor apartment on South Street, holding the baby in her arms. Today's flight was nothing, she reminded herself. Just a Convair 240 on a milk run. Something Tim had done hundreds of times. He could do it in his sleep. Not that he would, but still . . . On the kitchen radio Patti Page was singing "Tennessee Waltz." Laura began to dance around with the baby in her arms. Heather squealed with delight. Laura paused again at the living room window. This fog is crazy, she thought. They never had fog in January. And all this rain. It must be the January thaw.

Her three-year-old was still napping. If only she could get the baby to sleep, she'd be able to rest her back, which was killing her. She was pregnant with their third child, expecting in July. She and Tim were both secretly hoping for a boy after two girls, though neither would admit it. On Valentine's Day they'd be moving into their new house down the shore, with enough room for three children, not to mention two full baths. She'd never had her own bath—well, she'd be sharing with Tim, but still—a *grown-ups only* bathroom.

Their apartment was already feeling cramped. Even though her parents owned this house and lived upstairs, which was a huge help, she was ready for the move. They'd worked on the new house all weekend while her parents watched the girls. She measured for curtains in the bedrooms, and lined the kitchen shelves with wallpaper in a pretty pattern left over from her cousin's new kitchen, while Tim worked on building a cedar closet in the attic.

Before driving back they'd stopped for a shore dinner to celebrate their anniversary. She promised that next time she'd at least *taste* the lobster. Tim laughed. He was more adventurous than her in every way, but he didn't seem to mind. Only a month ago he'd returned from Korean airlift duty. Then it was a round-trip to Tokyo. She was so proud of her husband. He'd seen the world. Someday, when the children were grown, she'd travel with him.

She'd already prepared a meat loaf for supper. Tim loved her meat loaf. She just had to pop it in the oven. The potatoes were peeled, sitting in ice water, ready for boiling. She'd take out the frozen peas at the last minute. Birds Eye vegetables were a godsend, never mind what her mother said. Of course, nothing beat her mother-in-law, Helen's, cooking. She'd be at work now in the Osners' fancy kitchen, watching over Dr. Osner's little girl while preparing dinner for the family. Maybe someday, when Helen retired and had more time, she'd help out Laura, moving down the shore and taking care of the three kids. Then Laura could go back to school, get her degree in education and teach kindergarten or first grade. At the very least, Helen could show her how to fix those fancy meals she made for the Osners.

The baby jumped up and down in her arms until she started dancing again. She sang along with Patti Page. *"I was dancin' with my darlin' to the Tennessee Waltz . . ."*

Miri

Miri and Natalie rode the #24 bus from school, got off at the corner of Shelley and Magie, then walked down to the Osners' house. In the kitchen Fern was dunking Oreos in milk while Mrs. Barnes prepared dinner. Whatever she was browning on the stove smelled delicious. The salad leaves were drying in a cloth towel, waiting to be torn into an ebony bowl with Corinne's initials in silver. CMO for "Corinne Mendelsohn Osner." Someday, when Miri was married with her own house, she would have the same salad bowl with *her* initials in silver. MAM for

"Miri Ammerman McKittrick"—if she married Mason. But would Irene ever forgive her for marrying a boy who wasn't Jewish? Maybe she would just spell out MIRI and leave her husband out of it.

"Will Tim fly over our house today?" Fern asked Mrs. Barnes.

"I expect so," Mrs. Barnes said. "Any minute now, unless they were delayed by the weather."

Fern pretended to feed an Oreo to her cowboy bunny. "Roy Rabbit might be a pilot when he grows up."

"I hope he's smart," Mrs. Barnes said, "because you have to be smart to be a pilot."

"Don't worry," Fern said. "Roy Rabbit is very smart."

Natalie grabbed a bunch of green grapes and she and Miri headed for the den, where the windows looked down on a stand of Japanese cherry trees, bare now, but come spring she knew they'd be heavy with pink blossoms. She wished it could be spring now. Then she and Mason wouldn't have to worry about where to go to be alone and warm.

Natalie tuned the television to the Kate Smith show, though it wasn't quite four o'clock, while Miri made a quick phone call to remind Irene she was at Natalie's for the afternoon. Then both girls settled on the floor. Miri popped a grape into her mouth. Natalie rested her head on Miri's lap. "Play with my hair," she said.

Miri lifted one soft curl, then another.

"What are you thinking?" Natalie asked, looking up at her.

"Guess," Miri said.

"I'll bet it's about Mason."

"Not really."

"I'll bet you think about him every minute of every day."

"I think of him a lot but I wasn't thinking of him just now."

"Are you in love with him?"

"I've only known him thirty-eight days, not that I'm counting."

"My mother says she knew from the minute she first looked into my father's eyes she was going to be with him for the rest of her life. She says it came to her in a flash, like lightning."

"I haven't had that flash yet," Miri said, which was a complete lie. Didn't she know it the night they danced together in Natalie's finished basement? And if not then, at the Y, the first time they kissed? Who was she kidding? But what went on between her and Mason was private. That's how she knew it was special. Every other time she'd liked a boy she'd blabbed to all her friends about him. But not this time.

"Are we still best friends?" Natalie asked out of no-where, winding a piece of gray wool she'd found on the carpet around her finger.

"I can't believe you have to ask," Miri said.

"It's just that lately you've been so . . ." Natalie stopped, searching for just the right word. "Remote," she finally said, looking satisfied.

Miri was stung. "*You* go to New York for dance classes three days a week and you're calling *me* remote?"

Natalie sat up. "I didn't think you even noticed I was gone. You're always with Mason, or you're babysitting with Suzanne." Natalie smoothed down her curls. "Even at school you hang out with Robo more than me."

"I do not."

"You sit with her every day at lunch, laughing."

"You're at the same lunch table."

"But nobody laughs with me."

Miri looked at Natalie and realized it was true.

Christina

Mr. Durkee, who taught bookkeeping at Battin, asked Christina to assist with his late class. Christina was his star pupil. If she didn't mess up, she'd be graduating first among the girls in the business program.

Today she'd be working late at Dr. O's office. Mrs. Jones and her daughters were coming in for check-ups. Daisy scheduled their appointments after hours because Mrs. Osner was afraid if Dr. O's regular patients discovered Dr. O was treating colored people they might be upset, they might even switch to a different dentist. Dr. O, on the other hand, believed Mrs. Jones and her daughters deserved the best dental care. He had Daisy set up a plan for them with a sizable discount because, after all, she worked for the Osners and her girls were polite and doing well at school.

As long as she left school by 3:45 p.m. she'd make it to Dr. O's office in time. While the students were at their desks, taking a test, Christina grabbed her raincoat and umbrella. She was glad she was wearing old shoes in this crazy weather. She heard a plane overhead but when she looked out the window she couldn't see anything the fog was so dense.

Suddenly, the building rumbled. The girls looked up from their test papers, a few of them rushing to the windows in time to see a twin-engine plane thunder out of the fog, heading straight for them. One girl screamed.

Another crossed herself and started a Hail Mary. Christina was sure the plane was coming through the window into the classroom.

"Get back from the glass!" Mr. Durkee shouted. "Duck and cover!" But there was almost no time. The engine of the plane went quiet as it barely sailed over the roof of the school. The first explosion caused the windows to rattle, the second, louder explosion shook the building.

"Oh my god—Jack!" Christina cried. "Jack . . . Jack . . ." She ran from the classroom with Mr. Durkee calling after her, "Christina—stay inside. Christina!"

She flew down the two flights of stairs, then used the white marble steps from the first floor to the street, steps the students were not allowed to use. Outside, she rounded the corner of South and Williamson streets and raced toward the flames, toward Mrs. O'Malley's house, where Jack rented a room on the second floor.

Miri

Kate Smith hadn't even sung "God Bless America" when the program was interrupted by an announcement, an announcement so horrible it left her and Natalie immobile. A second plane had crashed in Elizabeth, this time near Battin High School. Before they had time to digest what they'd just heard, the sound of a long, low wail came from the kitchen. Without a word the two girls were on their feet, racing down the stairs. They found Mrs. Barnes doubled over, holding on to the kitchen counter. "No . . . please, God, no!"

Natalie pulled open the door to the finished basement, closed it behind her and disappeared. Miri grabbed a plastic glass from the counter, filled it with water and tried to give it to Mrs. Barnes, but Mrs. Barnes, who had always seemed so in control, so calm, no matter what, knocked it away.

The deep voice on the radio continued. "An American Airlines Convair, en route to Newark Airport from Buffalo, with stops in Rochester and Syracuse, has crashed and exploded . . ." Now Mrs. Barnes screamed, fell to the floor, banging her fists, pulling at her own hair. Fern squatted beside her. "Barnesy . . . stop, please stop." Miri had never heard Fern or anyone else call her *Barnesy*.

Mrs. Barnes didn't let up. She wailed, "Tim . . . Timmy!" "Barnesy!" Fern cried. "Barnesy, you're scaring me."

Miri didn't know what to do so she picked up the phone and dialed Dr. O's office. When Daisy answered, Miri cried it was Mrs. Barnes's son flying that plane and Mrs. Barnes was on the floor and wouldn't get up.

Daisy told her to stay with Mrs. Barnes, not to leave her for a second, and she and Dr. O were on their way. Miri knew from health class when someone was in shock you should keep them warm, so she sent Fern upstairs to get a blanket, then, as an afterthought, a pillow, too.

Fern came back with a pillow and quilt from Natalie's room and Miri draped it over Mrs. Barnes, who had gone quiet and white as a ghost, lying on her back on the floor. Miri slid the pillow under Mrs. Barnes's head. Her eyes were open, staring at the ceiling. Miri wondered if she was in shock or if it was something worse. Fern sat close to Mrs. Barnes, stroking her hand. "Barnesy, I need you to take care of me. Roy Rabbit needs you." She nuzzled Mrs. Barnes with her toy rabbit. But Mrs. Barnes didn't respond.

Laura

Laura heard the explosions but it was the general fire alarm that filled her with dread. She knew Tim was due in at about that time. The noise of the alarm woke the toddler, Evie, who started screaming. Laura ran to the girls' room, lifted Evie out of her crib and patted her back. "There, there, sweetie, everything's okay." That started the baby, Heather, crying. When word came over the radio that it was a plane, an American Airlines Convair, Laura knew for sure. She lay down on her bed with the toddler and the baby cradled on either side of her and began to sing, *"Hush, little babies, don't say a word, Mama's gonna buy you a mockingbird . . ."*

Steve

At first he and Phil didn't get what the commotion at the American Airlines counter was about. It wasn't until Phil's aunt screamed—a chilling scream you could hear throughout the terminal, a scream that would haunt him the rest of his life—that they understood something had happened to the plane. Phil rushed to his aunt's side with Steve right behind him, but she had already collapsed and two airline employees were trying to get her to her feet. Phil tossed the keys to the blue Ford convertible to Steve. "Drive it back to my house, okay?"

"Sure," Steve said. "Whatever I can do to help, you know?"

But Steve didn't have any idea how to help. He called his father's office from a phone booth. His father would know what to do. His father would offer to come and get him and Steve would say, *Okay.* But there was no answer at his father's office. He wished he'd never come to the airport. He wished he'd stayed at school, then gone to the Y to shoot baskets.

Nobody asked if he was okay enough to drive, which he wasn't, but somehow he made it back to Elizabeth, to Phil's house, where he pulled the blue convertible into the driveway, turned off the ignition, rested his head against the wheel and gave in to the emotion washing over him. He couldn't remember the last time he'd cried, felt his own tears hot and wet running down his face, his throat tight, his nose snotty. He took in a couple of big gulps, willed himself to stop, then got out of the car and started out for home, kicking at stones, leftover chunks of gray snow, whatever was in his way. *Fuck fuck fuck!*

Christina

Hundreds of people were running with Christina, all of them separated from the roaring fire by just a dozen yards. But only she was screaming Jack's name, until she turned the corner and saw it wasn't Jack's house on fire. It was the wooden house down the street and the house next to that, and where there used to be a three-story brick apartment building was rubble and thick black smoke—the whole area a blazing mess, with flames so blindingly bright red and orange she had to turn away. She covered her ears with her hands, against the screaming sirens.

There was no sign of the plane, or the people on it. She was stuck in a nightmare where something terrible was happening but she was powerless. She willed herself to move but she couldn't. Her feet were too heavy, as if they were encased in wet cement and she couldn't lift them. When she looked down she saw her feet were covered in mud up to her ankles—mud from the rain and the fire hoses.

Jack is safe, she told herself, *working for the electric company in Westfield or Cranford or some other nearby city. Jack is safe. Unless, because of the weather, he's not. No, he is. He has to be.*

Christina, who never showed her emotions in public, didn't try to restrain herself this time. She cried out as she saw a woman, her own clothes on fire, frantically pushing a small child rolled up in a rug at a neighbor. The woman tried to rush back into the flaming house, screaming, *My baby, my baby*, but others held her away. People were running from the burning houses. A boy with his jacket on fire was grabbed by a man, who threw off his overcoat and wrapped the boy in it, putting out the flames.

The girls from the modern dance club in their blue leotards were on the scene, with the gym teacher. Groups of other students who had club meetings after school were hugging each other and crying. A few of them called to her, but she didn't answer.

She caught a glimpse of Jack's landlady, and in an instant she was chasing after her. "Mrs. O'Malley . . . Mrs. O'Malley . . ." Christina called, until Mrs. O'Malley stopped. "Mrs. O'Malley, I'm Jack McKittrick's friend, Christina. Was he home? Is he okay?"

Mrs. O'Malley gave her a puzzled look. "Jack?"

"Yes, Jack McKittrick. He rents from you."

"Are you his sister?"

"No, I'm his friend, Christina."

"I always thought you were his sister."

What was she talking about?

"He's not home," Mrs. O'Malley said. "I don't know where he is."

"At work," Christina said. "He's at work. Right?"

"I hope so, dear."

THE WORLD MAY HAVE BEEN falling apart but at Dr. O's office everything was serene. Christina pulled down the hastily scribbled note taped to the office door apologizing for the emergency that had taken both Daisy and Dr. O away. She got out of her muddy shoes before unlocking the door with the key Daisy had given to her at Christmas. She was safe now. She prayed Jack was safe, too. She scrubbed her feet in the toilet, flushing again and again, wiped herself clean with disposable towels and changed into her white lab coat and shoes. She had no clean socks, no stockings. She'd have to wear her shoes with bare feet. She pinned up her dark hair, washed her face and gargled with Lavoris. Only then did she sit in Daisy's swivel chair, in front of the Remington typewriter and the leather appointment book, calmly calling patients, asking them to call tomorrow to reschedule.

She felt grown-up, helpful, even important, until her sister, Athena, phoned and gave her hell. "Why didn't you call us? We've been worried sick. Really, Christina—grow up! Take responsibility. Did you give a second's thought to Mama, who's going out of her mind with worry?"

"I'm sorry," Christina said. "I tried to call but I couldn't get through." This was a lie. She hadn't been thinking about her mother or Athena.

"You should have come here." Athena was using her holier-than-thou voice. "How far is the shop from your job? I'd say, five minutes, if that. And you should have stopped in at the restaurant to see Baba."

"You're right," Christina said. She'd learned the best way to avoid an argument with her sister was to agree. "I wasn't thinking."

"That's no excuse," Athena told her.

"In case you're interested," Christina said, "I saw it happen. The plane came right over Battin. I was outside on Williamson Street a minute after it crashed and exploded." She was getting worked up, her voice rising with her emotions. "I was there, Athena. I was there when people ran out of their houses screaming, on fire. Do you know what that was like? Do you even care?"

Before she could slam down the receiver her sister said, "Well, that sounds terrible but I don't see why you're angry at me."

This time Christina did slam down the receiver. The palm of her right hand was bleeding from digging her fingernails so deeply into it. She hated Athena!

She ran into the small, narrow lab where Daisy kept a row of white plaster-of-Paris figurines lined up on a shelf, each one a foot high, waiting for Dr. O to smash if he felt a temper coming on. Christina had witnessed his fury just once and it had scared her. How could this kind and generous man have such inner rage? What set him off? She only knew it never happened when there were patients in the office. She only knew that smashing one of the plaster-of-Paris figurines made him feel better. After, Daisy would sweep up the remains and Dr. O would carry on as if nothing had happened.

Now, as the rage boiled up inside of her, Christina grabbed one of those figurines and smashed it. She thought she would feel better, but she didn't. She slumped to the floor, her eyes closed against the headache coming on. She sat there, surrounded by the remains of Dopey, or whichever one of the Seven Dwarfs she'd smashed, until the phone rang. She went back to Daisy's desk and picked it up, praying it wasn't Athena again, or worse, her mother. "Good afternoon, Dr. Osner's office," she said, trying to sound professional.

"Is this Daisy?"

"No, it's Christina."

"Oh, Christina. This is Mrs. Jones. Someone called earlier to cancel our appointment."

Mrs. Jones's voice went very low and soft as if she were about to share a secret. "I was wondering if you happen to know if the pilot was Mrs. Barnes's son?"

Mrs. Barnes's son? Mrs. Barnes, who she'd met once, when Daisy sent her to the Osners' house with a package? Mrs. Barnes's son was in that flaming wreck?

"Christina? Are you there?"

"Yes, I'm still here." Her voice sounded small and unsure of itself. She cleared her throat several times.

"I'm asking because I know Mrs. Barnes from working at the Osners'," Mrs. Jones said, "and if . . . well, I'd like to be there."

Christina was barely able to hold herself together. She rolled out a piece of Scotch tape and stuck it to her arm as if that would help. "I'll call if I hear anything."

She went back to the lab, picked up the broom, swept up the mess and washed off the floor. She felt overwhelmingly tired, as if she hadn't slept for days. She felt if she didn't lie down immediately she would keel over.

She lay down on the sofa in the waiting room, where she smelled something terrible, something burned or burning.

What was it? She sniffed her arms, a handful of her hair. It was coming from her, her hair, her skin, the clothes she wore under the white lab coat. All of her smelled terrible. Maybe she would always smell that way, a reminder of what she'd seen. She could wash and wash and still it would be there. Christina Demetrious, the girl who smelled like fire and smoke, and death. She closed her eyes.

An hour went by, maybe two, then there was a knock on the office door. Daisy had instructed Christina to keep the door locked when she was alone in the office. "Who is it?" she asked.

"Christina? Christina, are you okay?"

She opened the door and fell into Jack's arms.

Miri

Miri was relieved when Dr. O and Daisy rushed into the house. Mrs. Barnes was still on the floor covered by the quilt. She still hadn't said a word. Dr. O bent down to check her pulse. As he did, he glanced toward the basement door, and for the first time Miri was aware of the music coming from downstairs.

"Is it true?" Mrs. Barnes asked Dr. O.

He answered, "Yes. I'm so sorry."

Mrs. Barnes nodded.

Dr. O helped Mrs. Barnes to her feet and led her to a chair at the kitchen table. Daisy brought her a glass of water and handed her a pill. But Mrs. Barnes's hands were shaking so badly Daisy had to put the pill into Mrs. Barnes's mouth, then hold the water glass to her lips. Mrs. Barnes swallowed without asking what it was.

"Is there anyone I can call for you?" Daisy asked.

"My other son, Charles. He'll call my daughter," Mrs. Barnes said. "She lives in Pennsylvania."

She has another son, Miri thought. A son and a daughter. That's good, isn't it? Suppose Tim was her only child? How many times had Rusty reminded Miri, *You're my only child. You're my life. So when it comes to doing stupid things, don't. Because I couldn't stand it if I lost you. Do you understand?* Now Miri thought she understood. There was a burden to being the only child.

"Daisy, will you try to find Corinne?" Dr. O asked, handing her an appointment book with a needlepoint cover. "I'm going to take Mrs. Barnes home." He draped a coat around Mrs. Barnes's shoulders and led her to the kitchen door.

Fern clung to Mrs. Barnes's leg. "I want to come with you."

"You stay here with Daisy until Mommy comes home," Dr. O said.

"No, I want to come with Barnesy!"

Mrs. Barnes looked down at Fern, as if for the first time. "You'll be fine, Fern Ella."

Fern didn't argue. She let go of Mrs. Barnes's leg. When Daisy asked if she'd like to hear a story, Fern choose *Madeline* from her bookshelf. "Madeline is brave," she told Daisy.

Daisy asked Miri to do something about the volume of the music coming from the finished basement. Miri opened the door and crept down the stairs, afraid of what she might find. "Nat . . . Natalie," she called softly. The only light was coming from the jukebox, the volume pumped way up. It took a minute for her eyes to adjust, for her to see Natalie crouched on the floor in the corner, rocking back and forth, mumbling to herself, like an old man davening on the High Holidays.

When Miri snapped on the overhead lights, Natalie covered her eyes. "Don't." But Miri left the lights on and pulled the plug on the jukebox. Now it was completely quiet. Eerily quiet.

"Come on, Nat," Miri said, grabbing her by both arms.

Natalie resisted. "I'm too tired."

"We're all tired." Miri hadn't realized how true that was until that minute. She felt heavy, as if she could sleep for a week.

Finally, Natalie stood. Miri practically pushed her up the stairs. In the kitchen, Natalie spied her quilt and pillow on the floor. She grabbed them and ran up to her bedroom, where she threw herself onto her bed, and held the pillow over her head.

Miri followed.

"They're out to get us," Natalie said, from under the pillow. "It's only a matter of time. Ruby says there's nothing we can do to stop them."

"What are you talking about? Who's out to get us?"

"I'm trying to tell you but you're not listening."

Miri lifted the pillow off Natalie's head so she could see her face, hear her words more clearly. "I am listening but you're not making any sense."

"You think any of this makes sense? Mrs. Barnes's son, and Phil's cousin, the one coming home from Syracuse. She was here New Year's Eve. Remember? Kathy Stein. She wore a green velvet dress. My brother kissed her."

"What about her?"

"She was on that plane."

"How do you know?"

"Ruby told me."

"No she didn't."

"You'll see."

Miri thought about shaking Natalie. Shaking and shaking until Ruby came tumbling out headfirst, her dark hair spilling toward the floor, her blue eyes outlined in black, her lips painted bright red to match her short red dress and at last her shiny black tap shoes. But despite all the color Ruby would still look dead because that's what she was—dead. She wanted to shake Natalie until she was the old Nat, the one Miri became best friends with in seventh grade.

When Miri didn't respond Natalie asked, "You think I'm crazy?"

"Are you?"

"Maybe," Natalie said. "I just want to stop seeing Phil's cousin dead, and Mrs. Barnes's son in his captain's uniform, all broken and burned."

"Stop it," Miri said softly. "Just stop it."

"You'll see," Natalie said. Then she closed her eyes and hid under the quilt.

IN THE KITCHEN, Daisy forked whatever was browning in the pan, put it on a plate, covered it with wax paper and slid it into the fridge. She tapped Ajax into the pan and started scrubbing, as Fern sang, "*Use Ajax, boom boom, the foaming cleanser, boom boom boom boom boom . . .*"

Miri said, "I have to go home. My grandmother will be worrying." She grabbed her coat and her books.

"Thank you for helping," Daisy said.

As she was leaving Steve opened the kitchen door and pushed past her. "Where's Mom?" he asked Daisy.

"She's on her way home," Daisy told him.

"She was playing mah-jongg at Ceil Rubin's house," Fern said. "They didn't have the radio on so they didn't know what happened." Fern looked at Daisy. "Right?"

Daisy nodded.

"What about Dad?" Steve asked.

"He took Mrs. Barnes home," Daisy said.

"Her son was the pilot of the plane that crashed," Fern added, hugging Roy Rabbit to her chest.

"Shut up about planes crashing," Steve shouted. "Just shut up!"

Daisy touched Steve's shoulder.

He flinched. "Don't!"

Miri asked, "Was Phil's cousin on that plane?"

Steve shot her a look. "How did you know?"

"Natalie told me."

"How did *she* know?"

Miri shrugged, pushed past Steve out the kitchen door and trudged up the hill to the bus stop. When the bus pulled up, Miri boarded and took a seat, forgetting to pay. The driver didn't say anything. Miri was thinking that just a little while ago she and Natalie were munching grapes in the den, waiting for Kate Smith to come on singing "God Bless America." Miri hoped if there was a god, and she was less sure about that every day, he would bless America and especially Elizabeth, New Jersey, and that he had the power to stop this thing that was happening.

· · ·

SUZANNE, in her yellow rain slicker and white rubber boots, was waiting on the front steps of Miri's house, a polka-dot umbrella opened over her head though it was hardly raining by the time Miri got home. "Where were you?" Suzanne asked.

"At Natalie's."

"Did you hear?"

"Yes, it's horrible."

"I know, but at least they say Betsy is still alive and so is Mrs. Foster. They're both at Saint Elizabeth's. My mother's on duty this afternoon."

"What are you talking about?"

"The crash. It hit the apartment building next to the Fosters' and set their house on fire. Penny . . . she didn't get out. Mrs. Foster tried, but the fire . . ."

Miri slumped to the porch steps, her hand over her mouth. She tasted bile coming up.

"Mother of god . . . you didn't know?"

Miri shook her head. It wasn't possible. It had to be a mistake. But even as she thought it, wished it, she knew it was true.

"BAD THINGS HAPPEN in threes," Irene said that night, doling out homemade vegetable soup and passing around warm bread—not that anyone was hungry, but Irene knew how to tempt them.

"Stop it, Mama," Rusty said. "You're scaring Miri."

"Darling," Irene said to Miri, "am I scaring you?"

"No!" Miri said defiantly. But she'd never get Irene's superstitions out of her head.

Later Suzanne came by again, to go with Miri to the

site of the crash, even though Rusty objected. "There's no reason in hell for you to go there. You've seen one plane crash. Why do you have to see another?"

"Because the Fosters lived in that house," Miri argued. "Because a week ago we were babysitting Betsy and Penny and now Penny is dead and Betsy is burned." Her voice caught, thinking of how Penny always folded her little eyeglasses and placed them on her bedside table before she went to sleep. And Betsy's tiny pink toenails, newly polished, making her toes look like little shrimp. Maybe Mrs. Foster knew to worry. Maybe she'd had a sixth sense about an impending disaster. She'd heard mothers know these things instinctively.

"There's nothing to see," Rusty told them. "Just rubble and burned buildings."

"We have to go," Suzanne said.

Rusty pursed her lips, closed her eyes, took a deep breath and reconsidered. "Just don't be too long. I want a promise on that."

"Okay," Miri said.

"Be back before eight o'clock."

Suzanne said, "I promised my mother the same."

Rusty nodded. "And take an umbrella."

A CHILL WIND SWEPT the open corner of South and Williamson streets. At the site, floodlights, combined with the fog and the light rain, sent up an eerie glow. Miri and Suzanne stood close. There was nothing to say. Nothing that would make sense of this.

On the ground floor of the Fosters' house there used to be a candy store, popular with the St. Mary's kids. Now there was a burned-out shell with no roof, and piles of rubble. There was no sign that it was hit by a plane. It could have been any kind of explosion. Except for the piece of the tail. Not that Miri could see it, but everyone said it was there. Somewhere.

"They say she had to choose between her children," a woman said to her companion. "She couldn't save them both. Can you imagine?" Was she talking about Mrs. Foster or someone else? Miri didn't want to think of Mrs. Foster trying to decide—*eeny, meeny, miney, moe* . . .

Suddenly Mason was behind her, his hands on her shoulders. "Hey . . ."

She whipped around. She'd thought he was at work.

"I have a friend who lived in that house," he said quietly. "The one that's gone now."

Miri and Suzanne both looked at him.

"Polina," he said. "She works at Janet. She has a little boy. Sometimes she kept Fred overnight."

"Are they okay?"

He shrugged. "They lost all their stuff. They have no place to live but they weren't home when the plane crashed, so I guess you could say they're okay."

Miri didn't know how to reply except to squeeze his hand to acknowledge his feelings. She wondered if Polina knew the Fosters.

"If only Penny and Betsy hadn't been home," Suzanne said. "If only Mrs. Foster had taken them someplace, to the library, maybe, or to a friend's house to play, a friend who lived in another neighborhood. If only . . ."

"*If onlys* don't work," Mason said.

A policeman moved through the crowd. "Go on now," he told them. "Time to get home."

. . .

THEY TOOK the bus back, got off at Suzanne's corner then walked to Miri's, where she kissed Mason goodnight at the front door, hiding Fred inside her jacket. Upstairs, Henry was sitting at Rusty's kitchen table, mopping up what was left of Irene's vegetable soup with a thick slice of bread.

"I shouldn't have let you go," Rusty said. "I don't know what I was thinking."

"It was an accident," Henry assured her. "A tragic accident."

"Twice in a row?"

"I know it doesn't make sense," Henry said, "but I'm asking you to believe me." He got up from the table and wrapped his arms around her. "Terrible things can happen, Miri. I'm so sorry about those little girls."

Miri dissolved when he said that, and when she did, Fred whimpered in sympathy. She unzipped her jacket. Fred cocked his head and looked around. "He can't stay at the Steins'," she told Rusty. "Phil's cousin was on that plane. And he can't stay with Mason's friend Polina, because she lived in the house the plane slammed into." She didn't wait for Rusty to give her permission. She grabbed a copy of the *Daily Post* from the pile on the table, went to her room and closed the door.

It didn't take long for Rusty to knock. "Miri . . ." The door opened. "It's okay for Fred to stay tonight. Just not in your bed."

But Miri had every intention of having Fred in her bed.

Elizabeth Daily Post

Special Edition

ANOTHER PLANE FALLS

Raging Inferno Destroys Block of Williamson Street

By Henry Ammerman

JAN. 22—It was a horrific scene of suffering and destruction, with bodies buried in the rubble that covered the wreckage of an American Airlines Convair en route to Newark Airport from upstate New York. The plane crashed today at 3:45 p.m. in heavy fog and driving rain, plowing into a block of houses on Williamson Street before exploding into an inferno.

Residents of the houses fled, some with their clothes aflame. Every available police and fire resource in the city was summoned to the struggle, but it would be hours before the search for bodies could even begin.

Ultimate Horror Only Feet Away

Students at Battin High School, across the street from the crash site, saw the plane skim the rooftop of their school just before the fatal crash. St. Mary's High School, catercorner from Battin, escaped destruction, but an after-school crowd of its students were gathered at a confectionery on the ground floor of 310 Williamson St. Knocked down by the initial explosion, they managed to escape before it burst into flames.

Dead and Missing

Six residents, including three young children, are missing and feared dead, along with all 23 aboard the plane. Among the passengers on the plane were Robert Patterson, former Secretary of War under President Truman, and four students at Syracuse University.

Less than six weeks ago, and one mile away, a Miami Airlines C-46 crashed into a warehouse of the Elizabethtown Water Company, landing belly up in the frozen bed of the Elizabeth River. That crash killed all 56 on board but spared those on the ground.

15

Distraction

This time Miri read Henry's story all the way through. After that she couldn't fall asleep, even with Fred gently snoring beside her. She thumbed through the paper until she came to the entertainment section, where the stories never made her sad. Gene Kelly had his appendix removed in Paris and was recuperating in Switzerland. Audrey Hepburn, twenty-one years old, opened in *Gigi* on Broadway, signed with Paramount Pictures and was engaged to be married. There was a pinup picture of Peggy Dow in a long gown. The caption read, NOW STARRING OPPOSITE ARTHUR KENNEDY IN *BRIGHT VICTORY*, PLAYING AT THE BRANFORD THEATRE IN NEWARK. The movie the Fosters went to see last Sunday night. Or didn't see. Miri wondered now if they went to a motel, like Suzanne said. If they did she hoped they had a good time because she couldn't imagine them ever having a good time again. She realized she'd been wrong. Even stories in this section of the paper could make her sad.

Rumors

At school the rumors were flying.

PETE WOLF: What did I tell you? This proves it! Some alien thing is trying to take over Earth.

ANGELO VENETTI: UFOs—they've been sighted in New Mexico. The Martians want to turn us into zombies so they can control our planet.

DERISH GRAY: They want to take dead children to the past, or the future, to show what life was like in the mid-twentieth century on a planet called Earth.

Miri tried not to listen, tried to believe what Henry had told her—that both crashes were accidents. But she wasn't convinced. That wouldn't explain why three schools were almost hit, first Hamilton, and now Battin and St. Mary's. And she remembered Leah telling them how close the first plane had come to the Elks Club on the day one hundred little kids were at a holiday party. But why would Martians come to Elizabeth, New Jersey? What was so special about *them* that made these creatures from outer space come here? Or was it a mistake? Did they mean to land in New York? Were they after only dead children to carry back in their spaceships or did they want living children, too? Is that what they were going to do with Penny, who liked to dress up in her pink ballet slippers and leotard, showing Miri and Suzanne what she'd learned in dance class that week—were they going to turn *her* into a zombie? She wasn't even sure what a zombie was. Something undead. Something that feasted on human brains.

They'd probably all be dead by June, Miri thought.

Forget prom and graduation. She just hoped it would be a quick death so they wouldn't suffer, so they wouldn't wind up horribly burned or blinded, or left without arms and legs. It was coming. She didn't know what it was but it was just a matter of time. She was beginning to believe they were jinxed.

DONNY KELLEN: McCarthy's doing the right thing, going after all the pinko Jew bastards like the Rosenbergs. They're the ones behind it. They should all be fried.

SUZANNE: Leave the Jews out of this. This has nothing to do with Jews. Plenty of Jews were killed on those planes.

DONNY KELLEN: You're such a Jew lover. That was just a cover to make it look like they're not responsible.

CHARLEY KAMINSKY (*to Donny*): You're an asshole, you know that? Stick your finger up your butt and take a whiff. That's you. A piece of shit!

Donny came after Charley but Charley socked him first, giving him a bloody nose. The other boys held Donny and Charley apart.

ELEANOR (*shouting*): It's sabotage, you idiots! We're under siege. Get it through your heads. Korea is nothing compared to what's happening here. Korea is a distraction. You don't hear Eisenhower saying nominate me for president, and I'll stop these crashes tomorrow. No, because he can't. Sure, he can stop the war in Korea. But he can't stop this one. Because our side doesn't know who we're fighting.

Everyone knew Eleanor was the smartest person in their class. So when she said *sabotage* the rest of them went scrambling for the Merriam-Webster dictionary.

Natalie watched but said nothing while the other kids went on and on, their stories of aliens, zombies and sabotage growing from possibility to probability. She shook her head once or twice as if to tell them they had it all wrong, but no one was watching besides Miri. What did Natalie know, or think she knew?

They had another safety drill before lunch, proving Mr. Royer, the principal, also believed they were jinxed.

A Condolence Call to Mrs. Barnes

On their way to pay a condolence call to Mrs. Barnes, Rusty insisted that Miri practice saying, *I'm sorry for your loss.* Mrs. Barnes lived in an apartment house on Elmora Avenue near Magie. *I'm sorry for your loss, I'm sorry for your loss,* Miri repeated. They'd left their house as soon as Rusty had come home from work, run a comb through her hair, freshened her lipstick and spritzed herself with Arpège.

"If she offers her hand," Rusty said, "you shake it."

"'I'm sorry for your loss,' shake shake."

"This is not the time for sarcasm, Miri."

When is the time for sarcasm, Mom? Miri would have liked to say, but she knew better. Instead she said, "I'm not being sarcastic. It's just . . . you're treating me like a six-year-old."

"You've never been in this situation and I'm trying to help you through it."

"Nobody's ever been in this situation."

"Not true, Miri. We've been through a war, remember? And we're fighting another one now. Some mother loses a son every day."

"Can you fight two wars at the same time?"

"You mean Korea and something else?" Rusty asked.

"Yes, Korea and something else."

"I hope that's never going to happen. Things are bad enough with Korea."

"So that means it's a good time to attack us, because we're busy fighting in Korea. Korea is a distraction, right?"

"I'm not sure what you're getting at," Rusty said.

"Never mind," Miri told her. She heard Eleanor's voice in her head. *Korea is a distraction.*

Corinne was at Mrs. Barnes's apartment, but there was no sign of the rest of the family, which surprised Miri. The small living room was crowded with family and friends who had come to pay their respects to Mrs. Barnes. Mrs. Jones was in the tiny kitchen with her daughter Jamison, serving up plates of sandwiches and cookies.

I'm sorry for your loss, Miri practiced inside her head. But it turned out she didn't get to say it to Mrs. Barnes because Mrs. Barnes was in her bedroom and didn't come out. The other son was there, so Miri said it to him. And the daughter from Pennsylvania with her husband and little girl.

"I'm sorry for your loss." She felt like an idiot saying it. Each of them took her hand and said, "Thank you." It wasn't as hard as she'd thought. But it felt wrong. She wished she could have told the truth—I was there when your mother heard the news over the radio, I was there when she screamed Tim's name and fell to her knees, I was there when Fern grabbed her leg and tried to go home with her, crying, *Barnesy*—that's what Fern calls her. Did you ever dream someone would call your mother *Barnesy*?

Rusty disappeared, leaving Miri alone in a room full of strangers. What was she supposed to do? She stopped in front of the family photos set out on the breakfront. Photos of Tim as a child, photos of him in his uniform, photos with his wife and two little girls.

Captain Timothy Barnes was handsome, better-looking than his brother or sister. Mrs. Barnes's daughter came up beside her. "Did you know my brother?"

"I know your mother," Miri said. "Is she okay?"

"Not really. I doubt she'll ever be okay again. Tim was her favorite."

Miri never thought about parents having favorites. When you're the only child you don't think that way.

Corinne came to her rescue. "I heard you were a big help on Tuesday, Miri. You've got a real head on your shoulders."

Miri knew that was supposed to be a compliment. As opposed to, *You have no head on your shoulders*. Or, *Use your head for once*.

"This has been very hard on Natalie," Corinne said, speaking in a hushed tone. "She's so sensitive, so imaginative. I suppose you know that."

"Yes." She didn't have the guts to tell Corinne that Natalie was acting cuckoo. Anyway, who was *she* to say Ruby wasn't living inside Natalie? Who was she to say that wasn't the aliens' plan all along? All of it was making her think the whole world was going crazy.

Jamison set a plate of sandwiches on the dining table, pretty little sandwiches on white bread with the crusts cut off, each decorated with a tiny pickle or slice of olive or sprig of parsley. Miri helped herself to a turkey sandwich. The potato salad had too much mayonnaise for her so she skipped that and took potato chips instead.

Corinne patted the sofa next to her, so Miri sat and bit into her turkey sandwich, taking small bites and chewing, chewing, chewing until there was almost nothing left to swallow, which she wasn't sure she'd be able to do anyway. She needed ginger ale. Why hadn't she poured herself a glass?

"I thought Natalie would be here," she managed to say.

"The children are at home. They went to the funeral this afternoon. Mrs. Barnes has been such an important part of their lives. She came to work for us when Fern was born. And Dr. Osner is back at the morgue."

Miri nodded.

"Where's your mother?" Corinne asked.

"She must be in the other room," Miri said, taking this as her opportunity to get away. "Actually, I think I'll bring her a sandwich." She prepared a plate for Rusty and carried it down the hall. It was a small apartment, with two bedrooms and one bath. The door to the smaller bedroom was open. Miri caught a glimpse of Rusty's brown skirt. She was sitting on the bed with a group of women. "Mom . . ."

Rusty looked up.

"I made you a plate."

"Thanks, honey. Come and sit."

Miri sat next to Rusty on the small bed, wishing she could lie down with her head on Rusty's lap, close her eyes and sleep.

Visitation

It took days to find the remains of the Sewing Machine Man and his wife, Mr. and Mrs. Galanos, who'd lived in one of the houses that had been destroyed. They'd been listed as missing and presumed dead. When they finally were able to identify them Christina didn't want to go to the church or the funeral home. She didn't want to see the son, who was staying with friends. But she had no choice. "We're going," her mother said. "Fix yourself up."

They waited on line to express their condolences. First Christina's grandparents Yaya and Papou, then her parents, then Athena and finally, Christina. "I'm very sorry," she said to the son, who looked like he hadn't slept in days.

"Do I know you?" he asked Christina.

"Christina Demetrious," she said. "My family knows . . ." She hesitated, then changed what she was going to say to, "My family knew your parents."

"Thank you, Christina."

That was it? She was free to move on now? Instead, she said, "My sister, Athena . . . you went to school with her."

"Thank you, Athena," he said, confusing her sister's name with hers. He didn't know what he was saying or what anyone was saying to him. By then the next person on line was grabbing his hand and blubbering about what good people his parents were.

He's in shock, Christina thought. Everyone is in shock. Maybe she was, too. She thought about telling him she'd been there, about how she'd seen the plane before it crashed. And then the flames . . . but why would he want to hear that? Athena reached in and pulled her away. "What were you telling him?"

"Nothing."

"It looked like more than nothing."

"Why do you care?"

"Just don't go saying too much."

"What would be too much?"

Athena didn't answer her question. Instead, she said, "You didn't even want to come, remember?"

"I thought I was supposed to be nice."

"Okay. So you were nice."

"I don't think anyone told him about me," Christina said. "That I'm the girl he's supposed to marry."

"Oh, so now you want to marry him?"

"I didn't say that. I just have the feeling no one mentioned Mama's plans to marry me off to him."

"I never knew you were in such a hurry to get married."

"I'm not." She felt like shouting at Athena, who was turning everything around. Where was Dopey when she needed him? She'd like to smash Dopey over her sister's head.

"I have to sit down," Athena said. She was pregnant again and starting to show. "I thought you were in love with Jack McKittrick," Athena said, tugging at her skirt. "So it's good to know you're keeping an open mind."

Christina was taken aback. "You know about Jack?" she asked Athena.

"Everyone knows about you and Jack McKittrick."

"Mama?"

"You better hope she doesn't. But I'm warning you, Christina, you're skating on thin ice."

Shiva

Steve went to Kathy Stein's house in Perth Amboy, where her family would be sitting shiva for seven days. Phil was already there, reciting the prayer for the dead with the other men. They had more than enough for a minyan without Steve and he was glad. He didn't know the Kaddish. He'd never been in a position of having to recite it.

Kathy's mother couldn't speak. She looked half dead. Her skin was gray, her eyes rimmed in red, her hair wild. Kathy's younger sister couldn't stop crying. She was surrounded by girlfriends, all of them crying, too. A group of boys stood around looking uncomfortable. *A nightmare*, Steve heard over and over. Yeah, it was a nightmare, all right. But you wake up from a nightmare, and this time there was no relief because when you woke up, the nightmare was still with you.

Steve didn't want to be there. He hoped Phil wouldn't stay long. Phil's mother was in the kitchen, helping with the platters of food that had been sent to the house, all wrapped in golden cellophane and tied with curly ribbon. Sandwiches, baskets of fruits, coffee cakes lined up in a row, like at a bakery. Surprisingly, Steve found himself hungry. He helped himself to a Sloppy Joe, potato salad, a pickle, then went back for more. He stuffed himself on coffee cake, slices of cantaloupe and pineapple, a couple of chocolate candies.

He wandered through the house, stopping to look at a tinted photo of Kathy on the piano, her bright eyes looking directly at him. *Happy New Year, Steve.* He would kiss that photo if no one were watching. Those sweet, warm lips, cold now, buried in the ground. Except he wasn't sure how much of a body was left to bury. Maybe just that arm with the charm bracelet. Her uncle had identified her by that bracelet, a high school graduation present from her parents. *Jeez.* He had to shake off these thoughts before he made himself puke. He could already feel the Sloppy Joe trying to decide whether to stay down or come back up.

Elizabeth Daily Post

SECRETARY PATTERSON TO LIE IN STATE

JAN. 24 (UPI)—The body of former Secretary of War Robert P. Patterson, who died Tuesday in a plane crash, will lie in state today in the 107th Regiment Armory at 66th Street and Park Avenue in New York. He once served in the regiment.

The body will be taken to Washington tomorrow for burial at Arlington Cemetery, with full military honors. President Truman and other high government officials will attend funeral services at the National Cathedral there.

Mrs. Patterson Writes a Note

In her Park Avenue apartment, Margaret Patterson, wife of the former Secretary of War, sat at the small French desk in her bedroom and started a note to Laura Barnes, widow of the pilot of the plane, inviting her and her children to spend a day in the country with her family. But she wasn't able to finish. Instead, she put the note in her desk drawer, closed her pen, took off her reading glasses and sipped the brandy she'd poured for herself. She didn't blame Captain Timothy Barnes for the loss of her husband. She believed he'd done everything he could to get that plane to Newark Airport. She blamed the weather.

Her thoughts went to Captain Barnes's young widow and those two little girls who probably wouldn't even remember their father. At least her children were older. They'd have their memories. And so would she. Not that memories were enough—they didn't keep you warm on a cold winter's night. They couldn't hold you when you were frightened or sad. But they were better than nothing. She was a professional wife. She would go on because that's what he would want. Maybe in the spring she'd send the note, inviting Laura and the girls to spend a day at their farm upstate.

Elizabeth Daily Post

THE LAST THREE MINUTES

By Henry Ammerman

JAN. 24—At 3:41 p.m. the American Airlines Convair had been circling for 10 minutes, waiting for another transport to land at Newark Airport. With the runway now clear, the tower told the pilot he was free to descend to 1,500 feet, instructing him to listen to radar advisories to aid his instrument approach in the rainy, foggy weather. "Roger," replied the Convair.

Five and a half miles out, the pilot was informed, "Coming up on glide path but you're 900 feet to the left of course."

At four and a half miles out he was "Nearing the course now, you're 400 feet left."

By four miles out, "You're on course now. The Elizabeth Court House is one mile ahead of you." He was coming over the center of town.

At three and a half miles out, the radar controller issued

a warning. "You're drifting 900 feet to the right of course and you're a half mile from the Court House."

Four or 5 seconds later, the reassuring orange blip disappeared from the radar scope.

"American 6780, this is Newark radar. We've lost your target, sir." There was no reply.

"American 6780, this is Newark radio. Do you hear?" Again there was no reply.

As the tower anxiously tried to make contact on other frequencies, calls came in from both the Newark Evening News and the Daily Post. A plane had crashed in Elizabeth.

Now they understood. There would be no reply.

Interviews

LAURA BARNES AGREED to talk with Henry Ammerman. "You know when you marry a pilot, it could happen," she told him. "You know, but you never expect it. He had so much experience. He was so smart and he always kept his head, never angry or quick-tempered, and on a milk run, of all things. I blame Newark Airport. Something has to be done about that airport before it happens again." She was red-eyed but composed, Henry wrote. He didn't tell her that her husband's wrists had both been broken from trying to hold the controls steady.

"Was it true what you wrote in the paper about the last three minutes?" Laura asked.

"As far as I can tell."

Days later Laura had a miscarriage, brought on by stress, the doctor said. The house down the shore was put up for sale. Laura never wanted to see it again. She mourned her lost baby but not the way she mourned

Tim. She would never love anyone the way she loved him.

Henry requested a meeting with the pilot's mother. He was told by her remaining son that she was prostrate with grief and could not be reached.

Sometimes Henry hated his job.

CHRISTINA FELT NUMB. She stuck a fork into the underside of her arm to see if the numbness was in her mind or her body. She felt the prongs digging into her skin. But she didn't care.

When Henry Ammerman came to interview them at Battin, Christina told him what she'd seen. But unlike some of the other girls, animated and anxious to be heard, jumping up and down, giving the reporter details of how Madame Hoffman, the French teacher, had fainted at the window of her classroom when she saw the plane crash into the brick apartment house, and how they sat her up and fanned her face while the president of the French Club ran to see if the school nurse was still in the building, Christina remained subdued.

Mr. Durkee proudly told Henry how calm his students had been, how they'd listened to his instructions to duck and cover, scrambling under their desks and staying there until after the last of the explosions. Christina didn't contradict him or any of the other girls.

"You know, Henry," Mr. Durkee said, "just forty-five minutes before the crash, a thousand girls were dismissed from school. Be sure your readers think about that."

"Good point," Henry said. As if he hadn't thought of that himself.

. . .

JANE KRASNER, in New Jersey for her roommate's funeral, talked to Henry about Kathy Stein. *Pale, brown-haired, and slender, Miss Krasner was obviously grieving,* Henry wrote. "Kathy was coming home to see a boy she'd met over the holidays. She really liked him. She wanted me to come with her but it was too expensive to fly and there wasn't enough time to take the bus. She said her father would pay for my ticket but I would never go for that. She was so generous and thoughtful . . ." Miss Krasner looked away. "I don't think I can go back to that dorm room we shared. I may take the semester off. Maybe I'll transfer to another school. Kathy was my closest friend. Sometimes it's like that. You meet someone and you know you're going to be best friends. You know it right away. Now she's gone. I'll never see her again. She was so beautiful, inside and out."

Phonies

When Steve read about Kathy in the paper, when he read she was coming home to see a boy she'd met over the holidays, a boy she really liked, he got into bed and stayed there for four days. He thought about dying but he was afraid to do it himself. His only solace was reading *The Catcher in the Rye*. Holden was his friend, the one person who could understand what Steve was thinking, and the unbearable sadness he was feeling.

Finally, his mother came to his room and said, "Get up, Steve."

"Why?"

"Because we need you to."

"That's not a good enough reason."

"We know you're sad . . ."

"Who's we?"

"Your family."

Steve snorted.

"Stop this, Steve!" His mother pulled the covers off him and just as fast, he pulled them back. "Can't you see what I'm going through?" she cried, burying her face in her hands. She turned away from him, her shoulders shaking.

What was this?

When she faced him again she was angry. "Don't do this, Steve. And give me that book!" She reached for it, but again, he was quicker, and shoved the book under his ass where she wouldn't dare try to get it.

"I need you to get up, shower, put on your clothes, have breakfast and go to school. I need you to do that for me."

Who gives a fuck about what she needs?

"Do you understand, Steve?"

"I understand." Part of him felt bad for her, his pretty little mother. But the other part knew she was a phony like all the other so-called adults in his life. Not one of them gave a shit about Kathy. She was just another dead person. Just one of the tragic twenty-three on just another crashed plane. *And hardy-har, Mother dear, it wasn't even a non-sked this time.* He should tell her that—tell her how he'd traveled back from Boston in a snowstorm in a non-sked, thanks to his father. What would she say then?

Maybe he would get up. Maybe he'd get up and go to school and pretend everything was okay, just like the rest of them.

He grabbed his copy of *Catcher*. "I'm not finished with you, Holden," he whispered to the book, "or you, either, Phoebe." Fern was his Phoebe, or could be if she played it right.

At school Phil acted all glad to see him, like nothing much had happened. "Were you sick? Your mother said you couldn't come to the phone."

"Yeah, sick."

"What kind of sick?"

"Just plain sick."

"You don't sound sick."

"What does *sick* sound like?"

"Okay, I get it."

No you don't, Steve thought.

Coffee Cake

Miri brought one of Irene's coffee cakes to Mrs. Stein once the Steins returned to their regular routines—Phil at school, Mr. Stein at his office, Mrs. Stein reading in her favorite chair. "I'm so sorry for your loss," Miri said.

"I still can't believe it." Mrs. Stein teared up. "My niece was a wonderful girl. And such promise. Even though we buried her and sat shiva, none of it feels real."

When Fred barked Mrs. Stein scooped him up and her mood lightened. "I'm so happy to see you, Miri, and Fred, too. Look at this cake!" she said, taking it from Miri. "It looks good enough to eat. What do you say?"

Miri nodded.

"And how about a cold glass of milk to go with it?"

Miri nodded again.

Elizabeth Daily Post

Editorial

BARKING AT THE MOON

JAN. 25—Elizabeth's second air disaster is now three days old. Our commercial airline death record has taken first place in the whole world. Show us, if you can, an official act or an official decision made that offers assurance there won't be more slaughter.

The governor, who is a lawyer himself, hides behind the opinion of another lawyer. The mayor calls for removal of Newark Airport "bag and baggage," which he should know is barking at the moon.

The Port Authority sticks to its old reliable routine of patterns and improvements to come, while crash experts give us an answer to everything except why the airport keeps expanding.

Let the governor order expansion work at Newark Airport stopped NOW—TODAY! That would be a gesture of sincerity which would reassure an aroused and grieving people.

Public Indignation

A few days after the crash, a "Public Indignation" meeting was held at City Hall, demanding authorities shut down Newark Airport. More than a thousand people came, not only from Elizabeth, but other towns along the flight paths.

Irene didn't want Ben Sapphire to go. "It could be too much for you, Ben."

"My wife died on one of those planes," Ben said. "I'm not sitting this one out."

"Then I'm coming with you," Irene told him.

"Take your pills just in case," Rusty said. But Irene ignored her.

"Come, Rusty," Ben said, "we'll give you a ride."

"Me, too," Miri said. She'd made plans to meet Mason there.

"You're not coming," Rusty told her. "You have to be eighteen."

"You didn't have to be eighteen to die," Miri argued. "Penny wasn't even eight."

Henry said, "I think she can come."

Rusty shrugged. "I hate this."

"We all do," Henry said.

MASON WAS WAITING for her with Christina and Jack, in front of City Hall. Miri still hadn't met Mason's older brother, but just as Mason started to introduce them a bum approached Jack, and Mason pulled Miri away, hustling her up the wide steps. It was the first time Miri had set foot inside City Hall, an impressive red-brick, white-columned building. She'd imagined it would be quiet, even serene, but not tonight. The noisy crowd spilled out into the lobby, leaving standing room only at the meeting. Rusty fought her way through the crowd to Miri and told her to keep to the side with Mason, away from the entrance. "I'll be over there," she said, pointing to a bench where Irene and Ben were already seated. "I want to keep an eye on Nana. I've got her pills in my pocketbook. If it gets to be too much, go outside."

"If it gets to be too much?" Miri said to Mason once Rusty was out of earshot. *"If it gets to be too much?"* As if two crashes weren't already too much. Mason nodded but Miri wasn't sure he'd heard a word she'd said.

The meeting started with Mayor Kirk saying something about umbrellas, but Miri couldn't hear well enough to understand. Then a representative from the airport promised the new runway, under construction, would keep planes from taking off and landing over Elizabeth. No one believed him, and when the crowd started booing, a police escort rushed him out of the building. After that tempers escalated quickly. The crowd wanted to blame someone or something.

Eleanor slipped in next to Miri. Miri was glad she wasn't the only one here from her class. "They don't understand it's sabotage, that we're a city under siege." Eleanor had to cup her hand and speak directly into Miri's ear, it was so noisy.

"Are you going to tell them?"

"I haven't decided."

"My uncle says they were accidents, that it was a coincidence."

"Sorry, but I don't buy that."

"I know it's hard to believe but—"

"Your uncle's a reporter, right?"

"Yes. He's sitting up front with the other reporters."

"They don't want us to know the truth. If we did, it would result in chaos."

"My uncle is an honest person."

"I'm just saying our *government* doesn't want us to know the truth." Eleanor walked away then, maybe looking for someone else to listen to her theory.

There was wild talk of blocking runways at the airport with a caravan of cars. Steve and Phil and Jack McKittrick were among those who volunteered to participate, sitting in their cars on the runways, preventing planes from taking off or landing.

Someone shouted that the pilot was at fault. "The first plane crashed into the riverbed, thanks to the pilot's skills. He didn't kill anyone on the ground. But this time . . ."

Mrs. Barnes's son stood and in a shaky voice said, "My brother was the pilot of the second plane. He was the best pilot in the world. You want to blame someone, blame *him*," and he pointed to Joseph Fluet, the investigator from the Civil Aeronautics Board. "*He* could have closed down the airport after the first crash. He had the power to do that. But he didn't, and now my brother is dead, his little girls are fatherless." His voice caught. "How many people have to die before something is done, before more families are torn apart like ours?"

As the crowd chanted, "Close down Newark Airport or we'll close it for you!" Fluet was rushed out of the hall by a police escort. *Two down*, Miri thought.

A woman stood on a chair, stuck two fingers in her mouth and let out a whistle so shrill Miri was sure a taxi in New York could have heard it. "We have a petition right here," she shouted into a bullhorn. "We urge each and every one of you to sign it. Tomorrow we're sending it to President Truman and other federal and state officials in vigorous protest—calling for the removal of Newark Airport."

Something bubbled up inside of Miri, a surge so intense she could taste it. She pushed her way through the crowd, calling, "Let me sign that. Let me sign that petition." Mason was right behind her, hanging on to her jacket. Was he trying to hold her back, or was he trying to protect her?

"Are you eighteen?" someone asked. "You have to be eighteen to sign."

"I'm old enough. Just give me the pen!" Rusty was waving frantically for her to stop. Just try and stop her. Just try and see what would happen. She didn't know what she'd do but she knew it would be something Henry would have to put in his next story. Niece or no niece. "Give me the pen!" she shouted, until Phil Stein handed one to her. She signed her name. *Miri Ammerman*, and her age, *15*.

Mason signed right after her. *Mason McKittrick*, *17*. He wasn't seventeen yet, but he would be soon. Miri supposed it didn't really matter.

Rusty made her way to Miri's side. "Enough is enough! Mason, will you walk her home?"

Mason nodded.

They didn't say much on the way home. Miri was seething, her gloved hands shoved deep into her coat pockets.

"What?" Mason asked.

"That," Miri answered, turning back toward City Hall. "And that!" This time she pointed to the sky.

"It's not what you think," he said.

"I don't know what I think."

WHEN SHE GOT HOME, Miri began to write a story for the school newspaper, but crumpled it up in frustration when she couldn't get it right. She tossed it into the trash and sat looking out her window for what seemed like a long time. Then she retrieved the story, smoothed it out and shoved it into her desk drawer. Why shouldn't her mind be as messed up as everything else?

Elizabeth Daily Post

A COMMUNITY PULLS TOGETHER

By Henry Ammerman

JAN. 26—The mayor calls it "The Umbrella of Death." Others are calling it "Plane Crash City."

No matter what you call it, the citizens of Elizabeth are reeling. An angry crowd of more than 1,000 gathered at City Hall last night, demanding the closing of Newark Airport following the second crash of a plane in 38 days. They did not believe that a new runway under construction at Newark Airport would make a substantial difference to the safety of the passengers on the planes or the residents on the ground.

They formed committees, threatened to stage a caravan of cars parked on runways, making it impossible for planes to take off or land, and signed petitions. Thousands more are expected to sign similar petitions in county churches at Sunday services. The meeting ended with a series of threats— Close Newark Airport or we'll close it for you!

Where Will It End?

When a man shouted, "Where will it end?" there were no answers to his question.

Captain Eddie Rickenbacker, president of Eastern Air Lines, said in a press conference called by the Air Transport Association that Newark was "a preferred airport" to pilots under any weather conditions. He said in most pilots' opinion "it is the best situated, the best equipped and the safest airport in the entire country." Ten pilots representing five airlines confirmed the statement. They said their personal choice in bad weather would always be Newark. But such talk had little effect on the people of Elizabeth. Indignation, which had run in angry undercurrents through the city, boiled to the surface.

Now the community is pulling together. The Red Cross is asking for blood donations for those injured on the ground, and for food and clothing for the displaced. Volunteers are needed to provide temporary housing. "It's time to take action," says Richard F. Green, Red Cross disaster director. "This could have happened to any of us."

16

Daisy

Christina told Daisy about Polina, the young mother who worked in the kitchen at Janet Memorial, who'd lost everything when the plane smashed into her apartment house on Williamson Street. "She has a little boy," Christina said, showing her a photo of a towheaded three-year-old. "My family can't take them in. We already have my sister, her husband and their little boy sleeping in the attic room, and my grandparents in my sister's old bedroom."

That was more than Christina had ever said about her family. Daisy lived in a small house in Linden with her older sister, Evelyn. They had a spare room as big as a closet. Daisy knew if she asked, Evelyn would say no. So she didn't ask. She brought Polina and Stash home that night.

Evelyn didn't make a scene in front of Polina. She waited until Daisy had made up the bed in the spare room, before giving Daisy hell. "You have no right—this is my house as much as yours. How dare you?" Daisy listened to her sister's whispered outrage, said she understood, then poured herself a drink, went to her room, closed the door, lit up a Camel and picked up a book.

Evelyn came around after a few days, thanks to Stash, who'd taken a liking to her. He chose to sit in her lap after dinner, asking her to read him a story. She began to bring him little surprises when she came home from work. A toy car, then a truck and finally a bus. He said he wanted to live with her forever.

Polina was still learning to speak English but Daisy had no trouble understanding her. The young mother was so grateful to have a roof over her head and a warm, safe place to stay with Stash, she couldn't do enough to help. "Please, Miss Daisy, I cook you supper tonight." She shopped for food, paid for it out of her meager salary and scrubbed Daisy's kitchen and bathroom without ever being asked. On Sundays Polina got herself up like a glamour-puss. Then she and Stash went off to church, taking the bus into Elizabeth from Linden. Daisy admired Polina's optimism. She'd lost everyone close to her in the war but she was committed to giving Stash the chance she'd never had.

Daisy drove Polina and Stash to Elizabeth every morning. Polina looked much younger without makeup. So lovely, with clear skin, plump arms and a nice bosom. Polina had to be in the kitchen at Janet Memorial at six. She dropped Stash off at the babysitter's house first. It was an hour earlier than Daisy usually came to work but she didn't mind. That extra hour gave her the time to catch up on billing and correspondence. If she finished in time she enjoyed relaxing in the waiting room reading magazines, sipping a coffee from Three Brothers, trying to think of a nice young man to introduce to Polina. There was someone who worked in the lab down the hall . . .

Miri

Miri went through her closet, pulling out shoes that didn't fit, skirts she hadn't worn since sixth grade, her old lime-green dress coat. Rusty said the rule for grown-ups was, *If you haven't worn it in five years, you'll probably never wear it again.* For kids it was two years.

Irene didn't agree. "When you've been through two world wars and the Depression you don't think that way." Irene saved everything. But even she was putting together a box of clothing.

"I wish I'd saved Estelle's things," Ben said.

"It's not like you sold them," Irene said. "You donated them to a good cause."

Miri went to Natalie's house to help her clean out her closet. Natalie grabbed armloads of clothes, still on their hangers, and threw them onto her bed. "Just give it all away," she told Corinne, when she came into the room. "Including my cashmere sweaters," Natalie said, scooping them out of her dresser drawer.

But Corinne hung all the good things back in Natalie's closet. "You're overreacting, Nat."

"I don't care about any of it," Natalie said, flopping down on her bed.

Miri was about to volunteer to take the cashmere sweaters herself, but Corinne saved her. "We'll give away anything you haven't worn in two years." So Corinne knew about Rusty's two-year rule. Two years meant since Miri and Natalie had been best friends. It felt like way longer than two years to Miri. She could hardly remember life without Natalie. That she was able to covet Natalie's cashmere sweaters at a time like this, when the people who'd lost everything in the crash had nothing, made her feel ashamed. She, after all, had Charlotte Whitten's hand-me-down dresses. Wasn't that enough? What was wrong with her? Why was she thinking such selfish thoughts?

At school they had a drive for pots and pans, canned goods, toys and books. The Red Cross was collecting boxes from all over town. Ben Sapphire was picking up and delivering. Irene was cooking and baking by day and knitting by night. After work, Rusty volunteered at the Red Cross house, putting together boxes of household goods and clothing to match each family's needs. Some nights Rusty would stay out late, serving coffee and sandwiches to the volunteers working at the morgue. It was much harder to identify the victims this time. This time they were all burned beyond recognition. Dental records were often the only way to find out who they were. Except for the pilot. He was the first to be identified by what was left of the stripes on his uniform.

The busier they kept, the better they felt. At least they were doing something positive.

Elizabeth Daily Post

WHAT WENT WRONG

Will They Ever Know?

By Henry Ammerman

JAN. 28—The initial findings in the probe of the Jan. 22 crash of an American Airlines Convair point to a sharp, almost vertical drop of the plane. When it was noted that this must have resulted from a radical equipment breakdown, chief CAB investigator Joseph O. Fluet said he was not yet ready to draw any conclusions.

But another official, speaking off the record, speculated that the pilot might have tried to pull the plane upward in a desperate effort to redirect the crash away from Battin High School, leading to a stall, which caused it to plummet directly to earth. He noted that the pilot, Timothy Barnes, had grown up in Elizabeth and had graduated from Hamilton Junior High and Thomas Jefferson High School. He lived only a few blocks from Battin.

Captain Barnes surely realized the possible implications of crashing into that particular building on a school day.

17

Miri

"Life goes on" became Irene's mantra. If Miri heard that expression one more time she was sure she would explode, just like the planes. If *life goes on*, then why shouldn't she go with Frekki Strasser to the Paper Mill Playhouse?

"Out of the question," Irene said.

"Because . . ." Miri prompted.

"Because you can't trust the Monskys."

"You think Frekki is going to kidnap me and send me to another planet in a flying saucer?"

"You'll discuss it with your mother."

"Ben Sapphire wants to take *you* to Miami Beach," she told Irene. "Who's to say he's not going to kidnap you and take you on a flying saucer?"

"I should be so lucky."

"You'd like to get on a flying saucer with Ben Sapphire?"

"What's all this about flying saucers?"

It was true that Ben Sapphire wanted to take Irene on a trip to Miami Beach. He reminded them his wife was heading there when her plane went down in the Elizabeth River. As if they needed reminding. Miri still saw that plane in her sleep. She could feel the heat. She'd wake up drenched with sweat and have to change her pajamas. Once she was awake she found it hard to get back to sleep. To calm her nerves, to take her mind off Plane Crash City, she'd look into her kaleidoscope, telling herself, *You're getting sleepy, you're get-*

ting very sleepy . . . If all else failed there were stories in the paper that gave her other things to think about.

ACTION! CAMERA!
One of many candid camera shots taken during the play
"Goodbye, My Fancy," presented by the Vail-Deane School
Dramatic Club, assisted by the Pingry Players.

You could tell the pretty blonde in the photo in the paper wearing the strapless dress with a full skirt was the lead. She was probably the most popular girl at Vail-Deane. Miri imagined herself at Vail-Deane, wearing a blue jumper and white blouse, the school uniform. All the girls at Vail-Deane were rich. They dated the boys at Pingry, who came from the same kinds of families. Some of the boys crossed themselves before basketball games. Miri had been to a game once with Suzanne, who had a cousin at Pingry. All of them went off to fancy colleges. Then they married each other and lived in single-family houses with big backyards, had chubby babies and drank themselves to death. Miri knew the part about drinking themselves to death wasn't necessarily true. She was just trying it out to make their lives seem less perfect.

Irene

Ben called Irene his "safety net." *Without you I'm lost. Your warmth calms me.* She could think of worse things for a man to say to her. Rusty once accused her of rescuing people the way some people rescue stray animals. The way Mason had rescued Fred. Miri had told her about that, about how he'd found Fred starving and wet in a snowstorm when he was just a puppy. No collar. No tags. Mason had nursed him back to health. Miri knew Irene would respond to that story. But she still wouldn't let the dog into her side of the house. Ben Sapphire, on the other hand, wasn't a dog. He was a grown man who owned apartment buildings in Jersey City and Elizabeth. And he considered himself *mishpocheh*, one of the family, with her blessing.

She told Rusty she was thinking of taking him up on his offer to go to Miami Beach. They would travel by train. "Maybe for a week or two, although Ben would like to stay longer."

From the look on Rusty's face you'd think she'd just announced that a man had landed on the moon.

"He has two bedrooms," Irene said, "one for him and one for me, and my own half bath, just a few blocks from the ocean."

Miri, who wasn't included in this discussion but was listening anyway, kept her mouth shut.

"I know his family," Irene continued. "He knows mine. What could go wrong?"

Now Rusty looked at her as if she'd lost her mind.

"You think I don't know he could have any woman he wants—with his real estate and his new Packard? Am I somebody who ever wanted another husband? I have everything I need right here. My family, good friends, plenty to do. But a little adventure—what could be bad?"

"You know what could be bad," Rusty said.

"You're worried I'll get pregnant?" When Irene laughed, Miri laughed with her.

Rusty, stony-faced, didn't. "I'm worried about your feelings, your heart—"

"I have pills for my heart."

"Not if it gets broken."

"Darling . . . thank you for caring so much."

Rusty shook her head and walked out of the room.

Miri stayed and gave Irene a hug.

Daisy

Longy had the last appointment of the day. "You know, Doc, you look like hell, no offense meant."

And it was true. Dr. O had dark circles under his eyes and was so pooped at the end of office hours he sometimes took a snooze on the couch before heading home. Daisy was worried and prayed it wasn't his heart. She'd been there when he'd lost his two brothers to back-to-back heart attacks while still in their forties.

"You need a vacation," Longy said. "Come to Vegas with me. We'll shoot craps. Eat the best steaks you ever tasted. I'll show you around town."

"Sounds good, Abe, but I can't get away now."

"Doc, sometimes when you think you can't, that's the time you have to." Longy could be very persuasive. "You like Betty Hutton?"

"Is the pope Catholic?"

Longy laughed. "She's playing in Vegas next week."

"I wish I could, Abe."

Before he left the office, Longy took Daisy aside. "Help me out on this, Daisy."

"I'll try, Mr. Zwillman."

"I'm worried about him."

"Me, too."

So Daisy cleared the following Thursday, Friday and Monday, without further discussion.

Corinne called Daisy the next morning. "Whose idea is this trip to Vegas?" She didn't wait for an answer. "Longy's, am I right?"

"Corinne . . ." Daisy took a deep breath. "He needs to get away. He's exhausted. It's beginning to affect him at the office."

"He could go away with me."

"That would be wonderful and I'd be glad to stay with the children."

"The children," Corinne said, as if she'd just remembered. "We can't both be gone at the same time, not now."

"It's just for a long weekend," Daisy reminded her.

"Yes, a long weekend, but with *Longy*."

Daisy laughed. "No denying that."

Corinne sighed. "All right."

Daisy said, "If you need anything, I'll be around."

"Thank you, Daisy."

On Wednesday, after office hours, Longy picked up Dr. O in a limo heading for LaGuardia. "We'll catch some winter sun if we're lucky," Longy called to Daisy.

"Catch some for me, too." Daisy waved goodbye.

Dr. O waved back.

Miri

Henry and Leah were planning their June wedding. They'd once talked about renting a big house down the shore, and everyone would come and stay for the weekend, but they'd changed their minds. The wedding would be smaller now, in a garden at the Hotel La Reine in Bradley Beach.

How could they be planning a wedding? Miri wondered. Because *life goes on*? Maybe this was true and maybe it wasn't. Life might go on but it didn't go on in the same way. It would never be the same for the Fosters. It would never be the same for the Steins. It might never be the same for Natalie. She didn't know who Natalie was anymore. She wasn't even sure about herself. Who was this girl who looked back at her from the mirror? If she'd once thought being in love could fix anything, she didn't anymore. It couldn't bring back Penny or make Betsy better.

SHE BEGGED RUSTY to let her go to the Paper Mill Playhouse with Frekki. "What's the worst that could happen?"

Rusty didn't give her an answer. When she turned and walked out of the room without another word, Miri knew she'd won.

AT 8:30 SATURDAY MORNING, Mr. Roman of Mr. Roman's House of Beauty, on Elmora Avenue, circled Miri, who sat in his chair. She was about to splurge on an Elizabeth Taylor cut, shampoo and set. Rusty, a big believer in long hair, would kill her if she knew. When Rusty caught her leaving the house so early, Miri had her excuse ready. "I'm going to the library," she'd said.

"Be careful," Rusty told her.

Did that mean don't let any planes crash into you? Did it mean don't let the aliens turn you into a zombie? Or did it mean look both ways before you cross the street and don't talk to strangers?

Mr. Roman's House of Beauty was already busy, with two women under the dryers, two more getting shampooed, and a second haircutter at work. The manicurist was polishing the nails of a lady Miri thought she recognized from the junior department at Levy Brothers.

Mr. Roman held up sections of Miri's hair. "Nice," he said. "Some natural wave, but you'll have to set the new cut in pin curls at night. Are you sure about this?" He was making Miri nervous. Was he trying to talk her out of cutting her hair? "Because once I start," he said, "there's no turning back."

"But how do you think it will look?" Miri asked, hoping for reassurance.

He kissed the tips of his fingers. *"Fabuloso."*

Was that an Italian word? If so, did it mean what it sounded like? Either way, the decision was made. Mr. Roman picked up his scissors and, *snip snip snip*, the process began. Was she making a big mistake or would she leave the shop looking like Elizabeth Taylor in *A Place in the Sun*?

She stuffed two pieces of Fleer's Dubble Bubble into her mouth, then blew bubbles so big they burst against her cheeks, until Mr. Roman told her he found such a habit distracting and not worthy of a lovely young lady. Under the dryer she read *Silver Screen* and *Photoplay*. Ava Gardner was on the cover of both.

Two hours later she paid with her babysitting money, trying not to think about the Fosters. Would they approve of her spending the money they'd paid her for watching Penny and Betsy on a haircut, while Betsy was being treated for severe burns and Mr. and Mrs. Foster were keeping a vigil at her bedside? Was she a terrible person for thinking of how she looked when they still didn't know if Betsy would live or die?

She caught a glimpse of herself in the mirror as she left the beauty parlor and at first wasn't sure who it was. She looked older, but nothing like Elizabeth Taylor. She shouldn't have let Mr. Roman use hairspray. She hated hairspray. She walked home without her hat, letting the cold winter wind whip her hair around. Before going inside she ran her fingers through it and checked herself in the mirror of her Volupté compact, a birthday present from Leah. That was better.

At home she'd have to hurry to get ready. Frekki was picking her up at 11:30. She prayed Rusty wouldn't hear her come in—anything to avoid an argument today. It was laundry day, vacuuming day—Miri was responsible for her room, which she'd cleaned last night.

But just as she opened the front door Rusty was coming up from the basement with the laundry basket. Miri braced for the worst.

"Cute," Rusty said, barely looking at her, which threw Miri for a loop. This was so unlike the reaction she'd expected, it worried her.

When she was almost ready, in her cashmere sweater and pencil skirt, Rusty brought her the strand of pearls her parents had given *her* on her sixteenth birthday. Pearls, even though Rusty's father had lost his business and was working behind the counter for next to nothing at his friend's bakery. Miri knew about the pearls, but until now, Rusty had never offered to let Miri wear them, and Miri had never asked.

Today, Miri thought, Rusty was trying to send Frekki a message. *See how well I've managed without any of you? See the daughter I raised without your help, in her cashmere sweater and expensive pearls?*

"Be yourself," Rusty said, giving her an extra long hug.

Miri understood. *Make me proud. This woman with the yellow Cadillac is nothing. She's no better than us. Remember that.*

INSIDE, the yellow Cadillac smelled of leather, like new shoes. Miri had never been in a Cadillac. Even the Osners didn't drive a Cadillac. Not that Corinne didn't want one, but Dr. O had a patient with an Oldsmobile dealership who gave him a good deal, so that was that.

On the drive to Millburn, Frekki chatted about the play they were going to see, an operetta, *The Desert Song*. She sang a few bars to Miri. *"Blue heaven and you and I . . ."* Her voice was low and smoky. On key. "I love musicals," she told Miri. Frekki might be a regular aunt taking her niece out for the day. Miri pretended that's what they were. She worried at first about what she would talk about with Frekki, this aunt she didn't know she had until recently, this aunt whose brother was Mike Monsky, the same Mike Monsky who was her father. *Her father.* It struck her as such a strange idea she wanted to laugh. And maybe she did, because Frekki looked over at her and Miri pretended the sound was a hiccup. Frekki didn't say anything about the latest plane crash. It felt good not to talk about it. But it made Miri wonder if people in other towns thought of it at all.

The restaurant across the parking lot from the playhouse had once been a real carriage house. You could still see the stable doors. Inside it was fancy, like Charleston Gardens at B. Altman and Company, where she'd gone last year with Corinne and Natalie. The same white tablecloths and a small flower in a glass vase on each table, lace at the windows. A slice of lemon floated in her water glass.

At first Miri thought it was a mistake but then she noticed lemon slices floating in everyone's water glass. She saw just one man in the restaurant, seated at a table with an elderly woman who looked like she could be his mother. At every other table were mothers and daughters, aunts and nieces, grandmothers and grandchildren. A few of the grandchildren were small boys, fidgeting in their best clothes. All the little girls wore party dresses. At a large table in the corner a group of teenage girls were celebrating someone's birthday.

A waitress dressed in black with a white apron handed Miri a menu.

CREAMED CHICKEN ON TOAST POINTS WITH BUTTERED PEAS

PORK CHOP WITH CREAMED MUSHROOM SAUCE

CHOPPED STEAK WITH CREAMY MUSHROOM SAUCE

TUNA CASSEROLE WITH CREAMED CORN

Everything was creamy. Ugh! She hated creamy sauces. At the very bottom was a children's menu.

SPAGHETTI WITH BUTTER

GRILLED CHEESE

HOT DOG

It would be embarrassing to order off the children's menu but better than ordering creamed something or other and not eating a bite.

Frekki leaned over and whispered, "The menu is so goyish, but they'll make you grilled cheese if you'd like."

The waitress gave Miri a look when she ordered grilled cheese but Frekki came to her rescue. "She can have whatever she wants," Frekki told the waitress. "Just charge me for a second tuna casserole and bring her the grilled cheese." Miri might like this woman, if only she were allowed to.

Frekki smoked an Old Gold while they were waiting for their food, her diamond ring sparkling in the sunlight, her nails polished dark red to match the color of her lipstick. "Nasty habit," Frekki said, as she flicked an ash into the glass ashtray on the table. "Take it from me. Don't start." Miri had already decided she wouldn't, even though it looked so sophisticated. All the movie stars smoked. Rusty limited herself to two a day, one after lunch and one after dinner. Henry smoked. Leah didn't. Corinne didn't but Dr. O and Daisy did. Irene didn't. Ben Sapphire smoked a cigar after dinner. Then there was Mason and his Luckies.

Everyone left the restaurant at about the same time and headed across the way to the Paper Mill Playhouse, an old mill turned into a theater, where Frekki snapped a picture of Miri, her coat unbuttoned to show off her birthday sweater and Rusty's pearls.

Before they were shown to their seats, Frekki bought Miri a souvenir program. At one point during the performance Frekki looked over at her and smiled. They came out humming "The Desert Song," the most popular song in the operetta. "I've always wanted a daughter," Frekki said. "I have two sons but they wouldn't be caught dead at an operetta."

"Maybe they'll get married and you'll have daughters-in-law who'll go with you."

"That'd be nice, though daughters-in-law don't always like their husbands' mothers."

"But if you're nice to them . . ." Miri thought of Irene and Leah, who liked each other.

"Yes, maybe," Frekki said. "I hope so. But that's still years away. You'll have to meet the boys. They're seventeen and nineteen. It's good for a girl to have boy cousins."

Cousins, Miri thought. *I have boy cousins.*

After the show they stopped for ice cream at Gruning's on the Hill. There was a line waiting for tables. But Frekki said, "Oh, look . . ." and she pointed to a table. Miri followed her gaze to a table with a man seated facing them. He waved to Frekki. Was this Frekki's husband, Dr. J. J. Strasser, who was such a good provider they lived in South Orange, and who had bought Frekki a yellow Cadillac and a big diamond ring?

She followed Frekki to the table. Suddenly, like a cat with its whiskers stiff, she knew this was not Dr. J. J. Strasser. Dr. J. J. Strasser would be older, she thought. He wouldn't look so much like Frekki, with thick hair and a toothy smile. He stood and helped Miri off with her coat, draping it over the back of her chair. When they were all seated, with their napkins on their laps, Frekki said, "Miri, this is my brother . . ."

Before Frekki could get out the rest, before she could say his name, Miri said, "I know who you are. You're Mike Monsky."

He said, "Yes."

Frekki added, "Your father."

He's not my father, Miri thought. *He doesn't even know me.*

Her body was telling her to flee. "Excuse me," she said, pushing back her chair and running, coming this close to colliding with a waitress delivering ice cream sundaes to some happy family. Another waitress pointed her in the direction of the ladies' room. Inside were little girls, teenage girls, their mothers, their grandmothers. She splashed her face with water at the sink. Someone asked, "Are you all right, dear? Do you need help?"

She waved her away. No, she didn't need help. And no, she wasn't all right. But she was going to pretend she was. She was not going to throw up in a stall in the ladies' room of Gruning's on the Hill, with all these fancy mothers and daughters watching and listening. She breathed through her nose the way Natalie did when she felt nauseous, which was often. That was better. She applied Pixie Pink lipstick. She patted down her hair, then fluffed it back up. She hated her new haircut. She'd already decided to grow it out and Mason hadn't even seen it.

The door to the ladies' room opened. "Hi," Frekki said to her. "Everything okay?"

"You planned this," Miri said. "You tricked me."

Two women blotting their lipstick glanced over at them.

Frekki gave them a weak smile. Miri knew she could make a big scene and embarrass Frekki. Maybe she would.

"I planned the meeting here, yes."

Miri raised her voice. "The whole day was a lie!" What did she care? There was nobody here who knew her or her family but there might be somebody who knew the great Frekki Strasser or her doctor husband.

Frekki shepherded her away from the sinks. "I wish you wouldn't look at it that way."

"How should I look at it?"

"As an opportunity. I thought you should meet your father and that he should meet you."

That stopped Miri for a moment. Then she turned and marched out of the ladies' room, shoulders back, head high, as if she were the Queen of Posture, and back to the table. Back to Mike Monsky. Her so-called father.

She took her seat at the table. The waitress asked what she'd like. "A dish of plain vanilla, please. One scoop."

"Hot fudge, nuts, whipped cream, Maraschino cherry?" The waitress held her pencil at the ready.

"Plain, please."

"Okay, just a single scoop of vanilla in a dish."

Isn't that what I said the first time you asked? Miri thought. But instead of screaming, throwing a temper tantrum, yelling at the waitress, who wore red-framed cat's-eye glasses turned up at the tops with tiny rhinestones in the corners, Miri said, "Yes, thank you." Saying it like that, with such authority, made her feel calm, in charge of her feelings.

Mike Monsky said, "This is awkward for both of us."

She knew he was looking at her but she refused to meet his gaze. "Maybe for you," she said. "But it's not awkward for me. I couldn't care less."

By the time Frekki came back to the table their ice cream had been served. "Are you two getting to know each other?"

Mike Monsky smiled a small, wry smile. "You might say that." Then he turned to Miri. "How's your ice cream?"

She hadn't tasted it yet. She lifted her spoon, dipped her tongue into it and said, "It's fine."

"How's Rusty?" he asked.

"She's fine." She was wondering if he was going to go through the whole family.

"I'm glad to hear that." He swirled his ice cream around, blending the scoop of chocolate with the scoop of vanilla like a little kid with a Dixie Cup at a birthday party. "So, you're fifteen now?"

"Why, did you forget when you shtupped my mother?" Frekki sucked in her breath.

Shtupped, a word she'd never said aloud until then. A vulgar word, Irene would say.

"What'd you do for your birthday?" he asked, ignoring her question.

"Had a pizza party with my girlfriends. My grand-mother baked the birthday cake."

"Aah, Irene," he said. "She was a great baker."

So, he knew Irene well enough to have tasted her cakes?

"My mother gave me this." She held up her wrist to show off her birthstone bracelet.

"Very nice," he said.

"Uncle Henry picked up the pizza at Spirito's. He's a famous reporter now."

"So I've heard."

He better not ask if she had a boyfriend. She'd throw her ice cream at him if he did. Because she had the power, she realized. She could do whatever she damn well pleased. And if he thought she couldn't because he was her father—ha!

"I live in California," he said, tapping out an Old Gold cigarette. Same brand as his sister, she noticed. Or maybe Frekki had bought the carton and he'd filched a pack. "Los Altos." She must have given him a blank look because he added, "San Francisco Bay Area. This is my first trip back since I enlisted." He fumbled around in his wallet and pulled out a picture. "My wife and sons," he said. "Your half brothers."

She didn't want to look but she couldn't help herself. The boys were little, maybe four and six. The wife was blond, pretty, not put-together-pretty like Corinne, but casual pretty. She was younger, with chubby cheeks, wearing Capri pants and a shirt. Posed like a movie star—leaning back against a tree with one foot on the ground and the other leg bent at the knee, her foot up against the tree, making it look as if the bottom half of that leg were missing. Miri passed the photo back without commenting.

"Jeffrey and Josh," Frekki said. "Those are your brothers' names."

"What's your wife's name?" Miri asked Mike Monsky.

"Adela."

"Adela. What kind of name is that?"

"It's an old family name."

"Is she Jewish?"

"That's a personal question, Miri," Frekki said.

"I thought we were getting personal."

"She's half, but we're raising the boys Jewish," Mike Monsky said. "I work in my father-in-law's business."

As if she cared enough to ask, *What business?*

He told her anyway. She knew he would. "Shoe stores," he said. "He's got a chain of shoe stores."

Did that mean Mike Monsky was rich?

As if he could read her mind he added, "He's got two sons working in the business, besides me. We were all in the Pacific together."

"Uncle Henry was in the war. He got shot in the leg."

"I'm sorry to hear that," Mike Monsky said.

"How about you?" Miri asked. "Did you get shot?"

"No, I was lucky."

"Rusty says they used to call you 'Lucky.'" This was a complete lie. She didn't know why she said it.

"Really? I never heard that."

"Neither did I," Frekki said.

"Lucky you didn't get caught getting someone pregnant before Rusty." She was getting in too deep now.

"That's a joke, right?" Mike Monsky asked.

She shrugged. "If you say so."

"My daughter's got a great sense of humor," Mike said to Frekki, who just shook her head.

Then he turned back to Miri and smiled. She didn't want to like his smile but she did.

"Please stop calling me your daughter," she told him. "You don't know me."

"You're right. But I hope I'll have the chance to remedy that."

Frekki looked at her watch. "I don't want to break this up but I've got to get home. We have company coming for dinner. Don't forget," she reminded Mike, "seven-thirty, in a tie and jacket."

"Go ahead," Mike Monsky told Frekki. "I'll make sure Miri gets home safe and sound and I'll see you later."

"Take the Cadillac." Frekki passed her car keys to him. "I'll take the Buick."

In the car, he turned on the radio. Pete Seeger and the Weavers were singing "So Long, It's Been Good to Know You"—a song that perfectly described her feelings about today. She bet he was sorry he'd turned to that station. Maybe he did it so he wouldn't have to talk to her on the drive home. Maybe it was to save her from having to talk to him.

When they got close to Sayre Street she told him to drop her off two blocks away, where there was less danger of Rusty or Irene seeing her in the car with him. He turned off the ignition and faced her. "You should know," he said, "I changed my last name to 'Monk' when I married Adela. My sister doesn't know and I'd appreciate it if you didn't tell her. I'd like to be the one to break the news."

"Why are you telling me?"

"You know why. Because you're my daughter."

She bristled.

"It would be your last name, too."

"My last name is Ammerman."

"You know what I mean." He reached for her hand. For one second she looked into his eyes and saw her own. Then she pulled her hand away, jumped out of the car and ran for home.

Later, she remembered the way his hand had felt, warm and strong. *My father,* she thought. That asshole was my father. She reminded herself not to like him. Reminded herself he'd abandoned Rusty before *she* was even born. She didn't know if it happened that way, but she assumed it had. *He planted the seed, then he flew the coop.* She vaguely remembered Rusty telling her that when she was small and asking about her daddy. She had no idea what it meant at the time. She'd imagined a chicken sitting on an egg. Now she heard Irene's voice in her head. *You can't trust the Monskys.* And it was true, wasn't it? Frekki had tricked her. And who was this guy who called himself her "father," really? He could be anybody. His stories could all be invented. No, she would not allow herself to like him.

RUSTY AND IRENE WANTED to hear about her day with Frekki. She told them about the restaurant, the show, ice cream at Gruning's. But she didn't mention Mike Monsky. Seeing him was her latest secret.

"PARK AND SPARK"

JAN. 31—In this so-called "modern age" of the hot rod and snazzy car, the problem of teenagers parking seems to be a big one for parents. But a smart girl will realize that if her popularity hinges on "park and spark" it will be short-lived. There's a price to be paid for free and easy necking. Girls know what a horrible nightmare a girl with a bad reputation must live through.

18

Christina

Christina wasn't thrilled about going on a double date with Mason and Miri. But Jack wanted to do this for his brother, so she would do her best to make sure a good time was had by all. It wasn't that she didn't like spending time with Mason and she had nothing against Miri, though she knew her only from Dr. O's office and as Natalie's friend. It was about not wanting to give up her time alone with Jack. She'd missed her chance last night because she'd had to go with her family to an engagement party for her least favorite of the cousins who worked at Three Brothers.

There would be no time to go to Jack's room tonight,

something she'd been doing lately. Jack wasn't allowed to have overnight guests, wasn't allowed to *entertain* women in his room, so he had to sneak her in, which wasn't that hard. Mrs. O'Malley knew her now, and understood she wasn't Jack's sister. But she also knew Christina was a good girl from a good family and that Jack was not going to take advantage of her so she was willing to look the other way if she caught a glimpse of Christina going up the stairs. It wasn't as easy with Christina's mother. If Christina was unable to be home by 11:30 p.m., she had to call and explain why. And it had better be a good excuse, like a snowstorm, something Mama could see for herself. As far as Mama knew, she was going to the movies with a group of friends tonight, which was almost the truth. She didn't add that the movie was playing in Newark or that it was *The Thing*, which they'd missed when it first came out last spring.

Miri

"What's going on?" Rusty asked Miri. "Why are you dressing up?"

"Mom, I told you I'm going on a double date tonight."

"On a Sunday?"

"Yes, because Mason had to work late last night. We're going with Christina and Jack."

"Who are they?"

"Mason's brother, Jack. And Christina from Dr. O's office."

"Christina goes with Mason's brother?"

"Yes, Jack McKittrick." Why couldn't Rusty keep any of this straight?

"How old is Jack?"

"I don't know. Maybe twenty-one or twenty-two."

"I don't want you going out with someone that old!"

"Mom . . . Christina and Jack are the chaperones. You know Christina from Dr. O's office."

"She seems like a responsible girl," Rusty said, more to herself than to Miri.

"Yes."

"Daisy says good things about her."

"See? And she's going to work for Dr. O full-time next year."

"Where are you going . . . that is, if I give you permission to go."

"To see *The Thing*." Here it comes, Miri thought, bracing herself.

"*The Thing*? I don't want you to see that movie. It's a horror movie. You won't sleep for a week."

She could have said, *It can't be anywhere near as scary as the real things I've seen*, but she didn't. Rusty had the power to send her to her room and keep her there. Instead, she argued, "Mom, please. It's just a movie. It came out last year. It's science fiction. Everyone at school has seen it, even the teachers." This last part was a stretch.

"I'll bet Christina would choose a different movie."

"Yeah, some love story, probably. You want me to see that kind of movie with Mason?"

"No, I do not!"

Miri decided to change the subject. "And then we'll probably stop for burgers."

"Not at the White Castle. They serve horse meat."

"That's just something Nana said to scare you when you were young."

"No, it's the truth. During the war they used horse meat."

"Well, the war is over." What happened to *happy-go-lucky* Rusty from last weekend?

"Korea isn't over."

"That doesn't mean they still serve horse meat." An image of Natalie at summer camp, astride a sleek black horse, popped into her head.

"No burgers at the White Castle," Rusty said. "Do you understand?"

"Okay. No burgers at the White Castle."

"How are you getting there?"

"Jack has a truck. He's a very safe driver."

"How do you know?"

"Because he uses it to get to work. He's an electrician. Christina says he's the best."

"Ha—she's no judge if she's in love. You tell him you're my only child."

"He knows."

"How does he know?"

What was this, the Spanish Inquisition? "Okay, I'll tell him."

"And I want you home by ten. It's a school night, after all. And get all your homework done first."

"I'm almost done with my homework."

Something was making Rusty act crazy tonight. Maybe she was getting her period. Maybe she had a spirit living inside her, too, like Natalie. Maybe it was only a matter of time before the dead moved into all their bodies.

Rusty came in for a hug. Surrounded by her familiar Mom scent, Miri thought, *There's so much I wish I could tell you, Mom, but I can't.*

• • •

THE MOVIE WASN'T as bad or as scary as she'd thought. After, at the White Castle, Miri ordered only fries and a Coke, while the others ate hamburgers. She didn't warn them about eating horse meat. They'd laugh at her, she knew, so she explained that she wasn't that hungry, probably because of the roast chicken Irene had served for Sunday dinner. Jack picked up the check for all of them.

Jack was proud of his '48 Dodge panel truck, keeping it clean and in good shape, his equipment stored in fitted wooden boxes. Miri and Mason sat on a little rug on the floor in the back and necked on the way home, sometimes falling over when the truck took a turn, making them laugh. Once, Christina slid open the little window between the front and back to look in on them. "What's going on? Are you two okay?"

"We're fine," they said at the same time.

"You're sitting up?" Christina asked.

"Like soldiers in a row," Mason said, tightening his fingers around Miri's.

JACK AND CHRISTINA DROPPED Mason and Miri off at her house. It was too cold to sit outside on the steps so they crept down to the basement, something they'd done a couple of times before. It was dark and dank even though Henry had painted the walls and the floor in a pale blue color and the oil burner kept it warm. A single bulb on a pull string gave them light. Piles of cartons were neatly stacked, along with summer furniture for the porch. They sat together on a beach chair until it collapsed, sending them both to the concrete floor, laughing. After that, they unwound a summer rug and lay down on it. The sisal was itchy but it would have been a lot itchier if they weren't fully dressed. They had to be very quiet. Had to whisper. Miri wasn't sure what would happen if they were discovered. Henry would probably be okay with it, and Irene never came to the basement. But Rusty—she never knew with Rusty.

"Let's play Trust," Mason said.

"How do you play?"

"You've never played Trust?"

"No. I've never even heard of it. Is it a board game?"

He took her hand and smiled. "You tell me something you've never told anyone else. Then I tell you."

"You tell me first," Miri said.

He turned toward her, propping himself up on an elbow. "My mom . . ." he began.

He'd never told her anything about his parents. He'd never mentioned either one of them except to say the kaleidoscope had been his mother's. She figured they were dead or he wouldn't be living at Janet Memorial Home.

"My mom," he began again, "she took off after my dad slugged her so hard he knocked out her front teeth and broke her nose and cheekbone. She said next time he'd kill her. 'I'll come back for you, Mason,' she promised the night she came to my room holding a small suitcase. 'I'll come back for you and we'll go away together.' I was eleven and I believed her. Instead they found her on the railroad tracks the next day. She either fell or jumped and the train rolled over her. At the time, nobody bothered to tell me. Easier if I didn't know, they thought. Jack *finally* told me. He said it was an accident but I think she jumped."

Miri didn't know what to say.

"Before she left," Mason continued, "she lay down next to me on my bed and said, 'He won't hurt you. He'd never hurt you. You just stay out of his way when he's drinking. Get out of the house. Go with Jack. Go anywhere. Just get out of his way.' I ran the night he came after me with an ax. Picked up Fred and got the hell out of there. That's the night Jack took me to Janet."

Miri could not stop the hot tears. She covered her face.

"Hey, come on, don't . . ." Mason said. "It's okay."

She shook her head. "It's not okay."

"Yeah, it is. Look, I'm here, aren't I?" He kissed away her tears.

Then it was her turn. What could she possibly confide that was anything compared to his story? How simple her life was next to his. How easy. She had just one secret to share with him. "My mom was never married. The guy who got her pregnant with me . . . his name is Mike Monsky and the day I got my haircut I met him. My mom doesn't know. No one does except my aunt, an aunt I never knew I had."

There, she'd said it. She didn't call him her *father*—because he didn't even know her, had never taken care of her, had never even seen a baby picture of her. What kind of father would that be? Better than one who chases you with an ax, she thought. But it's still cutting you up inside, isn't it?

Part Three

February–April 1952

19

Christina

Christina was at the store, helping her mother and sister get ready for Valentine's Day. They would soon be hosting a special evening for gentlemen only to choose gifts for their wives, even their girlfriends. Nia wasn't crazy about the idea but Athena convinced her to give it a try. "Stop worrying, Mama. The merchandise can only be returned for store credit, so we can't lose. But it won't be returned, because a wife would never insult her husband, who went to all this trouble to please her. Believe me, she'll wear it even if it's something she wouldn't normally be caught dead in."

"Unless she dies of embarrassment," Nia said. "Then she'd be caught dead in it."

"Are you making a joke, Mama?" Athena asked.

"Of course she's making a joke," Christina said. "Isn't that right, Mama?"

Nia just shook her head at her daughters.

Athena was counting on the gentlemen's desire to see their wives in black negligees. The younger ones, especially, but also the ones whose old-world wives wore black every day, though never at bedtime.

"Black," Nia screamed, pretending to faint, as Athena unpacked lacy black nightgowns. "Who would sleep in something black?" She blamed Athena's bad judgment on the pregnancy.

On the day that Athena brought in a window dresser to prepare the store for Valentine's Day, Mrs. Osner came into the shop for the first time.

Athena asked if she could help her.

"I need something to lift my spirits," Mrs. Osner said.

"How about something red?" Athena asked.

"I almost never wear red. But maybe you're right. Maybe I'm in a red mood." She selected a lacy red nightgown and a matching peignoir to go over it. "I'm a small," Mrs. Osner told Athena. "Do you have these in a small?"

"I'm sure we do," Athena said. Then she called, "Christina . . ." in her best voice. "Can you find these in a small?"

Christina stepped out from behind the curtain separating the dressing rooms and the stock from the front shop. "Oh, my goodness, Christina," Mrs. Osner said, surprised. "What are you doing here?"

"This is my mother's store," Christina explained. "My

mother's and my sister's. Athena, this is Mrs. Osner, Dr. Osner's wife."

"I'm so glad to meet you," Athena said.

Mrs. Osner smiled. "And I'm so glad you're carrying these elegant underpinnings. Saves me a trip to East Orange."

"Would you like to put something aside in case Dr. Osner comes in to shop for Valentine's Day?" Athena asked. "We're hosting a special night, for gentlemen only."

"I doubt Dr. Osner will be coming in to shop for Valentine's Day."

"I could drop a hint," Christina said.

"Yes, do that." Mrs. Osner flipped through the nightgowns and held up a silky white one, cut on the bias. And while she was at it she chose half a dozen pairs of underpants, two bras, two half-slips, two full and six pairs of stockings. By the time she was done she'd spent a fortune, more than a hundred dollars.

"When are you due?" she asked as Athena wrapped everything in tissue paper.

"Mid May," Athena told her.

"Lovely—a spring baby. My daughter Natalie was born in spring. Is this your first?"

"No, I have a little boy. He's two. He's home with my grandmother this morning."

"Well, Athena, you'll be seeing more of me. In fact, how about something for my daughter? She's almost fifteen. Something with hearts for Valentine's Day."

Athena showed her pajamas. White with tiny red hearts.

"Perfect," Mrs. Osner said. "Can you gift-wrap it?"

"Of course," Athena said, trying not to show how thrilled she was by a new customer spending so much money all at once.

"I'd better stop at Bob & Betty, too," Mrs. Osner said, "and pick up something for Fern. She's too young for your shop. Maybe slippers with pom-poms."

She wrote a check for her purchases and signed it *Corinne Mendelsohn Osner*. Christina knew plenty about Mrs. Osner's bank accounts. The statements came to the office every month because Mrs. Osner was hopeless at balancing her checkbooks. Christina knew Mrs. Osner came from money. She could afford to buy whatever she wanted whenever she wanted it. She didn't have to ask permission, like the other wives. She didn't have to save out of her household allowance every time she needed a new girdle. But Christina suspected the subject of money was often what led Dr. O to smashing one of the Seven Dwarfs. Christina remembered the last bill from Fishman's, the most expensive women's dress shop in the city, and how, after Dr. O had seen it, he'd exploded, smashing not one, but two of the Seven Dwarfs. Daisy hinted that every time the Osners had a spat, a shopping spree would follow. So, given what she'd just spent, Christina suspected a whopper.

When Mrs. Osner left the shop, Athena said, "Very nice, Christina. You have the makings of an outstanding salesperson. You know how to present yourself. You know how to make helpful suggestions. Why not come to work here after graduation? We could be partners one day. I'm not saying right away, because I'm the one with the experience, but in time we could expand into accessories. Scarves, gloves, bags."

"Thank you, Athena. I'll consider your offer." But Christina had no intention of working with her mother and sister, especially not her sister.

CHRISTINA DIDN'T DROP the hint about a Valentine's Day gift directly to Dr. O. Instead, she told Daisy that Mrs. Osner had put something away at Nia's Lingerie in case Dr. O decided to go shopping. Daisy went to the shop on her own, bought the silky white nightgown for Corinne and handed the gift-wrapped package to Dr. O the next day. "A little bird tells me this is what Corinne would like for Valentine's Day."

"Valentine's Day," Dr. O said. "Is it Valentine's Day already?"

"No, but it will be soon."

"Well, thanks, Daisy. It's very good of you to think of Corinne. Write yourself a check for the amount of the gift and I'll sign it."

Elizabeth Daily Post

KING GEORGE VI DIES

British Mourn Wartime Leader

20

Miri

The King of England died on February 6, and now Princess Elizabeth would be queen. She was twenty-five years old. Miri wondered how she felt knowing she'd be queen for the rest of her life. Was she sad that her father died but excited about being queen? Did she ever wish she were still a girl, a regular girl? Because Miri did. Sometimes she wished she were a little kid again. Everything was so simple then. Now she never knew when she was going to find out something terrible, something she didn't want to know. Sometimes her jaw ached in the morning. She wondered if Princess Elizabeth's jaw ever ached.

She wasn't going to tell Rusty, or anyone else, about this. She wasn't going to tell that sometimes she tossed and turned all night. Sometimes she woke up tired. Life felt harder than it ever had before. Sometimes she felt angry, frustrated, often sad. She thought being in love could cure anything but she was finding out that wasn't always true.

She and Suzanne had chipped in to buy a big stuffed panda bear for Betsy Foster but Suzanne's mother explained they couldn't visit her at the hospital. Betsy was still in isolation because of the burns. *Maybe in a few weeks*, Mrs. Dietz had told them. Miri agreed to keep the panda, wrapped in cellophane, in her room. The problem was, every time she looked at it, it reminded her of what had happened. She tried putting it in her closet on the shelf but it didn't fit upright, so she laid it on its back. Which in a way was worse, because then it reminded her of Penny in a coffin. Finally, she set it on its belly and covered it with a spare blanket.

And now—surprise—there was a letter from Mike Monsky. What was he thinking, writing a letter to her? She supposed she should be grateful he sent it in care of Frekki and Frekki put it in a plain envelope and forwarded it to her. Still, what if Rusty saw it? What if Irene did?

Dear Miri,
    I'm back in Los Altos and I've shown your photo, the one Frekki took of you in front of the Paper Mill Playhouse, to Adela and the boys. All three are anxious to meet you and hope you can visit over the summer.
                                            Yours,
                                            Dad (Mike Monk)

Dad? He had the guts to call himself *Dad?* And Adela wasn't surprised? She didn't get angry when she found out he had a secret child? Maybe she believed Mike *Monk* when he told her it was a surprise to him to learn he had a fifteen-year-old daughter. Maybe Adela believed whatever he told her. Or maybe they had a big fight over it.

Maybe Adela accused him of being a liar. *Liar, liar, pants on fire*, the little boys would have sung, circling their father. Why did he have to go and write to her? Why couldn't he just leave her alone? But was that what she wanted—for him to leave her alone? She didn't know. She folded the letter into smaller and smaller squares, then shoved it into a sock. It could have been a piece of lint. Toe jam in the bottom of her sock. Rusty would never bother to unroll a pair of socks. As far as Miri knew, Rusty never snooped around in her room. She was pretty sure Rusty trusted her. She was just covering all her bases.

TODAY SHE HAD a morning appointment with Dr. O and Rusty was going with her. "I need a pair of shoes," Rusty said. "And Dr. Osner said he'd fix my chipped tooth at the end of your appointment. Two birds with one stone."

The shoe store, Kolber Sladkus, was next to Three Brothers Luncheonette on the street level of the Martin Building, where Dr. O had his office. While Rusty was trying on shoes, black suede pumps with three-inch heels and a peep toe, on sale to make room for the spring line, Miri slipped her feet into the fluoroscope machine, where she peered into the viewfinder to see her bones, eerily green inside her shoes. Seeing her bones that way made her think of something from outer space. The boys at school were all walking around like zombies with their arms outstretched, making the girls scream. Winky Herkovitz said a flying saucer was causing the planes to crash. You couldn't see it. It was hovering above Elizabeth and when it wanted to cause a plane to crash, it did. What was it with the boys in her class? Was it that they liked the idea of spaceships and zombies? Was it too scary to think about what really made the planes crash?

Rusty paraded around the shoe store in her peep-toe heels, admiring them in the mirror. "What do you think?" she asked Miri.

"Nice," Miri said.

"They're for dress, not work. I might leave them at the office for special occasions."

How often did Rusty wear dress shoes? Maybe to the theater. Maybe to a holiday party.

Miri wasn't listening as Rusty went on about the shoes, until Rusty surprised her by asking, "How about it, honey? Would you like a new pair of shoes for Passover?"

"Passover? That's not until April this year."

"I know . . . but look at these patent-leather slingbacks. Aren't they cute?"

Rusty was acting strange today, but if she was offering new shoes, Miri wasn't going to argue.

Mrs. Kolber, who had fitted Miri for shoes as long as she could remember, brought out the slingbacks for Miri to try. "They're expensive," Miri said, eyeing the price on the box.

"You know what Nana says," Rusty told her. "They're your feet. You'll need them for the rest of your life. Treat them well."

Irene was proud of her pretty, well-shaped, well-cared-for feet. She massaged them with Pond's cold cream every night. No bunions for her from wearing shoes that didn't fit. Mrs. Kolber didn't have to pad Irene's shoes, like she did with some of her friends, to make sure she'd be comfortable in her everyday oxfords and her black pumps.

"You only live once," Mrs. Kolber sang. That was

probably how she got customers to shell out money for expensive new shoes.

Miri got out of her saddle shoes, pulled off her thick white socks and pulled on the peds Mrs. Kolber offered. When she slipped her feet into the new shoes and stood up, Mrs. Kolber pressed on her toes to see how close they came to the toe box, then told her to walk around to make sure she wasn't slipping out of the slingback. She'd never had slingback shoes. They made her feel like dancing.

While the shoes were being wrapped, Rusty wrote a check to pay for them. Instead of biting her lip the way she usually did when it came to parting with money, she was humming to herself. She hummed in the elevator all the way to Dr. O's office on the third floor. Miri wasn't sure about this happy-go-lucky Rusty. It made her nervous. On the way down the hall they passed the medical lab and Miri poked her head in the way she always did, to see the fat white rabbits in their cages. Natalie told her they had something to do with finding out if you were pregnant. Something about urine was involved. But neither of them understood how it worked. Once, Miri had a blood test at the lab to see if she was anemic. She wasn't.

In the waiting room of Dr. O's office, a little boy played with a small dog on the floor while his mother sat on the sofa and leafed through a magazine. As soon as Miri entered, the dog ran to her. "Fred!" Miri picked him up. "What are you doing here?"

"You know Fred?" the mother asked. Her English was heavily accented and she was good-looking, with big blue eyes, blond baloney curls hanging down her back, big breasts and just plump enough to make the boys whistle.

"Fred belongs to my friend Mason," Miri said, trying

to talk slowly, pronouncing every syllable in every word, in case she didn't understand.

"Very nice boy, Mason. I know from Janet. Always making us laugh. I'm Polina and this, my son, Stash."

Oh. Polina. Miri got a pang, thinking that Mason was friends with her.

Rusty looked up from the magazine she'd been flipping through. "I'm Rusty Ammerman, and this is my daughter, Miri."

"Very nice meeting," Polina said.

"Mason told me you live . . ." Miri began. "I mean *lived* in one of the houses that was hit but you were lucky because you weren't home."

"Very lucky. And lucky Miss Daisy took us home to stay. Miss Daisy so wonderful. Like mother to us. But we need find new place to live."

"Maybe we can help," Rusty said. "We have a family friend who owns apartment buildings."

Miri looked over at Rusty. Was she talking about Ben Sapphire?

"Would be so good," Polina said.

"How did Fred get here?" Miri asked.

"Fred!" Stash said, clapping his hands. Fred barked.

The door to the inside office opened and Christina stepped out. "I'm sorry," she said, "but we can't allow pets in the office, not even in the waiting area."

"Fred!" Stash said again, but Fred didn't bark this time.

"I know it's Fred," Christina said. "But even Fred can't be in the waiting room. It's against the rules."

Polina stood up. "Come, Stash. We take Fred for walk now." She turned to Christina. "Please tell Miss Daisy we come back later, for ride home." To Rusty she said,

"Very nice meet you." And to Miri, "Very nice meet you, too."

Before Miri could say anything else Christina ushered her into the office. "We're ready for you, Miri."

Christina was professional around her. She clipped on the white towel over the cape, and prepared the little pleated paper cup. How did they get the pleats into the paper? Miri wondered. Was it someone's job or was there a machine that did it? How come she'd never seen pleated cups anywhere but at Dr. O's office? She supposed other dentists also used them. But she'd never been to any other dentist. Christina poured a small amount of Lavoris mouthwash into the cup. Miri rinsed and spit before Dr. O came in, asking, "How's my favorite patient?" He probably said that to everyone but Miri liked hearing it anyway.

He began to poke around in her mouth, with Christina assisting. "What music would you like to hear today, Miss Mirabelle?"

Dr. O could whistle any tune, from the Top 40 to classical. Miri thought he'd surely win if he went on Arthur Godfrey's talent show. "Surprise me," Miri told him. And he did, whistling "How High the Moon." Miri relaxed, closed her eyes and thought of Mason. She cringed a couple of times during the drilling of the small cavity but it wasn't that bad. Just as Dr. O promised, she didn't need Novocain.

When the tooth was filled and Miri had rinsed, Dr. O said, "So how are you doing, Mirabelle?"

"Okay."

"Not worried about anything?"

"What would I worry about?" *Only everything.* Was he going to ask her about Natalie, and if so, what would she tell him?

"Does your jaw ever ache in the morning?"

"Sometimes." *How did he know? Please don't tell my mother if I have a terrible disease.*

"Looks like you're grinding your teeth."

Grinding?

"Understandable, given what you've been through. We can make you a device to wear at night to prevent the clenching and grinding."

"What kind of device?"

"Just something that fits over your teeth."

"Suppose I don't want a device?"

"Grinding can damage your teeth."

Damage?

"We carry anxiety in different ways."

Anxiety?

"Tell you what. We'll recheck in a month to see how you're doing. Okay with you, Miss Mirabelle?"

"Okay."

"Good." He smiled at her. "How come I haven't seen you around our house lately?"

"I was there on the day of . . . on the day of . . ."

"Yes, I know." He paused. "Well, I don't want to spoil Natalie's surprise. She'll want to tell you herself. She's in New York today, at dance class."

"But I'll see her tonight at bowling."

"Since when does Nat bowl?"

"She's our scorekeeper." Natalie couldn't take the chance of dropping a ball, or having someone else drop a ball on her foot.

"Ah, the scorekeeper," Dr. O said.

• • •

AT THE BOWLING ALLEY that night, Mason was tender, making sure her shoes fit, squeezing to check for enough toe room, just like Mrs. Kolber, choosing exactly the right bowling ball for her weight. She'd always been hopeless at bowling but now, with a few pointers from Mason, she was improving. Robo was the best in their group, gliding to the line, right foot behind her left, with a follow-through every time. Miri was paying attention to Robo's form, keeping a picture of Robo in her mind when it was her turn and it was starting to pay off. But soon Robo would be moving and Miri would have to find someone else to follow.

When Mason stopped by their station he ruffled Miri's hair, making the other girls sigh. Mason called her new haircut "cute" but Miri knew he didn't really like it. She assured him it would grow quickly, an inch a month, she'd heard, and just to be sure she'd already started to gently tug it, the way she did a pair of dungarees that had shrunk in the wash. She expected to be halfway there by summer, by the time of Henry and Leah's wedding. She was waiting until invitations went out to ask if she could invite Mason to be her date.

Mason pointed to a barrel-chested man, bowling in the next lane. "Joey Politics," he said. "He knows everybody and everything."

The girls looked over for a minute but really, what did they care about somebody called Joey Politics.

She told Mason about meeting Polina at Dr. O's office. "My mother's going to ask Ben Sapphire if he can find her and Stash a place to live."

"That'd be good." And just like that, he leaned in and kissed her, the first time they'd kissed in public, in front of Suzanne, Eleanor, Robo and Natalie. Then he kissed her again, until his boss called, "Enough, lover boy. You got a line waiting for shoes and I need a pin boy in lane six."

The girls teased her, humming the wedding march. "Have you set the date yet?" Robo asked.

"Stop!" Miri shouted, louder than she'd meant to, and they laughed, all but Natalie.

"It's freezing in here," Natalie said, wrapping a wool scarf around her neck. She was swathed in sweaters, and had her coat draped over her shoulders.

"If you bowled you'd be boiling," Suzanne told her, stripping down to a cotton shirt with her name embroidered across the pocket, like the ladies who played in leagues.

Miri threw her first strike that night, which she took as a sign that every day something good can happen. And today was a bonanza—new shoes, Mason's kisses and a strike.

Later, before Eleanor's father picked them up, Natalie took her aside. "Come to my house tomorrow morning. I have something to show you."

"Is it the surprise your father talked about?"

"He told you about the surprise?"

"Only that you have one. So what is it?"

"If I tell you it won't be a surprise. And don't say anything to the other girls, okay? I'm not ready to tell them yet."

Miri remembered the last time she'd gone to Natalie's, just her, and it turned out to be the worst day of her life.

THE SURPRISE WAS the finished basement. It had been transformed into a dance studio, with a mirrored wall, a barre and a wood floor. The jukebox still stood in the corner but instead of Nat King Cole and Patti Page, it held the kind of music you hear in movie musicals. *Blue skies smilin' at me . . .*

"Isn't it fabulous?" Natalie asked. "The floor is genuine maple, the best for tap." She hummed and did a couple of warm-up steps, then stopped and looked at Miri. "Say something."

"All the furniture is gone." Miri knew that wasn't what Natalie wanted to hear but she couldn't hide her disappointment.

"That's it?" Natalie asked, annoyed.

"No . . . I mean, it's great. But . . ."

"But what?"

"I'll miss the parties." This is where she and Mason met and danced for the first time. She'd been hoping Natalie would host another get-together soon. Maybe for Valentine's Day.

"We can still have parties," Natalie said. "The furniture is in the garage. Daddy and Steve can bring it back in anytime. Not that I have time for parties these days." Natalie pulled off one sweater, then another, and tossed them across the room. She stepped out of her dungarees and kicked them to the corner. Then she stood in front of the mirrored wall, in her long-sleeved black leotard, black tights, white little-girl socks trimmed in lace and black tap shoes with small heels and a Mary Jane strap. It had been ages since Miri had seen her without layers of clothing. The size of her took Miri's breath away.

"Why are you staring that way?" Natalie asked.

"What way?"

"Like you're in shock."

"Well, I am, sort of. You're so thin."

"I know. Isn't it great? Ruby's been coaching me. I eat green grapes and drink a ton of water. Dancers have to stay hydrated." Natalie posed. First position, second position, fifth position. "You know what I see when I look in the mirror?"

Miri was almost afraid to hear her say it.

"I see Ruby." She didn't wait for Miri's reaction. "I'm never alone now. She's given me the greatest gift a person can give. She's given me her life."

Miri felt something roiling inside her. She looked away, angry at Natalie for not eating, angry for acting crazy, angry for throwing away their friendship. But she was scared, too. Scared there was something really wrong with her. Scared that she and Natalie would never be friends again. That they'd never know what the other was thinking, that Natalie would never rest her head in Miri's lap while they watched television. Inseparable. That's what everyone said about them back in seventh grade. *Come back!* she wanted to shout. *Come back and be my friend.*

Natalie misunderstood Miri's expression. "You're jealous of Ruby?"

"Why would I be jealous of Ruby? She's dead."

"She's not dead," Natalie said. "Why can't you understand? Why won't you even try?"

"I don't like the way she's changed you."

"You've changed, too, since Mason. And just so you know, you're not the only one in love. I'm in love with this, with dance. Dance is my life. There is nothing else."

"Yes, there is. There's school and friends and your family. Some people would give anything for your family."

Natalie shook her head. "You don't know anything."

Miri didn't like the way Natalie said that, as if maybe there was something Natalie knew that she didn't. It hurt to think she had a secret she couldn't share with Miri. Not that Miri had shared her secret about Mike Monsky, but there was a difference between having a secret no one suspected and having one you dropped hints about, wasn't there?

"Maybe you should tell your parents about Ruby," Miri said. "Maybe they can help."

"Help? I don't need help. I've never been happier." She pressed the *play* button and the jukebox came to life. She snapped her fingers a few times and began to tap as Judy Garland's voice sang, *"Forget your troubles, come on, get happy."* She tapped across the room and back, then paused, looked at Miri and smiled a smile Miri didn't recognize, a hard smile—maybe it was Ruby's, maybe not, but it sent shivers down Miri's spine. She took a couple of slow turns around the floor, then began to turn faster and faster until she was spinning, spinning like some kind of whirling dervish right out of their social studies book.

"Stop . . ." Miri called. "Stop!" But Natalie didn't stop. Her eyes glazed over, as she twirled faster and faster, until her face turned almost purple.

Miri ran upstairs, found Dr. O and Corinne in the kitchen eating bagels. "What is it?" Corinne asked, reading Miri's face.

"Natalie," Miri said.

They both jumped up and followed Miri downstairs, where Natalie was still spinning to Judy Garland. *"Get ready for the Judgment Day . . ."*

Miri pressed the *off* button on the jukebox. The room fell silent, except for Natalie's taps. Dr. O grabbed her.

"Natalie . . . sweetheart . . ." He lifted her into his arms. "My god. She's light as a feather," he said to Corinne.

Natalie's feet kept moving. Somewhere she or Ruby was still tapping.

"Call Harry Reiss," Dr. O said to Corinne. Dr. Reiss was a doctor, but also their friend. He was at their New Year's Eve party, in the conga line.

"It's Sunday," Corinne said.

"Call him at home," Dr. O said.

"No."

"Call him, Corinne, or I'm taking her straight to the hospital."

"You have no idea what's going on in this house, Arthur. You're too busy solving everyone else's problems to see that your son is in despair and your daughter is losing her mind. You think giving her a dance studio at home is going to fix this?" She swept her arm around the room. "Don't you see . . ." Corinne began to cry. "I'm utterly alone. I don't even have Mrs. Barnes to help and she's never coming back."

"You have friends."

"I wouldn't tell my friends one word about what's happening to us. Not one word."

Miri didn't want to hear this, didn't want to witness the end of the perfect family. The end of her fantasies. Now Natalie was slumped against her father like a rag doll.

Miri snuck up the stairs and out the back door while Corinne's and Dr. O's voices rose and fell and rose again. She rode her bike home and collapsed into Irene's arms. "What's wrong, sweetie pie?" Irene asked, holding her. And for once, she didn't ask any more questions.

There's Plenty to DO and Plenty to SEE Wherever You Go in

Florida

From the Northwest Tip to the Romantic Keys,
You'll Find Infinite Variety.
That's Why So Many Thousands Come Down and Enjoy
the Glorious Sunshine
Outdoor Sports
and Scenic Wonders

Get in the NATIONAL Habit
Fly National Airlines
Airline of the Stars

Finest Aircraft! Finest Service!

21

Gaby

Gaby Wenders always wanted to fly. She'd wave to the planes as they flew across the wide-open fields behind her grandmother's house on their approach to Vandalia Airport between Dayton and Springfield, imagining the exciting lives of the passengers inside the silver ship—all of them rich and good-looking, all of them dressed in the stylish travel clothes she'd seen in her older sister's fashion magazines.

At thirteen, she'd stand in front of the mirror and practice. *Welcome aboard, ladies and gentlemen*, she would say in her new, well-modulated voice. *I am your lovely and perfectly groomed air hostess, Miss Gabrielle Wenders. Your pilot today is Scotty Champion.* She'd smile ever so slightly, her fingertips touching the silver wings on the lapel of her suit jacket. Captain Scotty Champion would be so handsome the female passengers would swoon at the sight of him. She might marry Scotty Champion someday, but not for many years, at least three, because she'd worked hard for her career and wasn't about to give it up for marriage.

In high school Gaby sent away for a brochure. She'd memorized it in the first week but she still liked to see it in print before closing her eyes at night.

Girls Wanted to Enter Flight Stewardess Training Group

Here is the Career Opportunity for Which You Have Been Waiting!

If you are interested and feel that you can meet all of the qualifications below, please write in detail and attach a full length photograph.

HEIGHT: Between 5'2" and 5'6"
WEIGHT: 135 pounds maximum
ATTRACTIVE: "Just below Hollywood" standards
PLENTY OF PERSONALITY AND POISE
GENDER: Female
MARITAL STATUS: Single, Not Divorced, Separated or Widowed
RACE: White
AGE: 21–26 years old
EDUCATION: Registered Nurse or Two Years of College
VISION: 20/20 without glasses

Must be a US citizen and available for training within 6 months. If you feel you qualify—

If? Gaby thought. *Come on!* She qualified with a capital Q. To get her parents' blessing she showed them a line in a magazine about how being a stewardess was a career for "Wives-in-Training." She knew they'd approve of that.

Getting her RN degree at the local hospital took two years, and Gaby worked for a year after that, until she could apply, which she did, on her twenty-first birthday. At the time she was still living at home with her parents and her younger brothers, her older sister long married, with four-year-old twins, another on the way and a husband who operated a forklift. They lived in a little white house near her grandmother's place. "You'll be able to wave to me," she told her young nieces, "the way I used to wave to the planes."

"Will you wave back?" one of the girls asked.

"Of course I will."

Gaby chose National Airlines, in part because she'd read that American received 20,000 applications the year before, for just 347 stewardess positions. Not that she doubted her qualifications, not for a minute, but Gaby went for National anyway, and was accepted, the only applicant out of 29 being interviewed on the same day. She was jubilant. Hard work and a positive attitude paid off.

She'd been careful about dating after high school, not wanting to get serious with some local boy who'd expect her to give up her dreams for his, produce two babies, preferably one of each sex, wear an apron over her shirt-waist dress and have dinner on the table every night at 6 p.m. No thank you. There was a young doctor at the hospital but he was almost as dangerous as the others. If she confided her dream to him he'd drop her like a hot potato. Still, she went out with him, not that he had much time off, but she never told her mother. And sometimes, when their breaks coincided, they'd get into his car and kiss until the windows steamed up. She'd stop him when he tried to get his hand under her skirt. "Please," he begged. "Just this once. I'm a doctor. Doesn't that count for something?"

Ha! Gaby had a goal, and no doctor or anyone else was going to dissuade her. She knew there would be plenty of nurses for him to flirt with once she was out of the picture. Nurses who would let him get under their skirts. She couldn't worry about that. If some other nurse got him to put a ring on her finger while Gaby was flying, well, so be it.

"Oh, Gabrielle," her mother cried as she'd packed her bag to head for training in Newark. "I'd hoped you'd meet a handsome doctor at the hospital and give up this crazy idea of flying."

Now, eighteen months later, she had no regrets about leaving Dayton or young Dr. Larsen. She loved her job. As far as she was concerned it was the best job in the world. In the stewardesses' dressing room at Newark Airport Gaby applied her makeup as she'd been taught in her program. A good base over the face and throat. Heavy enough to hide imperfections in the skin but light enough to look almost natural, a hint of color to the cheeks, brows penciled in, mascara to upper lashes only, no more high school lipstick. This month she was using Revlon's Love That Red.

She brushed out her hair, cut in a becoming style that never touched the collar of her suit jacket, and fastened her jaunty cap, which she had to leave on for the duration of the flight, not that she minded. She loved wearing her perfectly tailored and pressed suit, with the crisp white blouse and navy-blue heels, the leather bag swinging from her shoulder.

She wouldn't need her London Fog overcoat, with her name stitched inside, a detail that made her proud, in Miami. But she'd take the London Fog raincoat, just in case. She swore she would save these two coats, part of her uniform, forever. She pulled on her white gloves, as required.

A quick look in the full-length mirror proved her uniform was smooth over her posterior. You never knew when the chief stewardess might show up to run a checklist, observing the dress and work habits of the girls, an evaluation procedure most of them dreaded. Gaby could have done without the required girdle but understood it was part of the whole package, and it served her well whenever some passenger in the aisle seat, usually a smoker ordering a drink, let his hand, accidentally on purpose, run over her backside as she was serving him.

Some of the girls flirted with passengers, hoping they'd meet a rich guy to marry, but not Gaby. True, she sometimes went to dinner in Miami with one of her regular passengers, but she didn't call that dating. He was older, still very handsome, a real gentleman. He had a place in Miami on one of the private islands, and another in New Jersey, and was starting a business in Las Vegas. He sat in first class, always in the bulkhead seat, where he had more room to stretch those long legs. She'd heard his companions call him "Longy." But she called him "Mr. Zwillman" and he called her "doll." Oh, sure, he was probably married, but so what? She wasn't interested in marrying him. Or being his girlfriend. But dinner at the best restaurants in Miami Beach, ringside tables at the best nightclubs—that was something else. Vic Damone had joined them one night after his show. He'd signed her menu—*To Gaby. Your a nice girl.* Okay, so he'd forgotten *you're* is a contraction. With his voice and looks, who cared about contractions?

She didn't believe the girls who'd tried to tell her Longy was a gangster, that he'd killed people. That was malicious gossip. He was a businessman, a very successful businessman. And so polite. Always asking about her family. She enjoyed riding in his baby blue Cadillac convertible, looking up at the stars over Miami Beach.

"Has he given you jewelry yet?" Cleo, another stewardess, asked.

"No, why would he give me jewelry?" Gaby said. "I'm not his girlfriend."

"Then what are you?"

Gaby wasn't sure how to respond, so she just shrugged.

"Honey, you might as well get something out of it," Cleo said. "Ask him to take you shopping."

Later, Gaby realized that Cleo thought she was sleeping with Longy. What a revolting thought! Or was it? She was no fool—she noticed the way he looked at her. And hadn't he once asked if she could find him attractive? She began to imagine a romantic weekend in Havana. He was always flying to Cuba on business. Maybe next time he was on her flight, next time she went to dinner with him in Miami.

But Mr. Zwillman wasn't on her flight list tonight.

In the departure lounge, where music was piped in, "I'll See You in My Dreams" was playing. Gaby had seen the movie twice, once in Miami, and once in New York at

Radio City Music Hall. She'd written her mother about the plush red seats, the stage show, the Rockettes, to prove how glamorous her life was compared to what it would have been if she'd stayed in Dayton. Her mother wrote back, *Just be careful.* That was her mother's standard response to everything. *Be careful of what?* she wanted to ask, but she never did. She already knew the answer. *Be careful of life.*

Christina

Christina and Jack went to the early Valentine's Day party at Twin City Roller Rink. All the girls wore something red and the boys were given red bow ties to clip onto their collars. Christina's friend Gina told her she looked sexy in her clingy red jersey top when they went to the ladies' room to freshen their lipstick and comb their hair. "God, I wish I had your boobs."

Christina blushed but she knew it was true. She felt sexy tonight. She'd never worn anything red, let alone anything that clung to her body.

Later, when she and Jack were in his room, on his bed, kissing, she knew this would be the night. Not that she'd planned it. She just didn't try to stop it this time. On the bedside radio Tony Bennett was singing "Because of You." The volume was turned down so as not to disturb Mrs. O'Malley or the boarders. Between Tony Bennett's sexy voice, and Jack's warm breath as he nibbled her earlobe, she was lost in another world. Somewhere a cat was purring, which struck her as odd because Jack didn't have a cat, but who cared? Who cared about anything?

He unbuttoned her blouse, not for the first time, reached around and unhooked her bra, something she'd let him do before, even though she knew what that could lead to, she knew very well. He groaned when her breasts spilled out of her full B cups. *I dreamed I was bewitching in my Maidenform bra.* Moonlight streamed through the window. His hands were warm as he gently stroked her breasts, his fingers passing over her nipples, pausing just long enough to make them hard, then his breath was on them, as he kissed one, then the other. He pulled off his shirt so he could feel them against his naked chest. She closed her eyes, giving in to the rush between her legs. When he reached under her skirt, he hesitated for a second. She wasn't wearing a panty girdle tonight, just a garter belt, stockings and nylon undies. This was where she always stopped him, whispering, *No, Jack, we can't.* But she didn't stop him tonight. If he was surprised she couldn't tell. Her undies slipped off, then he was getting out of his trousers.

She kept her eyes closed. He was naked next to her and she was naked, though she didn't remember stepping out of her skirt or pulling down her half-slip—what did it matter . . . *sweet Jesus,* nobody told her it would feel this good to have his hands stroking her there. Someone else was singing now and the cat was purring louder, the cat was moaning, or wait—was it her? Yes, those sounds were coming from her. She felt something pushing against her, then slipping inside her. And she wanted it, she wanted it. Then a short, quick pain—did she cry out? Maybe, but she didn't say *stop.* She didn't say *no.* Her body tensed . . . *what if, what if . . .* But soon he stopped moving and let out one deep groan, and something warm was on her belly. Warm, like a dollop of thick sauce. He wiped it up with his underwear then kissed the spot where it landed as if it were sacred ground.

Natalie

Natalie lay against the pillows in her bed at Elizabeth General Hospital. Nurse Kirkegaard, who her parents had hired as her private duty night nurse, watched over her. Natalie was supposed to be sleeping but she never slept, not if she could help it. She was weak and tired but sleep was out of the question. She had a needle in her arm attached to a tube. "Just fluids to keep you hydrated," Nurse Kirkegaard explained.

"I want to go home," Natalie said.

"I know," Nurse K said, "and you will, as soon as you're able to eat, as soon as you're strong enough."

"I'm very strong," Natalie told her. "I can dance for hours without getting tired."

"Oh, you're a dancer?"

"Yes."

"My daughter is an actress. Maybe you've heard of her? Phyllis Kirk."

"Your daughter is Phyllis Kirk?" Now the nurse had Natalie's full attention. Phyllis Kirk was famous. The magazines were always running stories about her. Everyone knew she was from Elizabeth, had gone to Battin High. Everyone knew her mother was a nurse at Elizabeth General but Natalie never dreamed *this* nurse, who was middle-aged and stout and not beautiful, could possibly be her mother.

"She changed her name from Kirkegaard to Kirk," the nurse explained. "It's a stage name."

"I'm going to have a stage name, too."

"Natalie is a lovely name," Nurse K said. "Look at Natalie Wood."

"Yes, but I don't want people to confuse me with her. I was thinking of Ruby."

"Like Ruby Keeler, the tap dancer?"

"No, like Ruby Granik."

"The girl who was killed in the plane crash?"

"You know about her?" Natalie was surprised. She would never have expected Nurse Kirkegaard to know anything about Ruby.

"My daughter met her a few times."

"Really? Ruby knew Phyllis Kirk? She never mentioned that."

"You knew Ruby?" Nurse K asked.

"Yes."

"A tragedy."

"Yes." Natalie looked out the window at the night sky and thought about changing her name to *Ruby Night. Ruby Skye. Ruby Starr.* But she wasn't sure Ruby would want her to use *her* name. She yawned.

"How about a bedtime snack?" Nurse K asked. "I could make you a strawberry milk shake."

"I'd just throw it up," Natalie said. "It's better when I don't eat because I really don't like throwing up. I wish they'd figure out what's wrong with me so I can go home."

"Tomorrow you'll have some tests."

"I'm so cold," Natalie said. "I'm cold all the time."

Nurse K pulled another blanket over her, to stop her shivering.

"Am I going to die?"

"You're going to get well." Nurse K smoothed Natalie's hair, which had been falling out. Natalie had collected it and stuffed it into an envelope. You could see patches of her pink scalp.

"Did you know Phyllis had polio when she was a girl?" Nurse K asked.

"What? No."

"But she overcame it and so will you."

"You think I have polio?"

"No," Nurse K said. "I'm just saying that if Phyllis could get better, you can, too. And I'll let you in on a secret. Phyllis is up for a leading role in a very big picture opposite Vincent Price. It's going to be the first 3-D movie."

"What's 3-D?" It sounded like a bra size.

"I'm not sure myself but it's a very big deal. You have to promise to keep this to yourself."

"I promise," Natalie said. "I have a secret, too, but I can't tell you."

"You might feel better if you did."

"No." Natalie looked out the window again. "I tried telling my best friend but she didn't believe me. Either that or she thought I was crazy."

"Well, I'd believe you. Keeping secrets locked up inside isn't healthy. It can make you sick."

"You think that's why I'm sick?"

Nurse K took her hand. "Close your eyes and I'll sing you the same lullaby I used to sing to Phyllis when she was scared and couldn't sleep."

"But I don't want to sleep. If I do I might never wake up."

Gaby

Gaby welcomed her passengers aboard the first of two sections of the flight to Miami, due to leave at midnight. The second was scheduled for departure forty-three minutes later.

The passengers' names were on a seating chart, making it easy for Gaby to greet each one by name once they were seated. Mr. Venturini and Mr. Griffiths, friends headed to Fort Lauderdale for a week of fishing, asked if they could change seats. They wanted to sit together up front but had to settle for two in the same row at the rear of the plane. At least they didn't make a fuss about it. A priest, Father Good, sat at the emergency exit. He looked young and strong. He could handle it if he had to. Gaby wondered if he'd become a priest because of his name.

She had seen a married couple kissing goodbye at the gate. "See you in Miami, darling," the husband had said. Now the wife, sitting in the second row, explained to Gaby that she and her husband were celebrating their tenth anniversary but they never traveled on the same plane. This was nothing new to Gaby. Many couples flew separately. That way, if something bad happened, the children would be left with at least one parent. Some of them even divided the children, the wife flying with one, the husband with the other. Gaby wondered if she'd do the same. She didn't think so. She was no Nervous Nellie. She was a professional. Besides, flying was safer than driving.

She hung up the passengers' coats and handed out magazines. Neither of the two honeymoon couples wanted anything to read. They'd probably smooch all the way to Miami or else fall asleep from the stress of the wedding and arrive too tired to fully enjoy their wedding night. Not that Gaby was anyone to comment on that.

It was too late for a dinner flight. She'd be serving just a midnight snack and a beverage. Many of her passengers would sleep all the way to Miami. She'd probably have to tap their shoulders to wake them, saying, *We've arrived, sir.*

She delivered the paperwork to the cockpit. The captain was in the left seat, copilot in the right, flight engineer in the jump seat. He was engaged to one of the stewardesses from Gaby's class. All three were gentlemen. She'd flown with them many times. They kept their hands to themselves, which was more than she could say about some crews. She had to laugh when she thought about her fantasy pilot, Scotty Champion—if he existed she hadn't met him yet. And now that she knew something about a pilot's life she wasn't interested in marrying one—someday, when she was ready to get married, that is.

"Miss," one of her passengers, an anxious older woman in an aisle seat, called, "when can I use the restroom?"

"Do you need to use it?" Gaby asked.

"No. I'm just thinking ahead."

"After we take off and reach our cruising altitude, you'll be free to get up and use the restroom." Gaby smiled, trying to reassure her, betting this was her first flight.

"It's my first time flying," she told Gaby. "I'm visiting my son and daughter-in-law. They have a new baby."

"That's lovely, Mrs. Iverson," Gaby said. The passengers loved it when she called them by name.

Mrs. Iverson held up a tiny sweater she was knitting. "Do you think babies need sweaters in Miami?"

"I'm sure they do. I've worn sweaters, myself, especially in the evening."

She gave Mrs. Iverson two years, max, before she, too, made Florida her home. When Mrs. Iverson reached for Gaby's hand, Gaby let her hold it. "The weather's perfect all the way down," she said in a reassuring voice. "You'll get to see the moon. You just relax and breathe through your nose." Mrs. Iverson nodded. Gaby patted her hand.

"It will be so smooth you'll probably fall asleep and when you wake up you'll be in Miami."

SHE HANDED OUT silver wings to the children, always a big hit, and a deck of playing cards to anyone who wanted them. A mother and her teenage daughter took a pack. "Gin?" the mother asked her daughter, as she shuffled the cards.

"You know I always beat you," the daughter said.

"Maybe tonight's my lucky night," the mother said, laughing.

So far, no drunks. That was good news. A late-night flight meant drinking at the bar in the departure lounge before boarding, which could translate into trouble on board.

Tomorrow Gaby could lie on the beach all day, soaking up the winter sun. Never mind what her mother said about the sun ruining her skin. How would her mother know? She'd never sunbathed. She'd never been to Miami.

One more time down the aisle checking to make sure the passengers had their seat belts fastened. She turned off the dome lights and switched on the night-lights. Most passengers kept their reading lights on, except for the ones who were already asleep or planning to be asleep.

Gaby didn't like sitting in the rear jump seat, facing away from the passengers. She preferred to keep an eye on them. But rules were rules, and she strapped herself in for takeoff. The wheels of the four-engine DC-6 lifted off at 12:18 a.m., carrying fifty-nine passengers, a crew of four, and 2,953 pounds of mail, baggage and air-freight parcels.

The plane climbed to what she thought was 1,000 feet or less. One of the engines didn't sound right. Gaby had been on other flights where engines had conked out but this was different. It made a horrible sputtering sound. She couldn't be sure but it might have been two engines, because besides the sputtering noise, she heard what sounded like firecrackers. The plane dropped one hundred feet, and with it her stomach. The captain put full force on the power but the plane kept losing altitude.

Right then, she knew they would crash.

Christina

Christina rested her head on Jack's shoulder as he drove her home. She was already late, half an hour past curfew. She'd better have a good story ready for Mama. She'd tell her there was an accident on the road and she and her friends were stuck in traffic, waiting for the tow truck to remove the cars. She was never late coming home without calling to explain, so she hoped Mama would give her some leeway. How could she call when she was stuck on Newark Avenue? she'd say.

She felt herself drifting off when, suddenly, a big silver ship sailed by so low she swore she could see inside, swore she could see the passengers, their faces pressed against the windows. She wasn't sure at first if she was dreaming. She hoped she was dreaming. But no—she was wide-awake now, pointing to the sky as Jack swerved to the side of the road. The noise was thunderous. "What is it?" Her voice sounded as if it was coming from far away. And why was she asking, anyway? She already knew. She'd seen it before.

Jack shouted, "It's going down." He revved up the

engine, and followed the plane's path, which seemed to be heading for Westminster. "Jesus!" he cried, nearing Janet Memorial, as the plane fell from the sky. "Mason!"

Natalie

Nurse K had dozed off but not Natalie. She was looking out the window when something flashed in the sky. "What was that?"

"What?" Nurse K asked, awakening.

"In the sky. Didn't you see it?"

"No, dear. Now turn away from the window. Concentrate on something warm and beautiful. Do you like the beach?"

"Yes. I love going down the shore."

"Close your eyes and pretend that's where you are. Can you feel the warm sand under your feet?"

"Yes."

"And the sun on your back?"

"Yes."

"Dip your toes in the ocean. The water is very warm today."

"Should I swim?"

"Only if you want to. Only if the ocean is where you'd like to be."

Phil Stein

Phil was walking Fred before hitting the sack. School tomorrow, then a day off for Lincoln's birthday. Usually when he kept Fred overnight Fred did his stuff, and that was it until morning. But tonight Fred broke away, dragging his leash behind him, racing in and out of hedges. Phil chased him, catching glimpses of his red and yellow doggie sweater, as Fred jumped over low shrubs, scooting in and out of yards. What was wrong with that dog? "Damn it, Fred! Come back here." Phil heard a terrible noise, so loud his hands went to his ears. He looked up and saw a plane. *Not again, please, God, not again.* A loud explosion. The flames shot up. *What are you doing to us, God?* "Fred . . . Fred!" Phil cried, terrified that he'd lost the dog, terrified of what was happening. All at once the neighbors were out of their houses, coats thrown over their nightgowns and pajamas. Everyone was running, running toward the burning, mangled mess. He caught a glimpse of his parents. Until then he'd never seen his mother run. Didn't know she could. He gave one more anguished cry. "Fred!"

Miri

Miri awakened to the sound of thunder, but thunder in February? She ran into Rusty's room, gently shook her. "Mom . . . did you hear that? What was it?"

"What?" Rusty said, taking off her sleep mask, pulling out her earplugs. "Hear what?"

"I don't know. It sounded like thunder."

"It's nothing, honey. Go back to sleep."

Miri padded down the hall to her bedroom, telling herself it was nothing. She was safe, Rusty and Irene and Uncle Henry were safe. Mason was safe. Safe from his crazy father, who'd chased him with an ax. At the sound of a car starting up, Miri pulled back the curtain of her front window in time to see Henry peeling out of the driveway, taking the corner so fast he skidded, the tires screeching. Something wasn't right. She felt it in her gut.

She picked up the kaleidoscope from the top of her dresser and got back into bed, holding it first to her right eye, then to her left. Was there a difference? Not really. It was beautiful and calming either way.

Mason

Mason sat on his bed, facing the windows of the senior boys' dorm, thinking about Miri. He'd had an early supper with Jack. Burgers at Mother Hubbard's, then apple pie. Jack wanted to know about him and Miri. Wanted to make sure he wasn't moving too fast, that he knew the rules.

He more or less told him he'd never known anyone like her, so sweet, so trusting. He didn't say anything about their game of Trust. That was private, between him and Miri. He still couldn't believe he'd told her about his mother and about his father chasing him with an ax. Until now, only Jack knew. But it was his idea to play Trust, wasn't it? He must have known he'd tell her, must have wanted to tell her, to prove he trusted her, the way she trusted him. And now, as he sat at his window in the dorm at Janet, that was what was killing him. Because all the time he was living a lie. What if she found out about Polina? What was he supposed to do then?

Polina had volunteered to keep Fred overnight back in September, before he'd ever met Miri. She took him and Fred home with her to the two rooms on Williamson Street where she lived with her three-year-old kid, saying Fred could stay there. She unbuttoned her dress, showed him her breasts. *You like?* she asked. *You think I'm pretty?*

Yeah, and yeah.

You like to touch?

Oh, yeah. Keep asking. Please don't stop.

But she stopped when the kid came in and Fred barked. And the kid, who hardly spoke English, laughed. *Doggy?*

No, that's a story he'd never tell. A story that has no end, because every week he'd gone to her place until the crash destroyed their house. Every week. And sometimes he was thinking of Miri when he did it. And sometimes he wasn't thinking at all—he was just pumping her and it felt so good. She didn't want anything from him, only that, only to say she was pretty and he liked her. Easy to say because it was true. He was careful. He got a package of rubbers. He wasn't taking any chances. She was his first and she was a good teacher. She didn't have to say much. Just took his hand and put it where she wanted it. Took his dick and guided it where she wanted it, which was where he wanted it, too.

AS HE STARTED getting ready for bed, he felt the house shake, then heard the earsplitting roar of a plane. A few of the other boys woke up and ran to the window. In the clear moonlit night, they saw it heading straight for them. He and the other boys fell to the floor, flattened and braced themselves. Mason made it partway under his bed. But instead of smashing into Janet, the plane must have hit something else and seconds later it crashed into their playing field, taking down the swings, the softball backboard. One explosion followed another. Mason didn't stop to think—he raced outside in an adrenaline rush and charged across the field to what was left of the plane, its fuselage ripped apart. Three of the other boys followed. He pulled out a young woman hanging upside down in her seat. "I'm the stewardess," she cried. "I have to help."

"Okay, sure," Mason told her, "but first we have to get you out of here." He carried her in his arms while she kept insisting, "I have to help . . ." He got her out just before another explosion, handed her over to one of the other boys, then rushed back to the plane. He freed a girl trapped under her seat, and threw her over his shoulder. "My husband," she cried. "I'm not leaving without my husband. We just got married." Mason handed her down to another of the boys, then went back to find the husband buried under debris, and barely alive, if that. They were working as a team now. The boys from Janet and the other rescuers, police, firemen, nurses. He pulled out another victim, and another. An arm came off a corpse. A baby was charred and dead.

Then he was being restrained, held so tight he had to fight to free himself. "Let go!" he shouted.

"No, no more," Jack told him.

But Mason wouldn't listen. He broke away from Jack, with Jack following, in time to help Mason pull out a little girl, alive but in shock. "Mommy . . ." she cried again and again. Jack handed her over to a fireman, who carried her to an ambulance, then passed her to a nurse, who rode with her to the hospital. Mason was on his way back to the plane when an explosion sent him flying. Jack dragged him away from the plane. When he looked up he saw bodies, still strapped into their seats, hanging from trees like puppets in some kind of sick show. By then the field had turned into a muddy, bloodstained junkyard.

Christina

In the middle of the field Christina bent over a woman on the ground. "Please, girly, loosen my girdle. I can't breathe."

Christina knew exactly how to do it—the hooks up the side, the stays. "My mother runs a girdle shop on Broad Street," she told the woman. "Nia's Lingerie—maybe you know it?" Why was she making small talk while the woman moaned?

"My chest hurts. My legs are cold. Am I gonna die?"

"No." Christina tried to reassure her. She took off her coat and draped it over the woman, but when her eyes closed, when she lay so still Christina didn't know if she was unconscious or dead, she ran for help and led back a fireman, who checked the woman's pulse. "She's alive," he told Christina. "We'll get her to the hospital." He called for a stretcher and the woman was carried away, still draped in Christina's winter coat.

A small dog ran in circles, barking. "Fred?" Dear god, it was Fred, wearing the sweater she'd knitted for him! In all the horror, in all the chaos, Fred, the miracle dog, survived. She shivered in her clingy red top and held Fred tight to her chest, running with him to the Red Cross house across the street, slipping once, turning her ankle, getting wet and muddied. A miracle, too, that the Red Cross house wasn't hit. Christina had to call her mother, who would be worrying, who wouldn't know what was going on. Someone gave her a nickel for the phone booth. Someone else took Fred and handed her a blanket to drape over her shoulders.

"I've been worried sick," Mama said. "Where are you?"

"Another plane crashed."

"What?"

"On Westminster Avenue."

"Come home right now, Christina!"

"No, I'm not coming home. They need help here. It's terrible."

She heard whispering, then Baba got on the line. "We're coming," he told her.

At the sound of her father's voice, she choked up. "I'll meet you at the Red Cross house. Ask Mama to bring my winter jacket, dungarees, a sweater, socks and boots."

Baba came with meats and cheeses and loaves of bread, huge jars of mayo, mustard, pickles and sweets from Three Brothers. Mama came with him, carrying a bag from Nia's filled with Christina's warm clothes. Christina fell into their arms. "Baba . . . Mama!" There was no time to ask who Christina had been with or how she had wound up here, or what she was doing out so late on a Sunday night in the first place. She was safe. For now, that was all they cared about.

Christina helped them set up tables. "We'll make sandwiches," her mother said, more to herself than Christina. "Sandwiches for the rescue crews and the families who will come once they hear. But first, wash your hands," Mama ordered. "Use plenty of soap. Hot water."

Life is short, Christina told herself while scrubbing her hands. At least she wouldn't die a virgin.

Miri

In the morning Miri snapped on her radio, but instead of jokey morning banter and pop tunes, she heard the news that a third plane had crashed in Elizabeth. She'd been right about last night, about the terrible feeling in her gut. When she learned it had crashed in the field behind Janet Memorial, she threw her coat over her flannel pajamas, pulled on boots and ran the mile to the site.

Breathing hard, rushing by the scene of devastation, she banged on the front door of Janet with both fists, and shouted for someone, anyone. When the door was flung open Miri nearly fell inside. "Look at you," a woman said, helping Miri regain her balance. "You're half frozen. Come in, child."

"My friend lives here."

"All the children are safe, dear. Which one is your friend?"

"Mason McKittrick."

"Well, now—Mason McKittrick is quite the hero. Rescued I don't know how many last night. The stewardess, too, I hear. Pulled them out of the burning plane. The lucky ones are alive because of him and three of our other boys."

Miri felt such relief she began to cry. The woman put her arms around her. "Now, now . . . it's all right. Come along, the children are at breakfast. Polina's in the kitchen making pancakes." She led Miri into the dining room, where the younger children were sitting around a table.

"Can I see Mason?"

"Not now, dear. He's asleep. Those boys worked all night, fell into bed at dawn." Her voice went quiet, to almost a whisper. "He's got his dog with him."

"Fred!" Miri said. "Fred is here?"

"We bent the rules, just for the night. A brave boy deserves to have his dog."

Polina came in from the kitchen carrying a platter of pancakes. Miri almost didn't recognize her in a blue hairnet, an apron over her plain dress, sturdy shoes, no makeup. She looked younger, softer, than the day they'd met at Dr. O's office.

"Polina, this is a friend of Mason's."

Miri didn't think Polina recognized her and she didn't feel like reminding her they'd already met.

"What a boy!" Polina sang.

"What a boy!" the children repeated, reminding Miri of the way Penny and Betsy liked to imitate their parents. *Let's go, Jo!* But thinking of Penny and Betsy made her too sad.

"I didn't catch your name, dear . . ." the woman said.

"Miri."

"I'm Mrs. Traynor. Sit right down here"—she pulled out a chair at the table—"and let Polina bring you a nice hot cup of cocoa."

"Thank you," she said to Mrs. Traynor, "but I have to go. My grandmother will be wondering where I am."

"Not even one pancake?" Mrs. Traynor asked.

"No. Really. I have to go home and get ready for school."

"I'll tell Mason you stopped by."

"Thank you."

Elizabeth Daily Post

Special Edition

UMBRELLA OF DEATH HAS CLOSED

FEB. 11—Just hours after the crash last night of a National Airlines DC-6 into the field behind the Janet Memorial Home, the third such disaster in eight weeks, the Port Authority closed down Newark Airport "pending further investigation," and Mayor Kirk has promised it will be shut indefinitely. "The chaos, the horror, the terror is over," he said. "The Umbrella of Death has closed."

In Washington, E. S. Hensley, director of the Civil Aeronautics Administration's office of aviation safety, could offer no explanation why three major crashes have occurred in the same place within less than 60 days. "It could just as easily have been San Francisco, Timbuktu, or Saskatchewan," Hensley said. "Why the Lord let it happen at Elizabeth I cannot guess. There is no earthly reason."

22

Miri

At school, the boys were excited.

ANGELO VENETTI (*waving around the special edition of the paper*): No earthly reason. What did I tell you? But they won't write about the unearthly reasons.

They're scared the aliens will unleash a full attack
against us.

PETE WOLF: Yeah, but is it a plot against America or just a
plot against our city?

WINKY HERKOVITZ: Either way, we're in deep shit.

DERISH GRAY: But the mayor says . . .

WINKY HERKOVITZ: You're going to believe him?

DERISH GRAY: And Newark Airport is closed.

CHARLEY KAMINSKY: Indefinitely.

ELEANOR: Robo's father knew what he was doing moving
his family out of town. And just in time, too.

SUZANNE: How did Robo's father know?

ELEANOR: He's connected.

SUZANNE: To the aliens?

ELEANOR: To the mob.

SUZANNE: This is about the mob?

WINKY HERKOVITZ: Wake up, Little Suzy. Everything is
about the mob.

You should know, Miri thought, but she didn't say so.
She was willing to bet the kids at Robo's new school
wouldn't be talking about the latest crash. They'd probably be talking about the latest show at the Paper Mill
Playhouse. She felt like lashing out at all of them. She
was sick of their stories. If only she could be sure Uncle
Henry was right, that the crashes were accidents. But
she'd just read a convincing article in *Life* magazine,
"Making a Case for Interplanetary Saucers," that made
it all seem possible.

Miri turned and walked away. In a minute Eleanor
was by her side. "They're imbeciles," she said, nodding
toward the boys.

"They're scared but they won't admit it," Miri said.

"We're all scared," Eleanor said. "Aren't we?"

Miri nodded. They were all scared.

"I'm still not convinced it isn't sabotage," Eleanor said. "But if it is sabotage I believe your uncle will uncover it."

Miri was glad to hear Eleanor had confidence in Uncle Henry.

At lunchtime, she ducked out of the cafeteria to call Natalie's house. She'd called last night before she'd gone to sleep, before any of them knew their world would be shattered a third time. There hadn't been any answer, which made no sense. Even if no one else was home there would still be a babysitter for Fern. This time Mrs. Jones answered. "Osners' residence. Mrs. Jones speaking." Miri recognized her voice before she identified herself.

"It's Miri, Mrs. Jones. Can I speak to Natalie or Mrs. Osner?"

"Everyone is out. I don't know where."

"Do you know when they'll be back?"

"Sorry, I don't. Try them tonight." Mrs. Jones hung up first.

She called again before dinner. This time she got Steve. When she asked for Natalie, he said, "She's not here."

"Where is she?"

"Visiting relatives."

"What relatives?"

He didn't answer.

"Are you telling me the truth?"

"No."

"Let me talk to your mother."

"Say *please*."

"May I *please* speak to your mother?"

"Sorry, no can do." And he hung up.

Then Henry came home with the paper and Miri didn't call the Osners again.

Elizabeth Daily Post

AIRLINER SMASHES INTO SALEM AVENUE APARTMENTS

Explodes in Yard of Janet Memorial Home
Third Crash in 58 Days Brings Closure of Newark Airport

By Henry Ammerman

FEB. 11—Disaster from the sky rained down on Elizabeth for the third time in eight weeks. At 12:20 a.m., a Miami-bound National Airlines four-engine DC-6 taking off from Newark Airport sliced open the roof of a three-story apartment building on Salem Avenue. Spilling fuel as a wing tip ripped off, it set the apartment building ablaze before plunging to the ground and exploding in the playing field of the Janet Memorial Home.

Like a Swollen Cream Puff

Wrapped around the base of a tree was one of the plane's engines. Hanging like a huge dead leaf from the blackened top of another tree was a jagged piece of silver wreckage. The roof of the apartment building looked as if the plane had taken a gigantic bite out of it. The wreckage of the 101-foot-long aircraft stretched across the recreation field of Janet Memorial, and into Westminster Avenue, all brightly lit by roaring flames that took hours to bring under control. Nearby, silhouetted like a sentinel against the orange-red flames was another engine, one propeller blade pointed skyward.

The plane had broken apart like a swollen cream puff. Lying in Westminster Avenue was the forward section, the tomb of the three pilots. Unlike the two previous crashes, which claimed the lives of all on board, 38 survived this time, some seriously injured, some able to walk away.

Janet Home and Schools Nearby

Twenty-two passengers and three crew members aboard the plane died. Four occupants of the ravaged apartment building perished, three of them from the same family—Irving Zahler, 30, his 27-year-old wife, Marilyn, and their 4-year-old son, Monte. They had recently moved from Newark to the Salem Avenue apartment house, where Mrs. Zahler's parents live. Her father, distraught, said, "Planes come so low over our place you could make a malted milk from the vibrations." Mr. Zahler worked at Zahler Brothers Potato Market in Newark.

But the block-long pile of death and destruction providentially spared the 48 children asleep in the Janet Home, virtually next door to the ill-fated apartment house. Only a block away were two schools, Vail-Deane and Pingry, which would have been occupied by hundreds of students a few hours later.

Young Heroes from Janet

Many owe their lives to a group of four boys from the Janet Memorial Home. Led by 16-year-old Mason McKittrick, the teenagers rushed from their building and were the first to offer assistance. Ignoring flames and the threat of further explosion, they pulled survivors out of the wreckage. Setting up an assembly line, they passed the injured to others, who transferred them to safety, many of them laid out on gym mats, awaiting medical attention.

MIRI READ HENRY'S STORY, then read it again. *Swollen cream puff?* She'd always thought of cream puffs as soft and sweet. But Henry was using it to describe something hard and horrible. She worried, for a minute, he was losing his mind. Or was it that when something so unimaginable happens you need to find a new way to help people see it?

Elizabeth Daily Post

NO VALENTINE'S WEDDING

BOSTON, FEB. 13 (UPI)—Plans for a Valentine's Day wedding went awry because a tall bride-to-be has disappeared after leaving a note to her still taller fiancé, and her engagement ring pinned to a pillow. She said she just couldn't go through with the ceremony.

Walter James Curran, 27, of Philadelphia, waited in a hotel room for some word of his fiancée, Kathleen Lorna Flynn, 23.

The Valentine's Day wedding scheduled for Thursday was to climax a romance that began at a convention of tall people's clubs last year in Kansas City. Curran, a strapping six-foot-five engineer, made a radio appeal last night, urging his five-foot-eleven fiancée to return.

Mrs. Barton Flynn said her daughter "simply vanished into thin air" on a shopping trip, after getting out of the family automobile.

23

Miri

Miri tried to imagine what went wrong. What would make Kathleen, the tall bride-to-be, decide at the last minute she didn't want to marry Walter? Had she come to her senses and realized all they had in common was their height? Did she find him hopelessly boring? Or maybe she wasn't attracted to him. Maybe she was disgusted by the idea of having sex with him. Maybe she didn't like the way he smelled or the way he chewed his food or the way he mispronounced certain words. Maybe she never wanted to get married in the first place but her mother told her she'd better find somebody soon or she was going to wind up an old maid. He could have had a terrible temper or criticized everything she did. Or maybe she loved to dance and he wouldn't even try. Maybe he drank. Maybe she was in love with someone else. Miri wished she could talk to Kathleen and find out the truth.

SHE TRIED to convince Irene to invite Mason to dinner on Valentine's Day. "He's a hero. Everybody says so. Just ask Uncle Henry."

"He was very brave," Rusty said, backing up Miri, "rushing into a burning plane and saving the stewardess."

Miri said, "She's not the only one he saved."

"A hero is always welcome at my table," Irene said.

Miri threw her arms around Irene.

"What?" Irene asked.

"Thank you," Miri said.

"I'm not inviting him as your boyfriend," Irene told her. "So don't go getting any ideas. I'm saying it would be a *shonda* not to include him."

"Relax, Mama," Rusty said. "They're just kids."

"I remember when I thought *you* were just a kid, Naomi."

Irene used Rusty's real name only when she was dead serious. And it always shut Rusty up. She turned and walked out of the kitchen.

Miri felt bad for Rusty that night and went to her room, where she sat on the edge of the bed and held Rusty's hand. No words were necessary. They both knew what Irene meant even if she hadn't spelled it out, as if what happened with Mike Monsky was Rusty's fault. Well, in a way Miri supposed it was. She'd let Mike Monsky trick her into going all the way, hadn't she? Getting into that Nash with him, a car where the seat actually turned into a bed. She would never go out with a boy who drove a Nash. No boy was going to trick her into doing anything she didn't want to do. Which made her think, maybe Rusty wanted to do it. Maybe he didn't have to trick her at all.

She'd learned about the Nash a few years ago when Rusty was teasing Henry about his car. They thought she was asleep. "It's so old," Rusty had said. "And that rumble seat! You can't make love in a rumble seat."

"I suppose you think I should get a Nash," Henry said. "One with a seat that turns into a bed."

At which point Rusty threw her shoe at Henry. But Henry ducked and laughed.

"I will never get into another Nash as long as I live," Rusty said. "And neither will my daughter."

Miri kissed Rusty goodnight, something she didn't automatically do these days. Rusty gave her such an appreciative look she vowed to be kinder to her mother.

On her way out of Rusty's room, Miri spied part of a white box tied with a red ribbon, sticking out from under Rusty's bed. Could it be a gift from Longy? That would be disgusting! Or from Natalie's cousin Tewky? Even worse. Or wait, maybe it was for *her*. Rusty might have bought her something for Valentine's Day. Maybe paja-mas with hearts, or a set of day-of-the-week underpants.

She knew she was way too old for day-of-the-week under-pants but she'd always wanted them. Natalie said when she was young she'd never worn hers on the right days. *Too much trouble.* But Fern was obsessive about getting the days of the week right.

ON VALENTINE'S DAY the Other Naomi came home from the office with Rusty to join the family for dinner. Miri thought of the Other Naomi as "Miss Rheingold" because she'd been a finalist in the national contest. She lived in a studio apartment in Greenwich Village, a fourth-floor walk-up opening into a tiny kitchenette. Miri and Rusty once spent the night when Miss Rheingold got them tick-ets to see a production of *Peter Pan*. Miss Rheingold knew the guy who wrote the music and lyrics, Lenny Bernstein. She showed Miri his photo. He was sitting at a piano. *Good-looking, isn't he?* Miss Rheingold had asked Miri. The photo was signed *To Naomi, Best wishes, Lenny.* Now Miss Rheingold was thirty-one and single. Miri didn't know about Lenny. But she knew Miss Rheingold's fiancé had been killed in the war and she swore she'd never fall in love again, though she wouldn't mind marrying somebody rich. Miri didn't understand why Rusty enjoyed spending time with Miss Rheingold, except they were close to the same age and single. All of Rusty's old friends from Battin High were married and didn't include her when they threw par-ties or went out with their husbands on Saturday nights. She was a double threat—too good-looking, and with a reputation for being loose, which she wasn't. As far as Miri knew she'd never had another boyfriend—not since Mike Monsky got her in trouble. Once a month Rusty spent the night at Miss Rheingold's apartment and always brought the *Playbill* and theater ticket stub home to Miri.

Rusty could have entered beauty contests when she was younger and she'd probably have won first prize. She could have been Miss Rheingold for real, not some runner-up, except you weren't allowed to enter unless you were single and certainly not if you were a mother. Well, too bad. Miri never liked the way Miss Rheingold talked to her, using the same tone she used to talk to her cat, as if she were the cat's mother. Miri found that people without children either did that or they acted like you were the same age as them, which at this point, would have been better.

LEAH AND UNCLE HENRY WERE already there, making small talk with Rusty and Miss Rheingold, when Ben Sapphire came in carrying a box from Nia's Lingerie tied with a fancy red bow.

"For me?" Irene asked when Ben presented it to her. "Should I open it in public?"

"Why not?" Ben said.

Rusty and Henry exchanged looks. Leah looked down at the box of twenty-four valentines on her lap, one from each child in her class. Miri couldn't imagine why she'd thought the family would want to see them.

Irene raised her eyebrows and smiled at Ben without opening her lips. She untied the red ribbon and handed it to Miri, reminding her to roll it up and save it in the ribbon box. Then she took the top off the box, and peeked into the layers of tissue paper, finally pulling out a silky white robe covered with red poppies. She held it up for the family to see. "Is this beautiful or what?"

Ben Sapphire beamed.

"What a thoughtful gift," Irene told him. "How did you know I needed a new robe?"

"Who doesn't need a new robe?" Ben asked.

"Try it on, Nana," Miri said.

"Now? Over my clothes?"

"Yes," Miri said.

"Well . . . if you insist." Irene pulled on the robe, which fit perfectly. She tied it around her waist, and paraded around the room like a model at a fashion show. "Ta dah!" she sang, stopping to give Ben a peck on the cheek. "Thank you, dear friend."

"It's the least I can do," Ben told her.

Again, Miri caught the looks between Rusty and Henry.

"I saw a box just like that, with the same red ribbon, in Mom's room," Miri said. She didn't know why she said it. She was just filling up what felt like an awkward moment. She didn't want any awkward moments tonight. She wanted it to be perfect for Mason, though he hadn't yet arrived.

"No, you saw *that* box," Rusty said. "I hid it in my room so Nana wouldn't see it."

"Or are you suggesting Rusty has a secret admirer?" Miss Rheingold asked Miri.

"No," Miri said. "I mean, how would I know?"

Rusty laughed. "You think there could be any *secrets* in this house?"

"She should only be so lucky," Irene said. "Who wouldn't want a secret admirer?"

"How about one who's not so secret?" Ben Sapphire asked.

"Better yet," Irene told him.

When the doorbell rang, Miri jumped up. "I'll get it."

She opened the door to find Mason holding a single red rose and a box of Barricini chocolates. She would not tell him that Leah had brought boxes of candy, gifts from the mothers of her students, or that Miss Rheingold had brought a box of chocolate-covered cherries, all stashed in the pantry. He handed her the rose. "Happy Valentine's Day." He checked to make sure the coast was clear before he kissed her.

Fred was inside his jacket. "I had no place to leave him."

"He can stay in my room." Mason handed the dog to Miri and she ran up the stairs with him while Mason waited.

When she came down again she led Mason into Irene's living room. "Mason brought me a red rose for Valentine's Day." She made a big thing out of running water into a bud vase, trimming the stem and placing it just so.

"And these are for you." He handed Irene the box of chocolates.

"For me?" Irene said for the second time that night. Miri could tell she was pleased.

Miri introduced him to Miss Rheingold. "This is my friend Mason. This is Mom's friend Naomi."

"Miss Rheingold," Rusty corrected her.

"Please, call me Naomi," Miss Rheingold told him. She held out her hand with her bright red nails and Mason shook it. "Pleased to meet you, Mason."

"Same here," he said.

"So, this is the boyfriend?" Miss Rheingold asked Rusty in a whisper loud enough for everyone to hear.

Miri shot Rusty a look. What business was it of Miss Rheingold's?

"They're just friends," Rusty told Miss Rheingold.

But it was clear to Miri that Rusty had told her more.

"Friends are good," Miss Rheingold said.

"I couldn't agree more," Ben Sapphire said. "Friends make all the difference."

Miri stole a quick look at Mason, who was looking at the floor.

For a minute Miri's thoughts went to Natalie. But she didn't want to think about Natalie tonight or where or how she might be. She was glad when Irene called them to the table, where Henry proposed a toast to Mason, calling him a "true hero."

"I'm proud to have a hero at my table," Irene said.

"I'm not a hero," Mason argued. "I didn't even stop to think. I just did it."

"You saved the stewardess's life," Henry told him. "She'll never forget you. And neither will the others."

Mason's leg was jiggling under the table. Miri could feel it. He didn't want to be the center of attention.

"What do you call this?" he asked, holding up a spoon-ful of soup.

"It's soup," Miri whispered.

"Yeah, but what kind?"

"Potato leek," Irene said. "Do you like it?"

"Yeah, a lot."

Later, in the middle of the brisket, kasha, and peas, Mason said, "You know, I'm almost sure one of my grand-fathers was half-Jewish."

Irene put down her fork and looked over at him. The others waited.

"My mother's father. I never knew him and it was kind of a secret but when my father got mad at my mother he'd call her a—" Miri kicked him under the table and Mason dropped it. Was it true, or did he think he had to fib to get the family to accept him?

"I'd like to marry a Jewish man," Miss Rheingold announced. "Everyone says they make the best husbands. How about it, Henry? You know someone for me?"

"My girlfriends have first dibs on Henry's friends," Leah said in a serious voice.

Miss Rheingold smiled her beauty-pageant smile and said, "Of course they do. I was just joking. You never know where you'll meet Prince Charming."

"Well," Henry said, "how about seconds, Mason? You won't get a brisket like my mother's anyplace else in the world."

"I already know," Mason said, holding out his plate. "Sure, I'll have seconds."

Irene was pleased he liked her food. When she brought out a chocolate cake for dessert, frosted with white buttercream and decorated with red hearts, Mason licked his chops. "Boy-oh-boy, I can't believe you baked that!"

Miri couldn't decide if he was stuffing himself to impress her family or if he was really that hungry.

Later, they gathered around the television set that Uncle Henry recently brought home to Irene. He'd moved the old set, with rabbit ears, upstairs to Rusty's living room.

"That's some television set," Ben Sapphire said, when he saw the twenty-inch Motorola. Henry tuned in to *You Bet Your Life* with Groucho Marx. If they stayed late enough they'd get to see *Dragnet*, the new police show. *Just the facts, ma'am*.

"Did you know, Naomi," Ben Sapphire said to Miss

Rheingold, "Henry is making quite a name for himself. He's getting offers from big papers around the country. And newsmagazines, too."

"I had no idea, Henry," Miss Rheingold said. "You must be an ace reporter."

"He is," Leah said proudly. "His paper just gave him a big bonus. They don't want to lose him."

Everyone looked over at Henry. Ben Sapphire held up his glass of brandy and proposed a toast. "To our Ace. You're going places, Henry."

"Are you thinking of moving to another paper?" Miss Rheingold asked.

"I'm considering my options but I can't help feeling a twinge of guilt at finding success at the expense of tragedy."

"Come on, Henry," Ben Sapphire said, "that's what reporting is all about. You make a name for yourself reporting wars, bad politics, tragedy. Not the social section."

Miri didn't want to think about tragedy tonight. But it always came back to that, didn't it?

Steve

He'd swiped a photo of Kathy from her house when he'd been there for shiva. Just a little photo. Probably no one would notice it was gone. He bought a Valentine's Day card for her and signed it, *Love Steve*. Then he scrawled, *Hope it's nice wherever you are*, at the bottom. Maybe he was going cuckoo like his sister. But he didn't really believe that. He was just pissed off. He took the story he'd torn from the newspaper out of his desk drawer, the story about how Kathy was going home to see a boy she'd met over the holidays. A boy she really liked. He folded it and slipped it inside the Valentine's Day card. He laid her photo on his pillow and kissed it. "Happy Valentine's Day, Kathy." Then he went downstairs to the finished basement and grabbed a bottle of Scotch from the bar. Scotch, his father's drink of choice—he liked it on the rocks. His mother was more of a whiskey-sour drinker. One was more than enough for her. Back in his room he took a swig straight from the bottle. Jeez, the stuff was awful. It burned his throat. *Here's to us, Kathy*, he said. This time he poured himself a shot and gulped it down. It got easier. By his sixth shot he was blotto. He lay on the floor while his room spun around. *Whirlybeds*. It didn't feel good. He crept on all fours to the bathroom— spinning spinning—and puked his guts out. Then he fell back on the cool tile floor and everything went black.

Elizabeth Daily Post

SURVIVORS

They Live to Tell Their Stories

By Henry Ammerman

FEB. 15—The bus driver's classic call to "step to the rear" might be heeded by airline passengers. Most of the survivors of the National Airlines DC-6 crash on Feb. 11 had been seated in the rear of the aircraft. When the plane broke apart in the crash it left the rear section less damaged and more accessible to rescuers.

Gabrielle Wenders, the stewardess, was the only surviving member of the crew. She had been found hanging upside down, still strapped in her seat. "I don't know how I ever got out alive. It was a fiery nightmare. We were all so helpless. If it hadn't been for that young man, Mason McKittrick—a name I'll always remember—I might have died that way."

Chubby little Patty Clausen, age 5, was unharmed, but her mother perished. With her father hospitalized, hospital authorities put out a plea. "Can't someone take this most adorable child home? She keeps asking for her 'bow wow.'" The dog had been left in a kennel while the family went on vacation. Her uncle picked her up last night, but said he would wait before telling her of her mother's death.

Hospitalized newlywed Linda West, 25, was unaware of the status of William, her husband. They were married at noon on Feb. 10, and pulled from the wreckage 12 hours later. "When can I see my husband?" She begged her mother to bring him to her bedside. Her mother didn't know how to break the news to her daughter that Mr. West had died of a fractured skull and brain injuries the previous night.

In much better spirits was 17-year-old Cele Bell, who was anxious to get on another flight. "I want to go on vacation to Miami! I'd go tomorrow if I could," she told reporters. She had been traveling with her mother, who was pinned under her seat after the crash. But Cele was able to pull her to safety. They had been in the last two seats on the right side of the plane.

Of the 38 who survived the initial crash, two have died in the hospital. Some remain in critical condition, but the prognosis for most is good.

24

Natalie

Natalie's parents took her to New York, to the Central Park West office of some old man who smelled bad. Her mother assured her he was a famous psychoanalyst from Vienna, that he knew Anna Freud, daughter of the great man. Anna lectured frequently in the United States and Dr. Boltzmann might be able to arrange for Anna to see Natalie. Today's appointment with Dr. Boltzmann was a consultation, not a session, not that Natalie knew the difference.

The walls were paneled in dark wood, the floor covered with overlapping Oriental rugs. A faded red brocade sofa strewn with needlepoint pillows stood in the middle of the room, a crocheted afghan folded at one end. There was a big leather chair and two smaller chairs. Dr. Boltzmann sat in one of the smaller chairs, a cushion behind his back. She didn't like this. Didn't like that her parents were in the waiting room, not with her. Maybe the famous doctor had already seen them. Either way, she wasn't going to tell him anything. Half the time she couldn't even understand what he was saying, his accent was so thick. It reminded her of when they used to play Dracula. They'd run around the playground shrieking, *I vant to bite your neck!* She knew enough not to lie down on that faded sofa. She would never lie down on it, even if her parents brought her here every week. Instead she slumped in the big chair, feeling small, feeling like her old Raggedy Ann doll, which she still kept in her closet.

The famous doctor cleared his throat. It sounded like he had phlegm. Robo's father had phlegm. When he drove he often rolled down the window and spit it out. Natalie hated when he did that. She had to look away to stop herself from gagging. She thought she might gag here, in this dark, faded room.

"You can talk," the famous doctor said. "No one can hear you."

You can hear me, she thought. But she didn't say it aloud. Instead she said, "I don't want to talk."

"Ah . . . you don't want to talk and you don't want to eat."

"I want to eat but I can't. I have a disease."

"Not a disease. A condition."

"Did my parents tell you that?"

He shrugged. "We both want to help you get well. The parents and the doctor. Do you want to get well?"

That was a stupid question, a trick question, and she wasn't going to answer it.

"What would you like to talk about?" he asked.

"My hair. It's falling out."

"Do you pull it out?"

"No. Why would I do that?"

"Just now," he said, "you pulled out a clump."

She looked down and saw a golden-blond clump in her hand. How did it get there? She didn't remember pulling it out. She needed to ask Ruby about this. Ruby would tell her what to do. But lately, she felt Ruby had other things, other people on her mind. Natalie wanted to cry, roll herself into a ball and let the tears come. But she was not going to cry in front of this old man, in this old room, which smelled as musty as he did.

She wished she could twirl. Twirl and twirl until she was so dizzy she'd collapse on the floor. She'd like to slap her taps on the wood floor under the rugs, making more noise than this old doctor had ever heard. She couldn't believe her parents had brought her here. He was like a relic from the olden days. Something right out of a movie.

"Why are you here?" he asked. "What do you think?"

"I don't have to think—I know the answer. I'm here because my parents brought me."

"Why do you think they brought you?"

"To see you, obviously."

He ignored her sarcasm, not a good sign. "But why to see me?"

"Because their friend who is our doctor told them to."

"Yes, but why would he make such a suggestion?"

"Because you're famous."

"Ah, famous."

"And because they don't have any idea what's going on."

"And you won't tell them."

"That's right. And I won't tell you, either."

"Of course. Why would you tell me?"

"Because you really want to know, don't you?"

"Yes. I'd like to help you get well."

"I'd like to get well so I can dance again. That's what I do, you know. I dance."

"I hear you're a very good dancer."

"You heard that from my parents?"

"Is it not true?"

"Yes, it's true."

"So." A statement, not a question.

"Sew buttons."

"What is *sew buttons*?"

"Nothing . . . just an expression."

"To dance you have to be strong," he said.

"I was strong until I got sick. Now I just need some medicine to make me better."

Silence.

She yawned. She was just so tired.

When he called in her parents, when they were seated side by side on the sofa, the famous doctor suggested a rest home in the country for Natalie. He knew of one, just the right place for her, in Westchester County. But her father said it would be better if she could be closer to her family. He'd made some inquiries and suggested the Watchung Hills Children's Home, in New Jersey.

They were sending her away? She couldn't believe her father would send her away. But she didn't have the energy to argue. She'd argue tomorrow or the next day. She was sure she could persuade them to wait. Especially her father.

In the car, on the way home from the famous doctor's office, Natalie nodded off in the backseat, but she could still hear her parents talking softly about the children's home in Watchung. And then, something about how, at the end of the school year, they would relocate as a family. Her father had been asked to open an office in Nevada in a place called Las Vegas—a place with clean air, wide-open spaces, where the girls could ride horses. "Hell," her father said, "they can have their own horses."

Horses . . . Natalie thought. What did she care about horses? Fern was the one so obsessed with horses she wished she could *be* a horse.

"What about me?" Corinne asked. "I don't want to ride horses. I don't want to leave my home, my friends, a life I've worked so hard to create. I gave up everything to marry you, Arthur—my family, my roots, because I loved you the minute I met you—like a flash of lightning . . ."

The old flash-of-lightning story, Natalie thought.

"And now you're asking me to start all over in some strange place, surrounded by your gangster friends?" Corinne sniffled.

"It's an opportunity, Corinne."

"It's not one I choose to take."

"Suppose I say I want to do this?"

"There are many things in life we'd *like* to do, Arthur, but we don't because we consider the needs of those we love above everything else."

"We don't have to sell the house right away," her father said. "We can give it two years."

"What about your practice here—who's going to wait two years for their next appointment?"

"I've been thinking about bringing in a partner, or selling the practice. I've got a good offer from Myron Ludell."

"No," Corinne said. "It's a commitment I'm not prepared to make."

"And what if I say I'm going anyway?" Her father's voice turned angry.

"Is that what you're saying? Because if it is, you're going alone. I'm not going to let you take the children."

Natalie let herself doze. Dozing wasn't exactly sleeping. Dozing meant she could come awake whenever she wanted. Dozing meant she couldn't die.

Sometime later, after they'd come through the Lincoln Tunnel, her mother raised her voice, waking her. "It's all your fault," she cried, and for a minute Natalie thought Corinne was blaming her. "You and your crazy ideas. Las Vegas—some hick town in the desert. How many Jews are there in Las Vegas?"

"There will be more and more Jews," her father told her mother.

"Gangster Jews."

"Doctors, lawyers, accountants, businessmen. They're already constructing a medical arts center. It will be finished by the end of the school year. I'll have a beautiful office with the latest equipment, and plenty of patients to pay the bills. Daisy is willing to come."

"Daisy!" her mother said. "You've already talked to Daisy? Daisy before me? Well, that proves it. I've always suspected but until now I wasn't sure. You and Daisy—"

"That's ridiculous and you know it," her father said, his voice rising.

"Is it?"

The car swerved.

"Arthur!" Corinne shouted.

Had they forgotten Natalie was in the backseat?

Her father pulled off the road onto the shoulder, got out and slammed the door. He paced up and down, lighting a cigarette.

Her mother cried softly, then blew her nose. Natalie thought it best to keep quiet.

When her father returned to the car, he said, "I know this is the right thing to do for Natalie. Get her mind off . . . get her out in the fresh air."

"And what about her dancing?"

"There will be classes there."

"How do you know?"

"Entertainers have classes. And since when do we want to encourage her to pursue this cockamamie idea she has of becoming the next Ruby Keeler?"

Natalie held her breath when he said "Ruby"—*how did he know? How could he possibly know?*—but when he said "Keeler," Natalie understood he had no idea about *her* Ruby.

"We have to save her, Corinne."

"If we can't save her here, how can we save her there?"

"We have to try. I'm begging you to reconsider."

"And I'm begging you to forget this crazy idea. Who's behind it—Longy? And when it fails—and you come home *begging* for forgiveness—and there's nothing left of your practice or our marriage, then what? How will we live? How will we pay for treatment for Natalie, send Steve to college and Fern to Vail-Deane? You expect my family to support us? You've always resented my family money but now, all of a sudden, it smells clean to you? You're a fool, Arthur. I never thought I'd say that but it's the truth."

"I don't think you understand, Corinne. Natalie is very sick. If we don't do something we could lose her."

Corinne breathed in, teared up, waved a hand at her husband. "Don't ever say that again! There's nothing wrong with her. She's just sensitive. It's all been too hard on her. That's why she stopped eating."

"And I'm saying get her out of here so she doesn't have to worry about planes crashing into houses, into schools, so she doesn't have to think about death and dying."

Natalie slumped to the floor of the car, her hands over her ears.

Elizabeth Daily Post

FATHER OF ELIZABETH CRASH VICTIM
SUES FOR $250,000

FEB. 18—Thomas Granik of Sunnyside, Queens, filed suit today in Federal Court against Miami Airlines, Inc., for the death of his daughter, Ruby. She was a passenger in the airplane that crashed on Dec. 16 in Elizabeth. Mr. Granik said that the 22-year-old woman, a nightclub dancer, was the sole support of his family.

25

⸻

Miri

At school the following Monday, as Eleanor and Miri walked to English class together, Eleanor asked, "Are you still best friends with Natalie?"

Miri hesitated. "Yes," she said, but the truth was, she wasn't sure.

"Why was she absent all last week and again today?"

"I don't know. When I saw her last Sunday she wasn't feeling well."

"Have you talked to her?"

"No."

"Her parents?"

"No."

"Why not?"

"I've called a bunch of times but there's never any answer." She didn't say she'd talked to Steve or that she hadn't believed a word of what he'd said.

"I don't like the way this sounds," Eleanor said. "Why don't we just go over, ring the bell and ask what's going on?"

"I don't think that's the best idea. I think if they wanted us to know, they'd tell us."

She could see Eleanor digesting that. "Maybe you're right. Anyway, we've got a paper to put to bed."

Miri said, "I meant to tell you, I wrote a feature story." She hadn't planned to say anything about the story she'd started on the night of the meeting at City Hall.

"What's it about?"

"The situation."

"You mean *the situation*?"

"Yes, that. Not about Natalie."

"When can I see it?"

"I'll clean it up tonight and bring it in tomorrow."

"Good. We could use an interesting story about the situation."

THAT NIGHT Miri took the story she'd written from her desk drawer. Her own indignation spilled out as she quickly made changes, adding the latest crash to the story. She copied it over in ink. Then she took a bath, using Rusty's citrus bath salts. She slept well for the first time in a long time.

The next morning she handed the story to Eleanor. When they met in the cafeteria at lunchtime Eleanor said, "I like it. It makes you think. We can get it into the spring issue if we hurry. I'll run it by Tiny this afternoon."

Later, Tiny took Miri aside in homeroom. "Good story, Miri," she said. "Provocative."

"Thank you," Miri said. She wasn't sure *provocative* was a compliment but *good story* was.

"I'll have to show it to Mr. Royer."

"Mr. Royer . . . why?"

"As principal he has a veto over controversial stories."

"You think my story is controversial?"

Tiny smiled. "Don't you?" She didn't wait for Miri to answer. "But I'm on your side, so stop worrying."

Until then she hadn't been worrying.

ON WEDNESDAY, Tiny reported to Miri that after reading her story Mr. Royer said they couldn't run it in *Hamilton Headlines*.

Miri was speechless.

"He doesn't think it's appropriate. It could be seen as inflammatory."

When Miri still didn't respond, Tiny said, "I'm so sorry, Miri. I tried to explain but he was adamant. No stories about the crashes."

"That's crazy!" Miri said, finding her voice. "All the kids are talking about it. He can't pretend those airplanes didn't crash."

"I think he's concerned about how the parents might react."

"The parents? They don't read our paper."

"All it takes is one parent to start an uproar."

"Does that mean we're not supposed to have opinions?"

"I understand what you're saying and I agree with you. But I can't risk my job."

"Your job?"

"Yes. That's how it works. I'm a teacher. Mr. Royer is my boss."

"Then who stands up for us, the students?"

Tiny shook her head. "Welcome to the real world."

"I WROTE a story about the crashes for the school paper," Miri told Henry at dinner. It was one of the rare nights Henry was home in time to eat with them. "Mrs. Wallace, the adviser to the paper, called it 'provocative.'"

"Provocative!" Ben Sapphire said. "We need more provocative thinkers. Don't you agree, Henry?"

Henry glanced at Ben but didn't respond.

"She showed it to the principal," Miri continued. "He vetoed it, said it was inflammatory."

"Inflammatory!" Ben Sapphire said. "This is sounding better and better." Irene put her hand over Ben's, letting him know he should keep quiet. Miri didn't miss the gesture.

"I'd like to read it," Henry told her.

"Make that two of us," Rusty said.

After dinner Miri gave Henry her story. Tiny had returned it to her in case she wanted to revise it. "Maybe write about how the community is helping those in need," Tiny had suggested. "Something uplifting. Mr. Royer likes uplifting stories."

"I'm not writing for Mr. Royer," Miri had said. "I'm writing for the *student* newspaper."

Tiny gave her a sad look. "I know that, Miri. And I'm sorry."

"You already said that!" Miri felt bad lashing out at Tiny. She knew Tiny was on her side, but she wanted more. She wanted Tiny to remind him this is America. We have free speech. We have freedom of the press.

Henry went to his room to read the story. When he came out ten minutes later, he said, "If I were in charge I'd publish it."

"Really?" Miri asked. "You're not just saying that?"

"You know I'd never do that."

Miri nodded. She knew.

"That's not to say I agree with everything in your story."

Rusty grabbed the story from Henry and went upstairs to read it on her own.

While she was gone Miri saw clearly what she had to do. "Can I use your typewriter?" she asked Henry.

"Sure."

She'd had a full semester of typing. She could type thirty-five words a minute. At Battin next year, she'd take Typing for College, something they all laughed about. "Sounds like Typing for Chimpanzees," Robo had said. Miri wondered if they had Typing for Chimpanzees at Millburn High School.

"This is good," Rusty said, coming back downstairs, waving Miri's story. "I'm so proud of you, honey. You know how to speak your mind. But is this what you really believe?"

"I'm still not sure—" Miri began.

Ben Sapphire interrupted. "When do I get to read it?"

"When it's published," Miri told him.

Henry, seeing where this was going, said, "I don't have a stencil at the house but we do at the office. You want to take a ride with me?"

She got her coat.

"I type eighty words a minute," Rusty called. "You want me to come?"

"Thanks, Mom, but I can do this myself." She grabbed the story from Rusty.

Rusty looked disappointed, but Miri didn't care. It was *her* story.

The *Daily Post* office was busy but probably not as busy as it would have been during the day. Henry set her up at a typewriter, removed the ribbon and rolled in the stencil. She'd never cut a stencil for a mimeograph.

"You have to press down hard on each key," Henry told her. "It's different from regular typing."

Maybe she should have let Rusty help. It took a long time for her to cut the stencil. Henry didn't seem to mind. He was at work on another story at his desk. She went through a lot of correction fluid changing her typing mistakes. Finally, when she was as satisfied as she was going to be, Henry helped her run off a hundred copies on the mimeograph.

On Thursday morning she showed Eleanor her story. "I'm going to distribute it on my own."

Eleanor took a copy from the stack Miri was holding. She read the headline out loud. "'Zombies, Martians, Commies or Sabotage?'" Then she smiled, showing her braces, which she almost never did. "I like this. It's so *cheeky*."

Cheeky wasn't what Miri had in mind. Eleanor used expressions the rest of them had heard only in movies.

ZOMBIES, MARTIANS, COMMIES
OR SABOTAGE?

By Miri Ammerman

The first one fell a block from Hamilton, and 4
blocks from the Elks Club, where 100 children were
enjoying a holiday party.

They said it could never happen again.

But it did, skimming the roof of Battin
High School, 45 minutes after 1,000 girls
were dismissed for the day, and just missing
St. Mary's.

They said it was a coincidence but it could
never happen again.

This time it just missed the Janet Memorial Home
and at the end of that block, Vail-Deane School
for girls and Pingry School for boys.

Coincidence?

Some people think so, especially the adults in
our lives. But not everyone.

The students at Hamilton talk about it before
school begins, gathering in small groups outside
their homerooms. Everyone has a theory. Some
believe it is creatures from outer space, Martians
in flying saucers intercepting and causing planes
to crash. Others say it's zombies. Still others,
sabotage.

Could it be caused by Communists? Some say so.
But how could Communists cause three planes to
crash in a row?

Why is this happening?

Evidence points to a plot against the children
of Elizabeth, whether they attend public, private
or Catholic school—whether they live in an

orphanage, or in the best section of town. Children
are the one thing these crashes have in common. Hit
where there are children and teenagers. Hit where
it will hurt the most.

The adults don't believe it. They say close
Newark Airport and that will be the end of it.
Change the flight paths that bring planes in and
out over our city on their way to and from Newark
Airport and everything will be fine.

They want to protect us from the truth.
They can't admit this might be a force they
don't understand. Admitting that would be like
admitting they don't know the answers to our
questions, and how many adults in our lives would
ever do that?

Finally, the airport has closed. Will this be
the end of it? We can't say yet, can we?

We listen, but we must draw our own conclusions.
Prove to us that we're wrong. We're waiting.

ELEANOR SAID, "Give me a pile of stories. I'll help hand
them out. I'll bet the other staff members of the paper
will help, too."

Everyone was in, including Suzanne and two boys who
covered school sports. Until then, Miri had never given
them a second thought. Now she was grateful.

By lunch, the hundred copies were gone. Instead of
throwing the story in the trash, their classmates were
sharing it with friends. A group of eighth graders stopped
her in the hall. "You're the one who wrote that story,
right?" When she nodded, acknowledging she was the

one, a boy circled his thumb and index finger and winked. "About time," he said.

That afternoon Mr. Royer called Miri and Tiny to his office, an office Miri had never set foot in, in almost three years at Hamilton Junior High. The windows overlooked Cherry Street. A collection of Audubon prints hung on one wall. Miri recognized them because Irene had the same drawings hanging in her hallway. When she was little she'd memorized the names of all the birds.

Mr. Royer, in a rumpled suit, sat behind his desk. He was balding, plump and pink-cheeked. He didn't invite Tiny or Miri to sit, though there were two chairs in front of his desk.

"I'm requesting a meeting with your mother, Miss Ammerman."

"My mother works in New York," Miri told him. "The only time she can meet is at night."

"Why am I not surprised to hear that?" He muttered something about how women belonged at home until their children were grown.

Tiny, who had two children in elementary school, began to cough. She dug a Smith Brothers cough drop from a box in her purse.

HENRY OFFERED to meet with Mr. Royer in Rusty's place. The meeting was set for just after three on Monday afternoon, with Miri, Tiny and Uncle Henry. Miri told Mason on the phone that night she'd be late picking up Fred tomorrow. When Mason heard the reason he said, "I really like that about you."

"What?"

"I don't know. Just everything."

Miri laughed. "I hope I won't be expelled."

"Expelled? I don't think so."

"He expelled Suzanne's sister, Dorrie, when she was in ninth grade."

"What'd she do to get expelled?"

"I don't know. Neither does Suzanne. It was a long time ago. Her parents won't talk about it. She had to transfer to another junior high."

"Don't let Royer push you around. He does that if he thinks he can get away with it."

"I didn't know that."

"Now you do."

"Okay."

"Good luck," Mason said.

"Thanks. I'll need it."

"And you can tell him if he messes with my girl he'll have to answer to me."

"I really like that about you."

"What?"

"I don't know. Just everything."

THE FIRST THING Mr. Royer said to Uncle Henry was "I could expel her for this." *Expel?* He'd actually said the word out loud. "She defied my orders. Mrs. Wallace told her the story was not appropriate and what did she do— made copies and handed them out at school. Have you read the story?" Mr. Royer asked Henry.

"Yes, I have. I was impressed."

"It's hogwash!"

"Pardon me?" Henry said.

"Would you want me to allow the young Adolf Hitler to express his opinions in our school paper?"

Adolf Hitler! He was comparing her to Adolf Hitler?

"You can't be serious," Henry said calmly. "I hardly think that's a fair comparison."

Mr. Royer came out from behind his desk and began to adjust the bird prints on the wall, tapping the side of one drawing, then another.

Miri was stuck on *Adolf Hitler* so missed whatever Henry said next except it ended in *freedom of expression.*

Mr. Royer whipped around. "Don't lecture me on free speech, young man."

Tiny began to cough, just as she had the last time they were in his office.

"Do you need water, Mrs. Wallace?" Mr. Royer asked, annoyed.

Tiny shook her head. Again, she dug out a cough drop and put it in her mouth.

"I think the best thing for all involved would be for Miri to leave the school paper of her own free will," Mr. Royer said.

He was kicking her off the paper?

Tiny held a tissue to her mouth, got rid of the cough drop and cleared her throat a few times. "She's a good student," Tiny managed to say. "And a fine young reporter. She's never been in trouble. This would be very harsh punishment." She eyed the pitcher of water on Mr. Royer's desk.

Uncle Henry poured a cup and handed it to Tiny. She drank it down.

"You think this is harsh punishment, Mrs. Wallace?"

"Yes, I do," Tiny said with conviction, "and I'm concerned it will affect the morale of our other editors and reporters."

Henry said, "Why not give Miri another chance, Mr. Royer? I'm sure she understands now that your strong feelings come with serious consequences."

"I don't want another chance!" Miri said. "What good is a newspaper when its reporters can't write about what's on the minds of its readers?"

"That's it!" Mr. Royer said. "You're off the paper and you're on probation for the rest of the school year. One more incident and I promise you, Miss Ammerman, you will be expelled." He said the last few words very slowly, making sure they sank in.

Tears stung her eyes but she would not give him the satisfaction of seeing her cry.

Henry reached for Miri's hand. "Mr. Royer, with all due respect—"

"I suppose you're a bleeding heart, Mr. Ammerman . . . I suppose you think it's fine for students to break the rules."

"Sir, I don't think that at all."

"Well, I'm glad to hear it because this meeting has gone on long enough." He nodded at Tiny, then at Uncle Henry.

Miri half expected him to add, *Dismissed.*

She was so angry she was shaking, and so shaken by Mr. Royer's power over her, she wanted to scream. Was she supposed to be relieved she hadn't been expelled?

Out in the hall, she hugged Henry for coming and for standing up for her. She thanked Tiny, too. "This, too, shall pass," Tiny said.

Miri didn't know how to respond. Was that like

Time heals all wounds? She'd heard both expressions at Mrs. Barnes's house on the night of her son's funeral. They both sounded like bull to her.

"I promised to call Rusty and let her know what happened," Henry said.

"She's going to be mad."

"At Mr. Royer, not at you."

RUSTY WASN'T just mad, she was furious.

Who did he think he was, threatening to expel her daughter? She knew men like him, drunk with power, certain they could get away with anything and everything. Oh, she knew them, all right! She'd like to give him a piece of her mind. And maybe she would. She'd gone to Hamilton, too. So had Henry. But they'd had a different principal, one who'd joked with them. *How do you spell* principal? he would ask. *Remember the P-A-L on the end because the principal is your pal.* Ha! Mr. Royer was no *pal.* She bet he wouldn't dare behave that way toward her daughter if she had a husband. It was because she wasn't married, because she went to business, that he showed her no respect. A young uncle didn't count, even if he was a prominent reporter. Royer was a bully.

Henry urged her to let it go. Miri had just this semester left at Hamilton.

"And it should be a happy time for her," Rusty argued.

"She can join *High Spots* when she gets to Battin," Henry said. "That's a first-rate high school paper. I know Mr. Komishane, the adviser."

"Royer shouldn't get away with this."

"Maybe not. But Miri can handle it. If you go to see him it could be worse for her."

"You really believe that?"

"I do, Rusty."

"I'm not sure I agree."

"You don't have to."

Rusty said, "When you're a parent you'll understand." She knew she was saying that too often, whenever she was stuck. But she couldn't help herself.

ELEANOR CALLED an emergency meeting of the *Hamilton Headlines* staff. Tiny came, too.

They applauded when Miri came in. She looked around, her eyes misty. "I'm going to miss this," she said.

Eleanor said, "We've talked about going on strike."

Suzanne said, "Or resigning."

Eleanor said, "On the other hand, we can use this as a chance to write what we think."

Miri looked at Tiny.

"I won't be asking Mr. Royer's permission for any more stories," she said.

"But what about your job?" Miri asked.

Tiny shook her head. "There are other jobs."

Elizabeth Daily Post

CRASH PROBE REVEALS TWO ENGINES FAILED

Extraordinary Release of Preliminary Findings

By Henry Ammerman

FEB. 28—Both of the right engines failed on the National Airlines four-engine DC-6 that crashed into the Janet Memorial Home's yard on Feb. 11.

The CAB investigator also announced that the DC-6's radial 18-cylinder Pratt & Whitney "Double Wasp" engines are being disassembled piece by piece and nut by nut at the facilities of Pacific Airmotive Co. in Linden. This is the same type of engine that powered the Convair 240 that crashed near Battin High School last month and the C-46 that crashed into the Elizabeth River in December, when an engine exploded. The "Double Wasp" is one of the most widely used engines in aviation, with a reputation for reliability earned during the adverse conditions of World War II.

Crowds continue to gather at the crash site, which has taken on a carnival air, with a hawker selling bags of popcorn and families taking their children to see the remains of the devastation.

26

Christina

Christina's period was late. She was beside herself with worry. Jack said to give it another two weeks. It was probably the stress of the crash. He swore he'd pulled out in time. She was distracted at school but everyone knew she'd been at the scene of the third crash, everyone knew she'd tried to help the injured. Even Mama and Baba were kind. Athena said she was getting too much attention, that the family was babying her, that staying at the crash site that night might not have been the best decision she'd ever made. But the aunts and uncles threw a family party for her. Really, it was Jack who rushed into the burning plane. Jack and Mason and Mason's friends from Janet. But she couldn't tell them that. She didn't want to bring up the subject of Jack.

Finally, when they were alone in the kitchen, Mama asked, not unkindly, "You were out on a date with that boy?"

"Not so much a date," Christina tried to explain. "We're just friends. We went to Twin City, the roller rink."

But Mama was more interested in Jack than skating. "So who is this friend? He's a Greek boy?"

"His name is Jack McKittrick."

"McKittrick?"

"Yes."

"He's Irish?"

"Half, yes."

"And he's not a boyfriend?"

"No. But what if he was?"

"A boyfriend?"

Christina nodded. "I'm not saying he is . . . but just suppose . . ."

Mama sucked in her breath. It felt like she was sucking in all the air in the room. Christina felt dizzy, like she might faint. She steadied herself against the kitchen table.

Finally, Mama spoke. "Baba and I would be very disappointed, very concerned. And your Yaya and Papou—they would kill me for letting you have an Irish boyfriend."

"His mother wasn't Irish." Christina blurted this out, digging herself in deeper and deeper.

"She was Greek?"

"She might have been. She had dark hair and dark eyes. And I think her name was Eleni." Lies and more lies. She had to stop.

"Eleni," her mother said quietly. Christina knew Jack's mother's name was Elaine but that was close enough. She was probably Italian. Didn't Jack once tell her his mother made spaghetti sauce from scratch?

Christina's anxiety was showing up not just at home, where she left the cap off the toothpaste, and one time forgot to flush the toilet, leading Athena to give her hell, calling her *disgusting*—but at work, where she tried to be extra careful, not letting her mind wander. Still, Daisy sensed something was wrong. "Whatever it is, if I can help in any way, let me know."

"Thank you, Daisy."

"You know you can trust me."

"I do know. It's just that . . ." She was *that* close to confiding in Daisy.

"You've been through a terrible time," Daisy said.

"The death, the destruction—once was bad enough, but you've seen it twice, Christina. That would be hard on anyone. Dr. O has a friend, a patient, you've probably met him . . . Dr. Reiss?"

"Yes, I've seen him at the office several times."

"You could talk with him. I know Dr. O would be glad to set it up for you."

"I don't think . . . not now, anyway . . . but thank you."

Every time she passed the lab down the hall she looked in and saw the fat white rabbits in their cages. She could have a urine test to see if she was pregnant but she didn't want to be responsible for killing a rabbit, and the rabbit died whether or not you were pregnant. A lot of people thought it only died if you *were* pregnant. Ha! How did they think the technicians checked the rabbit's ovaries? No, she couldn't do that. Besides, she couldn't just walk in with a cup of urine and ask for the test. They knew her family from the luncheonette downstairs. They knew she worked for Dr. O. She would have to wait a few more weeks, wait for her period to come. She wasn't nauseous, though she was sometimes dizzy. She didn't crave certain foods—in fact she had very little appetite. And she didn't think her breasts were swelling, though Jack did.

She would not have sex with Jack, no matter how many times he said, "But, honey, if you're already pregnant it doesn't matter."

"And if I'm not?"

"Either way, I'll be more careful. I'll use a rubber until we know for sure."

"I can't, Jack. Please don't push me."

He was frustrated but not angry. He taught her how to give him a hand job. At first she didn't think she could touch it. But now she was more comfortable. Now she thought of it as a friend. She liked the way it responded to her touch. Jack put her hand on his balls. "Feel how tight they get," he whispered. "That's because it feels so good." Then he'd spurt, not on her if she was lucky.

At first she wouldn't let him touch her that way. "Are you sure I can't get pregnant? That is, if I'm not already pregnant?"

"Don't worry."

But worry was her new middle name.

When she let herself go, when she let him touch her there, she enjoyed it. She cried out when she got that good feeling. Why, oh, why hadn't they done it this way in the first place? Then they wouldn't be in this predicament. Now she was six weeks late. She wasn't ready to be a wife and she certainly wasn't ready to be a mother. There was talk of a doctor in south Jersey who could take care of it but it cost a lot of money and she wasn't sure it was safe.

One night when Jack met her after work he said, "How about a quick trip to Elkton?"

"You mean elope?" Debbie Reynolds had eloped to Elkton. And Willie Mays, too. Everyone knew about Elkton. They called it *Marry-Land* instead of Maryland. Usually it was a joke but Jack didn't sound like he was joking. Was he proposing to her?

"I've got it all figured out," he said. "We drive down early Saturday morning. Leave by six a.m. We get hitched, then drive back."

"You mean get married?" Christina had trouble getting out the words. Wasn't this moment supposed to be romantic?

"I can't stand seeing you so unhappy."

"I'm not unhappy. I'm worried."

"That's what I mean."

"I don't know, Jack."

"We love each other, don't we?"

"Yes."

"We want to spend the rest of our lives together, don't we?"

"Yes."

"Then let's do it. No one has to know. It'll be our secret."

"But if I'm pregnant I'll have to tell my family. There's no way to keep that a secret. And when they find out they're going to kill me. Or you. Or both of us."

"No, they won't."

She looked at him. Did he really think this could be solved so easily?

"We'll tell them it's because I've been called up."

She burst into tears. She'd prayed Korea would be over before Jack's number came up, even though she knew very well he was 1-A. Jack tried to comfort her but nothing worked.

"I haven't been called up yet," he whispered. "I was just saying it's what you could tell your family."

"You're saying I should lie to my parents?"

He didn't answer, which made her burst into tears again. Her life was turning into such a mess.

SHE HAD TO make up an excuse for not working on Saturday morning and felt guilty for lying to Daisy, telling her she was going down the shore for a family reunion. But Daisy said she'd cover for her. She told Christina to have a good day, told her she *deserved* a good day.

They set out on Saturday morning in Jack's truck, only to find out, when they reached Elkton, there was now a forty-eight-hour waiting period. Christina begged the clerk to make an exception. "Please," she cried, "you don't understand . . ."

"I think I do, dear," the clerk said.

They bought their license for a dollar, arranged for a pastor to marry them on Wednesday, April 2, because Christina would not marry on April Fool's Day, paid five dollars in advance for a corsage, then drove back home. On Wednesday, Christina skipped school. She'd write a note tomorrow about having a twenty-four-hour virus. All the girls were coming down with it. She wore her sheer white blouse, full black taffeta skirt, heels and her best jewelry—a small gold cross around her neck, which Yaya and Papou had given her for her sixteenth birthday, and an ankle bracelet from Jack. This was, after all, her wedding day. After the brief ceremony conducted by one of the marrying parsons, the witnesses threw rice. She kept twisting the slim gold band from Goldblatt Jewelers on her finger, a ring she wouldn't be able to wear in public.

Jack wanted to have sex before they started out for home, so they stopped at Boyd's motel and spent nine dollars on a room. But she was too scared to let go and enjoy it even though he used a rubber. After, they stopped at a diner for lunch. She ordered something called "Wedding Cake" for dessert, a white layer cake with lemon filling. Actually, it was pretty good.

That night she pressed her wedding corsage in her scrapbook, hid her ring under the false bottom of her jewelry box and cried herself to sleep.

A week later she got her period.

Elizabeth Daily Post

NO HOME LIFE FOR FLUET

MARCH 26—Joseph O. Fluet, the government's chief airline crash investigator for this area, hasn't been able to spend much time at his home in Great Neck, N.Y. According to his wife, he's been there for only two hours in the last month. Fluet is staying at the Elizabeth Carteret hotel. The lonesome Mrs. Fluet says she's weaving a rug to pass the time.

27

Miri

On most days Irene picked up the afternoon mail, but she was away for two weeks in Miami Beach with Ben Sapphire. Rusty tried to get her to promise to call home every night so she'd know Irene was okay, but Irene laughed at the idea. "Don't worry, darling, I'm a big girl. I can take care of myself."

"I'll look after her like she's a queen," Ben promised.

"I'll send postcards," Irene sang, looking smart in her new travel suit, and blowing them kisses as she and Ben left for Newark's Penn Station, where they'd board the Silver Meteor to Miami.

"Postcards," Rusty mumbled as the car pulled away.

So on this late-March day Miri was the one to pick up

the mail. She'd already walked Mason and Fred to Edison Lanes, where a bum came out of nowhere, pulling on Mason's sleeve, frightening Miri. He was filthy and he reeked of alcohol.

"Get off me," Mason told him.

"Come on, son. You're a big shot now, a hero," the bum said. "People must be throwing money at you. How about something for your dear old dad?"

She could see the anger in Mason's face, his jaw tightening, his teeth clenched. "I said, get off me!"

The bum looked at Miri. "Who's this? Your girlfriend?"

"Don't touch her," Mason said, shielding Miri with his body.

Fred barked.

"Well, well . . . it's Fred, is it?" He tried to pet the dog but Fred growled. Miri had never heard Fred growl.

"If you don't get out of here I'm calling the police," Mason said.

"I *am* the police, son."

"You *were* the police, but not anymore. And stop calling me *son*."

"Jacky always gives me a fiver."

"Yeah, to get rid of you."

"You want to get rid of me, son? Give me some change."

"Let's go," Mason said, grabbing Miri's hand. He led her inside but turned back to the bum once and called, "You better be gone when I come out. You hear? You better be gone!"

He wouldn't let Miri leave until the coast was clear. "I'm sorry you had to see that drunken excuse of a father," he told her.

That was his father? The father who'd chased him with an ax?

Miri was still reeling when she dropped Fred at Mrs. Stein's house. She walked home looking over her shoulder, making sure the bum who was Mason's father wasn't following her. It must be terrible having a father like him, Miri thought, someone you couldn't trust, someone so unpredictable. Better to have no father or a father in California you never had to see.

She let herself into the house, collected the mail from the floor, where it had come in through the slot in the door, and thumbed through it, separating Irene's and Henry's from hers and Rusty's. There was a postcard for her from Irene, showing a wide white beach with one palm tree leaning toward the blue-green ocean. The third postcard this week. Each one had a message beginning, *Darling Miri*. Then there would be a one-line message: *Wish you were here*, or *You would love this weather*, or *Having a wonderful time*.

She tucked the postcard into the waistband of her skirt and headed upstairs, where she dropped the mail on the kitchen table. On top was a creamy white envelope addressed to Naomi Ammerman in slanted handwriting that looked vaguely familiar. She turned it over to find an engraved return address.

Mrs. J. J. Strasser
Redmond Road
South Orange, N.J.

Why was Frekki writing to Rusty? She didn't like this. She sat at the kitchen table for a while, considering her options. Maybe she should steam the envelope open, read the letter, then reglue the envelope. Suzanne had done that once with a letter to her parents from her sister, Dorrie, the one who'd been expelled by Mr. Royer. She'd run off with a guy her parents didn't approve of, before she'd graduated from high school. Another option—she could open it, read it, then burn it, or hide it in her sock drawer the way she'd hidden the letter from Mike Monsky. But she wouldn't want Rusty to do that to her. Rusty, who said trust was the single most important part of a relationship. "Remember that, Miri. If you can't trust, you can't love." It was bad enough she'd hidden Mike Monsky's letter. But that was, at least, addressed to her. This was different.

Rusty would be home soon enough. Without Irene to cook for them, they'd been eating pizza, deli sandwiches or scrambled eggs for supper, but tonight they were going to have a roast chicken. Rusty had left instructions from Irene. Miri was to light the oven, season the chicken and put it in to roast. "You can't go wrong with a roast chicken, baked potatoes and fresh carrots," Irene told her before she'd left. She'd never tell Irene that Rusty had picked up Birds Eye frozen carrots instead of fresh.

At six o'clock Miri heard the front door open and Rusty sang, "I'm home . . ." She came up the stairs and into the kitchen, where Miri was basting the chicken, per Irene's instructions.

"It smells good in here," Rusty said, kicking off her shoes and getting out of her coat. She bent over and dropped a kiss on top of Miri's head. Then she picked up the mail and riffled through it. Miri was almost afraid to watch. She opened Frekki's note first. Her breathing changed as she read it. "What the hell is this?"

"What?" Miri asked. "Did somebody die?"

Rusty waved the note in front of Miri's face. "You met him? You met Mike Monsky and you never told me."

"Mom, I—"

"How could you keep such a secret from me? I'm your mother, for god's sake. How could you betray me this way?"

"Mom, I'd never—"

"Don't lie to me!"

"I'm not lying. What does it say?"

Rusty shoved the note at Miri, and she grabbed it, reading quickly. It said that Mike Monsky was in town and wanted to make a plan regarding their daughter, a plan that would include financial support and visiting rights. It said ever since Mike met Miri he'd been thinking about her. Frekki suggested they meet in the study of Rabbi Beiderman, who counsels many families in difficult situations. Rusty should also feel free to consult a lawyer. " 'Feel free to consult a lawyer'?" Miri asked.

"Feel free!" Rusty repeated. "Who does that bitch think she is?" Rusty went crazy, throwing her shoes against the wall. "He thinks he can walk into my life and destroy everything just like he did sixteen years ago? I'll kill him first."

Miri was sure that at that moment, Rusty meant it. Her ferocity scared Miri. "Did you think I'd never find out?" she asked Miri.

"Frekki fooled me. She never said he'd be at Gruning's."

"Gruning's! My god—you had ice cream with him?"

"I'm sorry, Mom. I didn't know what to do."

"You should have told me the minute you got home. I'd have stopped this immediately. I'd have warned Frekki and her brother, if they ever, *ever* contacted you again, I'd have them arrested. That's what you should have done. You can't trust him, Miri. Don't let that smile fool you, those eyes . . ."

"I don't trust him. I don't even like him. I never want to see him again!" This wasn't completely true. She was curious about her mother and him.

"What bothers me is you didn't tell me. You kept it a secret and now Frekki is asking for a meeting. I trusted you to go to the Paper Mill Playhouse with Frekki. I trusted you, Miri."

"But, Mom, I didn't know he'd be there."

"What's going on?" Henry called from the foyer. They hadn't heard him come in.

"A situation," Rusty called back.

Henry ran up the stairs two at a time and burst into the kitchen. "Mama?" he asked Rusty, and Miri could read the fear in his eyes.

"No," Rusty told him. "Mike Monsky has surfaced."

"Mike Monsky?" Henry said this as if they were talking about Frankenstein.

"And guess what?" Rusty said. "Miri's met him but didn't think she needed to tell me."

Henry gave Miri a questioning look but Miri didn't say anything.

"And now Frekki's cooked up some *mishegoss* about getting together with a Rabbi Beiderman," Rusty said. "To make a plan."

"A plan?" Henry asked.

Miri handed him Frekki's note.

Henry read it. "I know a good lawyer," he said. "I'm sure he'll advise us as a family friend."

The lawyer, Gregg Bender, came over after dinner. He and Henry were old friends. They used to play basketball together at the Y. Rusty made coffee.

"She doesn't want to see him," Rusty told Gregg Bender, offering cream and sugar for his coffee and a plate of store-bought cookies. "Isn't that right, Miri? Isn't that what you told me?"

"I did say that."

"There!" Rusty said. "You see? If she never wants to see him again why should we agree to have this meeting? Can someone please explain that to me?"

"Did you mean it?" Henry asked Miri. "Are you afraid of him?"

"No, I'm not afraid of him." *And no, I didn't really mean it but how am I supposed to let you know that without Rusty going crazy?*

"I understand how you feel, Rusty," Gregg Bender said. "But this is about Miri's future. As I see it, this could be an opportunity. Let's say Mr. Monsky puts away a nest egg for her education—"

"I've already started a savings account for her education," Rusty said. "Every week since I started working I've put something into it."

"So have I," Henry said, surprising Miri. "It's not a lot but it'll help pay for her tuition."

"Thank you, Uncle Henry," Miri whispered, afraid if she said anything more she'd start bawling.

"You see?" Rusty said to Gregg. "We have it all worked out. So why should we say yes to Frekki and her brother?"

"For one thing, to avoid this matter going to court," Gregg said. "To keep it *friendly*."

"Friendly?" Rusty gave a false laugh. "That's a good one!"

"For another . . ." And now Gregg looked at Miri. "Because she has a right to know her father."

"He is *no* father!" Rusty turned on her heel and headed for her bedroom. She slammed the door like a frustrated, angry teenager.

"This is very hard for Rusty," Henry said.

Gregg nodded. "I imagine so."

Miri wanted to say, *What about me? Don't you think it's hard for me?* But she didn't.

RABBI BEIDERMAN'S HOUSE was on a quiet street in Maplewood in a neighborhood of pretty old houses with flowering trees and lawns that would soon be green. Daffodils and tulips were sprouting. Miri might have sat in the rumble seat today if Henry still had his old coupe. But he'd given that to Leah so she no longer had to take the bus to work and he drove a new Chevy. He'd gotten a good deal on last year's model. Nobody wanted a maroon car. They passed a church as they turned onto the rabbi's street. Wasn't it strange for a rabbi to live near a church? The lawyer, Gregg Bender, was already there, parked in his car, waiting for them.

The rabbi was clean-shaven, dressed in weekend clothes, a tweed jacket over a blue oxford cloth shirt, no tie. She'd never seen a rabbi out of his robes. She'd never thought of a rabbi having a nice house on a nice street in a good neighborhood, wearing regular clothes, having a wife and kids. He welcomed them into a book-lined room with a sofa and four club chairs around a coffee table. Photos of his children at different ages were scattered around the room.

Henry made the introductions. "Glad to meet you, Rabbi," he said, shaking hands. "I'm Henry Ammerman, this is my sister, Rusty Ammerman, my niece, Miri Ammerman, and Gregg Bender, our lawyer, who is here as a family friend."

"Welcome to all of you," the rabbi said. "I admire your work, Mr. Ammerman. Please, make yourselves comfortable. We have coffee and Danish. Miri, would you like a glass of milk or orange juice?"

"No thank you."

Gregg Bender helped himself to a cheese Danish and a cup of coffee. Henry did the coffee thing, too. Rusty fidgeted with her pocketbook, pulling out a linen handkerchief, embroidered on one corner. She was probably hoping Frekki and Mike Monsky wouldn't show up.

But as the church bells chimed ten times, Frekki strutted in arm and arm with Mike Monsky, and another man behind them. Frekki said, "Hello, Rabbi. I'm Frekki Strasser and this is my brother, Mike Monsky, and my husband, Dr. J. J. Strasser."

Her husband, not her lawyer. Miri was surprised. She was sure Frekki would bring a lawyer. Miri tried not to look at Mike Monsky, who was focused on Rusty, who was picking nonexistent lint off her skirt. Only then did Miri notice that Rusty was wearing her new peep-toe pumps and the pale-green sweater dress that made her eyes look even more green. Her hair was loose, down to her shoulders. She looked especially pretty, though tense and unsmiling, twisting the linen handkerchief in her hands. Frekki wore a stylish wool skirt and matching sweater set in spring colors—navy and white. Miri was almost sure it was cashmere. A matching silk scarf was draped around her neck. Miri wondered how she got the scarf to stay in place. Her doctor husband checked his watch, explaining he was on call and might have to leave early. He hoped they would understand if he did.

"Let me begin by stating the obvious," Rabbi Beiderman said. "This isn't an easy situation for any of you. Miri, you're the one caught in the middle . . ."

Frekki interrupted. "She's not caught in the middle, Rabbi. She's the one who will benefit most from this arrangement."

The rabbi said, "Emotionally, Miri is in the middle."

Maybe this rabbi was smarter than she'd thought.

"Can we cut to the chase, please?" Rusty said.

"Rabbi, if I may . . ." Mike Monsky looked to the rabbi for permission to continue.

"Please . . ." the rabbi said, signaling for Mike Monsky to speak.

"We made a mistake sixteen years ago," he began, looking directly at Rusty.

He was calling her a mistake? Did she really have to sit here and listen to this?

"But the result of that mistake," he continued, "is a wonderful young girl who nobody in their right mind would ever call a mistake. I'm proud to call her my daughter."

"She's no more your daughter than I'm the Queen of Sheba," Rusty said.

"She's entitled to have a relationship with her father," Mike said.

"You call yourself a father?" Rusty asked. "I can show you fathers—responsible, loving men who are there for their families."

Henry leaned over and whispered something to Rusty. Rusty blew her nose in the linen handkerchief.

Frekki said, "Nobody doubts you've done a wonderful job, Rusty. You've raised a lovely daughter. But you can't deny her a father."

Rusty's face turned red. "I've never denied her anything."

But the truth, Miri thought. She wished she could shout at them to stop, but then everyone in the room would look at her.

As if reading her mind, the rabbi said, "Miriam, would you like to speak?"

She shook her head no. But there was plenty she might have said, if she'd had the courage. *I have a father*, she'd say to Rusty. *You might not like him but you can't pretend he doesn't exist. If you don't like him you should have thought of that before you got into his Nash with the seat that turned into a bed.*

Next, she'd look directly at Mike Monsky. *You think you can waltz into my life now and everything will be okay? You expect me to trust you just because you and my mother shtupped a couple of times? Trust has to be earned. You know who taught me that? My mother! You've never taught me anything, not anything good, anyway.*

Then, back to Rusty. *Stop arguing. Let him put money away for college. You know you worry about how you're going to pay. You think I don't know that for fifteen years you've done everything? You and Nana and Uncle Henry. You think I don't know what a family I have? A family I can count on. I don't need him. That's true. But if it turns out I want to know him, if it turns out I want to meet his other kids—so what?*

That doesn't change anything between us. I love you, Mom. Don't worry. You're not going to lose me. Ever.

Henry gave her a little nudge and she came back from her fantasy in time to hear Rusty say, "I don't want his money, Rabbi. I've managed all these years on my own."

"But the child is entitled, Mrs. Ammerman. I'm suggesting Mr. Monsky set up a fund for Miri," the rabbi said, "to help with college expenses. Perhaps the amount can be decided by your lawyers. You are entitled to nothing, Mr. Monsky. It will be up to Miri if she wants to see you or not. At fifteen, she can make that decision herself."

Her feelings for this rabbi just went from cool to warm.

"That sounds fair," Mike Monsky said.

Gregg looked at Henry, who nodded, and at Rusty, who shrugged.

Then the rabbi asked, "Do you want to see your father again?"

"I don't know," Miri answered.

"I understand," the rabbi said. "Personally, I think you owe it to yourself to get to know him, even though he hasn't yet had the chance to show you what kind of father he will be. I hope he'll be responsible, kind, supportive, but that's going to take some time, some proving. Maybe a week over the summer? Think about it."

Miri nodded. Rusty blew her nose again.

"Mrs. Strasser," the rabbi said, "thank you for bringing these two families together."

Frekki nodded.

"Mr. Monsky," the rabbi continued, "your wife is Jewish?"

"She's a convert, Rabbi. The boys are being raised Jewish. It's a way of life for us."

The rabbi said, "Good, very good."

Henry stood and shook hands with the rabbi. So did the others. Then Henry shook hands with Mike Monsky. When Mike extended his hand to Rusty, she didn't want to take it, Miri could tell, but finally, with Henry's urging, she held out her hand. Mike Monsky took it and said, "You're even more beautiful now than you were then."

Rusty gave him a kind of *ha*, without smiling. "You haven't changed," she said. "You've still got a line a mile long."

"It was always the truth," Mike Monsky told her, "whether you believed it or not."

Rusty turned, took Henry's arm and walked out the door.

"That wasn't so bad, was it?" Frekki said to Miri.

"I guess that depends on who you ask," Miri told her.

Mike Monsky put his hand on Miri's shoulder. "I hope you'll decide to give me a chance. I hope you'll come for a visit this summer, like the rabbi suggested."

"Maybe," Miri said.

"I'll write," Mike Monsky said.

Miri nodded.

"Can I have a hug?" he asked.

"Not here. Not now." And she hurried to catch up to Rusty and Henry.

LEAH HAD INVITED them to stop at Aunt Alma's house for brunch after the meeting. Before she got out of the car, Rusty changed from her new pumps into her comfy weekend flats. Leah came outside to greet them. Henry said something to her in private, probably telling her how it went at Rabbi Beiderman's, probably warning her not to bring up the subject.

Alma's house was small, and neat like her, barely big enough for two. Once Leah and Henry were married, she'd have it back to herself again. Miri wondered if she'd be sorry or glad to see Leah go. Inside, it was decorated in old-world style, with crocheted doilies on the arms of the sofas and chairs.

Rusty took one look at the whitefish salad, the lox and bagels, and said, "This looks like an after-funeral lunch."

Leah looked hurt. Henry put his arm around her. "Come on, Rusty—nobody's died."

Rusty was quick to apologize. "I'm sorry, Leah. I didn't mean . . . it's very sweet of you and Alma to have us over."

"I hear Irene is in Miami Beach," Alma said. "With that nice Mr. Sapphire."

"Yes," Rusty said. "And she seems to be enjoying it."

"Mr. Sapphire's apartment has two bedrooms," Miri said, feeling she had to defend Irene's honor.

"Maybe he could invite me down to stay in the second bedroom," Alma said. "I wouldn't mind getting away from this crazy weather. Spring or winter. Winter or spring. You never know from day to day. Pneumonia weather."

"Well," Henry said, "I'm famished. Let's eat."

"Me, too," Miri said.

Even Rusty helped herself to a bagel piled with lox, cream cheese and tomato.

They'd made it through. They'd survived the stormy seas of Frekki and Mike Monsky, at least for today.

"Are we going to tell Nana about this?" Miri asked.

"When the time is right," Rusty said.

"What do you think she'll say?"

Henry answered. "I think she'll say it's a good thing for a girl to know her father so she can make up her own mind about him."

Mike Monsky

He wasn't sure he should have let his sister talk him into this. She was a bossy big sister when he was a kid and she was still a bossy big sister, a bossy wife, too, he was betting. He was sure the good doctor who'd married her didn't know what he was in for. And now, J. J. Strasser wasn't thrilled about complicating his life with Frekki's long-lost brother or some recently found niece. That was pretty clear. But Frekki had some nutty idea this daughter of his had to be rescued, from what he didn't know.

He'd made the right decision staying on the West Coast after the war, marrying Adela. So he'd told a little white lie to the rabbi this morning about how she'd converted and how they were raising their boys in the Jewish faith. As if his in-laws would have gone for that. It was bad enough when their only daughter was marrying a Jew. And the Jew was going to be working in the family business.

But okay, according to his father-in-law he was a good-looking guy. You couldn't tell he was a Jew from just looking, and his own son had been Mike's shipmate in the Pacific. That counted for something, didn't it? That he'd even made it into the navy, which didn't favor Jews, was, in itself, a statement. This was no pasty-faced faggot who'd tried to get out of serving his country. As long as he, Rufus Collingwood, didn't have to meet Mike's family—and thank god he'd already changed his name to Monk. Mr. Collingwood had said this to Mike, face-to-face, man-to-man.

No problem there. Mike had told Frekki he and Adela had eloped, when the truth was they'd had two hundred to a sit-down dinner with dancing at the country club. Where he, Michael Monk, was now a member.

Mike and Frekki had grown up in the Weequahic section of Newark. In high school he was Mr. Popularity. The girls loved him. As a student, just so-so. Still, he'd gone to Rutgers, played basketball, joined Phi Ep, where he'd met Rusty at a party in February of his junior year. He fell for her before they'd exchanged two words. Hell, who wouldn't have fallen for her? She looked like a movie star, maybe Rita Hayworth with green eyes. Had he ever met a girl with green eyes? He didn't think so. She was tall and lanky. But he was cocky, came on too strong, scared her off. She was just a senior in high school while he was a BMOC. He reminded himself to take it slow and easy.

He couldn't take his eyes off her today in the rabbi's study. It all came rushing back. Her scent, the silky feel of her skin, the long hair wrapped around his fingers. And she'd loved it, hadn't she? She was always ready to hop into the Nash for hours of kissing, touching and finally—*Bingo!*—the night she gave in. After he demonstrated the bed-in-a-car, she wanted to do it again. He remembered because the Hauptmann guy, the one convicted of killing the Lindbergh baby, was executed in New Jersey the same night. Mike hadn't been strapped into the electric chair like Hauptmann but he'd been on fire for that girl.

It lasted until Fourth of July weekend, when he drank too much at a party down the shore and made a pass at some other girl—a mistake, and one that cost him. Rusty wouldn't stop crying and it was never the same between them. No more make-out sessions in the Nash or anywhere else. From what he heard, she was relieved when he enlisted. And so was he. There were plenty of other girls waiting. *Anchors Aweigh, my boys . . . Anchors Aweigh . . .*

His parents were ready to kill him. *A Jewish boy enlists in 1936, in peacetime? Are you crazy?* his father shouted. *Okay, so college didn't go the way it should have. You were sowing your wild oats. You'll go to summer school, make up the two classes you flunked. You'll do better next year. If war comes and we get the contract for military uniforms we'll be rich. You can work with me. Eli Tucker would give you a medical excuse. You have flat feet, like me, don't you? We'll be making the uniforms instead of wearing them. Come on, son. Say it was a mistake.*

And now, today, in the rabbi's study—sixteen years later and she looks the same, better, if that's possible. He's never cheated on Adela, not that he hasn't been tempted. But this was different. He doubted he'd have the strength to resist, should she be interested. Mother of his daughter and all that.

Elizabeth Daily Post

A-BOMB DRILL FOR TIMES SQUARE

APRIL 5—The New York Civil Defense Corps announced an air-raid drill for Times Square tonight. The exercise will be programmed as if an atom bomb had exploded and incendiary and high-powered bombs had rained down on the entire amusement area.

The drill is timed for the height of pre-show congestion. Traffic will be diverted.

28

Christina

Christina didn't feel married. She still lived at home and slept alone in her small bedroom with the faded pink floral wallpaper. She may have pressed her wedding corsage in her scrapbook, but she hadn't annotated the page, in case somebody—her mother, Athena—got suspicious and went looking for clues. At night she'd take her wedding ring out of her jewelry box where she kept it hidden, pulling on the secret tab that lifted the black velvet false bottom. And even then she kept the real bottom covered in fabric left over from Yaya's latest sewing project, making dolls for children who'd lost their toys in the crash. She'd lock her bedroom door, slip on the wedding band

and wave her hand around in front of the mirror to see how it looked. Then she'd take it off and kiss it goodnight before hiding it again. *Her wedding ring.* It must be real if she had a wedding ring. Sometimes she'd say *Christina McKittrick*, just to see how it sounded. She'd caught herself at school, scribbling her married name in her notebook, but she always stopped in time and erased the evidence.

After school and on Saturdays she'd hurry to Dr. O's office. Since she got her period, which she knew could have been a miscarriage, she'd been thinking about seeing a doctor, but she didn't know any gynecologists, and she certainly wasn't going to ask her sister to recommend one. Instead, she asked Daisy. She didn't have to tell Daisy anything more than she needed to see a doctor for lady troubles. "I'm so irregular," she said. "I don't want to worry my mother. You know how Greek mothers can be." She hated lying to Daisy. She wasn't irregular at all—her periods came every twenty-eight days, like clockwork, until recently.

Daisy wrote down the name and phone number of a doctor and Christina set up the appointment herself. Dr. J. J. Strasser had a fancy office in Newark. There were obviously pregnant women in the waiting room, and others who weren't, or if they were, they weren't showing yet. Christina twirled her wedding band around on her finger. It was the first time she'd worn it in public. But before it was her turn to see the doctor she chickened out, slipping it into her change purse.

Dr. Strasser listened to her story about why she was here. "I didn't get my period for two months and I've always been regular. Then I got it and it was especially heavy, with cramping."

"Get changed and we'll see what's going on. Have you had a pelvic exam before, Christina?"

"No." But she knew what was going to happen. He was going to put a speculum into her vagina. She'd read all about it last night. She was scared, but his nurse stood by her side and patted her hand. The speculum was cold and made her shiver, or maybe she shivered because she was scared.

"You're not a virgin," the doctor told her. "I doubt you're going to fool anyone into believing you are, but you never know."

"Actually, I'm married," Christina said. "But nobody knows. We eloped. I was a virgin until then." Technically, this wasn't true but she wanted this doctor to like her, to treat her well.

"You girls and your secret marriages," the doctor said. "If I had a daughter who did that I'd never forgive her."

What kind of father can't forgive his daughter? She was glad he wasn't her father. She believed Baba would forgive her anything. It was Mama she was worried about.

Dr. Strasser took out the speculum and felt around inside her with his hand, pressing down, making her even more uncomfortable. The nurse told her to breathe.

"I don't see any evidence of a miscarriage. Everything looks fine. Would you like me to fit you for a diaphragm, Mrs. . . ."

"McKittrick," Christina said, trying it out. "And yes, I'd like a diaphragm." She was so glad she'd read up on her choices last night.

"Do you have your husband's approval to use birth control?"

Her husband's approval? "Yes."

"If you use it properly—and that means *every* time— you shouldn't have to worry about being pregnant until you want to be."

After she was dressed and seated in his office, he said, "I see you're from Elizabeth."

She nodded.

"Plane Crash City."

"We don't call it that." She knew people who weren't from Elizabeth did. Wasn't there a story in the paper about letters to the editor addressed to Plane Crash City, New Jersey?

"Terrible," he said. "A tragedy."

"Three tragedies. And I saw two of them."

He looked up. "That would give you more than enough anxiety to miss your period."

"Yes."

"Newark Airport being closed is a real pain in the neck for me. Every time I want to fly to a conference or take a vacation I'll have to shlep into New York, all the way to LaGuardia or Idlewild."

"I'm sorry," Christina said.

He laughed. "You're a nice girl, Mrs. McKittrick. Good luck in your marriage."

"Thank you, Dr. Strasser."

"And don't forget. *Every* time."

"What?"

"The diaphragm. It doesn't work if you don't use it."

SHE ASKED HER PARENTS if she could invite Jack to the house, just to say hello. "He rescued all those people from the burning plane."

Mama and Baba looked at each other.

"We're friends."

"They're friends," Baba said to Mama.

Later, when the doorbell rang, Athena answered. "Hello, Jack."

"Hello, Athena."

"We were in the same year at school," Athena explained to Mama and Baba.

"And now?" Baba asked Jack. "What do you do now?"

"Now I'm an electrician, sir."

"Your parents are living?" Mama asked.

"I'm afraid not, Mrs. Demetrious."

"Family is everything," Mama said.

"Yes, it is," Jack said.

"You understand our Christina is precious to us," Baba said.

"Yes, sir."

"And she will marry a Greek boy someday. You understand that, too?"

"I understand your wishes for your daughter, sir. And I respect them."

"Good," Baba said.

Mama grabbed hold of Baba's arm, as if to steady herself.

Athena tried to hide a smile.

THAT NIGHT they made love using both her new diaphragm and a rubber, because she wasn't sure she was using the diaphragm correctly. She found it complicated and messy. First you had to put in the jelly and rub it around, making sure you got enough over the rim, then you had to squeeze it together and insert it into your vagina, getting it up far enough. She'd been practicing in her room at night. When she pulled it out she had to wash it, pat it dry and store it in its case, something else she'd have to hide, or maybe Jack would keep it. Yes, that would make sense. She supposed she'd get used to it. She supposed it would get easier. They were going to be married for a long time and she didn't want to be pregnant every year like Mrs. O'Malley's daughter, who'd already had five babies. But she still wasn't relaxed about going all the way. She supposed she had to give it some time.

Elizabeth Daily Post

ROSENBERGS GET PASSOVER VISIT

APRIL 9 (UPI)—Julius and Ethel Rosenberg, sentenced
to die for transmitting A-bomb secrets to the Soviet Union,
received a pre-Passover visit at Sing Sing prison from their
5- and 9-year-old sons. Meanwhile, following today's denial
of their last plea to the Court of Appeals, the couple's lawyer
said that he would be filing an appeal with the United States
Supreme Court.

29

Miri

Twice a week Miri sent a card to Natalie at the Watchung Hills Children's Home. *Heard you were under the
weather. Well, come on out!* Miri wasn't sure Natalie would
find any of the cards funny. Half the time *she* wasn't sure
they were funny. Sometimes she'd include a little note,
trying to keep it light, something about school, or about
a TV show. *Uncle Miltie dressed as Carmen Miranda Tuesday night. He wore a hat loaded with bananas, pineapples and
grapes. My mother laughed so hard she almost didn't make
it to the bathroom in time.* She'd bought all the cards at
once at the Ritz Book Shop, along with a copy of *Seventeenth Summer*. She and Natalie had read it together, at

the beginning of eighth grade, and Miri hoped when and if she had the chance to give it to her, it would remind Natalie of their friendship, because Natalie didn't answer any of Miri's cards or notes.

Irene suggested inviting Mason to their Seder on the first night of Passover, surprising Miri. Miri wore her new patent-leather slingbacks. Mason brought lilacs for Irene. They all missed Henry and Leah, who had gone to visit Leah's parents. But Miss Rheingold was there and Blanche Kessler from the Red Cross with her family and Ben Sapphire.

Corinne called a few days later, another surprise, saying if Miri would like to see Natalie she would pick her up at school the next afternoon, if that was convenient for her.

That night Miri wrapped the copy of *Seventeenth Summer* and tied it with one of the ribbons from Irene's collection. "She doesn't know you're coming," Corinne said on the drive to Watchung. "She doesn't want anyone to see her in this place but the doctors think it might be good for her to begin to reconnect to the outside world."

"Is she coming home soon?"

"Maybe in time for graduation. Just act as if nothing's changed. As if you're still best friends."

Aren't we still best friends? Miri thought, though she didn't say it aloud.

The Watchung Hills Children's Home, a big white house, sat on a hill surrounded by tall trees. The azaleas were in bloom. The grass was very green.

Inside, the halls were filled with music and children's laughter.

Corinne stopped outside Room 218. She knocked on

the door before turning the knob. "Everyone decent?" She didn't wait for a reply.

Miri hung back, anxious, not sure what she'd find inside the room.

"Nat . . . look who's here!" Corinne called, stepping back to make room for Miri. "I'll leave you two alone to catch up," she said brightly, as if there were nothing unusual about Miri visiting Natalie in this place. Then she disappeared.

From the look on Natalie's face, first surprise, then anger followed by disgust or maybe embarrassment, Miri could see Natalie didn't want her there any more than she wanted to be there.

"Hi," Miri said, trying to make her voice sound as bright as Corinne's.

"Hi."

"I'm glad you're feeling better."

"I'm alive, if that's what you mean." Natalie's voice had an edge to it.

In the other bed someone was sleeping. She had the covers pulled up so high almost her whole head and face were covered. One arm lay outstretched, attached to tubes.

Natalie was wearing regular clothes—dungarees, a shirt and a bulky cardigan sweater. She didn't look any different to Miri than she had that day she went cuckoo in the basement. Well, maybe a little better than that, but not much.

"You were there that day, right?" Natalie asked.

"Which day?"

"That day I went to the hospital."

"Oh, that day."

"You'll never believe who my nurse was."

"Who?"

"Phyllis Kirk's mother."

"Phyllis Kirk, the actress?"

"Yes, isn't that something? And she told me Phyllis is up for a big part in a Vincent Price movie. And it's going to be in 3-D."

"What does that mean?" Miri asked.

"I'm not sure."

Now the figure in the other bed sat up. She was so thin Miri was sure she'd been in a concentration camp. Next to her Natalie seemed almost healthy. Natalie, at least, had some color in her cheeks.

The skeleton said, "You have to wear special glasses and it looks like things are jumping out at you."

"How do you know?" Miri asked.

The girl shrugged.

"Lulu knows a lot," Natalie said.

So, the skeleton had a name.

"How come they let you see a friend?" Lulu asked Natalie.

"I don't know," Natalie said.

"Friends can make you feel worse about yourself," Lulu said.

"I don't want to do that," Miri told her.

"You don't want to, but you might anyway."

"Should I go?" Miri asked, hoping the answer was yes.

"Why don't you just shut up for once, Lulu?" Natalie said.

Lulu laughed. "So are you from Plane Crash City, too?" she asked Miri, swooping her free arm around like a plane taking off, then coming straight down, onto her bed. "Boom!"

"Come on." Natalie grabbed Miri by the sleeve and pulled her out of the room, then down the hall to a sunroom, where other kids had visitors, too. Many of the kids had braces on their legs. Some had crutches. Others were in wheelchairs, their legs straight out in plaster casts. "They had polio," Natalie explained. "They're learning to walk again. If you want milk and cookies they're on a table over there." She pointed across the room.

"What about you?"

"I don't drink milk or eat cookies."

"Okay." Miri helped herself to two shortbread cookies and a small cup of milk.

She sat down on a sofa next to Natalie.

"My hair is growing back," Natalie said.

"I didn't know you cut it."

"I didn't. It was falling out. From my condition."

Miri was dying to ask, *What condition?* But she was trying to act ordinary, like it was just another day. "It looks good. Like always."

"Lulu and I are the only freaks here. We didn't have polio, and we don't have cerebral palsy. What's happening at school?"

Wait—what do you mean freaks? Miri wanted to ask. Instead she said, "School . . . you know . . . the usual, except I was almost expelled."

"You, Goody Two-Shoes? What'd you do?"

"Wrote a story for the paper Mr. Royer didn't like, so I handed it out on my own." *And I'm not Goody Two-Shoes*, she wanted to add, but didn't. "The chorus is practicing for graduation. We're singing 'Younger Than Springtime.'"

"I hate that song."

"It's pretty sappy."

"What about you . . . are you still in love with Mason?"

"We're still the same."

"Why won't you admit you're in love?"

Miri didn't answer. Didn't say she was afraid to call it love, although it was love, and not puppy love, either. It was something much deeper now. Last week, in Irene's basement, she took his hand and placed it on her breast. It bothered her that he never tried to get to second base, never mind third. Why didn't he want to go any further with her? As an experiment she pulled her sweater over her head. His hands on her naked back were almost more than she could stand. But she didn't stop there. She reached around and unhooked her bra, showing him her breasts. Neither one of them spoke for the longest time. Then he said, "What are you doing?"

"I want you to touch me." She took his hands and placed them on her perfect A-cup breasts.

She could hear his breath quicken as he ran his hands over them. And *she* felt something, too, something down there, the way she did at night in her bed when she touched herself.

"It's not a good idea," he said.

"Why?" she asked, kissing him.

"Suppose I can't stop?"

"I'll stop you."

"You don't understand."

"I just wanted to make sure . . ."

"What?"

"That you like me *that* way." She put her bra back on, pulled on her sweater.

"And now?" he asked.

"Now I know you do."

She couldn't tell Natalie or anyone how much she cared. Probably Rusty once loved Mike Monsky, or thought she had. And look how that ended.

"What are the girls saying about me?" Natalie asked, bringing Miri back to the moment.

"They hope you'll get better soon."

"What do they think is wrong with me?"

"None of us knows what's wrong."

"Do they laugh when they talk about me?"

"No! Why would they laugh?" She would never say that they hardly ever talked about her. She was as removed from their lives as Robo, living in her new house in Millburn. Even more removed.

"Because it's funny, isn't it? I didn't even see the crashes, but here I am. My mother says I'm just very sensitive. Do you think I'm sensitive?"

"I guess. What about Ruby? What does she think?"

"She abandoned me a while back. Didn't even say goodbye. Didn't even say I'd be okay without her."

"Are you . . . okay without her?"

"What you see is what you get."

"Why are you talking in riddles?"

"That's not a riddle. A riddle would be more like, *What's soft and mushy and gray all over?*"

Miri didn't have a clue. "I give up."

"Natalie's messed-up brain. Get it?"

Miri was growing more uncomfortable by the minute. How long did Corinne expect her to stay here?

"Did you hear?" Natalie said. "My father wants us to move to Nevada. To someplace called Las Vegas."

"Nevada! But that's so far away, isn't it?"

"Only two thousand, five hundred miles. It takes five days to drive there. Some people fly. You have to make two or three stops. My mother swears she'll never go. They hate each other."

"No, they don't."

"Ever since the crash that killed Mrs. Barnes's son, all they do is fight."

"But New Year's Eve . . . the party, the diamond earrings . . ."

"All an act. God forbid Corinne's friends think there's trouble in paradise. One time she slapped his face at a party."

"No."

"She accused him of flirting with one of her friends. I found out from listening in on a phone call between my mother and Ceil Rubin. 'We all understand,' Ceil said. Then my mother started crying and I hung up the extension. That's one good thing about being here. I don't have to listen to them arguing. They never visit at the same time unless the doctors say they have to. Sometimes I think it would be fun to live in Nevada. No plane crashes. I'd have my own horse."

"But where would you go to school?"

"They have schools. At least I think they do. I'd go anywhere to get out of this place. But first I have to eat." She jumped up and grabbed a banana from the snack table. "I've been eating bananas without throwing up. Next is sweet potatoes. Did you know sweet potatoes are a perfect food? All the vitamins and minerals you could want wrapped into one tuber. Come on, let's go . . ." She grabbed Miri's hand and led her down the hall, back to her room. "I've been studying food groups in science. My tutor—did you know I have a tutor?"

"No."

"She graduated from Teachers College at Columbia. She's Lulu's tutor, too." Natalie pushed open the door to her room. "The trouble with Lulu is she wants to die. I don't want to die. I really don't."

Miri reached for Natalie's hand and for just a moment Natalie looked right into her eyes. "Will you miss me if I go?"

"You know I will." Did she mean *die* or move to Nevada?

Lulu said, "If I wanted to die that badly I'd be dead by now, Goldilocks."

"She pulls out her tubes," Natalie said. "She tricks the nurses. You know what she has? It's called anorexia nervosa."

"You have it, too, cutie pie." Lulu looked at Miri and pointed a finger at Natalie. "She has it, too."

"You never know if she's telling the truth or lying," Natalie said with a nod toward Lulu. "You can't believe anything she says. If she croaks I just hope she does it when I'm not around."

"I'll remember that, Golden One."

"See this banana," Natalie said to Miri, as she began to peel back the skin.

"Don't eat that in front of me or I'll vomit," Lulu said.

"She can't even look at food."

"I can if it's a picture in a magazine. Just not the real stuff. Not the smelly stuff."

"I have to go outside to eat a banana," Natalie said. "*Banana!*" she shouted, wagging it in front of Lulu.

Lulu gagged and reached for her call button. A nurse came into the room. "What now, Lulu?"

"She made me gag."

"I didn't *make* her gag," Natalie said. "I showed her the banana, that's all."

Miri snuck a look at her watch. She wanted to get out of there in the worst way.

"I think your mother is waiting for me," she told Natalie. She picked up the gift-wrapped copy of *Seventeenth Summer* from the chair where she'd set it down earlier and handed it to Natalie. "I brought this for you."

"I hope it's not chocolates."

"It's a book."

"Let's see," Lulu said as Natalie tore the paper off Miri's gift. "*Seventeenth Summer* . . . how sweet. Are you in love with her?" Lulu asked Miri.

"Don't answer that!" Natalie said. Then, quietly, she told Miri, "I already read it."

"I know," Miri said. "We read it together. I just thought . . . I thought . . ."

Lulu started singing, *"Be my love . . ."*

"Shut up, Lulu!" Natalie said.

"I've got to go," Miri said.

"Sure," Natalie said. "I don't blame you."

"HOW DID SHE SEEM?" Corinne asked on the way home.

"She was good."

"Argumentative? Angry?"

Miri nodded. "A little."

"That's better than depressed. She's eating again. Not

a lot. And only a few things. But that's progress. Green grapes, iceberg lettuce and bananas. Like a chimpanzee." Corinne gave a sharp laugh. "Oh, god—I don't know why I said that. Please don't mention that I said that, about the chimpanzee."

Miri wanted to say she liked chimpanzees, but she didn't.

Elizabeth Daily Post

Editorial

REASON HAS ITS LIMITATIONS

APRIL 14—The inflamed mob action which has been taking place in Egypt, Tunisia, Iran and elsewhere should point a major lesson to democratic western policy makers—the futility of placing too much faith in logic and reason when dealing with angry, impassioned peoples. Something similar can be seen even here in a few of the more violent and irrational proposals made to combat Newark Airport Expansion.

30

Steve

On April 15 Steve got an acceptance letter from Syracuse. Phil got in, too. Just the way they'd planned. Instead of celebrating, Steve went down to Williamson Street and walked around where Kathy died, all the time talking to her, trying to explain what was going on. Or maybe he was trying to explain it to himself. How someone his age, someone beautiful, someone he had dreamed about, someone he had kissed, could have stepped onto a plane one January afternoon and be dead an hour and a half later. How could that happen? How could that be real?

So, thanks, but no thanks, Syracuse. He was never setting foot on that campus again, never setting foot in that town, in the whole of upstate New York.

Phil was waiting for him when he got home, sitting outside in his car. "I figured you'd come home sooner or later."

Steve shoehorned himself into Phil's MG, an early graduation present from his parents. "I'm not going to Syracuse," Steve told him.

"Me neither," Phil said. "So which one do you want to go to—Rutgers or Lehigh?"

Steve shrugged.

"I say Lehigh," Phil said. "Put some distance between us and our families."

"Okay."

"We have to send back our forms with a check."

"Okay."

"Tomorrow, right?"

"Sure. Tomorrow."

"I'm counting on you," Phil said.

"Don't count on me too much."

"What do you mean? We're in this together."

"I got to go," Steve said, getting out of Phil's car.

He supposed by now his mother had told his father he'd gotten into all three schools he'd applied to. But maybe not. Because his mother and father didn't seem to be speaking these days. Life at home was no fun, to put it mildly. Natalie was lucky she was at that rest home. He hoped she was getting plenty of rest. Because there was nothing restful about living here. Only Fern carried on as if everything were okay. Maybe that was her way of dealing with it. Pretend everything is fine. Same as always. Too bad he couldn't do that.

Inside, his parents and Fern were waiting for him in the kitchen. "Congratulations!" they called out. Was this a surprise party? Were his friends hiding in the other room? He looked around, but no, it was just the family. What was left of the family. He supposed he should be grateful. A surprise party was the last thing he wanted. Besides, all his friends would be celebrating with their families tonight, except for the ones who didn't get into their first-choice schools.

"Look at your cake!" Fern sang. "It's your favorite. All chocolate. From Allen's Bakery."

"We're proud of you, son," his father said, throwing an arm over his shoulder.

His mother embraced him. "I never doubted you'd do well."

"Can we eat the cake now?" Fern asked, practically drooling over it.

"After Steve has his supper," his mother said. "I'll heat up the plate I saved for you."

"No, I'll have cake for my supper," Steve said, making Fern clap her hands.

His mother started to protest but his father said, "You're not going to be there next year to make sure he has supper before dessert. You might as well get used to it."

At which point his mother burst into tears and left the room.

"She's just emotional about you leaving home," his father said, trying to reassure him.

"Good Natalie's not here," Fern said. "She doesn't eat cake."

DESK-FAX SERVICE COMES TO AREA

APRIL 28—Western Union has introduced an electronic service which provides the busy businessman with a push-button telegraph office right on his desk. The device is the Desk-Fax, a machine which sends and receives telegrams by literally taking a picture of them.

Transmission is possible up to nine miles. The quality diminishes over longer distances because of the limitations of telephone lines.

31

Christina

Dr. O seemed tense at the office. Daisy was sweeping up more figurines than usual. Christina kept count of them. One day there were five dwarfs left on the shelf, and the next, only three. A few days later Daisy took her aside. "He can't decide whether to take the offer to open a practice in Las Vegas or not. His friends are building a modern medical-dental center and they're begging him to come. If he does, I'm willing to go with him. What about you, Christina—would you consider starting a new life after graduation?"

"You mean move to Las Vegas?"

"If he decides to go."

"I don't know. Jack would have to want to go, too."

"You should tell him there will be great jobs for an electrician out there. Think of all the hotels they're building."

"But it's so far away."

"It *is* far away. I can't deny that."

"My parents . . ."

"I know. It's hard to leave family behind."

"They'd never agree to let me go."

"But you'd have plenty of vacation time to come home and visit. And you could make it a two-year commitment, like going away to college, except instead of paying, you get paid. You'd make good money, too."

"But I wouldn't know anyone."

"You'd know me. And Dr. O. And you and Jack would make new friends."

"Jack is 1-A. He could get called up at any time."

"Let's hope that ridiculous war ends before then."

"Daisy—can I tell you something? You'd have to keep it to yourself. I mean it, no one can know. But if I don't tell someone, I'm going to explode."

"You can trust me, Christina."

"I know I can."

Daisy waited for more.

Christina finally bit the bullet and blurted out, "Jack and I are secretly married. We eloped to Elkton."

Daisy came out from behind her desk. "Oh, Christina." She put her arms around her. "I hope you'll be very happy." Then, "You didn't *have* to get married, did you?"

Christina laughed. "No. And that doctor you sent me

to . . . he fitted me for a diaphragm so I won't have to worry."

"When are you going to tell your parents?"

"I haven't figured that out yet."

"Well, don't say anything about Las Vegas yet. First, Dr. O has to make up his mind. But I have a feeling he's going to do it, and I admit I'm kind of excited about going. I'm starting to feel like a pioneer."

A pioneer, Christina thought. The Wild West. She'd have to learn to ride a horse, she supposed. The idea of it made her giddy.

Daisy

Christina and Jack were married! She knew Christina had something on her mind but a secret marriage had never occurred to her. She should have guessed. Hadn't she done the same at Christina's age—running off with Gerald Dupree, né Dorfman, to Elkton? *Gerald Dupree.* What a name. And *Daisy Dupree*—even better. A fabulous name, she'd thought at the time, a name fit for a stripper, or, even better, a movie star, which made her laugh—the only good thing that had come out of her hasty young marriage, annulled two weeks after they'd eloped.

But that was a lifetime ago. Gerry had been older, twenty-five to her eighteen. He'd been working for ten years by then, for the Stasio boys, number runners, then bootleggers. It was 1936, times were hard. She was a year out of Linden High School, where she'd won every award in the business program—for typing, steno, bookkeeping. She was lucky to find a job working as a secretary for an insurance agent in Newark. She wasn't his *número uno*, as he called his longtime secretary, but he liked Daisy, admired her for her organizational skills. With her first paycheck she went for an eye exam, got prescription glasses and the difference in the way she could see felt like a miracle.

Tall, with perfect skin and thick dark hair cut short, a good body, excellent posture, Daisy could have passed for twenty-five. Her older sister, Evelyn, had taught her a thing or two about using makeup, about flirting.

She'd met Gerald Dupree at a lunch counter, where they'd both ordered split-pea soup. When their checks came he put down the fifteen cents to pay for hers. She married him on a whim, two months later.

She knew what to expect on her wedding night, but nothing beyond that. In a motel outside Elkton, Gerry became frustrated with her. "What's going on down there?" he'd asked.

"How should I know?" she'd answered.

"I can't get in."

"I told you—I'm a virgin."

"I've had my share of virgins, baby, but this is something else."

He sent her to a doctor, who broke the news. She would never be able to have children, would never have normal sexual relations. She understood about not being able to have children. But what did she know about normal? What did she know about sexual relations? She didn't ask questions, and the doctor didn't offer explanations.

When she told Gerry she would not be able to have children he seemed more angry than disappointed. He didn't hold her or kiss her or say he loved her anyway. "Did he tell you why you couldn't have children?" he asked.

"Something about missing female body parts."

"Jesus, body parts! What body parts? You mean you're a freak? I married a freak? Did you know? You must have known."

"I didn't know."

"How could you not have known? You tricked me into marrying you."

"How did I trick you?"

"You gave me the come-on from day one. You were such a sexpot. Did you think I wouldn't find out? What did you think would happen when . . . oh, Christ, never mind. We'll get it annulled."

"What's 'annulled'?"

"It means, since the marriage was never consummated—"

"What's 'consummated'?"

"We never had sex. Do you know what that means?"

She wasn't an idiot. She just didn't understand what was happening.

"So now we go back to the way it was before we went to Elkton," he told her. "We go back to our lives before we met."

"Can I keep your name?"

This made him laugh. "*Dupree*? You want to be *Daisy Dupree*?"

"Yes."

"Fuck, Daisy! How're you going to explain that to your family?"

"That's my business."

"Be my guest."

· · ·

AFTER THAT, she'd reinvented herself. She'd learned to throw back a Scotch, to straddle a chair, smoke a pack of Camels a day and laugh at off-color jokes. She even told a few herself.

When her brother-in-law, Mel, said, *You've turned into a real broad, Daisy,* she'd said, *Good for me!*

She became strong, even tough if she had to be, a woman who made friends with men but who never let it get romantic. She was done with all that, with girlish dreams of houses with picket fences and little children calling her "Mommy." She was a female in every way but one. So she was missing some of her lady parts. So what? The doctor had referred to her as "juvenile" down there. Well, that was the only part of her that was juvenile. She'd never have to worry about why she wasn't getting pregnant, the way her sister, Evelyn, did. Maybe Evelyn was missing lady parts, too. She hadn't told Evelyn or anyone else about her *condition.*

She lived with Evelyn and Mel in the small house she and Evelyn had inherited from their father. When Mel was killed driving home one rainy night on Vauxhall Road, Daisy was there for her sister. After a few months she encouraged Evelyn to take a refresher course at Katharine Gibbs, using some of the insurance money she'd collected when Mel died. "Get a job," Daisy told her. "You'll feel better."

But jobs were scarce. The insurance agent was sorry he had to let Daisy go but the Depression was taking its toll, as if she didn't know. She learned to drive her father's old car, which had been sitting in the garage since her father's death. The mechanic down the street got it running in exchange for a few bags of groceries. She heard about a dental practice in Elizabeth, looking for an assistant. She was interviewed by the dentist and his wife. They hired her on the spot. They hoped things would improve soon, and when they did, they'd promised her a raise.

AFTER TEN YEARS working for Dr. O, he'd asked out of the blue, "I don't mean to pry, Daisy, but how is it a beautiful, accomplished woman like you has never married?"

She'd burst into tears, surprising herself and Dr. O.

"There . . . there . . ." he'd said, holding her, patting her back the way her father might have.

She felt so safe with him, trusted him so completely, she told him about Gerald Dupree and her condition.

He took a minute to respond. "Would you like me to set up an appointment with a specialist for you?"

"Yes," she said, surprising herself again. "I would."

The specialist confirmed the first doctor's findings. He gave a name to her condition, though she would never use it. She asked Dr. O to tell no one, not even his wife.

"You don't have to worry," he said. "You are an extraordinary person, Daisy. Among the finest I've ever known. I consider myself lucky to have you in my life."

"The feelings are mutual, Dr. O."

She'd thought after that day they'd have no secrets from each other.

Part Four

May–August 1952

Elizabeth Daily Post

COMMERCIAL JET FLIGHTS BEGIN

By Henry Ammerman

MAY 3—While Elizabeth awaits the CAB verdict on the reopening of Newark Airport, a new era of airplane travel began today with the flight of a British De Havilland Comet jet airliner from London to Johannesburg, South Africa. The British Overseas Airways Corporation plane carried a full payload of 36 passengers on this first-ever commercial jet trip. The journey was expected to take 24 hours, with intermediate stops in Rome, Beirut, Khartoum, Uganda and Northern Rhodesia.

With a top cruising speed of 480 miles per hour, the Comet is 50% faster than propeller aircraft such as the DC-6, and its proponents say it provides smoother and quieter travel.

32

Miri

On May 8 news spread that another plane had crashed in Elizabeth, smashing into Levy Brothers department store. Miri was eating lunch at her usual table in the cafeteria when she heard. She felt sick to her stomach and had to swallow again and again to keep down the egg salad sandwich she'd just finished. She thought of the lady who worked in the teen department at Levy Brothers, the one who was having her nails done the morning Mr. Roman gave Miri her Elizabeth Taylor haircut. Had she been at work today? Was she dead now?

The teacher who was lunch monitor that week shouted, "Everyone under the tables. Now!" She was one of the new, young teachers. She wore small pearl earrings that gave her face a glow. But now she wasn't glowing. She shouted, "Quiet, please! Another plane may be on the way. Cover your heads with your hands."

Kids were screaming. Someone vomited on the floor. The smell of sweat mixed with the vomit and the uneaten lunches. They had grown complacent, Miri thought, more interested in ninth-grade graduation and going off to high school than about planes crashing. They'd been moving on with their lives, which is what their parents urged them to do. They were trying to be regular kids, happy kids, to please their families. But this proved you never knew when something terrible would happen. Miri wished she could be with Mason. If she was going to die she wanted to die in his arms. Oh, god—please let him be all right. She and Suzanne held on to each other under the table. Some girls were whimpering. For once, the boys shut up.

Miri could smell her own sweat, the sweat of fear, the sweat that deodorant didn't prevent. Robo was probably so glad she'd moved away from Elizabeth. But not every-one could afford to buy a house in Millburn or South Orange or some other fancy town where planes didn't crash. Suzanne's eyes were tightly shut. Her lips moved silently. Probably she was praying. But praying wouldn't save them, would it? It didn't save the people on the planes. Not that Miri knew if they'd prayed, but she was betting they had. Was Suzanne praying to Jesus? Did it matter who you prayed to? Did anything matter?

It seemed like they were under the lunch tables for hours. Finally, an all-clear whistle blew. As they came out, they saw Donny Kellen, that idiot, standing on a table, shouting into a bullhorn. "April Fool! April Fool, everybody!"

"It's May, you asshole!" Charley Kaminsky yelled, throwing his half-finished plate of spaghetti and meatballs at Donny. That's when all hell broke loose. Kids rushed at Donny while he danced around on the table trying to avoid the food being hurled at him like bullets—half-eaten sandwiches from home, the daily special from the cafeteria, apples, oranges, candy bars.

Miri pitched her milk carton at him and clipped the side of his head. "Ow!" he yelled. "Stop . . . come on . . . it was just a joke! Can't you take a joke?"

A group of boys pulled him down from the table and started pummeling him.

Was he evil or just stupid? And why should they believe him when he said it was just a joke? He wasn't someone you could trust.

The young teacher couldn't begin to control the madness. "People, please . . . people!" But her pleas didn't stop them. She sent Eleanor to the office to get help.

Minutes later the principal's voice came over the loudspeaker, telling them it was a hoax. "Boys and girls," Mr. Royer said. Just the sound of his voice was enough to infuriate Miri. "There is no danger. There was no plane crash. Return to your tables immediately and give your attention to Miss Jensen."

None of them liked Edith Jensen, the vice principal.

She probably didn't like them, either. She marched into the cafeteria, grabbed Donny Kellen by the arm and demanded that he apologize. "Apologize to your classmates right now."

"But I didn't *do* anything."

"Apologize!"

"I'm sorry," Donny Kellen said. "I thought—"

"That's the problem," Miss Jensen said. "You didn't think. You never think. You probably haven't had a lucid thought in your life!" And she dragged him out of the cafeteria. Maybe Mr. Royer had already called the police. Maybe Donny Kellen would be taken away to jail, or juvenile detention. Miri was sure at the very least he'd be expelled. Finally, Mr. Royer could expel someone who deserved it.

That afternoon kids walked out of school without going to class, without waiting for bells or for teachers to dismiss them. They took off alone, or in groups. Some of the girls flirted with the boys, who flirted back by knocking their books out of their hands or snapping jackets at them. Suzanne wanted to go to Pamel's, the sweet shop on Broad Street, and celebrate with a banana split. But Miri wasn't in the mood to celebrate. It still felt all too real to her. It could have been another plane, it could have been anything. Was this how it was going to be? Always waiting for the next disaster?

She walked home alone, forgetting that Irene had gone to New York for the day with Ben Sapphire. She would have welcomed Irene's warm embrace. Instead, she headed upstairs to her room, where she would lie on her bed with the kaleidoscope, losing herself in its beautiful patterns and colors.

Upstairs, something felt wrong. Rusty's bedroom door was closed and it sounded as if she was sick. Rusty had never missed a day of work in her life—but now she was mewling. "Mom . . ." Miri opened the door to Rusty's room and wasn't sure at first what she was seeing.

Rusty looked over the shoulder of whoever was on top of her. "Ohmygod, Miri!"

Miri couldn't breathe, let alone speak. A man, naked, with a white backside, turned to look at her and Miri let out one cry, then covered her mouth with her hand and ran down the stairs, out of the house, up the street. That was Dr. O on top of her mother, and he wasn't checking her teeth.

Then Rusty was running after her, a raincoat thrown over a black lace negligee. "Miri, wait!"

Miri turned for a minute, in time to see Rusty trip over the negligee, too long for her raincoat to cover, her bare feet in her weekend moccasins. Miri didn't want anyone to see her mother this way. Didn't want the neighbors to gossip and ask each other what Rusty Ammerman was doing home in the middle of the day, wearing a black lace negligee and chasing her daughter down Sayre Street toward Morris Avenue.

Miri stopped, letting Rusty catch up with her. "You look ridiculous!" Miri told her.

"I guess so," Rusty said.

"Go home, Mom."

"Not unless you come with me."

Rusty tried to put her arm around Miri but Miri backed away, repelled. "Don't touch me!"

. . .

DR. O WAS GONE when they got home.

"I'm sorry this is the way you found out," Rusty said, wrapping the raincoat around her middle and tying the belt. "We were waiting until the divorce to tell you."

"What divorce?"

"Arthur and Corinne's."

"They can't get divorced. That will make Natalie sicker than she is now."

"Natalie knows," Rusty said.

"You told her but not me?"

"She doesn't know about her father and me. She only knows they're separating."

"I'll never forgive you for this. And I'll never trust you again, either."

"Honey—"

"Don't *honey* me . . . and don't act like everything's going to be okay, because it's not."

"I know this is a shock. I wish I could have told you sooner. I don't expect you to understand right away. But I hope—"

"What happened to honesty is the best policy? What happened to trust? All those things you told me when you accused me of betraying you? You probably lied about my father, too."

"I never lied to you about your father. And I'm not lying to you now."

"Did you tell him you were pregnant? Did he leave because of that?" How did this turn into a fight about Mike Monsky?

Rusty sat down. "He enlisted before I knew. Later, Irene wanted to tell his family but I wouldn't let her."

So that's how it was.

"I didn't want to marry him, Miri. It never would have worked, and by then he'd shipped out anyway."

"Does Nana know about Dr. O? Does Uncle Henry?"

"No one knows. We've tried to be discreet to avoid hurting anyone we love."

"Is this why Corinne and Dr. O have been fighting?"

"I can't answer questions about their marriage."

"He gave Corinne diamond earrings for Hanukkah. Did you know that?"

"No."

"Well, he did."

"I don't need diamond earrings to prove he loves me."

NATALIE PHONED Miri the following night. "I need to see you. Come to the house tomorrow right after school."

"The house? You're home?"

"No questions."

"But what about—"

Natalie didn't wait for her to finish. "Just don't be late."

Miri rode her bike to Natalie's right after school. She was relieved Corinne's car wasn't in the driveway. She didn't see how she could face Corinne.

Natalie was waiting at the door and rushed Miri up to her bedroom, closed the door behind them and blocked it with a chair.

Miri was surprised and uncomfortable. Should she be afraid? She didn't know. "How long have you been home?" she asked.

"Since Lulu died."

"Lulu died? That's terrible."

"Terrible things happen, in case you didn't already know."

"But it's so sad."

"A lot of things are sad."

"Are you going back to Watchung Hills?"

"Not if I can help it. Sit down and stop asking questions. I have a couple of things I want to tell you."

Miri wasn't used to Natalie bossing her around but she did as she was told, sitting on the edge of the twin bed, the one she used to sleep in almost every weekend, the one she thought of as hers. Natalie sat on her own bed, facing Miri. "One—you can stop this from happening. And if you don't I'll never speak to you again."

"Stop what?"

"Don't go all naïve on me."

"I thought you didn't know . . ."

"Well, now I do and you have to stop my father from marrying your mother and ruining my life, my little sister's life and my mother's life."

"How am I supposed to do that? They're grown-ups. They do what they want."

"Tell your mother she has to decide between you and my father."

Miri shook her head. She didn't think she could do that. Suppose she came out the loser?

"Two—refuse to go to Las Vegas."

"Las Vegas! What are you talking about?"

"Don't tell me you don't know. They're going to Las Vegas together at the end of the school year and you're going with them."

"No I'm not."

"If you don't stop them, you are. You're going to Las Vegas and you'll never see me or your boyfriend again."

"Stop!"

"Tell your mother to stop, not me. And just so you know, my father begged my mother to go with him. He was practically on his knees begging her to go. He promised Fern and me our own horses. But she said no. So my father found someone else to go with him. Your mother!"

"Why should I believe you?"

"I really don't care who you believe. I'm just telling you what's going on. And here's something else you should know. My mother's at her lawyer's office right now. She's going to take my father to the cleaners if they get divorced. There won't be anything left for your mother or you. I hope you'll be happy living on spaghetti."

Miri liked spaghetti but she wasn't getting into that now.

"I hate them!" Natalie shouted, pressing the sides of her head with her hands as if she were in agony. "I hate my father, your mother and I hate you!"

"What'd I do?"

"You found them."

"Who told you that?"

"My father came clean. He told my mother everything last night, and she told me. She says your mother is no better than a whore."

A whore! Her once-upon-a-time best friend was calling her mother a *whore*? Miri got a sharp pain in her chest. Maybe she was going to die, just like Lulu.

"What's wrong with you?" Natalie said. "You're turning purple. You can't scare me if that's what you're trying to do." Natalie grabbed her by the shoulders and shook, then slapped her across the face, which got her breathing again.

Miri jumped up. She had to get out of there, had to get fresh air into her lungs. She knocked over the chair blocking Natalie's door, flung the door open and fled down the stairs, shouting at Natalie, who was right behind her, "Never say that about my mother again! You hear me? *Never!*" Then she was out the kitchen door, and onto her bicycle.

Natalie followed her, screaming, "You know what they do in Las Vegas? They drop A-bombs in the desert. That's what they do for fun!"

Miri's fantasy was coming true but not the way it was supposed to. Corinne was supposed to meet her demise quickly, painlessly. She and Natalie were supposed to be sisters. They were supposed to be one big happy family, living in the red-brick house on Shelley Avenue. Not in some godforsaken place called Las Vegas, where they drop A-bombs for fun.

Christina

She waited until Sunday dinner, when they were all together around the dining room table—her parents, her grandparents, Athena and her husband, Thad, who hardly ever spoke at family gatherings, and their toddler, Alex, who was playing under the table. She waited until the lamb, the eggplant and the salad courses had been cleared from the table. Then, as her mother passed around little dessert cakes, Christina said, "Mama, Baba—you know I love you." She'd been practicing in her room. She hoped it wasn't a mistake to bring this up in front of the whole family but she wanted to get it over with all at once and she figured her parents would be less likely to go cuckoo in front of her grandparents and little Alex.

She had their attention now. Mama and Baba looked from one to the other.

"I've got an opportunity," she continued, "a wonderful job opportunity with Dr. Osner in another place—"

"What place?" her mother asked.

"Las Vegas," she said.

"Las Vegas." Her mother repeated this twice, then asked, "Where is Las Vegas?"

Athena said, "You don't mean Las Vegas, Nevada? You're not telling Mama and Baba you're moving to Las Vegas, Nevada?"

She had hoped Athena would keep her mouth shut, for once. She should have known better.

"How far is this place?" Mama asked.

"Almost as far as California," Athena said, holding her pregnant belly. She'd already gained close to forty pounds. Her maternity dress was snug across her middle.

Mama clutched her chest. "Nico," she said to Baba. "Do something!"

"I'm not moving there." Christina tried to reassure them. "Think of it as college. Two years of college but it won't cost you anything. Instead *I'll* be getting paid. And I'll come home for the holidays."

Baba said, "That Irish boy, he's going, too?"

Now Mama screamed. "No!" She banged her fist on the table hard enough to make the glasses and the silverware jump. Alex climbed onto Thad's lap and wrapped his fat little arms around his father's neck.

"You're breaking their hearts, Christina," Athena said.

"You don't understand," Christina said to her parents.

"Jack is 1-A—he could be called up at any time. You know what that means? He could be sent to Korea. Would you be happy then?"

Thad got up from the table and carried Alex, who had begun to whimper, out of the room.

Athena glared at Christina. "You have a way of ruining everything, even Sunday dinner. You do this and I'm the one who's going to have to pick up the pieces around here. It will all fall on my shoulders. You are the most selfish person I've ever known."

The grandparents began jabbering to one another in Greek.

Baba said, "Girls—you are sisters! Stop this fighting."

But Athena didn't stop. Her face heated up. "As if I don't already have too many fish to fry, between the store and Alex and the baby I'm about to have and a husb—" Before Athena could finish she cried out, "Oh!" Then "Oh!" again.

"What is it?" Mama asked.

"I think my water broke. I think I'm in labor. Somebody get Thad. Somebody get my bag!"

Everyone jumped up from the table at once. Everyone except Christina and her grandmother. Yaya moved next to her and rested her hand on Christina's. Christina put her head on the table and cried. She hadn't even told them her biggest news. She didn't see how she'd ever be able to tell them now.

Miri

Rusty and Dr. O wanted to take her out to dinner but Miri refused. She was not going to be seen with the two of them in public. "All right," Rusty said, "we'll eat here."

"Does he know you can't cook?"

Rusty smiled. "If you can read, you can cook."

"Are you quitting your job?"

"Not yet."

"When?"

Rusty shook her head. "Would you like pizza or deli?"

"Pizza from Spirito's. No sausage. Will Nana and Uncle Henry be eating with us?"

"No."

"Do they know?"

"Not everything. Not yet. We wanted to talk to you first."

"This sounds like fun."

"Sarcasm doesn't become you, Miri."

"Well, sorry about that, Mom."

"Look, I know how you feel . . ."

"No, you don't know!"

Rusty gave up. "Okay. Fine. Pizza from Spirito's. Tonight. Six-thirty."

Miri turned and walked out the door.

"Miri . . ."

"I'll be late for school."

"It's not even seven-twenty," Rusty said.

"Don't you have a train to catch, Mom?"

SHE WOULD HAVE to tell Mason about this. They had no secrets from each other. But what could she say? That she'd found her mother and Dr. O *doing it*? That Dr. O and Corinne were getting divorced?

These were her thoughts as she walked home from school that afternoon. She never expected to run into

Mason, standing in front of a small apartment house on Cherry Street. They hadn't planned to meet. Fred was staying with a friend so she didn't need to drop him at the Steins' today. She ran toward Mason, taking him by surprise, dropping her books to the ground and throwing her arms around him. "I'm so glad to see you!"

"Whoa . . ." he said.

"I have something to tell you," she said.

"I have something to tell you, too," he said.

"You go first," she said.

"Okay. The good news is, I'm going, too."

"Wait—going where?"

"Las Vegas. Isn't that what you wanted to tell me?"

"What do you mean, you're going to Las Vegas?"

"Jack's been talking it up. He says I can finish high school there, then come to work for him. He's going to teach me to be an electrician."

"Jack is going to Las Vegas?"

"Yeah, with Christina. Daisy's going, too. They're going to work for Dr. O in his new office."

"What else do you know?" Her mouth felt dried out. Her skin felt clammy.

"If you mean about your mom and Dr. O, yeah, I know about that, too."

"Does everyone know?" She steadied herself against a tree.

"Only the important people." Was he making a joke? He looked at her. "Why aren't you happy?"

Why wasn't she happy? She should be happy, shouldn't she? "I didn't want to leave you," she said. "I didn't want to go."

"So now you won't have to leave me because I'm going, too." He hugged her.

She didn't know whether to laugh or cry. Irene was right—some things were *bashert*, meant to be. Out of all the places in the world, she and Mason were going to wind up in Las Vegas together. She started to laugh. "But are you *sure* Jack is going?"

"Everything depends on Dr. O. If he goes, then Christina is going, and if Christina goes, Jack will go, and if Jack goes . . ." He lifted her off the ground and swung her around. Then he turned serious. "So long as Jack doesn't get called up. He says if he does, he could try to claim me as a dependent but he's not sure if that'll work or not. Christina wants him to try. We'd have to go to court."

"You mean Jack might have to go to Korea?"

Mason nodded. "He's 1-A."

"But Eisenhower says if he's elected he'll end the war."

"That's only *if* he wins. We don't even know if he's running yet. The election's not until November. He's not sworn in until January. And it could be somebody else. Joey Pol says it could be Adlai Stevenson."

"Joey Pol?"

"The guy from the bowling alley. Joey Politics. He says Stevenson's an egghead. Who knows what he'd do?"

"Uncle Henry says Stevenson is brilliant."

"Don't take this wrong, but your family leans to the left."

"Are you calling my family Communists?"

"Nothing like that. They're the best family I know."

"Then please take that back, about leaning to the left."

"Okay. I take it back."

They were interrupted by a little boy who ran at Mason, grabbing hold of his leg.

"Come see new house."

"I will," Mason told him. "Later."

"No, now!"

"Later, Stash. Okay?"

The door to the apartment house opened, and Polina came out, holding Fred on a leash. "Sorry so late," she told Mason. Her lipstick was bright red and her dress didn't leave much to the imagination, as if she were trying to look like Marilyn Monroe on the recent cover of *Life* magazine, beauty mark and all, one she didn't have when she was making pancakes for the kids at Janet.

"We are very happy here," Polina said. "A beautiful place."

"You should thank Miri," Mason said. "It's because of her you got the apartment."

"Mr. Ben's granddaughter?" Polina asked.

"I'm not exactly his granddaughter."

"But close to it," Mason said.

"Thank you and thank Mr. Ben," she said to Miri, right before she threw her arms around Mason. "Oh, this wonderful boy. I don't want to lose. I'll miss too much. Maybe we should go, too. What you think, Stash? Should we go with Mason, far away?"

She knew, too?

Stash said, "No, Mama. I like it here."

"He loves new apartment. But I love this handsome boy!" She squished those big breasts against Mason and was headed for a kiss on his mouth, but Mason turned his head at the last minute and the kiss landed on the side of his face, leaving a big red lipstick splotch.

Mason untangled himself, never taking his eyes off Miri, as if to say, *It's not my fault, I don't know what's going on here . . . don't blame me . . .*

For a minute Miri's eyes questioned him, while Polina went on and on. "This wonderful, strong, brave boy."

Polina must have noticed the look on Miri's face because she said, "Oh no! Mason, you have girlfriend and you didn't tell me?" She pretend-slapped the side of her head and tried to laugh, not a genuine laugh, a nervous laugh. "I love him like mother," she told Miri, recognizing her mistake. She could probably get fired for having a thing with one of the boys at Janet. "You understand? Like mother loves son."

Miri never saw a mother kiss her son that way.

"I hope my Stash grows up strong and brave like Mason."

Miri didn't say anything. She and Mason just looked at each other while Polina dug herself in deeper.

Stash tugged on Mason's arm. "Come for sleepover so we can play. Mama has big new bed. I have new bed."

Come for sleepover? Mama has big new bed? Miri felt the panic rising, her heart pounding, the urge to run too strong to resist. She took off, running for her life, leaving her books behind, leaving everything behind.

"Miri, wait!" Mason chased after her. "It's not what you think."

She stopped abruptly and faced him, this boy she loved totally, absolutely, this boy she'd trusted with all her heart, with all her soul. She was crying now, she couldn't stop, and she didn't care. She swiped her hand across her nose.

"She's the friend I was telling you about," Mason said, breathless from running after her. "She cooks at Janet."

"I know who she is."

"That kiss, it didn't mean anything. That's just the way she is. That's how it was in Poland when she was growing up. They kiss everyone on the lips. It has nothing to do with *us*."

"Really? That's what you expect me to believe?"

He waited too long to answer. "I never meant to hurt you. Why would I hurt you? You're the best thing that's ever happened to me."

"Stop! No more lies."

"Miri, please, listen . . . I wanted to tell you but I didn't know how. I tried to end it . . . and now it's over . . . I promise, it's over."

"I never want to see you again."

"Miri . . . don't do this." He reached out to grab her but she was faster. She stopped only once before she got home, to see if he was following, but he wasn't.

Mason

He couldn't stand the idea of losing her. And losing her because of what—some stupid kiss he didn't even want? Damn! He'd screwed up. He'd screwed up big-time. He should have told Polina he had a girlfriend a long time ago. Lately, Polina expected too much of him. She expected him to be the man of the family. She wanted him to quit school and get a job and move in and be a dad to Stash. But he wasn't ready for that.

In another month he'd be seventeen. He'd be able to get his license. He had enough saved for a used car. He just wanted to be a seventeen-year-old guy with a girlfriend, a dog and a car. And he wanted to get out of here, away from Polina. He wanted to go to Las Vegas with his brother, who would teach him not only to be an electrician, but a man. Sure, it was exciting to be with her at first. It was like a fantasy. This grown woman who knew what she wanted and wasn't shy about showing him. At first she made no demands. But now—now she wouldn't leave him alone. *Stashie misses you. I have big new bed just waiting. You come fill me up. I need you fill me up, Mason.* And what guy wouldn't want to fill her up? That was the problem. But he was done with her. Finished. Kaput.

Christina

Christina bumped into Zak Galanos in the hall at school. What was the Sewing Machine Man's son doing at Battin? She tried not to look at him but, too late. He did a double take.

"I know you, don't I?" he asked.

"You went to school with my sister, Athena."

"Right. Athena Demetrious. And you're the little sister."

"Not so little. I'm a senior, graduating in less than a month."

"And your name is . . ."

"Christina."

"Right. Christina." He smiled at her.

She didn't like this. It felt awkward. "What are you doing here?" she asked.

"I have an interview for a teaching position for next year."

Why on earth would he want to teach at the school

right across the street from where his parents died, from the hole in the ground that was once his house?

"What will you teach?"

"History, maybe a few classes of civics. Mrs. Rinaldi is leaving."

"I didn't know that."

"She wants to move someplace that's sunny year-round."

"Who doesn't?" She shouldn't have said that, given the fact that he was here looking for a job. A job in Elizabeth, New Jersey. A job in Plane Crash City.

"What about you, Christina? Are you going someplace sunny after graduation?"

"I'm thinking about it."

"Can I call you this summer? Would you go out with me?"

This was so embarrassing. And the second bell was ringing. She was going to be late for class. "I have a boyfriend."

"Serious?"

"Yes," she said, her voice so soft he had to lean in to hear her. What would he say if she told him she was married? "My sister just had her second baby—another boy. They named him *Ajax*, like the cleanser. They're going to call him AJ. I'll bet she tries for a girl next year."

"Send her my regards. And to your parents, too. They were very kind after the accident."

The accident. As if they'd fallen down the stairs.

"I saw it, you know. I was helping Mr. Durkee after school when the airplane . . . when it came right at us. We thought it was coming through the window of the classroom."

"I didn't know that."

"And after, I was there, when the fires and the explosion . . ." She felt dizzy. She needed to put her head down. She dropped the books she was holding and, as she fell forward, he caught her. Held her in his arms.

"It must have been terrible to see that."

"Yes." But no one *she* loved died. She reminded herself to breathe. Breathe deeply, like when the doctor inserted the speculum. When she recovered she said, "I'm late for class." She collected her books and started off down the hall.

He caught up to her. "Listen . . . in case you need someone to talk to, here's my number." He passed her a piece of paper.

She looked at it and nodded.

Miri

Henry found Miri, limp and exhausted, on the steps outside their house. She had no idea how long she'd been there, only that she was cried out, her chest so heavy she thought she might never get up. Some boy she didn't know had come by on a bike and dumped her books on the front lawn but she made no move to get them. When Henry pulled up and got out of the car she fell into his arms. "I know . . . I know . . ." He held her. But he didn't know. He couldn't know. "Come on," he said, "get in." He opened the car door for her and she got inside.

"Where are we going?" she asked, as he started up the car and pulled away.

"How about down the shore? How does that sound?"

She loved the shore and he knew it.

He drove for an hour and a half, stopping once at a phone booth to call Irene to tell her where they were, and not to wait for them for supper.

When they got to Bradley Beach they took off their shoes and socks, leaving them under the boardwalk, while they walked along the shore, letting the waves drizzle out across their bare feet. Rusty called the smell of the sea, the salty air "the ultimate cure for whatever ails you," but Miri didn't think it could wash away her sadness today, even if she jumped in fully dressed.

"You want to talk about it?" Henry asked.

"I hate secrets," Miri said.

"I don't blame you."

"Did you know?" she asked.

"About Rusty and Dr. O?"

Miri nodded.

"No one knew."

"Until I found them, you mean."

"I think they wanted to be found—not by you, not the way it happened, but they wanted it known. Otherwise they'd never have been at home that day."

"Natalie called Rusty a whore."

"Poor Natalie, if she feels that to defend her mother she has to bad-mouth Rusty. Someday she'll grow up and figure it out for herself."

"Figure what out?"

"There are two sides to every story."

"Always?"

"Almost always." Henry took her hand. "Rusty deserves to be happy," he said, "and so does Arthur. He's a good man, Miri."

As if she didn't know. As if she hadn't dreamed of having a father just like him. "How can a good man leave his wife and children?"

"We don't know about his marriage, Miri. We don't even know that he is leaving his children."

"Do you mean the children might go with him?" That would change everything, and not for the better, now that Natalie hated her. She was glad Steve would be going away to college. She didn't want to live in the same house with him. He barely acknowledged her existence. And Fern? Fern was a noodge but Miri wouldn't mind her that much. They could get a babysitter for her, maybe another Mrs. Barnes.

"You're asking questions only Rusty and Arthur can answer," Henry said. "I'm sure they're going to sit down with you and explain everything."

"Oh, no!"

"What?"

"Tonight. Six-thirty. Pizza from Spirito's. I forgot."

He checked his watch. "You're already late. You should call."

"Would you do it for me?"

"It would be better if you did it yourself."

She called from a phone booth along the boardwalk, feeding coins into the box as fast as Henry handed them to her. When Rusty answered, Miri said, "It's me. I forgot."

"We'll do it tomorrow," Rusty said. "No excuses."

"Okay. Tomorrow."

She didn't tell Henry until after they'd stopped at the hotel where the wedding would be, until after he'd shown her the garden where the chuppah would be draped with Grandpa Max's tallis and a white lace tablecloth brought from the old country by Leah's grandmother. Everything else would be decorated with peonies, Leah's favorite flower, in shades ranging from pale blush to deep pink. She didn't tell him until he asked, "Would you like to bring Mason to the wedding? I know we didn't send him a proper invitation but—"

"We broke up," she managed to say, holding back tears. *If only she could have a do-over she'd take a different route home from school, or she'd have gone to Pamel's with her girlfriends, or maybe to the library. Then she wouldn't have run into him or seen Polina and Stash.*

"You broke up?" Henry said. "I'm so sorry."

She leaned against him and nestled her head against his chest. "He has another girlfriend. All this time he's had another girlfriend."

Henry shook his head. "I can't believe this. Are you sure?"

"She cooks at Janet. She has a little boy. He says he tried to end it with her . . ."

"But you don't believe him?"

She shrugged. "Do you?"

"I don't know Mason as well as you."

"Would you ever lie like that to Leah?"

"Never."

"I don't see how he could have lied to me."

"Maybe he didn't know how to tell you. He's still a boy, Miri. He has a lot of stuff to figure out."

"I told him I never want to see him again."

"That's a strong message."

"I mean it." Was this her punishment for her fantasy about Dr. O marrying her mother? To lose her boyfriend, the best boyfriend any girl could have? No wonder he'd never tried to get beyond first base with her. All the time he was doing it with Polina. How could she, a fifteen-year-old girl, compete with that?

"I don't know how I can keep going," she told Henry.

"Miri, sweetheart—life is hard," Henry said, "but it's worth the struggle."

"Are you sure?"

"Very, very sure."

"I BROKE UP with Mason," she told Rusty that night, "and I don't want to talk about it."

"Oh, honey," Rusty said. "I'm so sorry. Is it about Las Vegas?"

"I *said* I don't want to talk about it, and *no*, it's not about Las Vegas. End of conversation." Let Rusty tell Irene. Let Rusty tell the whole world.

Henry

Leah said Miri would learn from this experience. She said it wasn't realistic of them to think puppy love could last. But learn what? Not to trust? Not to believe? Not to love? He didn't agree with Leah. He wished he could make Miri's sadness go away. But there was nothing he could do except be there for her.

Christina

Jack was beside himself. They were in his room at Mrs. O'Malley's. He paced up and down, punching his fist into his open hand while she sat primly on the edge of the bed. "And now Mason won't come to Las Vegas because of that little bitch."

"Do you know why Miri broke up with him?" Christina asked.

"No. Do you?"

"Because he lied to her. Because he's been . . ." She tried to put it delicately. "He's been sleeping with Polina, the girl who cooks at Janet, the one Daisy took in after she lost everything in the Williamson Street crash."

"Mason?"

"Yes, Mason. Polina told Daisy and Daisy told me. She thought I should know because of our . . . closeness."

"My little brother?"

"Yes, your little brother. Polina said Mason broke up with *her* right after Miri found out he was cheating."

"This is crazy. We're talking about kids."

"Polina's not a kid. But she has one."

"*Jesus, Mary and Joseph!* How do we know this is really true?"

"Why would Daisy lie to me? She's not a gossip. But you should ask Mason yourself."

"*Jesus, Mary and Joseph!*"

"I wish you'd stop saying that."

"What should I say?"

"I'm sorry, Jack." Christina softened. "It must be hard for you to hear this."

"What's hard is that he thinks he can't confide in me, that he thinks he can't come with us."

"Give him time. Let him cool off. I'll bet you anything he'll change his mind. If not right away, then as soon as he finishes high school."

"But that's another year. Who's going to be around to watch over him, make sure he's okay until then?"

"Any boy who can run into a burning plane, not once, not twice, but how many times?"

"I lost count," Jack said.

"Well, any boy who can keep his head straight through all of that is going to be okay."

"But you can't be sure, can you?"

"If you want to stay . . ."

"I didn't say that."

"Because if you don't want to leave him . . ."

"I didn't say that, either."

"All I mean is, I'd understand. And my parents would be over the moon."

"Until you tell them about us." Jack took a couple of practice swings with an imaginary baseball bat. "When are you going to tell them, Mrs. McKittrick?"

"When the time is right."

Fortunately, he didn't question her about when that would be. Because she hadn't the faintest idea. "Are we having our first fight?" she asked.

"We're never going to fight." He fell back on the bed and took her in his arms.

Miri

Miri found out from Dr. O that Mason refused to go to Las Vegas with Christina and Jack. *He's not going because I'm going*, she thought. Well, guess what? She'd decided to stay home with Irene and Henry. Henry and Leah could have Rusty's upstairs apartment and she'd move in with

Irene, downstairs. So Mason could go with Jack and she'd never have to see him again. Until Henry broke the news that he'd accepted a job with *The Washington Post* and he and Leah were moving to D.C. after the wedding. Just like that. He promised that when she visited, he'd take her to see the White House and all the other sites.

Okay, then she'd stay with Irene, and Ben could move in upstairs. When she announced her plan, Rusty said, "But Irene and Ben are coming with us."

"I don't believe you!" Miri ran downstairs to find Irene.

Irene said, "I should let my girls go without me? Are you crazy? Never!"

Ben said, "There's plenty of real estate opportunities in Las Vegas. Not that I need the money, but I like the idea."

LATER, at the twice-postponed pizza supper, once because of Miri, once because Dr. O couldn't make it, Dr. O said, "I can promise you this, Mirabelle. I'll love your mother and take care of her, and you, as long as I live. And I'll never give either one of you a bum steer."

"What about Natalie? Would you give her a *bum steer*?"

"Miri," Rusty warned.

"It's okay," Dr. O said to Rusty. "Mirabelle doesn't trust me yet. But I'm hoping, in time, I'll earn it."

"Stop calling me that," she said to Dr. O.

He looked hurt. "What would you like me to call you?"

"Miri."

"Okay," Dr. O said. "From now on it's Miri."

· · ·

RUSTY CAME to her room and knocked on the door before she opened it. "I wish it could have been different," she said. "I know people are saying I stole him away from Corinne but I didn't. You have to believe that, honey. Please."

"Did you fall in love in an instant, like a flash of lightning?"

"I wouldn't describe it that way. I was volunteering with the Red Cross. I'd bring him coffee and Danish at the morgue," Rusty said, "sometimes late at night. He needed to talk, to unwind. It was gruesome work, identifying burned and broken bodies."

"I don't want to hear about that."

"Okay."

"And I don't want to hear about the other stuff, either."

"I understand. But you should know that when Natalie got sick we decided to end it before it had even begun."

"So then, what . . . you changed your minds?"

"Staying apart didn't work out."

Miri could have laughed but she didn't.

Rusty tried to give her a hug. Miri stood stiffly at first, then relented. She knew she had the power to refuse but she was losing her will.

"It's going to be a great adventure," Rusty whispered.

Miri never thought about her mother being adventurous. If she was so adventurous how come she never went anywhere or did anything except get up and go to work every day, five days a week, and on weekends clean the house and do the laundry? When Miri put that to her, Rusty said, "Because I took my responsibilities seriously. I still do."

"Would you marry him if he were staying in Elizabeth? Would that be enough of an adventure for you?"

"I love him, Miri. Our lives together will be all the adventure I need. I'd stand by his side no matter what."

That was a powerful message for Miri. She loved Mason. But she wasn't standing by his side *no matter what*. And neither would Rusty, she bet, if the *no-matter-what* was Polina, or someone like Polina. If the *no-matter-what* was a pack of lies.

"Would you have gone without me?" Miri asked. That was really all she wanted to know.

"I could never leave you, Miri. How could you doubt my love?"

Even if she could doubt it, why would she? Why make life harder than it had to be? She was so tired from all of it. Too tired to fight it anymore. Too tired to run every time someone she loved disappointed her.

So, that was that. She was going. Mason wasn't.

Elizabeth Daily Post

JUNE WEDDING

JUNE 22—Miss Leah Rose Cohen, daughter of Mr. and Mrs. Seymour Cohen, of Cleveland, Ohio, and Mr. Henry Joel Ammerman, son of Mrs. Irene Ammerman and the late Max Ammerman, of Elizabeth, were married this afternoon by Rabbi Gershon B. Chertoff at the Hotel La Reine in Bradley Beach. The bride graduated from Ohio State University. The groom served in WWII with the Army in Europe. He is a graduate of Rutgers University and is a reporter for the Daily Post.

The bride wore a tea-length dress of white dotted swiss with a pink sash and carried a bouquet of New Dawn roses and peonies. The groom's sister, Mrs. Rusty Ammerman, of Elizabeth, was Matron of Honor. She wore a pale pink sheath. The two bridesmaids, Pamela Cohen, of Cleveland, sister of the bride, and Miri Ammerman, of Elizabeth, niece of the groom, wore matching dresses in deep pink cotton sateen.

The couple will honeymoon in Atlantic City, before moving to their new home in Washington, D.C.

33

Miri

It was a perfect day at the Jersey Shore, breezy but not so breezy their hairstyles were ruined or the chuppah was in danger of blowing over. Miri was annoyed that

Rusty thought she'd needed to lecture her that morning about how this was Henry and Leah's big day and no matter what else was happening, no matter what else they were thinking or feeling, they were going to be happy for Henry and Leah. As if Miri needed to be told. As if she would come to Henry's wedding and mope over her own loss. Although she felt her loss every minute of every day, her love for Henry was stronger.

Leah's mother was chatty but stayed close to Aunt Alma. She and Irene both wore beige at Leah's request, a color that didn't suit either of them. Irene draped a flattering pink floral scarf around her neck, and gave a matching scarf to Leah's mother, who was grateful. Leah's father didn't mingle. *Sy's arthritis is bothering him*, Leah's mother explained to anyone who asked. Dr. O and Rusty decided it was too soon to be out together as a couple so he didn't come to the wedding. But Ben Sapphire did, and he kept Leah's father company, making sure he had enough to drink to be cheerful, but no more.

Neither Leah's sister, who had just finished her sophomore year at Ohio State, nor Miri had ever attended a wedding, let alone been bridesmaids. They were seated together at lunch—chicken à la king with crispy noodles and rice. Pamela joked that the restaurant must be part Chinese, part ladies' tearoom, making Miri laugh, but it reminded her of going to lunch with Frekki before the play at the Paper Mill Playhouse.

After the wedding cake was presented, after Leah fed a piece to Henry, and Henry fed a piece to Leah, and the couple were toasted with Champagne, and the photographer, Henry's friend Todd Dirkson, captured it all, it was time for Leah to turn her back to the crowd and throw her bouquet over her shoulder. Rusty and Miri stepped out of the way. The bouquet landed in Irene's hands, who treated it like a hot potato, quickly tossing it toward Leah's friends, where Harriet Makenna caught it and promptly passed out. She was rescued by the photographer, who had met her when he'd covered the holiday party at the Elks Club.

Once upon a time Miri had planned to wear her bridesmaid dress with its detachable organza overskirt to the ninth-grade prom, but she'd decided against going. When her friends saw the depth of her sadness they accepted her decision. In the same once-upon-a-time she'd thought she'd wear the dress to Mason's junior prom, at Jefferson. She wondered if he'd go without her, if he'd go with someone else? She doubted it. Or maybe that was just what she was hoping. She couldn't imagine ever wearing the dress again.

Mason

Polina kept her job working in the kitchen at Janet, but Mason avoided her like bad food. The kid, too. He was done with all that. No more girlfriends. They wanted too much from you. They expected you to make them happy. Even when they said they wanted to make *you* happy. Maybe someday he'd feel ready to see Miri again but he couldn't think when that might be. He'd fucked up bigtime. He didn't expect her to forgive him. The question was, could he forgive himself?

Jack wouldn't let it go. Begged him to come with him and Christina to Las Vegas. Mason finally said, "Don't ask me again, Jack. I'm staying here, at Janet. I'll be fine."

"At least come with us for the summer."

"I can't. I've got a job. You know that. You're the one who set me up with your old boss. He's going to train me to be an electrician. Just like he trained you."

"He'd understand."

"No."

"Mason—you can't live your life avoiding Miri."

"Don't say that name around me. And yes I can. And I will."

"There'll be other girls, believe me."

"Cut it out, Jack, because you don't know."

"I know you're seventeen."

"That doesn't mean shit." He hoped Jack wouldn't cry. He looked like he might. So Mason gave him a bear hug. That way they didn't have to look at each other. Jack patted his back for too long.

"Hey, brother," Mason said, to get Jack to let go. "I'll write."

"Every week," Jack said, sniffling. "I need you to promise."

"I promise."

"And I'll call every two weeks," Jack told him. "On Sunday nights."

Mason nodded. Then he asked what he'd been thinking all along. "What about 1-A, Jack?"

"No word yet. I'll see you for Christmas, okay?"

"Yeah, sure, Christmas."

Steve

The morning after graduating from Jefferson High, Steve went downtown to the army recruitment center on Elizabeth Avenue and enlisted. He filled out all the paperwork, set up an appointment for a physical that afternoon, and he was in. It was that easy.

Phil was apoplectic. "Are you crazy? We're going to Lehigh, not Korea."

"You'll have to go without me."

"Steve—come on!"

"It's done."

"Do your parents know?"

"They will."

"They're going to go ape-shit!"

Steve shrugged.

He told his father first. He went to his office hoping to catch him before he left. His father was staying at the Elizabeth Carteret hotel these days, in the same room where Joseph Fluet, the guy who'd investigated the airplane crashes, had stayed.

"Hello, Steve," Daisy said. "Congratulations on your graduation."

"Thanks."

"I have something for you." She pulled out a package wrapped with manly paper and tied with a brown ribbon. "I hope you'll enjoy it."

"Thank you, Daisy."

"He's with his last patient of the day," Daisy said. "I'll tell him you're waiting."

When the last patient left, his father joined him in the waiting room. "How about supper at Three Brothers?" his father said. "I've been eating there a lot lately."

"Your girlfriend doesn't cook for you?" His father gave him a sad smile. So Steve said, "Sure, I like their burgers."

Steve waited until his father finished his moussaka,

then the baklava he'd ordered for dessert. He'd never seen his father eat Greek food. Steve didn't like baklava—too sticky for him. He was off desserts anyway, trying to get into shape before basic training. When he broke his news his father didn't take it well.

"Now?" he said. "You've enlisted now, when we're still fighting in Korea? No, son. I'm not going to let you do this."

"Too late, Dad. It's done."

"I'll get you out of it. I'll tell them you're not yourself."

"But I am myself."

"No, Steve. You haven't been yourself in a long time."

"How would you know?"

"I know my son."

"Not anymore. You don't have any idea who I am." Steve stood up. "Thanks for supper."

"Sit down," his father said. "We're not finished."

"I'm finished."

His father grabbed his arm. "You can't tell your mother about this."

"Says who?" Steve shook off his father, saluted him, then marched out of the restaurant. *Hup two three four . . . hup two three four.*

His father followed him out the door and down the street, calling, "Steve . . . I mean it, don't tell your mother. Not now."

Steve stopped. "You're not going to be able to fix this, Dad. I'm telling her."

"Then I'm coming with you," his father said.

"That should make Mom happy."

• • •

HIS MOTHER WAS in the den, sitting in her favorite chair, working on a needlepoint canvas. What was she making this time? A pillow for him to take to college? Fern was on the floor in front of the television watching *Hopalong Cassidy*. Natalie was probably locked in her room.

"Hey, Mom . . ."

"Steve! I thought you and Phil were going to a graduation party tonight."

"I had something more important to do."

His father stepped into the den.

"Daddy!" Fern ran to him, jumped into his arms.

"You're not supposed to be here," his mother said to his father.

"Steve . . . I'd like to talk to you privately," his father said.

"Sorry, Dad." He faced his mother. "I have some big news . . ."

His mother's face changed. Was she scared or expectant?

"I've joined up."

His mother put down her needlepoint. "Joined what?"

"You're in the army now," he sang, marching around the room. *"You're not behind a plow, you'll never get rich, diggin' a ditch, you're in the army now."*

Fern laughed.

"What is he talking about?" his mother asked his father.

"He enlisted," his father said.

His mother jumped up and lunged at his father. "You put him up to this!"

"Corinne . . ." his father said, setting Fern down.

"He's supposed to go to college, not the army," his mother shouted.

Natalie appeared in the doorway. "This sounds interesting."

"Did you know?" his mother asked his father. "Did you?"

"I just found out," his father said.

"He can't do this. He's a boy. He has no experience."

"Take another look, Mom," Steve said, pulling himself up to his full six-foot height, shoulders thrown back, eyes straight ahead.

"No!" Corinne cried. "I won't have him throwing his life away." She ran out of the den with Steve's dad right behind her. A door slammed. Voices were raised.

"Nice going, Steve," Natalie said.

"I figured you'd appreciate the drama."

"Will you wear an army suit?" Fern asked.

"It's called a uniform," Steve said. "And yes, I will."

"Will we have a cake to celebrate?"

"I doubt it," Steve said.

"How about a gun?" Natalie asked. "Will you get a gun?"

"Everybody in the army gets a gun."

"Don't bring it home."

LATER, when he unwrapped Daisy's graduation present he found something that looked like a handmade book, with long pages covered in red construction paper and black letters spelling out *Player Piano* by Kurt Vonnegut. Behind it was an old issue of *The New Yorker* magazine, dated January 31, 1948, with a paper clip marking a story, "A Perfect Day for Bananafish," by J. D. Salinger. He opened the card.

Dear Steve,

I convinced the manager of the Ritz Book Shop
to give me these galley proofs of a book that will be
published this summer. It is Mr. Vonnegut's first novel.
Something tells me you will like this writer.

Congratulations on your graduation.

Wishing you all the best, always.

Daisy

P.S. The Salinger story is one I recently came across
while browsing through a stack of old magazines.

For some crazy reason Daisy's gift made him cry. Maybe
because it meant somebody did know him, after all.

Elizabeth Daily Post

A FAREWELL TO ELIZABETH

By Henry Ammerman

JUNE 23—It is with some sadness that I write this, my last story for the Daily Post. I have been privileged over the past six months to report for you on the terrible series of airplane tragedies that has brought this city so much pain and unwanted national attention. As I leave the place of my birth for a job in a new one, the editors have invited me to offer some final thoughts.

The investigations of the Civil Aeronautics Board have now been completed. The results will be annoying and maybe disbelieved by those who saw sinister forces conspiring to bring about the three crashes in rapid-fire succession. Each plane failed for a different reason, and none of them indicate any pattern of sabotage or nefarious activity.

Dec. 16—The Miami Airlines non-scheduled C-46 that crashed in the Elizabeth River suffered engine failure, apparently from poor maintenance, which led to a catastrophic fire. The pilots had not been adequately trained to shut off fuel to a damaged engine.

Jan. 22—American Airlines Flight 6780, a Convair 240, was an incoming flight in poor weather conditions. The weather could have caused carburetor ice. While the plane had heaters to preclude this, it is possible the heaters were not activated. But without definite evidence, the CAB was mystified as to the probable cause of the crash.

Feb. 11—National Airlines Flight 101, a four-engine DC-6, suffered a sudden and unexpected reversal of its No. 3 propeller. Attempting to correct this, the pilot mistakenly feathered (shut off and locked) his other right-side propeller. With both the right-hand engines out, the CAB concluded "the aircraft did not maintain altitude and settled rapidly."

In both crash number one and number three there was a confluence of mechanical problems and mistaken action by the pilot. Perhaps if the Miami Airlines pilot had shut off fuel to the failed engine sooner, or if the pilot of the National plane had feathered the correct engine, they could have recovered altitude and made it back to the airport. Crash number two is more problematic but there remains a possibility that pilot action to overcome icing might have made a difference.

The one lesson we can surely learn from these events is that airplanes are complex machines, operating in a precarious environment—the air—where any emergency, be it from mechanical failure, human error or weather hazard, is fraught with peril. The risk is especially great when it occurs at low altitude, giving pilots little opportunity to take corrective action.

As if to underscore this point, just after midnight on Feb. 11, at almost the same time as the final doomed Elizabeth plane was going down, a Pan American airliner from Idlewild Airport lost an engine just after takeoff. But that pilot was free to maneuver over the Atlantic Ocean, unconcerned with multistory buildings or thousands at risk on the ground, and returned to the field in safety.

Every effort must be taken to safeguard heavily inhabited areas from takeoffs and landings. Let us hope the Port Authority will take this lesson to heart before reopening Newark Airport.

⬥⬥⬥⬥⬥

34

Miri

She was sure they would drive. *See the U.S.A. in Your Chevrolet*, even if their Chevrolet was an Oldsmobile. But she was wrong. They were going to fly. *Off we go into the wild blue yonder . . .* She couldn't keep songs about flying out of her head. And especially the ending of *that* song— *live in fame or go down in flame*—not that she'd lived in *fame* but still . . . She'd seen what it was like to go down in flame. And she didn't want any part of it. That was putting it mildly.

"I really don't want to fly," she told Rusty.

Rusty said, "I understand."

"If you understand, why would you make me do it?"

"I don't want you to spend your life avoiding travel. I want you to see the world."

"I'll drive."

"You can't drive across the ocean."

"I'll take a boat."

"Everyone will be flying, Miri."

"That doesn't mean I have to be like everyone else."

"No, but you don't want your fears to limit your possibilities."

"That sounds like something Dr. O would say, not you."

"But it makes sense, doesn't it?"

Miri shrugged. Did it? "Christina and Jack are driving to Las Vegas."

"Are you saying you want to go with them? Because I don't think that would be appropriate."

Before her world fell apart, Miri might have begged to go with them, Mason surely would have been along. She hadn't seen Christina or Jack since the breakup. She hated that word. *Breakup*. It reminded her of Henry's description of the third crash—*Like a swollen cream puff that had broken apart*. She felt as if she, too, had broken apart.

"I still don't see why we can't drive."

"The sooner we get there, the sooner we can establish residency." Rusty was losing patience, Miri could tell. "It takes six weeks before you can get a divorce. And we can't get married until the divorce is final."

Married. She sometimes forgot that her mother was going to marry Dr. O. He would be her stepfather. He'd be there for dinner at night, asking about her day, like a real father. But what about *his* kids? How would that make them feel? Sometimes, she didn't blame Natalie for hating him.

Christina

It didn't hit her until they made it to Las Vegas in Jack's truck, how far she was from home. She cried for two days when she saw the dusty road stop of a desert town with a couple of motels and flashy signs spelling out CASINO or BAR, surrounded by brown and red mountains, mostly untouched by vegetation. She expected green, not brown, and summer flowers, not cacti. She couldn't get out of bed. She wouldn't eat. Jack enlisted Daisy's help. Daisy had arrived before them to start setting up the new office. She'd been there a week when Jack and Christina finally made it. Daisy came to the cheap motel where Christina and Jack were staying until they found an apartment to rent, urged her out of bed, helped her into the shower and chose a sundress for her to wear to lunch at the Flamingo, a swell hotel with a pool, owned by some of Dr. O's friends.

"What have I done?" Christina asked Daisy, once they were seated with menus in front of them. She let Daisy order for both of them. "What am I doing here?"

"I'd say you're homesick, sweetie, but that will pass. Remember, you can always go back. You know what I'm going to do? I'm going to buy an open ticket on a plane from here to New York and keep it in my office drawer. It's yours, anytime you want it." Daisy reached across the table and touched Christina's hand.

"Thank you, Daisy. I don't know what I'd do without you." She picked up her burger and took a bite. She'd forgotten how hungry she was. "Um . . . good," she said.

Daisy laughed and took a bite of hers. "It is, isn't it?"

After lunch Daisy said, "I have something to show you." They drove in Daisy's new white Ford convertible to a long, low building, just out of town. "Welcome to the Las Vegas Medical Arts Building," Daisy said. Inside, she walked Christina through the hall to a large, almost finished suite of offices. "This will be your new home-away-from-home. The dental offices of Dr. Arthur Alan Osner and Associates."

Christina was overwhelmed by the scope of the project, by the newness of everything.

"We're interviewing dentists and dental assistants every day," Daisy told her. "All trained at the best dental schools in the country. General dentistry, orthodontia, oral surgery, periodontics, all in one section of the building. It's going to be a big operation. The biggest and best in the area. And you, Christina Demetrious, are my second in command."

"McKittrick," Christina said.

"What?" Daisy asked.

"Christina McKittrick. I'm married. Remember?"

"Of course," Daisy said. "Christina McKittrick."

There was no office furniture yet. But there were two card tables set up, each holding a typewriter. "This will be my station," Daisy said, leaning against one of the card tables. "And the other will be yours."

"I have my own station?" Christina asked. "My own typewriter?"

"You do."

"Can I try it?"

Daisy passed her a sheet of paper. Christina removed the cover from the new Smith-Corona and rolled in the paper. She stood as she typed CHRISTINA MCKITTRICK. MRS. JACK MCKITTRICK. CHRISTINA AND JACK MCKITTRICK OF LAS VEGAS, NEVADA. She wasn't alone, she reminded herself. She had Jack. She had Daisy. And Dr. O and his new family would be here soon. They would be *her* new family. Hers and Jack's. It would be okay. Never mind that Mama had fallen to her knees, wailing, when Christina left. Even though she'd promised to come home for Christmas, just like a college student, Mama cried, "No . . . Christina . . . don't go . . ." It took her father to get her mother to stop screaming. To get her back into the house.

"I hope you're happy," Athena said, the new baby in her arms. "I doubt Mama will live to see Christmas."

"What do you mean?"

"Did you ever hear of dying of a broken heart?"

"Mama's not going to die."

"But if she does, it's on your head, Christina." Athena turned and disappeared inside.

When Baba came back, he hugged her. "I don't know what you're doing but I wish you *Nase kala! S'agapo.* I'll always love you. You'll always be my daughter."

"I love you, too," she whispered into his neck. "Take care of Mama."

"Mama will be all right."

He pressed five crisp twenty-dollar bills into her hand. She didn't want to take them but he insisted. She longed to tell him she and Jack were married. But she couldn't.

Corinne

Thank god for Cousin Tewky, that's all she had to say. When he heard her on the phone crying and carrying on about Steve, about Arthur, about the whole family falling apart, Tewky flew in and took charge, presenting her with a tantalizing idea.

Come home to Birmingham. He had his eye on a charming house with a garden just a block from his own. Three bedrooms, plus a maid's, impeccably furnished, for rent with an option to buy. He'd already put a hold on it. He'd scouted out the best private schools for the girls. There was nothing to be done about Steve at the moment. Be proud of him, going off to serve his country. He's young. He's strong. He's smart. He'll go to college when he's out in a few years. Let Fern go with Arthur for the summer. Send Natalie to the dance camp she's begging to attend. If she loses weight the camp will be instructed to call immediately. If need be we'll bring in a doctor to evaluate the situation.

When she'd asked, "And then what?" Tewky had taken her hand. "Then we'll take action. There are rest homes in Birmingham, too. But I'm betting she'll be fine. Give yourself a chance to recuperate, Corinne. When Fern and Natalie get back from summer vacation everything will be set up. They'll be happy because their mother will be happy."

It was true, she realized. She hadn't been happy in a long time.

"You'll be the belle of the ball, dearest cousin," Tewky promised. "And I will be your dapper escort. Plus, I'm a very good dancer."

And just like that she stopped crying. Just like that she was Tewky's little cousin Corinne. He would take care of her and everything else. The house on Shelley Avenue would stay as it was. Tewky would find someone to live in and watch over it. If she wanted to sell in a year or two, they'd sell. For now, no decision had to be made. *No decision.* Such a relief. She felt very tired but the idea of going home to Birmingham filled her with hope.

If only she knew for sure what had gone wrong with her marriage. If only she understood how he could leave *her* for that woman. Miri's mother, no less. It was unthinkable.

And when, exactly, had they fallen so in love they were leaving town together, disrupting so many lives? Was it New Year's Eve, when Rusty twirled in the finished basement with Tewky? If she had never invited her to the party, would it have happened? She could kick herself every time she thought of that night. Of Arthur reminding her that Tewky was *that* way and she had no business foisting him on Rusty Ammerman. Had it started between them already? No, she didn't think so because that was the night, after all the guests had gone home, they'd made love to start the new year with a bang—to quote Arthur. And they'd laughed the next morning about their clothes, strewn around the floor of their bedroom.

So how had this happened? How could she not have known? Wasn't he just begging her to come to Las Vegas with him? If she'd said, *Yes, of course, darling—whither thou goest*—and all that, would they be leaving together to start a new chapter of their lives? Had she made a terrible mistake? Maybe. Would Steve be going off to Lehigh with Phil in September if she'd said yes to Las Vegas? Would Natalie get well in the dry desert air? She had to stop asking herself these questions. They only upset her and made everything worse.

Ceil Rubin gave a luncheon in her honor. Her friends promised to visit her in Birmingham but she knew they wouldn't. She promised to come back regularly to check on the house but she knew she wouldn't. Twenty years, just like that. Twenty years of marriage to Arthur, three children, friends, a life—

They toasted her. To starting over. They didn't need to say what they were thinking. Corinne was the first of their crowd to be divorcing. She wouldn't be the last, though no one would admit to being in an unhappy marriage. *You're lucky, Corinne. You have your own money.* Her mother always told her never to turn up her nose at the family money. And she never had.

Miri

Newark Airport was still closed and wasn't expected to open anytime soon, so on a warm summer day, Henry drove them to LaGuardia in Ben Sapphire's Packard. Ben had given the car to Henry and Leah as a wedding present and all six of them, plus Fern on Dr. O's lap, squeezed in for the ride.

At the departure gate Miri clung to Henry, not wanting to say goodbye. "I wish you were coming with us."

"Leah and I will come to visit soon, maybe over Christmas."

It would be Henry and Leah from now on. Henry and Leah, who'd been married for a week, and were going to Atlantic City tomorrow for their honeymoon. She would never have Henry to herself again. She'd have to share him with Leah, and already Leah was making it clear she didn't want to share Henry with anyone. "Everything will be different," Miri told him.

"Different can be good."

"I'm going to miss you so much."

"Not as much as I'm going to miss you." He held her tight until Rusty tapped Miri's shoulder, as if they were at a dance and Rusty was cutting in.

"My turn," Rusty said quietly, and Miri had to let go of Henry.

"Be happy," Henry told Rusty.

"I'll do my best," Rusty said. "You be happy, too."

When it was time to say goodbye to Irene, Henry hugged her tight. "I love you, Mama."

"Not as much as I love you," Irene told him, touching his face. By then all of them were holding back tears.

"Enough with the emotional goodbyes," Ben said. "We're going to Las Vegas, not the moon."

The plane, a silver Constellation looking to Miri like a huge, featherless bird with fancy wings, was ready for boarding. Irene carried her white leather train case with her pills, her makeup and her good jewelry neatly packed inside. She and Miri walked across the tarmac together.

"Aren't you afraid?" Miri asked her.

"What's to be afraid of, darling?"

"You know."

"It's going to be fine. I promise." Irene gave Miri her most reassuring smile.

"But you've never flown," Miri said. "How can you promise when anything could happen, anything could go wrong?"

"Anything could go wrong any day of the week. What's the point of worrying in advance?"

"How do you stop yourself from worrying?"

"I think of all the good things in my life."

"What about the bad things?"

"There's no room for them inside my head. Not anymore. Now I say live and let live, and I kick those other thoughts away. You can do that, too."

"I'm trying, Nana. I swear, I'm trying."

Irene squeezed her hand. "That's my girl."

SHE DID NOT want to flash back to six months ago, to that frigid December day when the ball of fire fell from the sky, exploding not once, but twice. She had pains in her stomach now, maybe from not eating anything since yesterday afternoon, when Suzanne had hosted a going-away lunch for her. Tuna salad and deviled eggs, all arranged on a pretty platter with pale blue ribbons tying up the napkins. The girls were careful not to mention Mason's name. Robo, who had come from Millburn, brought up the subject once. "Good riddance to him." Without saying a word Suzanne and Eleanor let her know she was out of bounds.

Miri handed the panda bear from its shelf in her now-empty closet to Suzanne, asking her to give it to Betsy in person as soon as Mrs. Foster said it was okay to visit. Suzanne promised she would.

They'd chipped in to give Miri a going-away present from Oakley's, a double box of stationery with a western motif—cowboys, cacti, broncos—decorating the lower-right-hand corner of each sheet, plus an Esterbrook pen in pastel green, with a bottle of green ink, exactly what she'd been hoping someone would give her for Hanukkah. "Something to remember us by," Suzanne said.

"As if I could forget any of you," Miri told them, choking up. She promised to write. They promised they'd write, too.

For a while she thought Mason might come by the house, but he didn't. Once she understood he was avoiding her the way she was avoiding him, she wanted to leave, the sooner the better. And now she was going. She was going to walk up the steps leading to the silver bird that would gobble her up, holding her in its belly until it reached its faraway destination, where it would spit her out. In one piece, she hoped.

The stewardess, in her famous uniform with the red cut-out TWA logo on her right shoulder, welcomed them onto the plane. Miri was reassured to see that the seating looked so much like a train. She was never afraid on a train. They were seated two by two—Irene with Ben,

Rusty with Dr. O and Miri with Fern. The stewardess handed the two girls silver wings to pin to their jackets. Fern's jacket was turquoise felt with appliquéd animals. She asked for a second pin for Roy Rabbit. Miri offered hers, then pinned one to Fern's jacket, and the other to Roy Rabbit's well-worn vest.

"Have you been to Lost Vegas?" Fern asked her.

"No." Miri resisted a laugh. It made sense to call it *lost* since it was in the middle of nowhere.

"Will you be my sister now?" Fern asked.

"Stepsister."

"Like in *Cinderella*?"

"No. My mother is very nice so you don't have to worry about having a wicked stepmother. And my grandmother is the best grandmother ever—except when she talks about boys, but you don't have to worry about that yet."

"I'm only coming for the summer," Fern said. "Mommy wanted me to go to camp but I wanted to go with Daddy."

"I'm glad you're coming with us." Miri never thought she'd say that, but there was something comforting about having Fern sitting next to her, her skinny little legs swinging up and down, her cowboy bunny clutched against her chest. She liked having someone to watch over, someone who needed her to be strong.

"Did you know Roy Rogers has a penis but Roy Rabbit doesn't have one, even though he's a boy bunny?"

"Yes, I know."

"I told you, right?"

"About a hundred times."

Fern said, "I flew one time when I was little, all the way to Birmingham, where my grandma lived. I got to sit on her hospital bed. Then she died. I didn't see her dead. Only sleeping." She was quiet for a minute, then she popped back up. "Do you know this song?"

She twisted her hands upside down, making goggles for her eyes with her thumb and second finger. She started to sing.

> *Into the air, Junior Birdman*
> *Into the air upside down*
> *Into the air, Junior Birdman*
> *Keep your noses off the ground.*

"Where'd you learn that?" Miri asked.

"Natalie learned it at summer camp and taught it to me."

By the time Miri figured out how to make the mask with her hands, the plane was on the move, picking up speed. Faster, faster, faster, until they were airborne. *Into the air, Junior Birdman.* They were flying. *She* was flying. She thought it would feel different, more like the ride at the amusement park that pins you against the wall with centrifugal force. That ride was both thrilling and terrifying but so was this one. Once they'd leveled off she pretended she was on a train, except when she looked out the window all she saw was sky with a bank of fluffy clouds under the plane. *Somewhere there's heaven*, she sang to herself. Because if there was a heaven, wouldn't this be it? Separated from earth by white fluffy clouds. She half expected to see angels wearing flowing white gowns playing harps. She half expected to see Penny, tapping on the window of the plane to get her attention. If only she believed in heaven.

"What?" Fern asked.

"Nothing. I was just singing to myself."

"What song?"

"Just some song I know."

"Teach it to me."

> *Somewhere there's music*
> *How faint the tune*
> *Somewhere there's heaven*
> *How high the moon*

"How high is the moon?"

"Pretty high."

"How do you know you can hear music there?"

"Because you can always hear music."

"That's good. Isn't that good?"

"Yes, it's very good."

IT WAS a long trip. First they landed in Chicago, where they changed planes. Between Chicago and Los Angeles a fancy lunch was served on a tray. Miri couldn't imagine how they managed to cook steak and French fries on a plane. The Parker House roll came with a pat of butter stamped TWA. She had never seen such tiny salt and pepper shakers. She thought about sneaking them into her bag but didn't want to set a bad example for Fern. For dessert there was ice cream with a chocolate chip cookie.

After lunch the stewardess handed out decks of cards. Miri and Fern played War until Fern's eyes closed. Miri covered her with a blanket and smoothed her hair away from her face. She was reminded of babysitting Penny and Betsy. But thinking of them made her too sad. She tried to read—Rusty had given her a copy of *The Member of the Wedding*, about a girl called Frankie who felt she didn't belong anywhere in the world. She wasn't sure if Rusty thought it would appeal to her because they were setting out for the unknown, because Rusty was marrying Dr. O or just because it was a good book. But she couldn't concentrate. She caught herself drifting off and shook her sleepiness away. She would not allow herself to sleep while she was flying, though when she'd gone to the restroom she'd passed Rusty and Dr. O, both dozing, and Irene and Ben, both asleep with their mouths partly open.

Before they landed in Los Angeles, the stewardess suggested they reset their watches to Pacific Time, which was three hours earlier than in New Jersey. They changed to a smaller plane for the short flight to Las Vegas. The stewardess handed out copies of the *Las Vegas Sun* as they boarded. Miri took one, and as soon as she was seated with her seat belt fastened, she thumbed through it. She stopped when she came to an intriguing headline:

Las Vegas Sun

MCCARTHY LOSES FACE IN VERBAL FIRE

JUNE 30—What was perhaps the most drama-packed and best-attended political meeting ever held in Nevada broke up in a scene of bedlam last night at War Memorial hall after the audience had listened to Sen. Joseph McCarthy of Wisconsin, who had purportedly come here to speak on behalf of Sen. George W. Malone, now seeking re-election.

McCarthy in his typical wild swinging fashion, with no regard for facts but with a hold on his audience that is frightening, called *Sun* publisher Hank Greenspun "an ex-convict" and "an admitted Communist, publisher of the Las Vegas 'Daily Worker.'"

Women shuddered and strong men controlled their emotions with difficulty as the attacks continued. They had never heard such disgraceful language in Nevada.

Cheers rang out when Greenspun responded and challenged the Wisconsin Senator to debate these "vicious lies." But McCarthy turned and ran like a scared rabbit.

TOO BAD Miri couldn't share that story with Eleanor. They could taunt Donny Kellen about his hero, McCarthy, except they'd heard Donny had been shipped off to military school. And who knew the next time she'd see Eleanor? Still, she liked knowing this was the newspaper Dr. O would probably bring home every day, or maybe it would be delivered to their house. It made life in Las Vegas seem real. They had a newspaper and the publisher's name was Hank, short for Henry. A good omen.

When Fern squealed, "Here come the bumps! Daddy—it's the bumps!" Dr. O turned in his seat to look back at Fern, to smile at her, to pat her leg.

The smooth air had turned choppy on the final descent into Las Vegas. Miri didn't like it. It wasn't like riding a bucking bronco. Not that she'd ever been on a bucking bronco but she'd seen them in cowboy movies. These bumps were unpredictable. The stewardess told them to keep their seat belts fastened until they'd landed.

Rusty turned to Miri. "How're you doing, honey?"

"I'm fine." A lie. She was so terrified she dug her fingernails into the fabric of her seat cushion. "How about you?"

"Good." But Rusty didn't look good. She was pale, with beads of sweat on her forehead and upper lip.

As they came lower and lower in their descent, the scene out the window looked to Miri like a moonscape, or how she imagined a moonscape would look. Sandy and flat with tall, dark mountains rising out of nowhere.

Lower and lower out of the wild blue yonder, lower and lower until the wheels hit the ground with a thud and the pilot reversed the engines, making a grinding noise. The captain spoke to them over the loudspeaker. "Welcome to McCarran Field, ladies and gentlemen. Enjoy your stay in Las Vegas. We hope you'll join us again."

She'd survived the trip. Even if she never flew again, which she was sure she wouldn't, at least she'd gone up into the wild blue yonder three times. At least she'd done that.

The passengers applauded as if they'd been watching a show. They were all yakking, thrilled to have landed at McCarran Field or maybe thrilled just to have landed. When they were told they were free to unbuckle their seat belts, Fern jumped into Dr. O's arms. Rusty, still looking unwell, draped an arm over Miri's shoulder. "We made it."

Yes, they'd made it, but this was just the beginning.

Las Vegas Sun

A-BOMB BLAST THRILLS

JULY 5—Thousands of holiday tourists on the Las Vegas strip celebrated dawn with the sight of an atomic flash at the Yucca Flat test site 78 miles away. The mushroom cloud was clearly seen, but there was disappointment at the slight shock.

A thousand soldiers, positioned in foxholes only 7,000 yards away from the blast, surged forward minutes after the explosion in a simulated attack to encircle and capture the devastated area.

"There were no casualties," the Army announced.

35

Miri and Natalie

Natalie came to visit after camp, just before school started. "Don't get the wrong idea," she said to Miri. "I'm curious, that's all. I still hate *them*."

"What about me?"

"I don't know about you. Maybe yes, maybe no."

By then they were living in a furnished stucco ranch house east of the city in a neighborhood of other ranch houses called Rancho Circle. They were all ugly and looked the same. The three girls shared a room. Irene and Ben rented an identical house across the street. Their furniture and boxes of stuff were in storage while Rusty and Dr. O looked for a permanent place. Miri hoped it would be better than this one.

Irene kept Natalie busy, kept her away from Rusty, who was pregnant but not yet showing and suffering from morning sickness that sometimes lasted all day. It disgusted Natalie to learn Rusty was pregnant. "So, you're not going to be the only child anymore," she said to Miri.

"So?" Miri was equally shocked to learn Rusty was pregnant, but she wasn't going to admit it to Natalie.

"So, you won't be the center of attention anymore," Natalie told her.

"I've never been the center of attention." But the truth was, it had occurred to Miri that she would have to share Rusty's love once there was a new baby. And maybe Irene's, too.

"I hope you like dirty diapers," Natalie said, "because they're going to expect you to be the babysitter."

"I like babies." She'd never lived with a baby, had never wished for a sibling, like some only children.

"I'm just warning you."

"Thanks for the warning."

"You have to admit it's embarrassing that she's pregnant at thirty-three. And he's eleven years older. I feel sorry for their baby. Think of it—when the baby is our age your mother will be almost fifty and my father will be sixty. They'll be more like grandparents than parents."

But Miri didn't want to think about that.

Some mornings Natalie and Fern rode horses together, and Miri would go along to watch. Dr. O drove them to a ranch twenty miles out of town. Fern named her horse

Trigger—no surprise there. Dr. O encouraged Natalie to name a horse, too. Natalie refused, saying he was just trying to buy her love, and her love wasn't for sale.

Miri knew from Dr. O that Steve had enlisted in the army the day after high school graduation. Natalie said it was her father's fault. If her parents had stayed together Steve would be going off to Lehigh with Phil Stein. Now Steve would probably be sent to *Ko-fucking-rea*. Miri had never heard Natalie use such language.

Nobody cared what Natalie did or didn't eat. She developed a taste for the whites of hard-boiled eggs dipped in salt water, like at a Seder, and on some days ate that three times a day. Dr. O was more concerned about Rusty's constant nausea. The doctor assured them the nausea was a good sign, a sign that it was a strong pregnancy. *Eat whatever you can keep down.*

Rusty told Miri she was hardly sick when she was pregnant with her. Miri said, "Maybe it's a boy this time."

"Maybe," Rusty said.

Irene and Ben took the three girls on a daylong trip to Hoover Dam, including a guided tour that Natalie yawned through, though she had to admit the place was impressive, *if you happen to like wonders of the world.* The tour guide, a friendly western type, was a different story. Natalie swore he'd made up his mind, from the moment he first saw her, that she was a stuck-up East Coast bitch. She acted like one, muttering, "Cowboy," loud enough for him to hear. But she didn't mind shopping for western boots, choosing a two-color style, the most expensive in the store. Irene didn't bat an eyelash. Just told her she hoped they were as comfortable as they were beautiful.

In the afternoons, in the scorching summer sun, 100-plus degrees, she and Natalie drifted on rafts at the pool at the Flamingo hotel, working on their tans. The pool at the Flamingo was the only thing Natalie liked about this ugly bone-dry place. At the Flamingo there was grass around the pool, the only grass Natalie had seen in Las Vegas.

Natalie bet the other kids at the pool were sons and daughters of gangsters. Her mother had told her about the Jewish gangsters who were building this town. She'd told her about Bugsy Siegel, who'd built the Flamingo, and Longy Zwillman, her father's patient, who had lured him here and was a partner in the fanciest new hotel in town, the Sands, due to open in December. These kids would be Miri's classmates at school. If Natalie stayed they would be her classmates, too. She talked to no one, but Miri did, to a girl whose uncle was involved in the casinos. Janine was her name. She would be a sophomore at the high school, too. Well, *la-di-dah*, Natalie thought, Miri would have one friend. Not that *she* cared. Why would she give two cents if Miri had a friend or didn't?

Natalie and Miri didn't talk about school or anything else. Miri had no idea Corinne told her if she didn't like it in Birmingham she could go to boarding school in a year. Which she was definitely going to do. Nobody knew about that, including her father.

One time Miri tried to draw her into the conversation, introducing her as her *stepsister*.

"Not so fast, cowgirl—there hasn't been a wedding yet, or am I missing something?"

"When they get married we'll be stepsisters," Miri said to Natalie.

"Why would I want to be your sister, step or otherwise?"

Miri was stung—not that she'd expected anything different, but still.

All Natalie really wanted was to see the mushroom cloud from an A-bomb, detonated every few weeks at Yucca Flats, not that far from town. But her father said absolutely not. Which made it easier to hate him. That and the pregnancy.

HER FATHER TOOK Natalie to the new office to check her teeth, then took her out to lunch, just the two of them. The whole time they were together she wanted to cry, she wanted to yell and scream and cry, then have him hold her and say everything was going to be all right. She wanted him to beg her to stay, to live with him, but then she remembered living with him would mean this godforsaken desert in the middle of nowhere. It would mean Rusty and a new baby and Miri. She and Miri would never be best friends again. She saw the writing on the wall. It was over between them.

She ordered a Waldorf salad without dressing.

ON HER LAST NIGHT in town Natalie rolled over in the twin bed next to Miri's, propped herself up on an elbow and asked, "Is it true about Mason?"

"Is what true?"

"That he had another girlfriend?"

"Who told you that?"

Natalie shrugged. "You can't trust any of them. Not even after twenty years of marriage. Just ask my mother."

Miri lay on her back, trying to dismiss the pain spreading through her body.

"I'm never going to let a boy break my heart," Natalie said. "Not that friends can't break your heart, too. And family. You think you can trust them, then you find out you were wrong. That's all I'm going to say."

She turned away then, leaving Miri awake, tears rolling down her cheeks.

FERN DIDN'T WANT to leave. She wanted to be flower girl at the wedding.

"We're not having that kind of wedding," Rusty told her.

"What kind are you having?" Fern asked.

"It will be a very quiet wedding in the rabbi's study. You won't be missing anything."

Still, Fern cried. "I want to be *your* sister," she told Miri. "I like you better than Natalie."

"Don't tell that to anyone else, okay?" Miri said.

"You mean it's a secret?"

"Not so much a secret as something only the two of us know."

"I wish I could stay here and ride Trigger to school. I don't want to go back to Mommy. She's mean. She only cares about good manners."

"Good manners are important."

"Natalie doesn't have good manners."

"She used to."

"But she doesn't anymore."

"No, she doesn't."

Miri went to the airport with them, to say goodbye. Fern wore her appliquéd jacket with the silver wings, a second set of wings still pinned to Roy Rabbit's vest. Natalie wore dungarees, her new western boots and a fringed jacket she'd seen in a shopwindow on Fremont Street. All that was missing was a ten-gallon hat. "Mommy's going to be surprised to see you wearing that," Fern said.

"That's the idea," Natalie told her.

"She's going to be mad."

"That's the idea."

"Are you going to be mean forever?" Fern asked.

"Maybe yes, maybe no," Natalie said, laughing.

Miri would have hugged her for old times' sake, but Natalie kept her distance, turning once, halfway out the tarmac to the plane, to wave to her. "So long, cowgirl," she called. "I'll see you in my dreams."

"Not if I see you first," Miri called back.

Dr. O was accompanying the girls to Birmingham. They'd have to change planes and he didn't think they were experienced enough travelers to do it on their own. Natalie disagreed.

Rusty was teary-eyed saying goodbye to him.

"I'll be back in five days," he promised.

"That's five days too many," Rusty said.

When Dr. O kissed Rusty goodbye, Miri looked away. Getting used to her mother in love was going to take time. Getting used to her mother pregnant—that was a whole different story.

The plane's engines revved up. It taxied to the runway, then picked up speed until it rose into the air. *Into the air, Junior Birdman*, she imagined Fern singing, her hands making upside-down goggles over her eyes.

Miri waved at the plane even though the passengers couldn't see her. Inside her head she said a little prayer to keep them safe, to return Dr. O to Rusty, and the girls to Corinne.

Rusty took a cracker from her pocket, put it in her mouth and chewed. "I think I'm starting to feel better," she said to Miri.

"I'm glad."

They stood together, mother and daughter, their hair blowing back in the wind.

"I think I'll learn to ride a horse," Miri said.

Rusty didn't miss a beat. "I think I'll learn to drive a car."

"We can learn together because you can get a license here at fifteen."

"Fifteen? Who told you that?"

"This girl I met at the Flamingo."

"You made a friend?"

"It's too soon to call her a friend."

Rusty drew her close. "We're going to be okay. This is all going to work out. I can feel it in my bones."

Miri wished she could feel it, too. Until she could, she hoped Rusty was right.

Thirty-five Years Later

February 10, 1987

The flight attendant gently nudges Miri. They're coming into Newark and her seat back has to be returned to its upright position. She's still a nervous flier, still digs her fingernails into the fabric of her seat cushion for landings. She could have waited until tonight and come with Christina and Jack on the company plane but she wanted to do this on her own.

It's not the first time she's flown into Newark Airport. The flight path no longer brings planes in or out over residential Elizabeth. Not since the airport reopened in November 1952. But that doesn't stop her from thinking about it every time. It doesn't stop her from rushing to the doctor before a flight, sure she has a sinus infection, hoping to be told it's not safe for her to fly. She closes her eyes, sings a little song inside her head until they're safely on the ground. Then she's up and on her way with all the other passengers.

Outside, she grabs a taxi to the old Elizabeth Carteret hotel, the hotel where Joseph Fluet stayed during the investigations, where Mr. Foster stayed while Betsy and Mrs. Foster were in the hospital, where Ben Sapphire stayed when he wasn't sleeping on Irene's couch. And where Dr. O went when Corinne kicked him out of the house. Miri had been inside the hotel just once, for a bar mitzvah party back in seventh grade. She can still remember the dress she wore, one of Charlotte Whitten's, though she didn't know it at the time. Black velvet top, sweetheart neckline, white net skirt. She tries to imagine Eliza wearing a party dress and gets a picture in her mind of her fifteen-year-old daughter, named for the city she's returning to, galloping on her beloved horse in one of Charlotte Whitten's dresses from Bonwit's. She laughs out loud. When is the last time *she* wore a cocktail dress? No, wait—she remembers—Frank Sinatra's opening at the Sands, where they celebrated Rusty's sixty-fifth birthday. He'd dedicated "Fly Me to the Moon" to Rusty, which made her night.

Miri didn't want a big bash for her fiftieth. She made Andy promise, no surprise party. She hated surprise parties. Christina threw a barbecue at the ranch anyway, but at least it wasn't a surprise. She and Andy danced the Hustle, the Bump, the Funky Chicken, to prove to their sons, Malcolm and Kenny, both college students, and to teenage Eliza, how young they were, how hip, never mind that their kids had moved on to new dance fads. Andy is a great dancer, much better than she is. He's still trying to get her to loosen up on the dance floor. He's a skier, a mountain biker, an easygoing, well-liked guy. He's made a name for himself in forensic dentistry. She fought him on that one. She had enough disasters in her life. But he won, promising not to bring the details of his work to the dinner table.

Her hotel room is nothing to write home about, but it's clean and light, looking out over Jersey Avenue. Christina and Jack are staying in a suite at the Pierre in New York. They offered her an adjoining room, but she opted for Elizabeth, explaining she was having dinner with Henry and Leah, who would also be staying at the Elizabeth

Carteret. And she's been thinking about a story based on the thirties gangland slaying that took place in a suite on the eighth floor of this hotel. She's never lost her fascination for the Jewish gangsters.

She sits on the edge of the bed and dials Eliza at school. It's midafternoon there so she's surprised when Eliza answers in a sleepy voice. "Hullo?" She didn't expect her to answer at all, thought she'd just leave a message on her machine, the way she had this morning.

"Hi, honey. Are you all right?"

"Why wouldn't I be all right?"

"I expected you to be at class. Or at the stables." She means to sound soft, maternal, but knows she sounds judgmental. The school, in the mountains of Colorado, was highly recommended by the counselor they'd consulted. It was supposed to do wonders for children like Eliza, bright but unmotivated, who would rather shovel manure than read.

"You're calling to check up on me?"

"No, I just wanted to tell you I'm at the hotel. In Elizabeth."

"I can't believe you actually went."

"Well, I did."

"It just seems really stupid to me. It's not like it's your high school reunion or anything."

"No." Miri resists a laugh. To Eliza a high school reunion must seem like one of life's major events.

"Well, it's your dime and your time. Just don't expect me to tell you to enjoy yourself."

"No, of course not." Miri no longer expects anything from her daughter, except to be challenged, berated and humiliated.

"So I'll see you when I see you," Eliza says. A statement, not a question.

"President's Weekend," Miri reminds her. "Tahoe."

"Oh, yeah. I forgot." Eliza yawns loudly. "Will everyone be there?"

"I hope so." Miri doesn't ask who Eliza means by *everyone*. Maybe the boys and their friends.

Silence.

"Eliza . . . are you still there?"

"Where else would I be?"

"Okay, then," Miri says, trying her best to keep it upbeat, positive. "Take care and I'll see you soon. Bye, honey."

Eliza shouts, "You know I don't like goodbyes!" She slams down the receiver.

How is it that Miri, who longed for a daughter after two sons, has wound up with an angry, sullen child like Eliza? She's still trying to figure out where it went wrong but can't put her finger on it.

She unpacks, hanging up her suit for tomorrow, and sets her toiletries on the little shelf above the bathroom sink. She studies herself in the mirror. It's unsettling how different she looks away from home, away from the familiar reflection in her bathroom mirror. Last time she looked at herself in a mirror in Elizabeth she was fifteen and growing out her Elizabeth Taylor haircut. Now she's fifty. *Jesus, fifty!* And her hair is long, lightly permed, with golden highlights. An improvement, she thinks. She's in good shape, runs five miles a day, but instead of running from someone—Rusty, Mason, Natalie—the way she did that year, she runs to clear her head, to give herself a burst of energy that carries her through the day.

Christina has been trying to prepare her for seeing Mason tomorrow by dishing out small bits of information—his wife, Rebecca, will be visiting her ailing parents in Sarasota, his daughter and twin sons are all at college—but Miri hasn't been willing to talk about it. "Please . . ." she said to Christina. "That was so long ago. We were just kids." She knows Christina doesn't buy her nonchalance but she lets it go.

Miri can't admit she's nervous about seeing him. *Come on, who wouldn't be nervous about seeing her first love? Who wouldn't want her old boyfriend to find her attractive?* If you don't want that, you don't go to high school reunions, you don't go to the thirty-fifth commemoration of the worst year of your life. Besides, she's not fifteen anymore. She's not that girl whose heart was broken on a sunny afternoon in May. She's a woman, married with three children and a career. She's responsible, dependable, mature. *Right?* she asks herself. *Right,* she answers.

She stays up too late that night, watching *A Place in the Sun* on TV. She'd seen it with Rusty at the Regent movie theater *that* winter, the year it won six Academy Awards. They'd each gone through two handkerchiefs, bawling over the young Elizabeth Taylor and Montgomery Clift. Rusty planned to come with her to Elizabeth for tomorrow's commemorative event, but Dr. O's health is too fragile, even though Fern is a doctor and offered to stay at the house.

THEY GATHER the next morning at the site of the third crash, in the field behind Janet Memorial. The old home is in disrepair, no longer used to house children in need, children without parents or family to care for them. She wonders where those children go now. It's a bright, sunny day, mild compared to the bitterly cold winter of 1952.

Miri stands between Christina and Henry, oversize sunglasses covering half her face, a cashmere shawl thrown over her new suit.

She and Christina had gone shopping for today's event. They'd each bought a designer suit with big shoulders, right out of *Dynasty*. They'd laughed their heads off in the dressing room. Christina is the best friend Miri always wanted. The real deal. When it comes to dynasties, Christina and Jack have their own. *Irish Jack*, that's what they called him in the early days. He'd built his dynasty slowly, shrewdly—though he swears he didn't have a clue back then, just knew he wanted to work hard and be successful for Christina and their girls. An understatement, if ever there was one. Went from being an electrician to an electrical contractor to a general contractor to owning one of the biggest commercial construction companies in the West, with IRISH JACK lettered on the side of his plane.

THE MAYOR, Thomas Dunn, who was a Sixth Ward councilman that winter, speaks from a platform. "The fifty-eight-day period that ended here on February eleventh, 1952, at twelve-twenty a.m., was the most memorable of my life, outside of World War Two. Our mayor at the time called it 'The Umbrella of Death.' Others referred to our town as 'Plane Crash City.' But we know better. We know our city survived the American Revolution. George Washington slept here, as we learned as schoolchildren. We have been and always will be a proud revolutionary city, a welcoming city to immigrants from all over the world, where your parents and grandparents and even great-grandparents settled. Today I welcome all of you and ask that you bow your heads in remembrance of those we lost, both on the ground and from the air. One hundred sixteen died in that fifty-eight-day period, senselessly, needlessly, randomly. It could have been any of us."

Already, Miri feels herself choking up.

Three clergymen take turns reading out the names of the dead, beginning with the first crash. Miri waits for the familiar names. Ruby Granik, twenty-two, Estelle Sapphire, fifty-nine. Then the second crash. Kathy Stein, eighteen. Penny Foster, seven. She lets out a small, unexpected cry when Penny's name is read. Henry reaches for her hand. Christina passes her a packet of Kleenex. She wipes her eyes, glad she didn't use mascara, and blows her nose. When all the names have been read, a children's chorus sings a medley—"April Showers," "Pennies from Heaven," "Keep on Smiling." Someone with style has orchestrated this day of events.

After, they form a circle and toss flowers into the center. Most of them have daffodils or tulips but Miri special-ordered a dozen sunflowers through a local florist. Penny loved sunflowers, was always drawing pictures of the sunflowers in the print hanging over her family's fireplace. Then they join hands and close their eyes for a silent prayer.

The ceremony lasts just half an hour. Their personal remarks are to be saved for the luncheon to follow at the Elizabeth Carteret hotel. The mayor makes an announcement that the lunch will be hosted by Natalie Renso, who will be signing books following the program.

Miri looks around the circle but can't find Natalie. She thought Natalie might show up to honor Ruby. Instead, she spots Gaby Wenders, the stewardess, in her old uniform. She must be in good shape, Miri thinks, to fit into that uniform thirty-five years later. And next to Gaby, the boy who rescued her, the boy who saved her life. Miri half expects to see the boy he was then. The boy she loved. Instead, she sees a grown man. Still, her knees grow weak. *For god's sake*, she thinks, trying to remember what her yoga teacher has taught her about breathing in stressful situations.

He makes the first move, walking briskly across the field to where she is standing. "Miri," he says. "*Jesus . . . Miri . . .*" He wraps his arms around her. Now she can't breathe at all. When he lets go, she pushes her sunglasses up so she can get a look at him. Did she hope he wouldn't be attractive?

He grabs her hand. "I'm so glad to see you."

"I'm glad to see you, too." The voice that comes out doesn't sound like hers.

"Can I give you a ride to the lunch?" he asks.

Christina and Jack have a car, so do Henry and Leah, but Miri says, "Sure," and walks with Mason around the block to his red Mazda RX-7. She almost laughs because Andy drives the same car.

"I'd know you anywhere," he says, "even with the *hair.*"

"I'd know you, too, even without it." He's not really without it, just has less on his head, more on his face.

He laughs. And just like that, she's fifteen again. Except she's not.

. . .

THEY'RE SEATED at different tables at lunch. She's with Christina and Jack, Henry and Leah, four others. He's across the room with Gaby and her handsome husband, their grown children and young grandchildren, and two men who were boys at Janet then, boys who helped rescue the trapped passengers.

None of her old crowd is here. Suzanne lives in Seattle, married to a neurosurgeon. Miri tries to see her every year. Robo is divorced and has a gift shop in Westfield. Aside from two years at Boston U, she's never left New Jersey. Eleanor is a professor of mathematics at Purdue, married to an economist. She hasn't won the Nobel Prize yet and didn't laugh when, a few years ago, Miri mentioned the possibility. *Some things aren't funny*, Eleanor told her.

Miri and Mason steal looks at one another through lunch. Miri doesn't blush the way Rusty does, but she feels her checks flush. She drinks two glasses of wine, too fast. It goes straight to her head. *You go to my head . . .*

She must have sung that line out loud because the woman next to her, a daughter of the Secretary of War who was killed when the second plane crashed, says, "What?"

Miri knows she sometimes sings a line from a song out loud when she means to sing it only inside her head. "I was just thinking of an old song," she says.

"Don't you love the old songs?"

"I do," Miri says. "My daughter finds me hopeless that way."

"Mine finds me hopeless in every way."

"Yes, that, too." They laugh.

"My father was a wonderful person," she tells Miri. "I've never stopped missing him."

"My uncle, Henry Ammerman, wrote about your family," Miri says.

"The young reporter?" the woman asks, eyeing Henry, who is seated on Miri's other side. "I remember him. I was at the apartment the day he came to talk to my mother."

"Henry talked to everyone after the crashes. Everything I know about writing I learned from him."

"You're a writer?"

"Reporter, now columnist, for the *Las Vegas Sun*."

"Las Vegas . . ." she says, in a tone Miri has heard a million times, as if ordinary people can't possibly live there.

The program begins as dessert is served, plates of cookies and some kind of mousse that Miri pushes away. The mayor introduces Henry Ammerman. Oh, god, it's going to be in alphabetical order? She's going to be next? She doesn't want to go next. Doesn't want to get up in front of these people at all, especially not in front of Mason.

"He was a young reporter for the *Daily Post* then," the mayor says. "Today, he's a prizewinning journalist for *The Washington Post*. Ladies and gentleman, Henry Ammerman." Enthusiastic applause.

Henry speaks well, painting a picture of Elizabeth at that time—the fear, the chaos, the adolescent rumors involving spaceships, zombies, sabotage, ultimately of a community coming together. Miri is as proud of him today as she was then. She smiles at Leah. Miri has never been as close to Leah as she'd once hoped. She supposes it has to do with the distance between them, which has become more than geographical. Leah was maternal to her during her college years, when she chose American University, with a major in journalism. But Miri was into trying her wings when she came to Washington, and Leah wanted to clip them. The last thing Miri needed was another mother. She offered to babysit her little cousins once a month, more if she found she had a free weekend. She'd had plenty of experience by then with her brothers, William and Stuart, born a year apart. She'd spent her high school years surrounded by babies and toddlers.

By senior year Leah was lobbying for her to stay in D.C. "There's not one good reason for you to go back to that ridiculous town."

"There's my family," Miri said. "And a job offer from the *Sun*."

"You can do better. Go to New York. Don't waste all that talent."

When Miri said, "I'm just going home for the summer," Leah didn't buy it.

"There's a boy, isn't there? The one you met over the holidays."

Well, yes, there was someone she'd met over the holidays, a dental intern working for Dr. O. But so what? Half the girls in her graduating class were already engaged, showing off their diamond rings every chance they got.

"What's his name?" Leah said.

"Andy. He's from San Francisco. Went to Stanford." She hoped Leah would be impressed.

"Andy."

"Yes."

"You're just twenty-two, Miri."

She knew how old she was.

"Give yourself a chance."

"I'm not getting married."

"You will."

"Someday."

"Just don't settle."

"I won't settle."

She didn't give a hoot about a diamond ring, and the idea of one had probably never entered Andy's mind. When they became engaged a year later, he gave her new skis and a black pearl to wear around her neck on a chain. She still wears it, is wearing it now. He was a young dentist then and insisted on checking her teeth, like a horse dealer buying a mare. "Nice," he'd said, once he had her in the chair. "Healthy gums." Before she'd even closed her mouth he'd asked, "Will you marry me?"

"This is a proposal?" she'd said.

He'd nodded, embarrassed, and brought out a bottle of Champagne he'd hidden in the cabinet. He filled two pleated paper cups and passed one to her.

"I must be the first person ever to be proposed to in a dental chair."

"Is that a *yes*?" he said.

She gulped down the Champagne, held out her cup for more. "Yes!"

Her family was happy. Marrying Andy would mean she'd stay in Las Vegas. Henry was always supportive. If she was happy, he was happy for her. They didn't marry for another year. When they did, Ben Sapphire gave them a bungalow.

THE MAYOR CALLS Miri's name. She still goes by *Ammerman*. If she'd taken Andy's name, *Zinn*, she'd be at the end of the program. She thinks about walking out the door and not coming back. But Henry comes to her side, takes her arm, walks her up to the podium, the way he walked her down the aisle on her wedding day, sharing her with Dr. O, who was on her other side. Two of the best fathers any girl could have.

She hadn't invited Mike Monsky to her wedding. They'd found out pretty quickly there wasn't going to be much between them. The first summer he'd picked her up in Las Vegas and driven her back to Los Altos, where she never even met Adela, who'd had such a severe migraine she'd moved into her parents' house for the duration of Miri's visit. And that visit was cut short when Mike's kids came down with chicken pox. The following year it was worse. Adela greeted her, then left with the boys to spend a week with her parents in Santa Barbara. By then she'd had it. If Mike Monsky wanted to see her, he could come to Las Vegas, or take her someplace neutral. But it never worked out. She wasn't disappointed. She had a lot of people in her life. He was just a complication.

Frekki stopped by once, with Dr. J. J. Strasser, when Miri was a senior at Las Vegas High. They were on their way to a medical convention in L.A. She'd invited Miri to lunch at the Sands. "I just wanted to make sure you're okay," Frekki said.

"I'm fine," Miri told her. "I got into American University, my first-choice college."

"Well, good for you," Frekki said. "I hear you've seen your fa . . ." She hesitated before saying the word, then changed it to "Mike."

"Yes. Twice. But we're both so busy, there's not a lot of time to visit."

"I understand," Frekki said. "I'm meeting him for lunch in L.A. He's flying down for the day, without Adela or the boys." She sighed deeply.

Miri nodded.

"I hear he's changed his name to *Monk*."

"Yes." Was she just finding out?

"Well, I can't say I blame him. *Monsky* was always a mouthful."

Miri took a bite of grilled chicken and chewed it very slowly.

When she'd announced her marriage to Andy, Frekki sent a crystal bowl from Tiffany's.

Mike Monk sent a $100 check.

AT THE PODIUM Miri takes the leather-covered journal from her purse, opens to the first page and signals to Henry, she's okay. She begins to read into the microphone, glancing over in Mason's direction just once. His head is bowed.

After enough time it fades and you're grateful.

Not that it's ever completely gone.

It's still there, buried deep, a part of you.

The stench is gone from your nostrils now

Unless someone leaves the kettle on to boil and forgets about it.

The nightmares have tapered out.

There are more pressing things to dream about, to worry over, to keep you awake at night.

Aging parents, adolescent children, work, money, the state of the world.

Life goes on, as our parents promised that winter.

Life goes on if you're one of the lucky ones.

But we're still part of a secret club,

One we'd never willingly join,

With members who have nothing in common except

a time and a place.

We'll always be connected by that winter.

Anyone who tells you different is lying.

The final speaker is Gaby Wenders. She introduces the *boy heroes*, especially her hero, Mason McKittrick. Then her husband, Dr. Larsen, her children and grandchildren present a plaque to Mason. The oldest grandchild, maybe five, says to Mason, *Thank you for our Gaby*. There's not a dry eye in the house.

After the presentation to Mason it feels as if the program is over. People stand and begin to say goodbye to one another, when the doors swing open and Natalie makes her entrance, swooping in like a high-fashion gypsy, the "Queen of New Age," as she's known, her Santa Fe jewelry jangling on her wrists and around her neck. A buzz goes through the crowd and people take their seats again. After all, she's Natalie Renso. She's famous. You can see her on TV, at readings and book signings, in fashion magazines. Most people don't know *Renso* is *Osner* spelled backward, the kind of code name children come up with in third grade. But it's worked well for Natalie. She steps up to the podium, waits for the whispering to die down and begins.

"It was the winter that changed our lives," she says. "The winter we learned who we were, and what we were made of." And that's it. She doesn't say a word about Ruby. Just that she'll be happy to sign books—please write the name of the person you'd like her to sign for on a Post-it.

Even Lee Patterson, daughter of the Secretary of War, lines up to get her signature. "My daughter would never forgive me if I didn't bring her a signed book."

Miri does not get in line. She hangs back.

"Did you really sleep with Warren Beatty?" someone asks Natalie.

"Why not?" Natalie answers. "Everyone who had the chance did." She laughs, and the crowd laughs with her.

CHRISTINA DOESN'T LIKE whatever's going on between Miri and Mason. You'd have to be an idiot to miss it. The two of them making goo-goo eyes at each other all through lunch. Jack tells her to let it be, they're adults, they're not going to do anything stupid, anything that would mess up their lives. Instead, she tries to convince Miri to fly home with her and Jack today. The plane is waiting at Teterboro. But Miri says she's staying another night.

"Fine," Christina says. "I'll stay and fly back commercial with you tomorrow."

Miri looks at her. "No."

"No? What do you mean, *no*?"

"I mean that's crazy. Fly back with Jack and I'll see you day after tomorrow. I still need to talk to Natalie, away from her adoring fans, and I want to stop by the cemetery on the way to the airport tomorrow."

"Don't do anything I wouldn't do," she tells Miri.

"Never," Miri tells her.

"Is that a promise?"

Miri hugs her. "Don't worry."

But that's a phrase that's always worried her, even coming from Miri, her dearest friend.

CHRISTINA IS RETRIEVING her coat from the cloakroom when an attractive silver-haired man says, "Hello."

"Hello," she answers.

"I went to school with your sister . . ."

He doesn't have to finish. It's the Sewing Machine Man's son, Zak Galanos. He seems nice enough, still teaching, though not in Elizabeth. His wife is an elementary school principal. They have two children. This was the life her mother wanted for her. A decent Greek husband, a couple of kids, a house in Cranford or Westfield. She never dreamed her life would turn out so different. A life of such wealth it embarrasses her. It's laughable how her family's attitude toward her changed as her fortunes grew. She's heard her nephews refer to her as their rich aunt Christina from Vegas—and sure, she helped put them through college, helped Athena open a new store at the Short Hills mall. She made sure her parents were comfortable at their retirement home, and when it was needed, she paid for round-the-clock care.

She came for her mother's funeral three years ago, and her father's, a year later. Even her parents accepted having an Irish son-in-law. They couldn't resist their four beautiful granddaughters, the oldest, Nia, named for her mother, born when Christina was just nineteen, the bundle of joy who kept Jack out of Korea. It wasn't until five years later that they were ready for more children, three more girls in a row. She convinced Mama and Baba to come to Las Vegas for Nia's eighteenth birthday. Sent the plane for them, with IRISH JACK painted on the side. They were impressed. She took them to see their favorite entertainers—Dean Martin, Liberace and the Greek chanteuse Nana Mouskouri—made sure they had ringside tables, everyone making a fuss over Irish Jack's in-laws. And when her mother needed an emergency root canal, Dr. O was there to hold her hand as the young, gifted Dr. Kyros, *a Greek dentist, Mama*, performed the procedure. Dr. Kyros was married to a former chorus girl and together they made tall, beautiful children with perfect teeth.

Okay, she'll fly back with Jack today but that won't stop her from worrying about Miri.

MASON IS HOSTING a small reception for Gaby and her family in his hotel suite, at 5 p.m. He invites Miri. She's the first to arrive and is embarrassed. She's changed into pants and a sweater, western boots, the cashmere shawl draped over her shoulders. She feels more like herself. She's flossed, brushed her teeth and gargled with mouthwash. Ever the dentist's wife. She checks out the room, looks out the window. Anything to avoid sitting down facing him.

He can tell she's uncomfortable and says, "I'm sure the others will be here any minute."

He smiles at her, looking into her eyes. But she quickly looks away. "Do you come to Elizabeth often?" she asks.

"Almost never. It's changed, and not for the better."

"I heard Janet closed."

"In '62, when the state eliminated orphanages. End of an era. It's been condemned since the seventies. Kids break in at night to party. Makes me sad."

He offers her a glass of wine.

"Just water," she says.

"I read your piece on Longy," he says, handing her the water glass.

She laughs. "I was a senior at college. Sold it to the *Las Vegas Sun*. A heady experience. They hired me based on that story."

"I like your theory that he never would have hanged himself, that it was a gangland slaying disguised as suicide."

"I still believe that."

"Jack sent other stories, too. The one about the fire at the MGM Grand."

"I don't really specialize in disaster, but when there's a disaster, like my uncle Henry, I'm there." That was the disaster that led Andy into forensic dentistry, but she doesn't tell that to Mason.

"Vegas must be a good place for stories," Mason says.

"If you like weird stories, it's great."

"Well, I'm proud of you." Again, he looks into her eyes. Again, she looks away. Gulps down the whole glass of water. She's saved by a knock on the door. Gaby and her family, and a few minutes later, the boys from Janet. And Phil Stein.

"Oh my god," she says. "You're Phil Stein, aren't you?"

"I am."

"I loved your mother."

"And she loved you. Never stopped talking about you, even after you moved away."

"Is she . . ." It's awkward, asking if a parent is still living.

He shakes his head. "She died years ago. Complications of diabetes and a stroke."

"I'm sorry. She was so kind to me."

"She was a good person. I'm still trying to convince my sister of that."

"Mother-daughter relationships can be difficult," Miri says.

"Tell me about it. I gave Mom a dog for her sixtieth birthday. My sister almost killed me. The dog reminded Mom of Fred. Remember Fred?"

"We have a dog named Fred," Miri tells him, "and another called Goldie."

"*Goldie*. My mother would have loved knowing that."

They both laugh. "Do you have a family?" she asks.

"Divorced," he says. "Like half our generation."

"Sorry."

"But I have two kids. You?"

"Still married," she tells him. Then adds, "Happily."

"One of the lucky ones."

She nods.

"I was at your stepbrother's funeral. Steve Osner. He *was* your stepbrother, wasn't he?"

"Yes. The family was devastated."

"A military hero. He was my best friend all through school. The way Corinne threw herself over his coffin . . . I'll never forget that moment."

No one had told Miri about this. Rusty had been asked not to attend the funeral. She'd understood. She was pregnant again, anyway, and as sick as the last time. Daisy went with Dr. O to the funeral, as much to look after Dr. O as to mourn Steve.

"If only I'd been able to convince him to go to Lehigh with me," Phil said. "Neither of us could stand the idea of Syracuse after my cousin's death. You remember Kathy?"

"I do, and her green velvet New Year's Eve dress."

"It was an awful time."

"Yes."

"But Steve went and enlisted the second he graduated." He shakes his head. "Maybe to prove something to his parents. Who knows? He was enraged by the divorce. Shipped out to Korea after basic training."

"He walked into enemy fire, didn't he?" They didn't talk a lot about Steve's death but Miri knows Dr. O blamed himself.

"Tossed a grenade into a bunker on Pork Chop Hill," Phil said, "blew himself up along with the enemy. And you know, the war was basically over by then. But they kept fighting over that stupid hill, as if it mattered, as if it would make a difference. Such a fucking waste, excuse my language."

"Dr. O's never gotten over it. I doubt you ever get over a child's death. He and Rusty named my second brother Stuart. It would have been too hard to have another son named Steven."

It's bittersweet, chatting with Phil, then Gaby, who takes Miri aside and asks if it's true about Longy. "Was he really a mobster?"

"I'm afraid so," Miri says.

"He sent me a basket of flowers after the crash. He was such a gentleman."

"Yes," Miri says, then adds, with a straight face, "and he was good to his mother."

She doesn't mean to be the last to leave. Or does she? Before she reaches the door, Mason says, "Sit awhile, Miri. Talk to me." He brings her a glass of wine. She sinks into the sofa, tucks her feet under her. She's more relaxed now.

"Hungry?" Mason asks.

She shakes her head. Looks right at him for the first time. "Do you ever think about how young we were? My kids are older than we were."

"Miri . . ." Hearing him say her name like that in a soft, slightly hoarse voice takes her back to the basement in Irene's house, to the night they played Trust. He rests his hand on her arm, and just that is enough to make her tingle.

"I didn't know how to hear your side of the story," she says. "I didn't believe there could be another side to the story."

"My side of the story is easy," he says. "I was an idiot."

"I didn't know how to forgive you."

"I never blamed you for not forgiving me. No girl in her right mind would have forgiven me."

"I couldn't compete with her."

"If it matters, I was never with her again. A few months later she married a guy who owned a bar, had another kid and died at thirty-nine of ovarian cancer."

"That's sad."

"Yes."

As she sips her wine, she can feel the pull. But she's not going to do anything stupid. Never mind the devil on her shoulder whispering, *Life is short and then you die.*

He leans in, kisses her gently, waits to see if she responds. She does, then changes her mind. "I can't do this."

"I know," he says. "Neither can I."

It's all about remembering, it's all about being fifteen and in love for the first time. She can almost smell the winter air outside the Y, feel the oil burner's warmth in Irene's basement, see the kaleidoscope, the colors, the patterns—which reminds her—she jumps up, walks across the room and pulls a tissue-paper-wrapped package tied in red and white bakery string from her bag. She hands it to him. "I thought your daughter might like to have this."

He rips off the paper, holds the kaleidoscope up to his eye, then hands it back to her. "Remember what I said when I gave it to you."

She remembers.

He pulls her to her feet, hits the switch on his tape player and Nat King Cole sings, *"Unforgettable, that's what you are . . ."* He's thought of everything. They dance, holding each other, swaying, the way they did at the Y. Is this what she wants? Is this why she came here? She loves the idea of the kids they were, the sweetness between them.

She sometimes thinks of Mason when she and Andy are making love. When she's not sure she can get there—something new, something perimenopausal—as soon as she puts herself back—ohmygod—as soon as she's there, she calls out, *Yes, yes, yes!* And Andy is happy he's satisfied her so well. Does Mason imagine her when he's with Rebecca? Does he imagine Polina?

"Do you ever wonder about what might have been?" Mason asks.

"Who doesn't?" She collects her shawl, her bag, the kaleidoscope. When they say goodnight at the hotel room door he touches her face.

She goes back to her room, kicks off her boots, falls back on the bed and calls Andy. She needs to hear his voice.

"Are you okay?" he asks.

"Yes . . . but I miss you."

"Miss you, too."

"See you tomorrow," she tells him.

"I'll meet you at the airport."

"But I left my car there."

"So what?"

She tears up.

"Ask me about the snow on the mountain," he says.

"How was the snow?"

"Perfect."

SHE MEETS Mason for breakfast the next morning, then he drives her to the cemetery to visit Irene and Ben. The cemetery is close to Newark Airport, not exactly a peaceful site, but it's where they wanted to be, with their families and old friends. She places a stone on top of each headstone. Ben Sapphire, the stepgrandfather she came to admire, and Irene Ammerman Sapphire. She misses Irene, her nana, who loved her unconditionally, who taught her, by example, to take another chance on love. Miri wipes the tears from her eyes, then blows her nose.

"She gave me her recipe for brisket," Mason says.

"No."

"Yeah, she did. And I passed it on to Rebecca. Every Friday night we have Irene's brisket. It's not exactly the same, not quite as good as I remember, but it's good. I look forward to it."

"Irene would love knowing that."

"She knew."

"You kept in touch with her?"

"Holiday cards, the occasional note."

"She never told me."

"She didn't want to upset the cart. One summer, when she and Ben were vacationing down the shore, she invited me and Rebecca and our kids to lunch."

"I can't believe she kept you a secret from me!"

"She wanted to see for herself that I was happy. She already knew you were."

"She never stopped trying to rescue people, to fix what wasn't right."

"Rebecca fell in love with her."

"Who didn't?" She stops, then asks, "You and Rebecca?"

"Up and down. But I think we're going to make it."

"I hope you do."

He checks his watch. "I have to get you to the airport . . . if you're really going."

She gives him a *you must be kidding* look.

He shrugs and smiles. They walk back to his car. "I'm glad we got to spend time together."

"I'm glad, too." She feels satisfied, happy.

At the airport he kisses her goodbye in the car. "If someday . . ." he begins.

"Yes, *if* . . . But for now . . ."

"I get it," he says, kissing her one last time.

SHE'S MADE A PLAN to meet Natalie for coffee in the first-class lounge at the airport before their flights. How long has it been since Natalie visited them in Las Vegas? She gave a lecture at the library on "channeling your past lives" during one of her book tours, but that was years ago, and she flew in and out of town quickly, with no time for family. Fern, who'd come in from Shiprock with her girlfriend, Ora, also a doctor on the Navajo reservation, had been disappointed. Now the two of them run a family clinic outside of Las Vegas.

Natalie spies her first. "Hey, *Brenda Starr* . . . how's it going?"

"Not so bad."

"You look better today. Yesterday, you looked like a corporate executive in that suit."

If Miri thought Natalie would be different now that she'd achieved fame, she was wrong.

"How was it seeing Mason again?" she asks.

"Like seeing a long-lost friend," Miri tells her. "Like seeing you."

"I saw your goodbye kiss. I doubt if that's how you'd say goodbye to me."

Miri feels her face flush. "It didn't mean anything."

"If you say so."

Change the subject before this escalates, Miri tells herself. "So, Warren Beatty?"

"You like that story?"

"It grabbed my attention."

"He was great."

"So, it's true?"

"Maybe yes, maybe no."

"We're back to that?"

"Ask me another one, Girl Reporter."

"How did you know Kathy Stein was on that plane?"

Natalie pauses for just a moment. "Ruby told me."

"No, really . . . how did you know?"

"Sorry if you don't like my answer but it's the truth. Next . . ."

Miri reminds herself not to push it. "Corinne?"

"She and her hubby spend winters in Palm Beach, summers on Nantucket. They play golf. I don't know how they can stand it. But, then, I never understood my mother. I suppose you see a lot of Fern."

"I do. It's nice for Dr. O."

"You still call him that, after all these years?"

"I tried Arthur but it never felt right."

They get their coffees, carry them to a quiet corner, where Miri says, "He's sick."

"I heard."

"We're hoping you'll come to see him."

"I was waiting for his eightieth birthday."

"You probably shouldn't wait that long."

"August? Are you saying August is too long to wait?"

Miri nods.

"Shit."

"Yeah."

ON THE PLANE Miri is seated next to a young girl. "I'm Lily," she says. "I'm nine. My dad is a pilot."

"Is he flying this plane?" Miri asks, sure that if he is he'll be extra careful with his daughter on board.

"No. He flies to Europe," she says, kicking the seat in front of her. "I just came back from Portugal. Have you been there?" She doesn't wait for Miri to tell her she hasn't been to Portugal. "You should go. They have a lot of tiles there. Do you like tiles?"

"Yes."

"Everything is tiled except your toothbrush."

Miri laughs.

"You think I'm joking but I'm not," Lily says. "Are you going to Vegas to gamble?"

"No," Miri tells her. "I live there."

"Me, too. With my mother. My dad lives all over the place. Do you think it's weird?"

Does she mean weird that her parents live in different places?

"Vegas," she says. "Do you think it's a weird place to live?"

"I've lived there since I was fifteen. My children grew up there."

"And they turned out okay? Because my dad thinks it's not a good place to grow up."

"They're fine." Well, she thinks, two of them are anyway, but she's not getting into that.

"What were you doing in New Jersey?" Lily asks.

"Visiting old friends."

"Was it fun?"

Miri thinks before answering. "In a way it was. Yes."

The flight attendant stands at the front of the cabin. "May I have your attention?" She demonstrates the proper way to fasten your seat belt. Then she says, "In the unlikely event . . ."

Lily leans close and says, "This is the part I don't like. Why do they have to say that?"

"It's just a safety rule," Miri tells her, trying to sound as if she means it.

"Are you scared?" Lily asks.

"No. Why would I be scared?"

"You're digging your fingernails into your armrests."

Miri tries to laugh. "Just an old habit," she tells Lily.

But Lily can see right through her. She reaches for Miri's hand. "Will you hold my hand until we're up?"

"Sure," she says. Lily reminds her of Fern on their first flight to Las Vegas. But she doesn't tell her that. Instead, she says, "I have a daughter. She's fifteen. Her name is Eliza."

"Do I remind you of her?"

"A little."

"Is she dead?"

"What? No! Why would you say that?"

"Because you seemed sad when you said her name."

"I'm not sad. I just miss her. She's at school. I'll see her next weekend." Miri closes her eyes. Who is Lily, really? What are the odds that the two of them would be seated together on this flight? *In the unlikely event . . .* she hears the flight attendant saying in her head. Life is a series of unlikely events, isn't it? Hers certainly is. One unlikely event after another, adding up to a rich, complicated whole. And who knows what's still to come?

Lily looks out the window, then back at her. "My dad says unlikely events aren't all bad. There are good ones, too."

"Like meeting you on the plane," Miri says, making Lily smile.

DAISY SPENDS TIME with Dr. O every day. An hour here, an hour there. Sometimes they tell each other jokes. Sometimes they reminisce. Other times they're quiet. He sleeps, she reads. Rusty says it's such a help to be able to call on her, to count on her. She still goes to the office three days a week. She still looks good, maybe because she gave up smoking when she moved to Las Vegas, maybe thanks to her condition. Who knows? That was so long ago.

She can't imagine life without Dr. O, her oldest, dearest friend, more than fifty years of working together, fifty years of friendship, of knowing everything about the other, except for one—she never knew, she never guessed about Dr. O and Rusty. How he managed to hide that from her she doesn't know. Proves that everyone, even the person closest to you, can have secrets.

RUSTY'S LET her hair grow and doesn't color it. She wears it in a braid hanging down her back. There's something about her still-lovely face, silver hair and clear eyes that makes people turn and stare, the way they did when she was in her prime. She's a western woman now, though she's never felt comfortable on a horse, or driving long distances on her own.

When Miri and Christina ask if they can plan an early eightieth birthday celebration for Dr. O the last weekend in March, she gives her blessing. That's five weeks from now, she thinks. Who's to say what will happen in the next five weeks? He's made his wishes clear. No more treatment. Palliative care only. Don't try to extend his life. He's had a good run. *Thirty-five fantastic years with you, my love.* When he says that, she dissolves. She can't bear the idea of losing him.

"You're strong," he tells her.

"Not anymore."

"I need you to be strong."

She nods. For him she'll do anything. If he needs her to be strong, she'll be strong.

"I never expected to make it to eighty," he says. "And I'm not talking about cancer. I expected God to strike me down for wanting you."

She smiles. "Arthur, you're becoming religious in your old age?"

"I've always been religious deep down. I never wanted to hurt anyone, not even when I was drilling a tooth."

She kisses him. "Is it any wonder I love you?"

"No funeral," he reminds her for the tenth time.

NONE OF THEM KNOWS if Natalie will show up for his early birthday party, but at the last minute, she does. She brings fifteen-year-old Ruby with her, the youngest of her three children, each by a different father. She's never seen the point of marriage. They stay in a two-bedroom suite at Caesars Palace, arranged by Christina. A car and driver are at Natalie's disposal, delivering her and young Ruby to Miri's house for Dr. O's party. It's a sunny afternoon, warm enough to set up the buffet on the deck.

Eliza hits it off with Ruby Renso. "What exactly is our relationship?" Miri hears Ruby ask Eliza.

Eliza answers, "Well . . . your grandfather is married to my grandmother. That must make us something-in-laws."

"Yes," Ruby says. "Something-in-laws."

Before sunset Eliza and Ruby come to her. "Mom," Eliza says with more enthusiasm than Miri has heard in ages, "Ruby's invited me to Santa Fe for the summer."

"Actually," Ruby says, "we live on a spread in Tesuque, outside of Santa Fe."

"Can I go?" Eliza begs. "Please . . ."

Miri has to think fast. "Let me talk to Natalie about this and see what we can work out."

"Does that mean yes?" Ruby asks Eliza.

Eliza says, "It means *We'll see*."

"Great!" Ruby says. "At least it doesn't mean no!"

Miri laughs. So do Malcolm and Kenny. "She's going to be okay, Mom," Kenny says of Eliza.

"I hope so," Miri says.

"At least we didn't give you any trouble," Malcolm says. "Right, Kenny? We were perfect children."

Ha! Miri remembers the pot plants in the closet, the acid trip to the mountains, the fake IDs falling out of Kenny's wallet when they were stopped by the police on their way to hear the Grateful Dead. But they've made it through. They're good young men.

When the trio begins to play "It Had to Be You," Dr. O gets up with help from his and Rusty's sons, and he and Rusty slow-dance. Their grandchildren circle around them. They end with a kiss and immediately the trio plays "A Kiss to Build a Dream On." The other guests get up to dance, led by Miri and Andy. She's felt closer to him since the trip to Elizabeth, more appreciative. If he's noticed, he hasn't said anything. He looks down at her and smiles. "Nice party."

Tears spring to her eyes. "Thank you."

"Love you," he says.

"Love you, too."

· · ·

NATALIE ASKS for time alone with Dr. O the next day. Can she be trusted not to upset him? Miri wonders. Not to accuse him? Is it any of her business? She checks with Rusty, who asks Dr. O, who says yes, whatever Natalie has up her sleeve he can take it.

Twenty minutes later Natalie comes out of his room. Miri is waiting. "Thanks for encouraging me to come now," she says. "I needed to apologize to him. Instead, he apologized to me."

Natalie hugs Rusty for the first time since she was a young girl. "Thank you for making my father happy."

Rusty breaks down.

CHRISTINA ARRANGES for the plane to fly Natalie and Ruby back to Santa Fe.

At the airport Natalie looks hard at Miri, then hugs her. "So long, cowgirl," she says softly. "I'll see you in my dreams."

"Not if I see you first," Miri whispers into Natalie's hair.

Natalie strides out to the plane with Ruby. She turns back once and waves. Miri returns her wave.

"You okay?" Christina asks, as the plane takes off.

"I'm good," Miri says, then adds, as if the thought has just popped into her head, "I think I'll take a leave from the paper."

Christina looks at her. "This is sudden."

"I'll be able to spend more time with Andy, meet you for lunch."

"And . . ." Christina says.

"Maybe I'll write a book. I might have a story to tell."

"It's about time," Christina says.

As they lock arms, starting back to the car, Miri begins to sing. *"Somewhere there's music, how faint the tune . . ."*

Christina joins in. *"Somewhere there's heaven, how high the moon . . ."*

"Or maybe we can put together a sister act," Christina says. "I know a guy who knows a guy who owns a hotel with a lounge in Vegas."

Author's Notes

Although this book is a work of fiction, and the characters and events are products of my imagination, the three airplane crashes are real. I grew up in Elizabeth, New Jersey, and was in eighth grade during the winter of 1951–1952, a student at Hamilton Junior High, so I have firsthand memories of that time and place.

I have tried to depict the crashes as accurately as possible and for that I have depended on reports in two now-defunct local newspapers, the *Elizabeth Daily Journal* and the *Newark Evening News*, to supplement the official investigative reports of the Civil Aeronautics Board. I have drawn heavily on the colorful writings of the reporters for these newspapers, freely adapting some of their descriptive phrases—a plane that falls "like an angry, wounded bird" and another that has "broken cleanly in half like a swollen cream puff."

My thanks to Irvin M. Horowitz, Melville D. Shapiro, Earl K. Way of the *Elizabeth Daily Journal*, and to that newspaper's editorial writers. Also, to Angelo Baglivo, Joseph Gale, Joseph Katz, Albert M. Skea, Arthur

Swanson, Frank Eakin, Alfred G. Aronowitz, Armand Rotonda, and Cortlandt Parker, Jr., of the *Newark Evening News*.

I feel as if I know these reporters and am ever grateful for their stories. I like to think their combined DNA has seeped into my hero, Henry Ammerman. At a time when television was still new, it was up to print journalists and photographers to paint a picture for us, to tell the stories not only of the crashes but of those who were on the planes, and those who were left behind.

Thank you to Mary Faith Chmiel, director of the Elizabeth Public Library, and to Nancy Smith, senior reference librarian. Thanks also to the Newark Public Library and its interlibrary loan staff. To Robin Henderson, reference librarian, and Christine Bell, assistant, at the Monroe County Public Library in Key West, all of them helpful and resourceful. Thank you to Tom Hambright, who runs the history room at the Key West library. He set me up at a microfilm reader and warned me to take cover whenever he opened the door to the dusty closet where he kept his treasures.

Thank you to Tom Meyers, Fort Lee Office of Cultural & Heritage Affairs, for information on the Riviera nightclub, including the New Year's Eve, 1951, dinner menu, and Pupi Campo's Riviera Latin band.

I worked on this book from January 2009 to November 2014. During that time I was inspired by books, articles, and blogs.

Replacement Child by Judy L. Mandel is a book I recommend to anyone curious about the true story of one family who was caught up in the tragedy of the second plane crash.

But He Was Good to His Mother: The Lives and Crimes of Jewish Gangsters by Robert A. Rockaway.

Notorious New Jersey: 100 True Tales of Murders and Mobsters, Scandals and Scoundrels by Jon Blackwell.

Viva Las Vegas: After-Hours Architecture by Alan Hess.

Thanks to The Mob Museum in Las Vegas for a fascinating tour, and to Steve Franklin, our guide to the neighborhoods of '50s Las Vegas.

Diane Norek Harrison for her blog post: "Elizabeth Memories: Elmora Avenue in the 1950s."

Nat Bodian for "Looking Back at The Tavern: A Great Newark Restaurant" in Old Newark Memories.

Stu Beitler for his submissions to the GenDisasters website.

Thank you to the friends and family members who listened and shared memories while I went on and on about my story. I didn't keep a running list, so forgive me if I've left out any of your names:

Pamela Chais for coming up with the title (before she ever read the book).

Corky Irick for bringing me a Speed Graphic camera like those used by news photographers of the time.

Jim Ackerman for sharing a family story that inspired the character of Mrs. Barnes.

Myrna Blume, who reminded me about the La Reine Hotel in Bradley Beach.

Joanne Tischler Stern, who has the best memory of all my school friends and who enthusiastically answered my questions.

Myrna Seidband Watkins, Mary Weaver, Roz Halberstadter, Ronne Jacobs, Robert Silverman, David Hofmann, ReLeah Lent.

Bob Kallio, who lived at Janet Memorial Home during that time, for the scrapbooks he donated to the Elizabeth Public Library.

And to David Kaufelt, my Key West bro—who was in seventh grade at Hamilton when I was in eighth. How great to find a boy from long ago and become good friends in Key West fifty years later. I miss you.

To my family—my brother David, who spent twenty years in the Air Force and has never lost his fascination with planes. My daughter, Randy, who became a commercial airline pilot and was my go-to source for questions about how planes and navigation systems work. My cousin Josh Rosenfeld. To Larry, Amanda and Jim, and to Elliot. All of them patient, encouraging and loving. At the end of the day, these are the people who know me best and nonetheless still care about me.

To my assistants in Key West, Patricia Bollinger, Joanne Brennan and Marianne Noordermeer—I couldn't do any of it without you.

And thanks to so many at Knopf, but especially: the production and design team—Maria Massey, Cassandra Pappas and Kelly Blair, who designed a jacket that captures both the time and the story; Anke Steinecke, for her legal expertise and Ruthie Reisner, for dedication above and beyond the call of duty. And to the publicity and marketing group who make it sound like fun (even though I know better)—Paul Bogaards, Josefine Kals, Danielle Plafsky, Nicholas Latimer and Maggie Southard.

Thank you to Sonny Mehta, who was my publisher in London in the seventies. We meet again and I couldn't be more thrilled.

To my agent, Suzanne Gluck at WME, who waited and waited, never pushing (and yes, she's really a fabulous agent).

And to my smart, funny, generous editor, Carole Baron. For five years we chatted about the book I was writing (though I wouldn't show it to her or anyone) over long breakfasts at Sarabeth's whenever I was in New York. We'd reminisce about the fifties, the Jewish gangsters our fathers knew, the music we danced to, what we wore, what we read, what was going on in our worlds. This was truly a collaborative effort. Carole and I worked for nine months after I finally sent her the manuscript. Without her, I'm not sure I would have finished this book. For this one and for *Summer Sisters*, thank you, Carole. You are my sister.

Finally, to my loving, supportive husband, who has been there for me for thirty-five years. When the deadline loomed, he "stepped up to the plate" and said, *I can be your Henry Ammerman*. He took the stories in my research notebook and reworked them. I was a tough city editor, but he came through every time, always in good humor. Without his months of work, his dedication to Henry, the story and to me, you probably wouldn't be reading this book for another five years, if then. He is my "Henry" and my everything else. How lucky I am to have him in my life.

—JUDY BLUME
Key West
February 22, 2015

P.S. from "Henry Ammerman"—I'd like to throw in a thanks to what William Gibson calls the "global instantaneous memory prosthesis." When you need it quick the Internet *knows*, like The Shadow from the radio show of our youth.